Praise for *Tinisima*

"In lyrical, erotically charged language, Poniatowska delivers a fast-paced, almost impressionistic portrait. . . . Poniatowska shines in describing the early, idyllic years with Weston in the 1920s, capturing the indolence and sensuality of post-revolutionary Mexico." —*Los Angeles Times*

"A beautifully produced, barely fictionalized biography . . . Poniatowska's account of Modotti's final years is somber and riveting. . . . In Poniatowska's hands the contradictory, impulsive, and adventurous Modotti is never less than divine. Her meticulous account of Modotti's dark sojourn in the Soviet Union greatly contributes to your knowledge of a woman who will fascinate for generations to come." —*The Washington Post*

"Fascinating . . . the clipped, declarative style of Poniatowska's story lend just the right distance to allow the novelist real perspective on Modotti's life." —*Chicago Tribune*

"The picture of Tina Modotti that emerges [in *Tinisima*] is that of a romantic protofeminist misunderstood and abhorred by the macho society around her, a woman whose camera mattered far less—to her and her contemporaries—than her tragic fall from grace. It is a telling picture, one that says much about Mexico's turbulent past, and about its nostalgic present."
—*The Nation*

"I read *Tinisima* as if it were the north star, a torchlight, a guidebook, a grave by the side of the road warning me to watch that curve. All too often a remarkable woman's life is reduced to her association with a male mentor or to her romanticized martyrdom at the hands of love. Poniatowska rescues all of the Tinas from this oversimplified fate, the Tina of hearsay and the Tina of history, the Tina who gave birth to herself several times in one lifetime as real women do after the great passions of life—

child laborer, garment worker, stage actress, Hollywood vamp, artist's model, photographer, spy, lover, wife, nurse, revolutionary. Without a doubt *Tinisima* proves Modotti not only lived in interesting times, she made them interesting."

—Sandra Cisneros

"The great Mexican writer Elena Poniatowska uses her imagination and skills as a journalist to recreate Tina Modotti's life, conveying not only the character of that wild and sensuous Italian refugee, her notorious love affairs, alleged crimes, and leftist politics, but also the '20s, a vibrant time of change, revolutions and art." —Isabel Allende

"An intensely imagined, sensuously detailed account of the extraordinary life of photographer and militant revolutionary Tina Modotti. She tells this novel in an urgent present tense, segueing among short, vivid scenes with cinematic virtuosity."

—*Publishers Weekly*

PENGUIN BOOKS

TINISIMA

Born in Paris in 1933, novelist, essayist, and journalist
Elena Poniatowska is today one of Mexico's leading literary
and intellectual figures. She is especially noted for developing an art form that blends journalism and fiction. She is
the author of more than forty books, including *Nothing,
Nobody: The Voices of the Mexico City Earthquake*; *Frida
Kahlo: The Camera Seduced*; *Massacre in Mexico*; and the
novel *Dear Diego*. She lives in Mexico City.

Tinisima

Elena Poniatowska

Translated by Katherine Silver

PENGUIN BOOKS

PENGUIN BOOKS
Published by the Penguin Group
Penguin Putnam Inc., 375 Hudson Street,
New York, New York 10014, U.S.A.
Penguin Books Ltd, 27 Wrights Lane, London W8 5TZ, England
Penguin Books Australia Ltd, Ringwood, Victoria, Australia
Penguin Books Canada Ltd, 10 Alcorn Avenue,
Toronto, Ontario, Canada M4V 3B2
Penguin Books (N.Z.) Ltd, 182–190 Wairau Road,
Auckland 10, New Zealand

Penguin Books Ltd, Registered Offices:
Harmondsworth, Middlesex, England

First published in the United States of America by
Farrar, Straus and Giroux, 1995
Published in Penguin Books 1998

1 3 5 7 9 10 8 6 4 2

Originally published in Spanish as *Tinisima* by Ediciones Era.

Grateful acknowledgment is made for permission to reprint the following: Excerpts
from *Edward Weston's Daybooks*, with permission of Aperture. Copyright © 1981 by
Center for Creative Photography, Arizona Board of Regents. Excerpt from *The Letters
from Tina Modotti to Edward Weston*, with permission of Center for Creative Photography. Copyright © 1986 by Center for Creative Photography, Arizona Board of Regents. Excerpt from "Canto LXXXI" by Ezra Pound, from *Cantos of Ezra Pound*, with
permission of New Directions Publishing Corp. Copyright © 1948 by Ezra Pound.

THE LIBRARY OF CONGRESS HAS CATALOGUED
THE FARRAR, STRAUS & GIROUX EDITION AS FOLLOWS:
Poniatowska, Elena.
[Tinisima. English]
Tinisima / Elena Poniatowska; translated by Katherine Silver.
p.   cm.
ISBN 0-374-27785-0 (hc.)
ISBN 0 14 02.6876 6 (pbk.)
1. Modotti, Tina, 1896–1942—Fiction.   I. Silver, Katherine.   II. Title.
PQ7297.P63T5613   1996   863—dc20   96-33810

Printed in the United States of America
Set in Adobe Garamond
Designed by Abby Kagan

Acknowledgments

One of the great legacies of Tina Modotti's extraordinary life and photography was to unite in friendship those who have written books about her. Mildred Constantine was the first, with *Tina Modotti: A Fragile Life* in 1975. Amy Conger is the author of the enlightening *Edward Weston in Mexico 1923–1926*. Sarah M. Lowe has prepared the most complete catalogue of Tina's photographs and cleared up many obscure points. Christiane Barckhausen has thoroughly investigated Tina's militancy and life in Italy, Germany, and France. She is the only person who has worked with the archives in Russia and she has unearthed much information about Vittorio Vidali. The wonderfully creative Riccardo Toffoletti, founder of the Comitato Tina Modotti, organized the Tina Modotti Congress in Udine in March 1993, and was kind enough to invite me—along with many Italian scholars—to Tina's birthplace.

The list of acknowledgments in the Mexican edition of *Tinisima* is enormous. I could have put together a book of more than a thousand pages of interviews alone. In Trieste, Italy, Vittorio Vidali, Tina's last and only living lover, gave long and detailed accounts of his life and Tina's in an interview that lasted a week, resulting in 350 pages of questions and answers. My only regret is that most of the people I spoke to over the past sixteen years are gone, and perhaps I didn't thank them enough.

Manuel Alvarez Bravo's and Mariana Yampolsky's insights on photography are most appreciated. Dianne Nilsen at the Center for Creative Photography was also a great help.

Edward Weston's *Daybooks*, Amy Stark Rule's *The Letters from Tina Modotti to Edward Weston*—intelligently compiled and annotated—and Antonio Saborit's remarks and Tina's letters in the Archivo General de la Nación in Mexico were indispensable to my work.

I especially want to thank Katherine Silver, John Glusman, Susan Bergholz, Becky Gallagher; my dear friend Bell Chevigny, who has given me steadfast support these last years and who carefully read the final version; Sarah M. Lowe, who was so willing to share her knowledge and photographic materials, as was Spencer Throckmorton; Ellen Calmus, who has translated the poetry of Neruda and many others; and above all, Beth Jorgensen, to whom this book is dedicated. Her concern for my work has been an inspiration.

Wonderful institutions gave me access to their archives: CEMOS (Centro de Estudios del Movimiento Obrero Socialista), Fototeca del INAH, Archivo General de la Nación, Biblioteca Nacional, Archivo del Partido Comunista de Trieste, Comuna di Udine, Instituto Friulano per la Storia del Movimiento de Liberazione en Italia, the Hoover Institution at Stanford, the Schmidt College of Arts and Humanities at Florida Atlantic University, among many others.

Tinisima is intimately linked to them all.

For Beth Jorgensen

Tinisima

1

At the Red Cross station, the families of patients are huddled on the floor, waiting passively for God's will to be done. The news about the attack on Julio Antonio Mella, exiled Cuban student and revolutionary leader, on January 10, 1929, spreads through the streets like the wind, and comrades from the Communist Party begin to arrive.

The combination of cold and fear makes Tina tremble uncontrollably. Enea Sormenti pats her reassuringly on the arm and speaks to her in the language of her childhood. Now, now. More soft caresses, until Tina gives up and lets her head fall on his shoulder. She realizes that tears are running down her neck, that her hair is a mess, that she is freezing.

"Non si può fare altro. Aspettiamo, Tina, aspettiamo."

Dr. Díaz Infante emerges from the operating room. "Technically, the operation was a success. We stitched up the bullet wound. The bullet that entered the thorax continued through the epigastrium and the abdominal cavity. Another bullet entered his arm. That one caused less damage."

"Did he speak?"

"No. He was unconscious when he arrived. The truth is, there is very little hope. The fact that he's an athlete . . . Perhaps with God's help . . ."

This small ray of hope unleashes more tears. Let him live, she pleads, even if I never see him again, just let him live. Another surgeon comes through the swinging glass doors. Tina looks at him and knows what he is going to say.

It's almost two in the morning. Her friends surround her. They hug each other. Luz Ardizana does not budge from Tina's side. Sormenti takes off his black felt hat, just like the one Julio wore, and speaks gravely to her. "Devi essere forte d'ora in avanti."

"Can I have him, Doctor?"

"I'm sorry, señora, it's against the law."

"My God," Tina says, pressing her fists together. "At least let me see him."

"You must wait until they take him to the Juárez Hospital for the autopsy. You can claim him there afterwards."

"I am his wife," Tina lies, "and I insist on seeing him right now."

The doctor is walking away. "When they're ready to take him to Juárez, talk to the people carrying the stretcher. Did you bring a sheet?"

A sheet? Who walks around with a sheet to wrap a dead body in? Someone offers to go home to get one. No, he lives too far away. Someone else lives closer. What time is it? Make sure nobody follows you. Maybe it's better to buy a new one. No, everything is closed. There is fear in the air. Probably everyone is being shadowed. If this happened to Julio . . . Better not be in the streets. Maybe we could borrow one and return it later.

The police commissioner and his assistant appear at the end of the hallway, carrying large folders under their arms. They do not remove their hats when they reach Tina. They have nothing to do with the victim, much less with his loved ones. Like an auctioneer, the commissioner reads off the list:

One pair of black pants.
One black jacket.

One purple undershirt.
One shirt.
One brown sweater.
One pair of suspenders.
One brown coat.
One black belt.
One red notebook and pen.
One newspaper: *El Machete*.

"Write this down," he says to his assistant. "Upon taking inventory of the deceased's clothing, a bullet hole was found in the back of the brown coat, in the back of the black wool jacket, in the back of the knit sweater, in the back of the shirt, and in the back of the purple undershirt."

He picks up each item of clothing as it is mentioned. He sticks his little finger through each hole, then carelessly tosses the garment on his desk.

"The bullet exited through the undershirt and the shirt, but not through the sweater, jacket, or coat. It would appear that the bullet, after passing through the body, remained in the sweater and fell to the ground, probably when the victim was lifted . . ."

"Are you going to give me his clothes?" Tina asks in a pleading voice.

"Who are you?"

"I am his comrade, his partner. May I have his clothes?"

"We are not giving you anything. We do, however, have some questions for you. I recommend that you think very carefully before answering; anything you say can be used against you. Do you recognize the writing in this notebook as that of your comrade, or husband?"

"Yes, it is."

"I have found nothing besides this scribbled name and number. Do you know who Magriñat is?"

"Yes, and that is his telephone number."

"Where is the gun?"

"What gun?"

"The one that killed your comrade, or husband?"

"How should I know?"

"Did you pick up the bullet that killed him?"

5

"What? I didn't even think of it. I picked up his hat because I thought he would need it."

"His body will be in the Forensic Services of the Juárez Hospital."

"I want to take a picture of Julio. My camera. Someone please go get it. Luz, can you bring it from my house? You have the key."

As Tina focused her camera on his face, still so young, still so brave, she remembered what Mella had told her about his childhood. He had been brave since he was small, ever since Longina, the woman who took care of him, led him by the hand along the sea wall in Havana. "People are only afraid of what they don't understand," his nanny said to him. "You can do anything you set out to do." One afternoon she made him follow her up a small hill. He was at the bottom, trembling. "You can do it, come on up here, kid." On hands and knees, bellowing with rage as he slipped on the pebbles, the boy clambered up. At the top, Longina held her hand out to him. When he got there, creeping over the ground like a worm, he wept with joy and Longina kissed his wet cheeks. Julio Antonio never forgot the lesson.

Within the four walls of his home, he had also told Tina, Longina's voice was the only sign of life. In the living room, with the curtains drawn so as not to let in the sun, his mother, Cecilia, sat waiting. She was always gazing through the window toward a sea which had nothing to do with the gray ocean she knew in England. If she went outside, she took a parasol and a wide-brim straw hat to keep the tropics off her fair skin. She hated the Cuban sun, blamed it for her terrible migraines. It was because of the sun that she stayed indoors, waiting. In her light dress, with her needlework on her lap, she watched her sons, Julio Antonio and Cecilio, without seeing them. She waited angrily. Her passive resistance permeated the whole house. A time bomb, that house; a time bomb, his mother. When the boys sitting at her feet got rowdy—especially Julio Antonio—she would say in her awkward Spanish: "Vayan con su manejadora," Go with you nanny. Some afternoons around six, the hour when the sun abated, the heat had produced such a stupor in her that she spent hours under the white mosquito netting or in the hammock or the rocking chair, her eyes gone violet, quiet, concentrated, ready to explode. That was the hour when Nicanor

Mella would come to visit. Longina would serve tea or orangeade and Mella would kiss his sons. Then Cecilia would tell her to take them for a walk and the last thing Julio would see would be his father's courteous bow as he asked, in English: "How are you today, Cecilia?"

"Not well," she would answer, vindictively.

"Can I do anything to help?"

"It's up to you," she would say in a cutting voice.

Though Julio didn't understand them, those words would rankle in his earliest memory. And all his life he would run away from women who didn't feel well, women in soft shawls, vaporous women who stretched out their too-white legs like the hands of a clock, waiting, waiting.

When the Cuban President Zayas (called "The Chinese" because of his eyes) had received Julio as part of a commission of fifteen young students, Mella in the middle of the most appalling silence had complained that the fossils they had for teachers only cared about getting their paychecks. "We don't even have formaldehyde in our biology labs." Rhetoric, routine, and corruption had taken over the university and now, to add insult to injury, they were going to give an honorary degree to Earl Crowder, the American consul. Mella waited for an answer. His classmates had blanched and were looking desperately toward the door. The elderly President Zayas, taken off-guard, replied that he would ask the president of the university and the Minister of Education to meet with him. And with these words he dismissed them.

That crazy boy had dared to make demands of him, would you believe it, of him, the President of the Republic. What did he and his little friends know about the pressures being brought to bear on Cuba? Just yesterday that old fox Crowder had told him, "I wonder how you Cubans are going to be able to get out of this mess without a loan from J. P. Morgan." Making an enemy of a country the size of the United States would be suicidal.

Julio Antonio's real name was Nicanor MacPartland; he was the illegitimate son of the tailor who used to visit his mother. He'd been rebellious from the time he was very young. During his life he had risked death many times: in jail in Cuba, when he staged a hunger strike; in Central America, where he was considered a subversive and the enemy of the government; in Belgium, where he was with the radical Henri Barbusse—and each time he had survived. Now, as Tina focused her camera on his lifeless face, she could hardly believe that he was not about to open his eyes and tell her that they had to hurry up and get out of there.

Since three in the morning the group of comrades has occupied the hallway of the autopsy unit of the Juárez Hospital. Blood, urine, and chloroform turn round and round on this wheel of misfortune. A trash can next to the women's bathroom overflows with bandages, toilet paper, and a whole day's worth of bloody rags that nobody has bothered to remove. Sormenti looks at Tina. She leans against the white tiled wall, Graflex in hand. She is exhausted. She no longer cries; she only trembles. Sormenti takes off his coat and lays it gently over her shoulders.

"I'm not cold."

"Keep it anyway."

They allowed her to take a picture of Julio Antonio, of his head. They didn't leave her alone with him, not even for a moment. She clicked the shutter and walked out with her head held high. Later she would tell Luz Ardizana, "On the pretext of setting up a shot, I was able to caress his cheek. Only that, my hand against his cheek, one second, without their noticing."

Tina hands her Graflex to Sormenti and lights another cigarette, striking the match against the wall. All night her temples have been pounding so intensely that she hopes they will explode and give her some relief. Then she would be laid down next to Julio. Yet here she is, still alive.

"Who's responsible here?" asks a nurse.

"The lady . . . All of us, we are all responsible."

"We're almost finished."

"We've been here since three in the morning. It's now two in the afternoon. No autopsy can take that long."

"Yours isn't the only one. Everyone has to wait his turn."

Tina stubs out her cigarette on the radiator, and the butt rolls across the floor. She automatically slips another into the corner of her mouth and lights it with a match she shields in the palm of her hand.

8

Among those waiting for Julio Antonio's body are three Cubans: Sandalio Junco, Teurbe Tolón, and Alejandro Barreiro Olivera. "Those three are good comrades," Julio once said. Tina now looks at them for traces of Julio, in their speech, in their sad conversation.

"So this is life," thinks Tina. "This passage, this waiting." She walks up and down the corridor. "You've already smoked a whole pack," Sormenti reminds her. "Put on the jacket, you're still trembling."

"Yes, but not from cold. From anger."

"You have behaved like a true Communist. Your bravery . . ." The expression in her eyes stops him in mid-sentence.

Her bravery. She closes her eyes and hears the buzz of her comrades' voices. The slamming of a door returns her to reality. She is in a hallway, and she is waiting for Julio's body as one waits for a suitcase on a train platform.

"You know," says Rosendo Gómez Lorenzo, the chief editor of *El Machete*, the Communist Party newspaper, to his comrades, "without a bribe, we'll be here forever. It's the only way to get things moving."

Sormenti is the only one with any money.

The comrades decide to hold Julio Antonio Mella's wake in the main hall of the Communist Party headquarters at 54 Mesones Street. The coffin, windows, and walls are draped in red and black cloth. The weak bulbs emit a dim light. Tina retreats to a dark corner and for a moment is soothed by the familiar sounds. She sees everyone as if from afar, silhouettes outlined in the shadows. Whenever anyone approaches to offer condolences, the wrenching pain returns.

Tina begins to sense a certain tension among her comrades, a surge of motivation and activity in those who are usually so slow to act. The atmosphere is changing into that of a battlefield. There is still silence in the room where Mella's body lies in state, but on the stairway, along the corridors, and in the street below, the level of activity increases. Tina goes out to the balcony and wants to describe the scene to Julio: "Look at how hard they are working! They're painting banners, distributing freshly printed leaflets. In the last few hours they have organized more acts of protest than in the last three months combined. How hard you worked just to set up a meeting! How angry you got when nobody showed up! Afraid, you'd say, they're all afraid. Look at them now, Julio!"

Telegrams announce the arrival of delegations from other regions. The first protest will take place tonight. Groups wait in the corridors and demand the presence of Comrade Modotti.

Tina thinks, "I must pull myself together; I must be the calm and collected comrade they all know." She is confident she will not collapse; fatigue muffles the pain. Luz Ardizana keeps an eye on her.

"Tina," says Luz, "you should change your clothes. Your skirt is stained."

She sees Julio's dried blood. She feels Julio's head in her arms. She hears Julio's voice: "I am dying for the revolution." Or did she simply imagine those words? Because she and Julio had become one, immense and indivisible, like life itself; now her black strapped shoes tread the sidewalk alone, unaccompanied by Julio's long stride.

Twenty minutes later, Tina returns, breathless, and tells Luz, "I couldn't get into my house. It's swarming with policemen."

"What are they doing there?"

"They're searching my house. They didn't know who I was, so I asked them what was going on. They told me a crime of passion had been committed. My books and clothes are strewn all over the floor. They emptied out the drawers. I don't even know how I made it back. I don't even know what bus I took."

"Calm down, Tina. I'll get you some clean clothes."

Luz looks toward the door; two strangers wearing hats have entered. They look over the crowd.

Gómez Lorenzo announces that a cable has been sent to Bertram and Ella Wolfe in New York, requesting that they notify the *Daily Worker* about "the Mella assassination and the grave situation for the working class in Latin America."

The first time Tina and Julio were left alone in the office of *El Machete*, her entire body entered into a state of expectation, like that of a hunting dog who remains perfectly still yet totally alert. She tried to close her lips, to quiet the trembling in her belly. He took her hand and led her into a small room called "the archives" and there they made love, first standing up, then on top of the scattered newspapers. Neither of them worried about someone coming in on them. Tina lost herself and became Julio. She was Julio, he was Tina, there was no difference between her desire for Julio and his desire for her. Julio was the strongest part of herself. She looked at him and saw reflected in his eyes the Tina she aspired to be. "I want to be the woman in your head, Julio, I want to be as you see me." Julio was her path to knowledge, her finest idea of herself.

Once he moved into her place on Abraham González Street, Tina could not imagine living any other life. It seemed to her that she had always bought coffee at the corner of López and Ayuntamiento, then walked home to grind it in the small wooden mill she held between her knees. Julio could never resist such a sight, and he'd pick her up and carry her off to bed. He told her about her knees: the most beautiful he had ever seen; about her legs— the color of polished clay.

No matter what kind of day it had been, she eagerly awaited the night. Her lips swelled in anticipation. Julio took her by the hand or lifted her in his arms and carried her to bed. Tonight Julio would make love to her in a new way. He would seat her on his belly, swing her around, move her up and down the length of his penis until she would fall on his chest, her head pressed against his, her face buried in his neck; Tina, skinless or a sack of skin emptied of herself, emptied of a long day of work and all her worries, all forgotten, her mouth open, ecstatic, her breath on Julio's shoulder, her smothered shouts, her hand stretched up, extended.

Whenever she had to go out, she would return as quickly as possible, her body longing for his hand on her thigh, his arm around her waist. Yes, she was his woman, his comrade. She had never before felt that she belonged, not with Robo, not with Edward, not with Xavier. Only with Julio. When he was inside her, she was overwhelmed by almost unbearable pleasure, the air around them electrified by each breath they took, charged with this mysterious impulse as they let themselves fly with no consciousness of being transported.

Whenever he had to leave, she would watch him through the window as he walked away, until his hat became a black spot moving along the sidewalk, until he no longer had a head, until he was gone.

But Tina gladly let her house be turned into a train station to keep him home as much as possible. The Cuban immigrants practically lived there. She heard them repeating endlessly: "Today that Mussolini of the Caribbean will fall." If Julio wasn't there, his comrade would welcome them graciously; though at first they came for Julio, they soon began to come for her—but Tina never suspected that.

She would offer them "un cafecito," then disappear to make the bed or straighten up the house while the men talked. There were days when victory seemed imminent; others when, as she washed out a cup or a spoon, she grew afraid for both of them, afraid to be consumed by the language of the struggle that never led anywhere: secrecy, paranoia, living for the future, looking over your shoulder as you walk down the street. "But I have chosen this!" she reminded herself as she wiped the cup and returned it to the table. "I musn't let fear turn me into a hypocrite."

Tina lived in a whirlwind, sharing with the Communists their danger, their secrecy, their struggles. Before, her friends had been aesthetes; now they were militants, carpenters, railroad workers. At their house on Abraham González Street, Tina and Julio welcomed the exiled leaders of workers and peasants from all over South America, the Caribbean, Central America. She felt inspired by their passions, the danger they lived with, the strength of their ideals. She accompanied Julio to his meetings and listened to him speak. With Julio by her side, she could face anything. Even the sea. Julio had asked: "How can a girl born on the Adriatic not know how to swim?" He was a rower, a swimmer, a human merman. She would have to know what it meant to be surrounded by waves and to plunge into them, head first. They would be born again together, naked, their bodies clasped in this immense amniotic fluid. The sea was their womb.

A few months before he was murdered, Julio had an article published in *El Machete* in which he denounced the Bay of Havana as a graveyard for hundreds of "suicides" and "the disappeared." He rattled off the long list of murdered leaders and the circumstances of their deaths.

"They will hunt him down in Mexico," thought Tina. "Machado himself will give the order."

One afternoon, Tina took out her Graflex and photographed Julio's typewriter. He had written the first sentence of his next article: " 'Technique will become a much more powerful inspiration for artistic production; in time it will find a solution in a more sublime synthesis, the contrast between nature and technology.' Leon Trotsky."

Tina watches as Julio's curly head of hair and his shoulders emerge from the water. Suddenly, a wave snaps his neck. On the beach, she sees only a Cuban flag, a flimsy paper flag clinging to the sand like a delicate membrane. A second wave. Now the flag is torn to small pieces that wiggle like worms on the edge of the water. A soldier appears out of nowhere and bends down to collect them. "It's paper, only paper," shouts Tina, but the man, tall and robust, puffs out his chest and says, "There's something else." The water reaches the toes of his boots, but he doesn't seem to notice. His boots reflect the sun as he pokes his stick around in the sand, searching for more paper worms. "There's something else, I'm sure of it, there's something else." Tina also looks but only sees the bubbles as the water retreats over the wet sand.

Mella's Typewriter. Tina Modotti, 1928. Courtesy the Museum of Modern Art, New York. Gelatin silver print, 9 3/8 x 7 1/2 in.

2

*I*n the courtroom during the preliminary investigation into Mella's murder, Tina listens as they read the statements she made at the Juárez Hospital and the Red Cross. Her words sound cruelly impersonal. Julio had an appointment to meet Magriñat at La India Cantina on the corner of Bolívar and República del Salvador while she waited for him at the cable office at the corner of Independencia and San Juan de Letrán.

". . . and at 21 hours, Mr. Mella arrived and walked with the witness toward Balderas, continued along Morelos Avenue, until they turned down Abraham González Street. Just as they turned the corner, she heard two shots and Mr. Mella, who had been holding her arm, took a few steps forward, then collapsed before reaching the street. She was aware that the attack had come from behind; she could smell the gunpowder. Mr. Mella had told her that Magriñat, during their meeting, had warned him that two assassins had been sent from Cuba to kill him. After he had been shot, Mr. Mella said, 'Pepe Magriñat had something to do with this.' Then he turned to a bystander and said that Machado had ordered his murder. 'I am dying for the revolution,' he added."

"When first questioned, you stated that your name was Rosa Smith Saltarini, but your name is, in fact, Tina Modotti. Why did you give a different name?"

"Because I was, I am a photographer. I wanted to protect my clients."

"You said you were an English teacher living on Lucerna Street."

Silence. The court reporter takes a moment to insert the carbon paper into the Underwood.

Rosa Smith Saltarini, twenty-two years old, widow, from San Francisco, California, English teacher, living at 21 Lucerna Street. "What made me say Saltarini," she wonders through her fatigue. Saltarini is actually one of her names; she never did know how to lie. The name means "those who jump" and had been the nickname of her grandfather and great-grandfather, who used to jump like goats through the fields of Udine. Tender images of Istria and Friuli fill her mind. She sees her grandfather leaping over streams; she sees herself, Mercedes, Gioconda, Yolanda, Benvenuto, their feet high in the air, and hears their mother shouting for them to come in; it's time to eat, and because only happy people jump, they joyously jump into the house and settle themselves down in front of their bowls of polenta.

Julio had so totally absorbed her that she had not thought about her childhood in Udine for a long time. It was as if Julio's death had tossed her back into the world, as naked as the day she was born.

Also, if she called herself Rosa Smith, then it would not be her, Tina, who now sat under this bare light answering questions, nor would it be Julio in that coffin, because Julio Antonio never loved Rosa Smith.

"Please answer the question. Is Tina your real name?"

"It's actually Assunta, but they call me Tina."

Tina remembers that her mother calls her Tinisima. "Is that your only name?"

"Assunta Adelaide Luigia . . ."

"I see nothing of this in the file. And your family name?"

"Modotti."

15

"Please spell that for the record. And your mother's maiden name?"

"Mondini."

Suddenly, Tina is not a photographer. She is nobody except a family name that is spelled out with difficulty, with indifference, almost with disgust, every letter underlining the fact that she is a for-eign-er and therefore prohibited from getting involved in Mexican politics.

Tina then confirms that she is a widow and that Mella was married to a Cuban woman named Olivín, to whom he wrote frequently requesting a divorce.

Yes, she has been a card-carrying member of the Communist Party since 1927, and yes, she cried from happiness when she joined because becoming a member was her greatest dream. Yes, she and the deceased were united by a common ideal, a desire to change the world.

Suddenly the questions and answers begin to sound malevolent, as if they are pushing her into a trap; all she wants to do is return to Mesones and sit down next to Julio's body.

Yes, she believes that wealth is unfairly distributed and should be taken away from the rich and given to the poor.

Yes, she admires the Russian Revolution, she thinks it is the most important thing that has happened on earth and that other countries have a lot to learn from it.

Yes, socialism, yes, socialism, yes, socialism.

She walks back to 54 Mesones, where Julio's body lies in state. She is flanked by two policemen and leans on Luz Ardizana's arm for support. Luz tells her she shouldn't respond so honestly to such manipulative questions. "All I want is for them to find the murderer," Tina says wearily. She looks down at her feet, focusing on the immediate task of not tripping, not wasting time. Walk, move. One minute in the street is a year without Julio.

As she enters the large hall of Party headquarters, Tina no longer feels like a victim. She looks around and sees members of all the groups that formed part of Mella's life in Mexico: the Radical Jewish Workers' Club, the Railroad Workers' Union, the Venezuelan Revolutionary Party, the Young Pioneers, the National

Federation of Communist Students. Those who worked with Julio on the opposition Cuban newspaper approach her shyly, holding their hats in their hands; she stretches her arms out to them in gratitude. Shudders of fear ripple through the mourners: by appearing here, they, too, have put themselves in danger.

The police agents in the crowd can be easily identified: their arrogance contrasts sharply with the sad yet defiant look of the others. In the street, men, women, and children gather around the banner of the Communist Party. The young people carry signs: "Mella's Murder: Machado's Crime; International Women's Group." "Machado: Murderer." There are so many mourners the Security Committee is unable to check everyone's identification.

The flags of the Party and the Young Communist League lead the demonstration. Everyone shouts: Long live Mella! Long live Mella! Mella is here! Me-lla, Me-lla. Long live the Cuban proletariat! Long live Mella's Cuba! Long live the Communist Party! Long live Lenin! Long live the Soviet Union!

Tina dreads the moment they will reach the cemetery, when she will be parted finally and forever from Julio. A rumble from deep within finds its way out through her lungs and burns in her throat. A sob escapes.

"Tina."

"Yes?"

"Now."

Six comrades from the Central Committee lift the coffin draped in the red flag with its hammer and sickle, and carry it into the street. She feels comforted by the warmth of the crowd, their breath, their bodies.

The funeral march begins. The knot tightens in Tina's stomach. The January sun sends out piercing rays. Tina watches the coffin obsessively, careful not to let it get even a few feet away. When they reach the beautiful courtyard of the law school, where Julio Antonio Mella had been a student, the comrades set the coffin down in a place of honor. One well-dressed student with graceful gestures picks up the microphone.

"I am Alejandro Gómez Arias, and I speak on behalf of the non-Communist minority in this school. Mella has united us more effectively than all the flags in the world. He has died for those who cannot see the writing on the walls. We can be certain that death saw him approach with those clear, steady green eyes. He must remain for us an inspiration, an example to follow. May you rest in peace, Julio Antonio Mella."

Everybody wants a turn at having the honor of carrying the coffin. The procession continues down San Ildefonso, then comes to a stop on Brasil. As shoulder pushes against shoulder, Tina is reminded of her stay on Ellis Island, where she and the other refugees were kept in quarantine before being admitted to the United States. Then also she was surrounded by fearful faces, by women with scarves on their heads and children in their arms. Such misery, to be shoved together like cattle, the smaller children sheltering between the legs of the bigger ones. Then she had also felt dizzy, suffocated; then she had witnessed the same defeated gestures. They are carrying Julio's body, Julio's dead body. In the hospital, she had caressed him. Oh, Julio, if only I could give you back your warmth!

When they reach Madero Street, one voice begins to hum the "Internationale"; the others join in.

They pass Bellas Artes, still under construction. It looks like a half-dressed skeleton. At Abraham González Street, they stop where Mella was shot. "How strange," Tina thinks. "I don't feel anything, absolutely nothing."

As they approach the cemetery, Tina sees thirteen red flags set around a newly dug grave. The Cuban comrades open the coffin for a few seconds, allowing Tina a glimpse of Julio Antonio's face for the last time. He is paler, less beautiful than when she photographed him at the Red Cross. Not a single tear falls on her cheek. Her eyes are dry and burning. Now she wants only to be alone, to curl up in bed and rest her head on her pillow, at home . . . What home?! The police have taken it over!

The mourners brace themselves against a strong blast of wind. When Rafael Carrillo, the young leader of the Mexican Communist Party, turns around two feet in front of Tina, the crowd grows silent. Even those passing out carnations hold still.

"Julio Antonio Mella has fallen in the thick of battle, face to face with the implacable enemy; this afternoon, we have come to bid him farewell. His remains may soon be taken to the faraway land of all revolutionaries, to our dearly beloved Moscow, where he may rest next to the other great leaders of the struggle for international Communism. Those of us who remain will take up our battle positions, for we have no right to rest."

Rafael removes the flag from Mella's coffin before it is slowly lowered into the grave. Tina tosses in her carnation, unleashing a red avalanche. Luz Ardizana shatters the silence with a loud shout, "Adiós, Julio." Rafael Carrillo tosses in a handful of soft earth; the others follow his lead.

The mourners descend to the gate of the cemetery and begin to disperse. Tina turns around one last time and realizes that Julio is already part of eternity. His grave occupies a tiny spot on the land at the foot of the volcanoes.

Four days after the murder, Judge Pino Cámara puts Tina under house arrest on the fifth floor of 31 Abraham González Street, with guards in attendance around the clock.

Luz Ardizana leaves her own apartment at dawn to buy the morning papers and returns to read them. She has never felt so edgy, not even when she was in prison. She bolts the door and spreads the newspapers out on the bed. Mella's assassination has paralyzed the entire Party; nobody seems to be able to do anything other than follow the news.

Luz puts on her thick glasses and picks up *El Universal*, then *Excelsior*, *La Prensa*, and *El Nacional*. "The police strongly suspect that Tina Modotti knows the identity of the murderer but has refused to tell the authorities . . ." "Tina Modotti and her Communist comrades have given their version of the tragedy that occurred on Abraham González Street . . . They believe that the individual who murdered the Cuban student was hiding behind a low wall." "Tina tells of her love and maintains her innocence." "Protests in South America." "A sordid story." "Communists prepare a vigil on the 24th of this month in honor of the dead student." "A message from Moscow regarding Mella's death. Many countries send cables protesting the crime." "The mystery is yet to be solved."

Luz scans the columns of small print. A picture of Julio Antonio's body at the Juárez Hospital jumps out at her—"a twenty-four-year-old man, 182 centimeters tall, 84 centimeters wide at the thorax, 86 centimeters around the abdomen . . ."

She is struck with horror as she follows the path of the bullet, and continues reading: "The stomach smelled of gas and had remnants of food—garbanzo beans—pallid lungs, lifeless heart, a small amount of urine in the bladder . . ." Julio's organs on the butcher's block; the journalists buzzing around them like flies. What did they do with his intestines? Did they stuff them back inside or throw them, still warm, into the trash can? Did they bury Julio with his organs intact? Her vision is blurred by tears, and she cannot continue reading.

From far away, one could easily mistake Luz for a teenage boy. She always wore pants, a black jacket with a masculine style, and though her neck was somewhat delicate, her hair was cut just like a young boy's. Her alert, inquisitive eyes shone out from behind her Coke-bottle lenses.

Julio Antonio used to lift her up on his shoulders so she could write on the walls from eight feet above the ground: "Down with shortages." "Death to the oppressors of the people." "Down with the government." From this height, she could also plaster the walls with posters where city workers, whose job it was to take them down, couldn't reach them. Invariably, the police would insult her when they caught her. "So what do we have here? A little dyke? You like to feel like a man? What's your name, Lucha or Lucho? You should really go home and pick up your knitting needles, little lady. What you need is a good fuck, a really good fuck to set you right."

Over the next few days, Luz continues to be horrified by the vulgar exhibition of Tina and Julio's intimacy. Tina and Julio are on everybody's tongue, their home open to the world, their bed in shambles, their caresses tossed about like pages of a discarded newspaper, the life they shared made so transparent it disappears. It's true, revolutionary camaraderie allowed for the breakdown of certain mores, but the appearance in a major daily of a photograph of Tina naked has left them all exposed. And it isn't so much her breasts that cause a sensation, but rather that dense crop, that dark triangle behind which hides the world's greatest sortilege. Had anybody seen such a bush before?

• • •

At home, the guards follow Tina to the bathroom and wait outside the door until she is finished. Despite such humiliations, Tina manages to remain dignified and aloof. Her comrades warn her that Valente Quintana, the prosecutor in charge of the case, is not to be trusted, but quickly reassure her that the Party will not abandon her.

She cooperates with Pino Cámara, the judge, and listens to every word of the hearings that are held each morning. Always accompanied by her guards, Tina returns to the court in the afternoon to find out if anything new has come up. She is cordial and polite to everyone, from the lowliest clerk to Pino Cámara. She is particularly cooperative with José Pérez Moreno, police reporter for *El Universal*, who is conducting his own investigation and seems to be more professional than the rest of the gossip-mongers.

The courtroom could be a church, Valente Quintana the priest celebrating Mass, and the journalists his altar boys. They take their cues from him, kneeling at the right moments and carrying out the ritual with the utmost obedience and dedication.

During one of the first hearings, Tina is asked to describe how she was walking with Mella "on that fatal night." Without hesitating, she gets up, runs over to Quintana, and takes his arm.

"This is how I was walking with Julio: I was next to the wall, and he was on the outside. I was holding on to his left arm—like this."

She is so intent on faithfully reproducing the scene that she doesn't hear the giggles or notice how the men exchange glances. From that moment on, not even the bailiffs can take their eyes off her.

"How can you explain the fact that two bullets hit Mella on the left side, one entering his left elbow, which you were holding, and yet you were not harmed?"

"I cannot explain it. It's bizarre, isn't it?" she asks, turning the interrogation back on Valente Quintana.

Disconcerted, she brings her hand up to her elbow as if looking for a possible wound, then places it on her head and remains thoughtful. She responds with a degree of innocence that might disarm her fiercest enemy.

"I don't remember exactly how our arms were linked, but I was walking next to the wall; I felt a flash of powder on my right cheek, look, right here."

Tina obsessively reviews the details. She tortures herself trying to pick apart, step by step, what happened, and between one cigarette and another she relives each moment.

The first thing Tina saw was his bright smile under the wide brim of his hat. With four long strides he crossed the telegraph office, then reached his arms out to embrace her. She felt a great weight lift off her chest.

"How did it go, Julio?"

"Okay. Did you send the cable?"

"Yes. What did they tell you?"

"Let's get out of here."

"What did you talk about?"

"I'll tell you when we get home."

"Tell me now."

"Two Cuban hit men have come to Mexico. Magriñat says I'm their target."

Tina felt the weight return. Julio Antonio put his left arm around her shoulder and his head against hers. Once outside, a blast of cold air pushed them on their way.

"You see, Tinisima, that ass who runs Cuba thinks I'm more dangerous here than in Havana," he said, attempting a joke. Tina took two steps for every one of his.

They crossed Balderas Street. Mexico City was deserted. All one and a half million residents had shut themselves in their houses since the Cathedral's bells rang eight times. There was not a soul on Independencia Street; even the policemen in their navy-blue uniforms had turned in for the night.

"Let's walk on Morelos, Julio. It's wider, better lit."

Julio hooked his arm through hers. Tina wanted to bury herself in him, merge with him into a single nocturnal fragrance.

"Just a few more feet," she thought. "We're almost there."

They turned left at the corner of Abraham González Street. A sharp report rang out of the darkness. Another shot followed the first. Julio was no longer holding her. Julio, Julio. A shadow darted behind her. Julio. He was in front of her, staggering. He took three steps, one more, then collapsed. She ran toward him, screaming at the top of her lungs. Help, Julio, help. A car, please help, a doctor, have mercy! She was conscious only of the smell of gunpowder on the burnt sleeve of her jacket and Julio's head in her arms. "Pepe Magriñat had something to do with this," he murmured. Julio, bleeding to death, gathered his remaining strength. "I am dying for the revolution."

"No, Julio, you're going to be all right, Julio." She kissed him on the forehead.

Tina's lap was soaked with blood. Julio was as light as a feather. He was leaving; almost gone.

"Señor, a car, please, a doctor, he needs a doctor. He needs to be taken to the hospital!"

She was no longer alone. Shadowy figures surrounded her in the darkness.

"My love."

Tina kissed him again and again. She caressed his forehead, his hair.

"Señor, his hat, over there, that's it. Give it to me, please."

As Tina gives her testimony, she moves constantly, every question provoking a physical response. Luz makes a mental note: "I must tell her not to talk with her hands, not to move so much. She's so Italian." Every once in a while, Tina runs her tongue over her dry lips, and the men stare at the corners of her mouth, her pink tongue, her cheeks, which grow redder in the heat of the interrogation, the strands of hair that fall out of her bun. More convincing than her assertions is her body, her hands which always find the gesture when her voice cannot find the words, then fall on her lap, where she presses them against the curve of her belly. Luz decides that the reason these men find Tina so compelling is that they have never seen a woman so in touch with her body, as if she had just finished making love and the tingling of her flesh was palpable. To attract is part of her nature. The journalists write: "the beautiful protagonist of this tragic event," "the attractive Venetian with black, deep-set eyes." And José Pérez Moreno adds his sartorial touch: "Tina Modotti appeared in a tailored blue suit, a blue blouse, and a beige felt hat."

The columnists, using material collected by "the foot soldiers on location," pontificate solemnly: "We can no longer see Tina Modotti as an innocent adolescent, but rather a dangerous adventuress who knows more than she wants to tell . . ." Tina is discredited because she is a woman. She is weighed and measured like merchandise in the marketplace. Everyone in the courtroom possesses her: the clerks, the judge, the bailiffs. They mount her and don't want to let her go. Julio Antonio is just an excuse. She's the one they are interested in.

Tina is bewildered by the many witnesses who give their accounts with such confidence when questioned by Quintana. She doesn't understand how so many people witnessed the murder on such a deserted street. Why didn't they help? Policeman number 72, Miguel Barrales, saw the shots come from a car that raced away down Paseo de la Reforma. The owner of the Sanitary Bakery heard the shots and sent his clerk to see what was going on.

One man saw Tina walking with two men. The boy from the butcher's shop saw them walking down the left side of the street, not the right, as Tina insists, and they didn't turn on Morelos, but on Paseo de la Reforma. A student, Alvaro Vidal, heard the dying man say more than Tina heard.

"They have ordered my murder, and I am dying for the cause of the proletariat. I am resigned to my fate. This attack comes directly from the government of Cuba."

Mr. Victoriano González, owner of a garage on Abraham González Street, brings in a .45 caliber bullet. Lint from Mella's jacket was found on it.

"This is the bullet that killed him."

"Where did you find it?"

"On the street, a few feet from the sidewalk. It looks like a car ran over it."

Quintana holds the bullet between his thumb and forefinger. "This is the bullet that caused the fatal wound. It remained between the sweater and the pants and probably fell out when the victim was lifted into the ambulance. Mr. González's find has now definitively established the scene of the crime."

The allegations become more absurd and more offensive and have less and less to do with the crime itself. Nevertheless, Valente Quintana listens respectfully to each and every one. Tina was seen sitting on a park bench kissing a man only two weeks before. Someone else witnessed her immodest behavior in a dance hall. Another watched her undress one night by Chapultepec Lake. An anonymous witness states in a letter that when he had to travel to Cuba he left Tina, his lover at the time, in the care of a friend, who then had sex with her. Tina becomes furious as she listens. She wants to say that she is not a good dancer, that no one takes care of her, that she has control over her own body, that nobody has ever taken advantage of her.

Tina feels the animosity of Valente Quintana more strongly than the support of her comrades. Alone in Mexico, with no family, officially a foreigner, how could Tina fight those lies without a public tribunal? Outside the courtroom, the life of the Party has become completely chaotic; everyone is working on the Mella case. They freely publish denunciations in *El Machete* and *The Hammer and Sickle*, but these cannot hope to compete with the attacks on the Communists that are published in the major dailies. In fact, the Communists seem virtually invisible, their influence nil, this in spite of their support for strikes and their excellent relations with Makar, a functionary at the Embassy of the Union of Soviet Socialist Republics. *El Machete* only appears monthly; who knows when *Cuba Libre* will appear again.

She closes her eyes. The water envelops her as she sinks deeper and deeper into the sea; near the corner of Morelos and Abraham González, the hired assassin hiding in the shadows aims his gun at Mella; one bullet in the back, another in the elbow. A current of cold water pulls Tina farther away from shore. Suddenly she is carried to another beach. Julio is crossing the street, but he doesn't reach the other shore. Tina shouts "Help! Help!" but only bubbles come out of her mouth. "Nobody hears me. Nobody understands me." Again she hears the words: "Pepe Magriñat had something to do with this," and she now sees Magriñat, the murderer, enter the courtroom, an enormous, glistening water serpent, and she remembers Julio's rasping voice: "Pepe Magriñat had something to do with this."

Magriñat doesn't take his eyes off her as he answers the judge's questions.

"I simply don't believe you, señora. It would have been natural for you to turn around to see who fired those shots."

Perhaps, yes, perhaps he was right, it would have been natural. Why had she not even tried? I could have saved him, but I didn't. I would have given my life for Julio, yes, my life, yet the bullets didn't touch me. Magriñat makes a good impression in the courtroom: he is dressed in a navy-blue suit, and his hair is slicked back with Vaseline. He wears all the symbols of respectability, of prosperity: a white handkerchief in his pocket, shined shoes, a modest tie. His friends are other businessmen, family men. He is the owner of a company that installs neon signs. Every day he rises early in the home he shares with his wife and children and goes to work. Mella, on the other hand, was a rebellious student, a foreigner, an enemy of law and order, involved with an adventuress of questionable morals with whom he shared a studio, an Italian, just look at her . . .

Tina looks at herself in a large mirror of water. A wave lifts her up, then tosses her down on her face. Foam and blood pour out of her mouth. Someone pulls her out of the water, gives her mouth-to-mouth resuscitation. "We're just going through the motions," she hears a voice saying, "because this woman has been under for too long." The strong smell of tar permeates the air and reminds her of New York when she arrived on a ship full of immigrants.

"No matter what we do, she'll never come around," says the lifeguard. She hears the faraway sound of the sea. "I hear nothing but the sea, only the sea."

Since January 12, 1929, the newspapers have been full of intimate journals, news of rendezvous, love letters. Now *Excelsior* is reporting that among the photographs the police found at Tina Modotti's house was one of a child, with the inscription: "For Julio from his daughter, Natasha." Another portrait by Tina, "a talented photographer," shows Julio Antonio lying naked in a field, his head resting on his arm, as if in a deep sleep or pretending to be dead. *Excelsior* affirms that the newspaper is in possession of even more compromising photographs.

The campaign to implicate Tina intensifies. Julio's name wasn't

Mella but Nicanor MacPartland: bastard and lover, womanizer and braggart. From Mexico, he wrote numerous letters to Silvia Masvidal, a beautiful girl, as could be seen from the photographs printed in *El Universal*. One thing was clear: Mella sure got the good-looking ones.

The readers live this soap opera by installments, a chapter each morning with their café con leche, a pubic hair left on their tongues after their lips touch the inside of Tina's silky thighs. At first Tina was convinced that Julio's sacrifice would bring many around to the cause, but now she sees that nobody gives a thought to his martyrdom. She is the compelling subject: la italiana. And rather than her ideals, the public wants to know everything about the tumult in her heart.

Finally, *Excelsior* publishes an article, albeit on the back page, that sends a ray of hope through the gathering darkness. "According to various artists," the article begins, "the photographs of Tina Modotti and Julio Antonio Mella are artistic nudes rather than examples of immoral photography."

The article reports on a press conference held by Diego Rivera and Miguel Covarrubias at which the artists showed photographs of nudes, drawings in pencil and ink, reproductions of universal art, "that nobody with a minimum of artistic education could ever qualify as immoral." The artists also discussed the photos of Tina taken by Weston on the roof of their house in Tacubaya.

The article then states that the editor in chief stands by his editorial writers, claiming that they based their opinions on other photographs in the possession of Rodrigo de Llano, head of *Excelsior*. Rodrigo de Llano received Rivera and Covarrubias at six in the afternoon and showed them a photograph of Julio Antonio Mella naked "in front of the changing rooms, a photograph routinely taken for entrance into the Havana Sports Club." Rivera and Covarrubias explained that "Julio Antonio Mella, one of the best rowers in Cuba, was required to pose for this photograph, as he would have been to join any sports club in the world. Taken more than three years before he had even heard the name Modotti, this has absolutely nothing to do with her." The photograph of Tina that was published, Rivera and Covarrubias asserted, was an artistic nude taken by the photographer Edward Weston. Miss Modotti was his professional model.

Finally, someone is defending her.

Of course it is Diego Rivera, that's why the press pays attention. Soon after the campaign against Tina began, Diego descended from his scaffold, interrupting his work on his mural to dedicate himself to her cause. He called meetings, took up collections to send cables and mobilize the international press, and demanded a reconstruction of the facts. From early in the morning he could be found at Party headquarters, dictating messages and haranguing the comrades. Journalists swarmed wherever he went. They wrote that he had a bad smell, but still they buzzed around him. The minute he walked in the door, he began to speak in a loud voice. He shouted even when saying hello. When he and Lupe, his wife, arrived at a meeting, they made so much noise they were nicknamed "the screechers." Under such dire circumstances, Diego's defense was more than welcome: only his magnetism could move people to action.

Since Julio's death, Tina goes to bed with her clothes on, resting her head on Julio's pillows. She tries to keep herself from falling asleep because then she begins to search for him. She cannot even close her eyes without feeling his skin, the weight of his arm, some part of herself under Julio's body, some part of his body pressed against hers. Sometimes, in the middle of the night, they would wake up and seek each other in the warmth of the bed, in the sweetness of their sleep.

"Give me your hand." Tina feels herself pulled down by an ocean current. "Julio, I'm drowning. Julio, I can't." Her feet drag through the sand. If she could only anchor them at the bottom she would feel safe, but the bottom of the ocean, out there in the silence, is beyond her reach.

Tina awakens with strange sounds coming out of her throat. Her mouth is full of phlegm, her ribs are about to explode, her body is covered in a cold sweat.

"Open up, open up."

The guards in the adjacent room react quickly; they have probably been spying on her through the keyhole. She runs to the bathroom and vomits green bile, as putrid as the wave that crashed over her. She returns to bed. At dawn, she hears the pendulous snores of one of the guards through the crack in the door. Tina remembers a sentence she heard Jorge Cuesta say one night at Lupe Marín and Diego Rivera's house: "We're a bunch of poor devils."

The next day, Tina sits down on her bed. One of the policemen comes in and hands her a newspaper. The headline: "The Mata Hari of the Comintern." Despite herself, she reads on. She is especially disappointed when she sees that the article was written by José Pérez Moreno. "I thought he had more sense than that."

The article states: "She doesn't have a photography studio, but she takes portrait photos at her home. She described to us her initial involvement in the anti-Fascist revolutionary movement.

" 'Why are you anti-Fascist?'

" 'Because I am against tyranny, especially in my own country, where the common people live in misery.' "

Tina lights another cigarette. How ridiculous her words sound as she reads them! A person's life deserves respect. But her past and present are being spread across every paper in the country. Cuban agents may have murdered Julio, but Mexico—cruel, xenophobic Mexico—was flaying Tina alive. What were the journalists insinuating when they repeated over and over: "Mella was shot down next to her, and she didn't even get a scratch"?

"She knows more than she's letting on," Pérez Moreno concludes in his article. He is becoming obsessed with the case, with Tina. Modotti is so different from the other women he knows. Her answers are frank yet accommodating. It's such a pleasure to listen to her and, of course, look at her. "What would it be like to live with a woman like that," he wonders. The women in his own family are like servants. No matter how late he comes home, they bring him food and drink and sit down with him. "Do you want anything else? More coffee, perhaps?" They are all submissive, shy, doing their best to be invisible. They just put up with life, with men. Tina gives him a glimpse of a life lived fully. She enters a room with her energetic step, and everybody smiles without realizing it. Pérez Moreno looks forward to seeing her at court every day. He likes everything about her: her thick hair, her eyes, her waist, the curve of her full lips. He fills his articles with details about every item of clothing she wears.

All he has to do is look at her to know that she is a woman who knows how to love a man, without resentment, without pity, 29 without disgust. She loves them, and that's all there is to it. She takes them into herself until they become flesh of her flesh.

"She wore a short black skirt, a gray sweater with a black belt, smoke-colored stockings, and a small black velvet hat decorated with two silver cherries.

"Her face shows signs of exhaustion; she probably spent another sleepless night."

His readers like his vision of Modotti, and they express their approval with phone calls and letters. Circulation has increased since January 12.

3

After four days of hearings, Tina realizes they will use anything they can to incriminate her. As Luz watches her
friend, she is amazed by her strength and unpredictability, by the
mystery of such a powerful life force that seems to say to her: "Yes,
Luz, here I am, you can count on me!"

That morning, when Tina takes the stand, Valente Quintana
approaches her aggressively and dangles a letter in front of her.

"Have you ever seen this?"

Tina is visibly affronted. "What, you've read even that?"

"Yes, it was brought to our attention, and I thought it should
be added to the file."

"But what does it have to do with anything?" asks Tina.

"This typewritten letter is dated Moscow, June 5, 1928. Do
you remember it? You must have received it less than six months
ago."

"I don't understand why my private life has to be made public."

"Just answer the questions. Did you conceal the contents of this letter from Julio Antonio Mella?"

"I never concealed anything from Mella."

"And this person who mysteriously signs with an X, is he in Mexico?"

"No, sir. He's in Moscow."

Tina thinks with horror, "Now they're going to smear Xavier, too."

The judge intervenes. "Since we have already read the letter and the witness looks exceptionally tired, would you be so kind, Mr. Quintana, as to summarize it for us?"

"An individual, identifying himself only as X, affectionately addresses this woman and advises her to consult a lawyer before traveling to Europe, that her return to Mexico may be facilitated by applying for Mexican citizenship before she leaves. He states that he does not like the idea of her having to work to pay for the trip and that he would give her the money if he were not a prisoner."

"He's not a prisoner," Tina blurts out. "That's just his way of saying that he is studying at the university."

"He then recommends," Quintana continues in a more pompous tone, "that she should look for the best transatlantic route and bring a lot of documentary photographs to sell in Moscow, where he says she will find a fantastic agent. He repeats that first of all she should find the best way to get her passport in accordance with the laws of this nation of barbarians. He then says that he does not want to return to Mexico to be killed by a .45. He urges her to make the trip and signs in pencil with an X.

"We have analyzed this letter thoroughly," Valente Quintana continues menacingly. "X, who is obviously Mexican, calls his country a 'nation of barbarians' and confirms our suspicion that the .45 pistol, the one that killed Mella, is yours and that you are perfectly adept at handling it. We also know that both you and Mr. X are devoted Communists. What's more, X not only signs with an X, but he does so in pencil, to be able to erase it all."

"Oh, mamma mia," Tina exclaims. "He is an artist, he draws, and a pencil is what he had in his hand. The pistol was his. He left it with me, but I no longer have it. You twist everything around."

"I must ask you to please control your outbursts. I understand this is painful, but it is your duty to cooperate with the authorities."

"But that's what I have been doing. All I want is justice for Mella."

Tina protests to Judge Pino Cámara: "I am the daughter of poor Italian workers, but we never opened each other's letters." She remembers something her father used to say about prying into other people's business: "The punishment is in the crime." And here in the courtroom they not only betray her privacy, but Pérez Moreno and the entire Mexican press vilify her in black and white.

Once, she and Julio played at reading each other's most secret thoughts, but there was mutual respect, and they never used their discoveries to hurt each other. Everything that was beautiful has been vulgarized, like that day in the forest of the Desierto de los Leones when Julio fell asleep naked, and she photographed him.

She and Julio had taken off their clothes and left them in one big pile. Then Tina put on Julio's underpants and ran off, and he ran after her. She was never shy about being naked; she'd compete with the others to see who could get undressed faster so they could dance unfettered by buttons, collars, belts, snaps, with her arms held high, her breasts bouncing like two pears. Once she and Julio shyly told each other about their first sexual experiences; but now the two of them were being spread over the pages of those sordid Mexican newspapers, transformed into scorpions that wounded each other with poisonous stings.

Tina feels even worse after *Excelsior* publishes Julio's diary. The man in the diary is Julio, but it is also someone else; he is her man but also belongs to others. The passionate tones are familiar, but they are not addressed to her. Julio never told her about Silvia Masvidal, or about Edith. He spoke only about Olivín, and only with reference to the divorce that would allow them to marry. Olivín had left Mexico with their daughter, Natasha. Silvia Masvidal, *Excelsior* explains, was the woman he loved most. But there were others: Edith, Margarita, and Tina, his last lover.

Excelsior does not bother to mention that the diaries are from 1920, nine years before the murder. Tina, like the other readers, falls into the trap.

Julio Antonio Mella's memoirs, obtained exclusively by Excélsior, *have aroused great interest. Their journalistic success cannot be attributed solely to the fact that they are the intimate notes of the famous hunger-striker, but rather to their intrinsic value . . . If Julio Antonio had attempted to write a book for publication, he would not have awakened as much interest as he has with his sentences that so admirably express his spiritual state.*

His emotions pulsate on every page; it seems he could not live without loving and being loved.

His journals were full of extractable quotes like *"True happiness does not consist of having everything one desires but rather of desiring things one does not have and struggling to acquire them."*

Another entry began: *"I got up late, did nothing. I sent Silvia a cable. How difficult it is to have no word from her! This afternoon I went rowing in Chapultepec. I was sad as I watched this sunset whose purplish hues reminded me of her large, mysterious eyes. I thought only about how happy I would be with her by my side."*

Tina looks out the window of her apartment. Sometimes she watches the street corner from this window. The people down there never raise their heads. "He gave up his life," thinks Tina, "on that sidewalk; his blood is on the soles of their shoes, and they don't even know it."

She feels excluded. To whom did he direct all these secrets? He never showed her his diary. She doesn't know the people who send their condolences, or the woman who takes her by the arm on the way out of the courtroom and says to her, "I traveled to Veracruz with him; I was supposed to be his contact; I can come and go from Cuba whenever I get the order." Tina moves away defensively: real contacts tend not to be so communicative.

Suddenly, Julio is a stranger to her. She makes an effort to shake this vision of Julio and Silvia Masvidal, to replace it with one of Julio and Tina. Who was Julio, really? Dozens of men and women have traveled with him, shared his life with him. Didn't Belén Santamaría once shout angrily at her that she, Tina, was just a stepping-stone in his life, that he was destined for great things on his island, things that he must do without a woman by his side? That no married man could lead an enterprise as vast as the liberation of Cuba? Julio had the stature of a continental leader and would return to Cuba a single man, single, do you understand, chica? Just he and the Cubans. Tina would have to disappear. Didn't she realize the magnitude and greatness of his mission?

Julio is no longer by her side to calm her down, reassure her. She faces the storm alone. And the future? What would have happened? Would there have been a place for Tina? Julio said they would live together on the island, and Tina was prepared to share his fate. Once that tropical Mussolini was defeated, Julio would build a new socialist Cuba along the lines of the Russian Revolution. He would form a Central American and Caribbean anti-imperialist league, break relations with the United States, offer the peasants education, medicine, and decent food. Cubans would learn to produce for their own needs, they would develop their own science and technology. They would even make cameras. Yes, Tina, you will make films in the streets of Havana, surrounded by your students, films for the people and by the people; you'll see, my love, what a country my country is, we will make love morning, noon, and night, the arts will blossom like the large red flowers of the royal poinciana tree, the petals of your lips will burn at the hour of love, our island is guided by the light in a woman's eyes; Cuba needs your eyes, as I need your saliva, the tears from your eyes.

Exhausted, drenched in a cold sweat, she tosses and turns in bed, a moan of pain accompanying each movement. Is she the only one who has been left with these images of love? Are there others he loved the same way? He is the only one she has loved with such yearning, such passion, such a willingness to be completely open. Often, after they went their separate ways, Tina would sit down on a bench in the Ciudadela before going to work. She loved him so intensely that getting away from him for moments was her only salvation. Memories of last night's lovemaking played havoc with her senses. She began to shiver: her lips would remember his smile of satisfaction, the hair falling over his forehead, the weight of his legs, his hands on her back, her neck, her belly. She could almost feel his mouth on hers, Julio on top of her, yes, Julio, convulsing, exploding in spasms; yes, Julito, yes. She would pull herself together as she went over each moment one by one. She had loved Weston, her teacher, but never with such urgency, such a compelling ache.

Half an hour later, Tina would get up from the park bench and somehow or other make her way to 54 Mesones. Maybe he'll finish early today and come pick me up. Once inside the office, she would jump each time the door opened. I hear Julio's steps. It is Julio. No, it isn't. When will he come? My heart aches; I can't live like this. It is late. What happened to him? What's happening to me? I'm being consumed by love. I don't think I'll be able to work, she repeated to herself. The attraction between them was so fierce that when he finally entered the office she would feel the beating of her pulse in her belly. I'm crazy: to desire a man like this is madness. I am feverish; each day is a new delirium. I used to be a normal woman, and now I can't do anything but wait for him.

She didn't understand anything except Julio's gestures, Julio's hands on her body.

Sometimes they made love as if it were a game. The bed, the sheets, the blankets, everything spun around them, as light and playful as feathers. Sometimes Julio would arrive home in a serious mood; then, neither the blankets nor anything else would dance. There was something desperate in the way he would bury himself in her. One night Tina was awakened by his sobs; she took him in her arms and sheltered his head between her breasts until their desire returned. Mella clung to her like a drowning man, pulling her down, her name coming in one long sigh: Tina, Tina, Tina, Tinaaaa. Again, the tears on her shoulder. For the sake of modesty, she didn't turn on the light or look at him. She felt his sobs and let them come as she caressed him softly, softly, softly.

The next morning a warm yellow light crept over their bed, their feet, their knees. When it reached their bellies, Julio awoke. He was no longer the same man as the night before. He woke up to the world, the sun, the transparency of the air. Day came to greet him and again they made love, laughing, pressed to each other, their legs white with semen, musk, sandalwood, their skins shining.

It was the quality of light, the way it advanced over the floor and encroached on the whitewashed walls that grounded their morning lovemaking. This was their way of settling themselves into the day, into life. "We have the same surface area," Julio would say and laugh. "We have the same perimeter, the same mouth." They came together. They became one another. Merged into one. Tied together. Afterwards, at the breakfast table, it was difficult not to share even their bites of food, don't swallow yet, wait for me. When Julio lifted his cup, Tina instantly did the same, just one, you and I, eating from the same plate with the same fork and knife, the same morsels in our mouths. Any other way would have been inconceivable.

36   "When did you first meet Julio Antonio Mella?"

"I first saw him during the Sacco and Vanzetti campaign, but I didn't talk to him until many months later."

In 1927, at the huge demonstration in support of Sacco and Vanzetti, Julio Antonio Mella was the only speaker. "Look at that handsome man," commented a girl standing in the crowd next to Tina. Yes, he was electric. For some reason, people put their hopes in him. He would save Sacco and Vanzetti: in fact, he would save everyone in the crowd. He was their spokesman: they would have said the same things if they had known how. He had the capacity to think and communicate his thoughts. He had sexual power as well: he could satisfy them all.

Tina waited among those who approached him after the ovation. They all wanted to raise him on their shoulders. Julio, smiling, refused. When Tina finally offered him her hand, she felt his eyes upon her as a precious gift: his gaze raised her above the crowd, singled her out.

"When did he begin to pursue you, romantically?" Quintana asks.

"In July of the following year. He moved into my apartment in September. We only lived together for four months."

"Were you seeing anybody else at the time?"

"I already said that I had broken up with somebody else when I met Mella."

"Where did you first meet Xavier Guerrero?"

"In Los Angeles. The government sent him there in 1923 to set up an exhibition of popular art. That was before I moved to Mexico."

"Did you know that he was a Communist?"

"Yes."

"Did you love both Guerrero and Mella?"

"Not at the same time."

"On the eighth of last month, were you living with Mella?"

"Yes."

"And yet you received money from Guerrero. We found among your papers this message from Moscow, dated a month ago: 'Dear Madame: In the name of Minister de Negri, I am pleased to send you the enclosed check for the sum of twenty-five dollars, entrusted to me by your husband and my friend, Mr. Xavier Guerrero. Yours affectionately, Omar Josefe, Commercial Attaché to the Mexican Delegation in Germany, Holland, and the U.S.S.R.'"

Whispered exclamations of interest and surprise.

Quintana raises his voice above the buzz. "You are Mrs. Guerrero, your husband is in Russia, and you have just said you were involved with nobody else."

"I'm sure Omar Josefe addressed me as Mrs. Guerrero to expedite matters. Correspondence between Communists is difficult."

"Guerrero supported you financially while you lived with Mella?"

"Xavier sent me those twenty-five dollars out of decency. I helped pay for his ticket to Europe. He was always very kind to me."

"Did you tell Mella about your relationship with Guerrero?"

"I was always honest with him and with Guerrero. The only thing Mella didn't know was how difficult it was for me to decide to live with him. He interpreted those months of indecision as a lack of love or courage. I didn't love Guerrero anymore, but I didn't want to hurt him: so I waited, because I wanted him to know about it before I changed my life . . ."

Tina bites her lips. Again, she's saying more than she needs to.

"Yes, we have realized that you make men suffer; we have read the letter the dead man sent you from Veracruz."

"That is my private business."

Julio was so upset, there was so much anguish in his scribbled words. "So explain it to me. What kind of love is this that drives me to desperation? I love you serenely and wildly, as I've told you many times, as something definitive in my life. You say that you love me and will be mine. But when? How? Oh, Tina, is it fair? If you love me, what right do you have to make me suffer so. You are ashamed to be seen with me or, as you said, to hurt him. Are you still that interested in him? Tina, it's not in me to beg, but in the name of all the love between us, give me something concrete, something I can hold on to . . . I'm suffocating."

Quintana turns to her solemnly. "You have contradicted yourself more than once."

"You are constantly setting traps for me. Your questions are all insidious."

"I'm sorry, but my questions are not designed to please you. Just tell me, what were Guerrero's political views?"

"He was and is a Communist, a member of the Mexican Communist Party."

"Which of the two, Mella or Guerrero, had stronger ideas about Communism?"

"They were the same."

"Did you have strong feelings for Guerrero?"

"At a certain time, yes."

"And did you, while living with Mella, think it proper to receive money from another man?"

"Yes, from a friend."

"I am talking about a person who was romantically interested in you. Is it honest, legal, or ethical to receive such presents?"

"If I had known they were being offered with some romantic intention, I would not have accepted them. There are many ways to give a gift."

"Would you please tell us if Guerrero expressed strong feelings toward you?"

"Yes, he did, but his love for me was secondary to the most important thing in his life: the revolution. He was willing to sacrifice himself for it."

"Do you really believe that when a person has strong feelings for someone, they can be sacrificed for an idea?"

"If the person is truly committed, yes. The loves of revolutionaries are always secondary to their political convictions."

"When you began to be intimate with Mella, did you completely break with Guerrero?"

"Yes, no, I mean, I continued sending him weekly magazines; he had asked me to keep him informed about Mexican politics."

"How did the break occur between you and Guerrero?"

"I sent him a letter in August or the beginning of September. Letters take about twenty-three days to reach Moscow. The reply was hand-delivered. Since he was a well-known Communist, his letters didn't always get through."

"And afterwards, did you receive money from him?"

"Only that check for twenty-five dollars. I gave it all away to needy friends. Anyway, Xavier's financial situation was never very good."

"And yours?"

"I have always worked to support myself."

"Did Mella ever travel without you?"

"He went a number of times to Veracruz, Puebla, Atlixco, and other towns to participate in activities related to the struggle for   39 workers' rights. He once went to Durango as a representative of the National League of Peasants."

"Did you tell Mella about your relationship with Guerrero?"

"Yes. I already told you, at the very beginning."

"How did Guerrero treat you?"

"I told you, he was always very kind."

"Do you recognize this letter?" Valente Quintana says as he approaches her.

"It is from Julio Antonio, from Veracruz. Are we going to go over this again?"

"Señora, we are investigating a homicide. This letter is signed Nicanor MacPartland. Did you know about Mella's secret political activities?"

"The secrets, no."

"Then explain this sentence: 'I don't want others to know what you know.'"

Tina feels Julio's absence as a sharp stab in her belly.

"Since he's dead, I can say it. Julio traveled to Veracruz with the intention of going into Cuba to start the revolution, but he didn't want anybody to know."

Someone blew the whistle, and the comrades returned from Veracruz with defeat in their eyes and their shoulders weighed down. Those were days of mourning. Tina took Julio in her arms and felt his tears on her shoulder. Now again they are flowing, wetting her neck, her breast, oh Julio, as Valente Quintana asks aggressively, "So he only wanted to make a revolution in Cuba? Do you realize that while looking for a murderer we have uncovered a conspiracy?"

"Only in Cuba."

"Now then, please explain this sentence: 'You know that with me you have nothing to fear.'"

"I already told you. I was nervous, indecisive. I couldn't commit myself to him. It was incomprehensible to him that I should hold back for months, and he interpreted my behavior as a rejection. I thought about going to Moscow to talk things over with Guerrero. Julio thought that if I saw Guerrero again I would stay with him. While Mella was away for a week, I had time to think things over, and I decided to write to Xavier."

All eyes are glued on Tina as Quintana reads the text of this letter in court. Tina wonders if they have obtained it through supernatural means, until she remembers that she kept a carbon copy of it among her papers.

X, there is no question that this is the most difficult, painful, terrible letter I have ever written in my life. I have delayed writing, partly to be sure of what I want to say, and partly because I know what a terrible effect this will have on you.

I need all my tranquillity and serenity of spirit to clearly explain the situation to you, without ambiguities, and without being overwhelmed by emotions, something that seems almost impossible if I start to think what this letter will mean to you.

X, sometimes when I think of the pain I will cause you, I think I am a monster rather than a human being. At other times I feel that I am the poor innocent victim of a terrible fate, that there is in me some kind of hidden force that directs my actions in spite of me. But I am the first to dispel notions such as "fate" or "hidden forces." So what's left? Why do I act as I do? I truly believe that my feelings are intrinsically good, that I consider other people's feelings before my own, that I am never cruel for cruelty's sake. And now, when I must be cruel, I suffer perhaps more than you do.

But now is the time to tell you what I must tell you. I love another man. I love him and he loves me, and this love has brought about what I never thought possible: I have stopped loving you.

X, I could tell you a long story about this love; how it was born, how it grew to the point where I decided I must tell you; how I have struggled with myself to eradicate him from my life (I swear to you I have even considered suicide, but I knew that was simply a cowardly solution). I could tell you how torturous this dilemma has been for me; I have thought about everything, especially about you. But more so I have thought about the consequences of my actions on our revolutionary activities. This has been my greatest concern, even greater than my concern for you. And I have reached the conclusion that no matter where I am, with you or somebody else, the little good I might do the cause, our cause, will not suffer, because working for the cause is not, for me, something external, the result of loving a revolutionary, but is rather the result of a very deep commitment inside myself. And I owe a lot of that to you, X. You are

41

the one who opened my eyes, you are the one who helped me at a time when I felt the ground of my old beliefs breaking up under my feet. And to think how much you have helped me. I pay you back like this. How terrible, X! The only thing that makes me feel a bit better is knowing how strong you are, knowing that you will overcome the pain I am causing you. I only hope that you do not ever doubt the sincerity of my love for you, and I swear to you that the feelings I had for you were the greatest pride of my life. And yet this has happened. How is it possible? I don't know myself. I don't understand, but I do feel that what is happening now is inevitable, and I can act in no other way.

I considered waiting to tell you all this personally, when you returned or going there to tell you; I thought it would be more honorable, more faithful than telling you in a letter. But I realized that I couldn't continue writing to you in the tone that had always come so naturally but that now would be false.

I feel I should not love you anymore: I feel that would also be your wish, and I promise that by the time you return I will have left. I don't expect a response from you, but I would like to be sure that this letter reaches you, because I don't want to change anything in my life until I am sure it has.

"The epilogue," Quintana adds triumphantly, "is a cable from Moscow: 'Letter received. Goodbye. Guerrero.'"

Pino Cámara adjourns the session. Tina is about to leave with Luz Ardizana when a man with a white beard steps in front of her. A court official introduces him. "This is Dr. Maximilian Langsner, the criminal psychologist who got the Canadian murderer, Boohar, to confess. We have asked the doctor to examine you under hypnosis to discover the truth."

"If I agree, that is. I'm under investigation, but I'm not part of the circus," Tina responds arrogantly.

The professor sits down in front of her. "We can speak English if you like."

"I will answer in Spanish. I have nothing to hide."

As Langsner begins asking questions, Tina calms down under the weight of his unblinking, hypnotic eyes.

"You have called attention to yourself with your cheerful, composed demeanor throughout this ordeal. You have not even dressed in mourning."

"Julio Antonio is not dead for me."

"Did you love Julio Antonio Mella?"

"Yes."

"And you believe he is not dead?"

"He survives in his work, in the effect he had on his friends, in his thoughts."

"Do you believe in reincarnation?"

"No."

"Are you religious?"

"I am a Communist."

"Tell me, how do you think human beings perpetuate themselves?"

"Through their ideas. Perhaps through their children. I, myself, don't have any."

"Why is that?"

"I don't know."

"I understand you were once married. Who was your husband?"

"The American poet l'Abrie Richey; he died of smallpox in Mexico. He is buried here."

"Do you ever visit his grave?"

"Rarely."

"Is there a gravestone?"

Tina doesn't answer.

"Is there some kind of marker on the grave?" he repeats, thinking Tina hadn't understood.

"Yes, there is a gravestone."

"Who had it made?"

"I did."

"That's what I wanted to know," he says with satisfaction. "When?"

"In 1923, when I came to Mexico."

"Did you already hold your current political views?"

"In the United States I worked in a garment factory and became interested in union activities. I heard songs about Joe Hill, Tom Mooney. My brothers are activists. I only joined the Party a short while ago."

The room gets hotter. Tina begins to nod off. This man is

hypnotizing her with his flat, monotone voice, each word a drop of water, tick, tick, tick, tick, taking her slowly back to her past.

"Are you tired?"

"Yes, very."

"We can stop now. We'll soon have another opportunity."

Pérez Moreno is dozing on the bench. Tina acknowledges him with a cursory nod, then continues on her way. He approaches Dr. Langsner. Tina manages to hear part of his response.

"I'm going to see her again, but at this point it looks like a crime of passion; she is a woman with a very strong temperament . . ."

Tina does not care to hear anymore. She walks out leaning on Luz's arm. As they go out the door, the two policemen assigned to guard her take their places behind her.

"What kind of country do we live in?" shouts Diego Rivera, furiously shaking his walking stick in the air the next morning. "Because if this hypnotist's act weren't so laughable, it would be pathetic."

Curious bystanders, some of whom have been waiting for hours, as well as employees of the court, gather around him. Everyone wants to hear what Diego has to say.

"This was no crime of passion. It was a political crime," Diego shouts. "Why don't they investigate Magriñat? Why are the authorities protecting him? Hasn't anybody realized that he is the murderer?"

Diego's harangue threatens to incite a political demonstration. The police force him away from the courthouse. Diego, undaunted, continues outside on the sidewalk.

"In Cuba, Magriñat had a reputation for being a pimp, a gigolo, a gambler. And yet, whom do they watch night and day and keep under house arrest like some kind of common criminal, whom do they interrogate endlessly? Tina Modotti. For what mysterious reason has Magriñat not been arrested?"

"Rumor has it that it was Modotti's pistol that killed Mella," José Pérez Moreno informs him.

"Poor Tina, all she needs is for those political puppets to make her confess that she killed the man she loved. They should be looking for Magriñat's weapon, not hers," adds Diego.

"I was there when she sold that gun," blurts out Carleton Beals, an American journalist. "And I am prepared to sign a written statement to that effect."

"Give it to me. I'll publish it," Pérez Moreno offers enthusiastically.

"I had commissioned some photographs from Tina for *Creative Arts*," Beals continues, "and while I was there to pick them up, Fritz Bach, a German journalist, arrived. Tina showed him the gun. He tried to take it apart, but didn't know how. He then asked Tina how it worked, and she said she didn't know anything about it. Bach said he was going to take it home to look at it more carefully. He took it and left. I got the photographs from Tina and left also."

"You see. Bach has the gun, but you journalists didn't even try to find that out," Rivera scolds Pérez Moreno.

"I have another theory," Pérez Moreno asserts. "What if the Communists had him killed, and the Italian is trying to protect them? One order from Moscow, and it's done. You people are always doing things behind each other's backs."

Rivera shouts at the top of his lungs and just barely refrains from breaking his stick over Moreno's head. "That's all we need! Why in hell would we kill him when he was the most loyal, dedicated . . ." Pérez Moreno gets quickly out of shooting and shouting range, and disappears.

Diego's presence in the courtroom irritates the judge. He is disgusted by Diego's filthy, wrinkled pants, his unbuttoned shirt, his shirt pocket bulging with hastily folded papers. "He turns my courtroom into a marketplace." Whenever he's not demanding the floor, he takes out a little notebook and begins scribbling, arousing curiosity in those sitting near him. The bailiff told the judge that he saw a sketch Diego had made of him in his robes and that it was hilarious. Diego makes him feel insecure. More and more people are on his side every day. Not even the primmest, most proper secretary is offended by his appearance. "Maestro," over here. "Maestro," over there. Everything is excused because, after all, he is an "artist," a "bohemian." None of the guards dares mess with him, not with that hefty pistol peeking out from under the loose jacket that covers his belly. What is it about this man that makes people watch his every movement, that attracts attention to everything he does? Diego has become Tina's one-man defense committee, even though he doesn't have a clue about courtroom procedure and talks whenever he feels like it. That poor Italian, so trusting, wasting away before everyone's eyes, poor thing, as if she lived in the clouds. At home, Pino Cámara hides the newspapers from his children. Modotti has become more famous, or infamous, than La Malinche.

As Judge Pino Cámara leaves the courtroom, he approaches José Pérez Moreno. "Valente Quintana has just been removed as chief prosecutor," he states dryly.

"What a scoop! Thank you, Judge, thank you very much."

"The order came from the President. He's feeling pressure from certain sectors of public opinion."

"Public opinion or Diego Rivera's opinion?"

"He is being replaced by Colonel Talamantes, chief of the Mexico City Police Department."

To sleep is to float. The tide reaches the bed. Tina is tossed about on the waves, drifting out on green, blue, and purple liquid before dropping to the bottom of the ocean. Julio told her he once heard the bellow of a female shark in heat, a sharp intermittent sound, yet he remained in the water despite the danger. A cry, almost human, rises from the depths; the female is searching for her mate. Tina's own bellow grows within her, crosses over the watery walls, rises to the level of the water, and sticks in her throat. When will the tears stop pouring down her cheeks and wetting her pillow? She arches her back and begins to tremble, stifles a groan, blinks, then places her hands between her thighs as Julio grows inside her, making her grow. Julio in the depths of her eyes, anchored to the bottom of the ocean. She hears his voice.

"Tinisima."

"We're burying you, Julio."

"How can I die if you still live?"

She shouts, "Julio!" The ebb and flow of the waves as they wash over her body, her tear-stained face. Julio disappears, but the undertow brings him up again. She will drag him out by his hair full of sand and foam; she will place her mouth over his cracked lips, breathe flakes of salt into his chest until he has been restored.

"Tinisima."

The wind carries the sound of Julio's laughter. Suddenly, everything is erased, and except for the hum of the sea at the foot of the bed, all has returned to silence.

She is pulled, gasping, back from the depths. With trembling hands she lights another cigarette. Her chest hurts, and her head is about to explode. The current wants to drag her out to another dream. Tina presses the cigarette between her lips and inhales deeply, pushing the smoke out through her nose to keep the sea out of her mouth. The cigarette is her only life raft. She must concentrate on it as she swims against the current. For the rest of the night, she sits on the edge of the bed, her head resting against the wooden backboard. Each breath is painful. If she's not dreaming about Julio, she's remembering him. There's no relief.

At dawn, Julio is lying in the room. Tina feels him breathing next to her, he is about to touch her. Julio is there, his hat on the hook, his toothbrush in the cup, his shoes, his enthusiasm. "I saw something you have to take a picture of, Tinisima. Let's go look at it before it's gone. A street corner, a woman in the market . . ."

So many times he carried the Graflex, and when asked if he was a photographer, he'd point to her and say, "I'm her assistant." She would give anything for just one more stroll with him through the hot, almost deserted city. How they both loved the naked pride of Mexico's sky, the humble, reduced figures of its people, their houses, the violence of the colors, those strident roses that suddenly appear out of the forest of green. "What a spectacular country!"

She still hears his voice, sailboats anchored in the room.

4

$\mathcal{T}$ina makes a print of the last photograph she took of Julio while he was alive. The picture also includes David Alfaro Siqueiros, Sandalio Junco, Teurbe Tolón, and Alejandro Barreiro, all members of the Committee for the Defense of the Proletariat.

She places the print on her bedside table, lies down on the bed, and falls asleep with the light on. When she wakes up, she shouts, "Open up."

From the other room, there is only silence.

"Open up."

Then she realizes what has happened. She is free.

Once Valente Quintana is removed from the case, the crime-of-passion theory is discarded and the political-crime theory adopted. Magriñat is again brought in for questioning. This time, when asked about his itinerary after he parted from Mella at La India Cantina, he defiantly asserts his right to go wherever he pleases. He destroys the good impression he previously made. It becomes clear that Magriñat had had plenty of time to send a gunman out after Mella.

The Communists accuse Magriñat. They claim to have more than a dozen witnesses who can testify that he is a gambler and professional assassin, that in Mexico he has worked as an agent provocateur. What's more, he has a prison record and Modotti doesn't. True, she gets around, plays it a bit loose, but that's the way women are in the Old World. Just looking at her, you wouldn't necessarily get that impression. She has some gray hairs, and there are lines around her eyes. She's too thin. Poor woman, they've really ground her to the dust.

The testimony of Mr. Frovlán C. Manjarréz, governor of Puebla, is decisive. In Cuba, there is no political repression, there are only dead bodies. He lived in Havana for two and a half years and is well informed. "It is highly probable that Havana gave the order for Mella's assassination, just as the Communists claim." Mr. Manjarréz tells about Colonel Masso, who was shot on the terrace of his house in Havana. The Cuban government does not brook opposition.

On Saturday, Judge Alfredo Pino Cámara formally charges José Magriñat for the murder of Julio Antonio Mella, and orders that he be held without bail until trial.

The first thing Pérez Moreno does when he hears the news is rush over to Tina's apartment. After running up the stairs, he is disappointed to find Luz Ardizana, that skinny woman with glasses, in the doorway talking to the reporter from *La Prensa*. Is she giving him any exclusive information? What a disagreeable person! Tina appears and apologizes for receiving them in her kimono, "which shows off her ivory complexion," he writes afterwards.

"We want some details."

"You people never give up. Nothing has changed."

"But you are free."

"That's relative . . ."

She lets out a sigh that reveals her doubts, and abruptly asks, "Do you think they'll let Magriñat go?"

"No, not now. The judge is holding him without bail."

"I'm very much afraid of that man," she blurts out.

"You? Why?"

"I don't know, but I have the feeling that if he gets out of prison, he will try to hurt me, even more than he already has."

Tina's neighbor, Frances Toor, tells Luz Ardizana that every night, at the same hour, she is awakened by a loud scream.

"She needs calcium for her nerves. I'm going to take her to a doctor! And to think she looks so calm, as if she has everything under control."

"Yes, but at night . . ."

"We have to help our poor comrade," says Enea Sormenti one morning when he sees her enter the offices of *El Machete*. "She needs to get away for a few days, take a rest."

"She won't want to."

"Let me handle it."

Sormenti walks over to her desk and gives her an order. "Get out of here, Tina. What are you doing here with those horrible circles under your eyes? You look like a bunch of wilted spinach. Go get some sunshine!"

A few days later, as she descends from the crowded train that brings her to Juchitán, in the Isthmus of Tehuantepec, the humidity in the air immediately changes her mood. During the whole trip she clutched her bulky Graflex on her lap to keep it from being bounced around. "Other women carry their children," she thought. "I carry my camera."

The seduction has begun. The banana groves, the hammock on the terrace, the royal poinciana trees, the comforting, eternal sound of the cicadas and other rumblings one never hears in the city. She sleeps better than she has in months. "This is like returning to the womb," she thinks and smiles as she awakens in the sweet softness of the hammock. She begins to spend her time with the local women. Na'Chiña is their shepherdess.

Parrots screech from the treetops, iguanas stretch out in the sun, the breeze teases the curtains and pushes open the windows. The accusations recede. Nocturnal rainfall, so gentle that Tina doesn't feel it in her hammock on the terrace, drips off the foliage.

In Juchitán, people go freely in and out of houses that are always open. The children play in the mud along with the chickens and the pigs. A kind of Dionysian effervescence permeates the public spaces. Juchitán is one big public space—market, cantina, plaza—full of people of all ages, peasants from the outlying areas, everything bursting with exuberance, like the painted gourds, the iguanas, and especially the women, who carry earthenware trays overflowing with fruits on their heads.

"I'll never laugh again," she had thought, but the sound in her throat takes her by surprise. María Henestrosa and Catalina Pineda tickle her ribs while they help her try on an embroidered sleeveless blouse with her flowered skirt. Voices speaking Zapotec tumble over the clothing stand in the marketplace under the arcade of the Municipal Palace. "Look, this will fit you because you're so small; hey you, give her something in red velvet." The vowels hang in the air: "gunabadiiidxa tuuunga naa. Xiindi gune." Reina, Cirila, Isabel, Alfa, and Gudelia surround her, besiege her with their breasts, their braids that hang down to their thighs, the sweat that soaks their bodies. "You're sad, aren't you? Sadness is no good for anybody. Just get rid of it." Tina blushes. "Something tells me you are living in the past. Enjoy the moment, you're young. And what are you doing all the time with that black box? Mr. Gómez warned us that it can see through our clothes. And anyway, what do you need it for? The only thing we women need is that black flower between our legs, the one everyone wants to get hold of. Here, being a woman means shouting through the cornfields that stretch from sea to sea, letting yourself flow like the hair that tumbles over your shoulders before it is braided up again with red and yellow and blue ribbons."

All those grueling months and not a single woman in the Party had been so open with her. She is amazed by these women who establish such intimacy with so little false modesty. "Hey, you, get moving over there." They duck as they walk past the fly-covered meat hanging from the eaves; they sidestep the stinking puddles, the baskets of fish on the ground; they walk past piles of tamales wrapped in banana leaves, chile peppers, totopos, the large brittle tortillas baked in a hole in the ground. "Come on, let's go." Some have a dark shadow over their upper lips. "Trim that mustache, María." And they open their legs when they sit down to eat, spreading the totopos over their knees. "Move it, girl, what are you afraid of?" Tina is so shocked by their conversation that she is never quite sure she understands them correctly. They talk about the sun, the moon, the birdie that pecks, then stop to hold their bellies as they laugh heartily at the pun Tina finally understands. Tina no longer dwells on her pain. They grab her around the waist, caress her hair, stroke her chin, pamper and pet her until her eyelids droop from pleasure. "You're very pretty, but you'd look much better with gold teeth. At least buy yourself a chain, something that glitters." "Take off that horrid black skirt; these blouses let in the air, and why are you wearing a bra when you have such beautiful little breasts? Take off your stockings, don't be so hard on yourself. In this heat we should all be running around in our birthday suits. Who'll see you? You'd think the earth was a mirror." They undress her, touch her, tickle her, sweep away her misery. Their carefree steps emanate green, water, wood. "We'll take you to a vigil to exorcise you."

One afternoon, she reluctantly tells Na'China that she lost her lover. The old woman shrugs her shoulders. "So what? What are you worried about? Tomorrow we'll go to the market. There are lots of fish there to choose from. Don't keep moping around, you're only hurting yourself." That night, the hammock envelops her in the same sweet sleep as the night before. She awakens feeling cleansed, without a single tortured thought. "We'll cure you in spite of yourself," Na'China said. Why close herself off from the lives of men and women who continue to breathe around her? What joy to be alive!

That morning she buys a pair of dangling earrings, her first act of vanity since Julio's death. Tina blossoms. Her place on this earth is no longer a narrow sidewalk in Mexico City. Instead, it is this avenue bordered by palm trees. Here she doesn't meet those skittish city rats; here her companions are women whose freedom makes them queens of the earthenware jugs, women who catch tortoises and rabbits, lobster and deer, the stars and the rain in their skirts. They talk about the phallus like some everyday object that they can take into their hands, as if it were their own little treasure they could place in their private cache whenever they wanted to.

Life is so easy in Juchitán! The rain dangles from the sky until it suddenly falls, only to gather itself up and fall again. The women run into the sea. With their skirts and blouses still stuck to their skins, they are off to the orchards to pick chirimoyas and avocados.

To take photographs has been easy, too. As a matter of fact, they have been the easiest photos she had taken in her life, they all came to her naturally, she hardly had to ask the women to stop, they were slow, they walked into time like statues, they posed for her without knowing it and their inner potentiality eliminated all self-pity, all sentimentalism. "My work is good." Tina's heart jumped. They carried themselves regally and like them Tina did not want life to bow her head. The columns of the Juchitán market were Doric and she wrote to Edward on the back of one of the photos: *"Too bad the woman moved! Does the marketplace not look like a Greek temple?"*

Tomorrow, Tina will be on her way back to Mexico City.

"Enea, look at the pictures I took."

Enea Sormenti shuffles through them as if they were a deck of cards.

"Bene. Bene. I don't know anything about art, but they look okay to me."

As if he were looking at a child's homework. Her experiences in Juchitán, the lushness of its women, their strength, their attitudes; it all crumbles around her.

"There weren't any courts there or journalists holding notepads, trying to condemn me with every one of their insidious questions."

"Yes, I can imagine. Hey, you, Tachuela, come here a second. What about that meeting . . ."

She'll have to keep it all to herself: Na'Chiña's tenderness, like that of young corn, the hammock, the foliage. Here, the only subject is politics. She should have known. She can't even tell Luz Ardizana about her trip. "I'm so glad you had a good time. You needed a break so you could get back to work."

"How did you end up in this country?" Na'Chiña had asked her. Tina remembers the question and closes her eyes; she feels that she has lost something along the way and begins to spin out her memories, some aloud, some to herself. There, before her, stands Na'Chiña: her interlocutor and unlikely accomplice.

5

In 1915, when Tina was nineteen years old, she met Roubaix de l'Abrie Richey—otherwise known as Robo—at the Pan-Pacific International Exposition in San Francisco.

"Look at that distinguished-looking man," Mercedes, Tina's sister, said to her.

Perhaps Tina fell in love with the way he looked at her, a look that made her feel he wanted to discover her. "This artist is searching for something deeper within me, something he will help me find." She imagined she would like to live with a man who made batiks and could lose himself in poetry, the poetry of forms and of words. Tina was a seamstress. What couldn't the two of them do together!

He was six years older than she, and she felt protected when she was with him. He seemed to infuse their relationship with the tenderness that flowed so easily from his entire being.

In 1918 they were married and soon thereafter moved to Los

Angeles. They lived and worked in a studio that became the meeting place for what John Cowper Powys, their friend and intellectual mentor, referred to as "the sect."

If it was a sect, Powys was the center around which it revolved. He imposed his ideas, while the others sat in awe at his sarcasm, his humor, his brilliance. Tina would sit devotedly at his feet as if he were an object of worship.

"I believe in nothing, not even that I believe in nothing. My skepticism is authentic, even though I can't believe this, or even that I don't believe it."

Tina smiled, and John realized how intently she was listening to him.

He addressed himself more directly to her. "I am not a materialist, because my liberty is not limited by any idealistic notion of life."

"So you must be an infidel," commented Ramiel McGehee, the dancer, wrapping his robe more tightly around his waist.

"I know that I don't know, or that maybe I do. The Catholic Church, for example, is a beautiful and admirable work of art created by humanity to satisfy its own needs; it is a romantic and charming escape from the banalities of existence."

The Mexican poet Ricardo "Rodion" Gómez Robelo rejected his words with a wave of his hand.

Powys continued. "And as proof of my respect for my religious friends, I also accept that I cannot explain what I have just said."

"Yours is a hodgepodge of philosophies," Gómez Robelo stated.

"No, I am simply a hedonist. I masturbate continuously; it is my main mental-health exercise. And if more men would do it, they wouldn't attack other people. Masturbation is a private and political ritual. Don't you agree, Tina?"

Tina searched for a response, attempting to rise to his level. My God, what should I say? She took a long drag of her cigarette and slowly exhaled. The smoke encircled her head.

"I am beyond good and evil. I was born before Original Sin."

Powys's smile reassured her. "You are Powysian par excellence."

Tina loved Powys because she had seen him go out of his way to avoid stepping on plants; she had seen him pick up fallen leaves and caress flowers. For him, everything was alive; he apologized to the stones for stepping on them. Tina completely agreed with Powys about vivisection. Making four-legged animals suffer to help

55

two-legged ones was unjustifiable. "As long as they are used for experiments, a cure for cancer will never be found," said Powys. "It goes against the laws of nature."

Powys also spoke about George Eliot, Melville, Tolstoy, Nietzsche, and Dostoevsky, who particularly interested Ricardo Gómez Robelo.

"One night when I was a law student, I went to a whorehouse," Gómez Robelo said. "I knelt before a prostitute and kissed her feet. 'I am not kissing you,' I told her, 'I am kissing all of suffering humanity.'"

This purely Dostoevskian act won him Powys's acceptance and Tina's affection. From that night on, the sect nicknamed him Rodion Romanovich Raskolnikov.

Mention was constantly being made of Grushenka, Zosima, underground spiritual forces, vertigo, turbulence, ecstasy, the risk in being a charlatan. For John Cowper Powys, man's only censor was man himself, for he was a being condemned to be free. Pleasure is a doorway to freedom. Tina, at his feet, devoured his words.

One day, Ramiel McGehee brought with him to the studio Edward Weston, a small man with a powerful chest and an imperious air. Tina was attracted to him the moment he sat down next to her. They stretched out on handmade batik pillows and listened to music.

"Americans are so flat, and this city is flatness incarnate. Like uncooked pizza dough. We Italians take that dough and make pizza, we smother it in cheese and salami." Tina kneaded invisible dough and threw her arms up into the air, showing off the luxurious black triangle under her arms. "Americans lack imagination."

"Americans eat what others make, Tina." Ramiel laughed. "What does Robo think about all this?"

"Oh, he's an aristocrat. His vision is clouded by his dreams. He is too refined to think about pizza. Compared to him, I seem depraved . . ."

"Is he very sensitive?" Weston insisted.

"He is not of this world. He can sit for hours looking out the window without doing anything."

"You are tragic; he is romantic," Gómez Robelo pronounced. "You tend toward catastrophe; he prefers escape. You live on the edge; he lives in the clouds."

"We are all exiles in search of paradise."

"But you, Tina, you are paradise," Ramiel said.

"Thank God for the Richey–Modotti ghetto."

"The only thing we truly have is our bodies," asserted John Cowper Powys. "We can change countries, but not bodies. There is no greater source of pleasure than the body."

Ramiel asserted that the dancer's body could defy gravity. "I shall demonstrate it this very moment." And in one great leap he crossed the entire room. Powys looked on with delight.

"Don Juan ignores what Onan knows," Gómez Robelo said, quoting Machado.

Weston launched into a monologue about the creativity of the female body. "Women," he said, turning to Tina, "are allowed a whole series of movements that are prohibited to us. I would love to walk like you, Tina, but can you imagine what they would say to me in the street?"

"It's the damn bourgeoisie that imposes those limits," Tina said.

The sect was also united by Ezra Pound and his poetry, Hinduism, the new sciences, meditation, sensuality, the esoteric, and by a pervasive sense that they were for one another the only bulwark against the vulgarity of the world. By drinking saké they came closer to Japan and its essential nature; the West was the inventor of all that was superfluous. Europe was heavy and drab. One need only look at those awkward, prematurely aged European bodies, trapped in their tailored suits. But have you seen those marvelous saffron-colored Hindu silk blouses in that shop on Sawtelle Boulevard, on the way to Santa Monica?

"This is the only paradise from which we do not want to be exiled, Tina."

Gómez Robelo, art critic and director of the Museum of Fine Arts in Mexico City, had, in fact, been in exile before the triumph of the Mexican Revolution. Having served as attorney general to Victoriano Huerta, later considered a traitor, he had been thrown out of Mexico by Venustiano Carranza in 1914. He was an erudite man who dazzled them one night reciting Keats, Shelley, Byron. His specialty was Edgar Allan Poe. Nobody could compete with Powys's lucidity—Blake spoke through him—but Gómez Robelo had more charm. In spite of his ugliness—his thick lips and angular face—he was seductive, like Cyrano de Bergerac. "How amusing! A Mexican Edmond Rostand, without his Roxanne!" agreed Powys.

"I think he's attractive," Tina declared. "Maybe because of his ugliness, and because he always says that his only passion is his passion for beauty. Toulouse-Lautrec fascinates him because he himself is a Toulouse-Lautrec."

Gómez Robelo didn't respond.

"Publish your poetry, Rodion," Robo said. "I will illustrate it."

"I can design the book," Ramiel McGehee added.

"He makes magnificent books," John Cowper Powys said, lending his support.

Robo insisted on illustrating *Sátiros y amores—Satyrs and Loves*—a title that delighted Powys. Tina was his model for the line drawings. He drew a rose in place of her sex and a circle of petals around her nipples. On her head, he placed a Spanish mantilla; at her feet, a skull with a snake in its teeth. Robo and Gómez Robelo were obsessed with death, but Gómez Robelo was even more obsessed with Tina: her white face, her deep black eyes, that dangerous way she had of crossing her legs while smiling imperceptibly.

Robo translated:

> *White as if some internal light*
> *illumined her transparent flesh.*
> *Enigmatic eyes of the Orient;*
> *deepest black; a firefly at the center.*

Every time they met, Gómez Robelo discovered a new Tina he had never glimpsed before. She questioned him about the pyramids in Mexico. He told her about Diego Rivera, a muralist who turned his back on Rodin and Impressionism and looked instead to Mexico's pre-Hispanic past for his inspiration, to "those who built the pyramids." He explained that today's Mexican painters were the descendants of the indigenous muralists; they were workers themselves who identified with the working masses. Tina told him that the first thing she had done when she arrived in San Francisco in 1913 was to go to work in a garment factory. She would never live without working. She had worked since she was a child, and she would continue to work until the day she died. She told him about the Italians in San Francisco, more than fifteen thousand of them, how they had turned that port into an Italian city with their pizzerias, their bakeries, their theaters, their shouting, and their songs.

Had Gómez Robelo heard about the 'filodrammaticas'? She had played in Dario Niccodemi's *La Nemica* and still knew by heart the great final scene in the second act. Acting in Hollywood had never given her as much satisfaction as she had derived from those skits they performed in the streets and neighborhood squares. Then she had been an actress, a true actress!

"I am so ignorant," Tina complained one afternoon.

"You have talent, and that is much more important than the accumulation of information," responded Weston.

"How do you know I have talent?"

"By watching the way you move. Look at yourself now, for instance. Even the way you stretch out your arm is intelligent."

"You really think so?"

Weston's voice became soft and caressing. "I think you are remarkable. There is nothing better than natural intelligence, and yours is particularly sharp."

Tina felt intensely attracted, perhaps unconsciously, to this strong man who encouraged her. But it wasn't until Edward showed her some of his photographs that she fell irrevocably in love with him. She was especially impressed by his nudes of Margrethe Mather. After seeing them, she decided: "I want to be at the genius's side." The fact that a man of his stature would even look at her endowed her with a solidity she had never felt before.

During the week, Tina went to work early in the morning at Metro-Goldwyn-Mayer. The directors always cast her as the typical Italian girl, the vamp, the Apache. "They can only picture me with a knife between my teeth." She hadn't gotten a single role that she considered worthwhile. Lawson Butt had been her lover in *The Tiger's Coat*. "Don't remind me of that movie. It is so mediocre!" "I prefer *I Can Explain*." "What can you explain, Tina?" "Hey, have you met Sherwood Anderson?" "I haven't met anybody. In Hollywood, you don't meet people. Every day they give me my lines, and I memorize them. Early the next morning, I'm sent to the makeup artist, then I go onstage. The lights blind me. I do what the director tells me to do, the scene is repeated, I never give my opinion, the shoot is over, and . . . I'm back in the studio with Robo. I don't even think they know my name. Yesterday I heard someone say, 'Call that exotic girl.'"

"But you know you are a good actress," said Edward encouragingly.

"Yes, but nobody else cares. If I don't bring in money, nobody gives a damn about me in Hollywood. *Riding with Death* is as bad as the others."

Weston invited Tina to his studio so he could photograph her. Their desire for each other was implacable. "What insanity! What's come over me?" Tina said to herself. Passion conquered her from within. She now lived only to be called on by Weston, to hear him say: "Come to the studio." Tina wrote to him on April 25, 1921: *"One night after—all day I have been intoxicated with the memory of last night and overwhelmed with the beauty and madness of it . . . How can I wait till we meet again?"*

She turned periods into dashes and exclamation marks into lightning bolts. *"Once more I have been reading your letter and as at every other time my eyes are full of tears—I never realized before that a letter—a mere sheet of paper could be such a spiritual thing— you gave a soul to it!*

"Oh! If I could be with you now at this hour I love so much. I would try to tell you how much beauty has been added to my life lately! When may I come over? I am waiting for your call."

Tina and Weston's love engulfed the entire group; everyone shared in the delirium. Pain, jealousy, envy, desire, passion: the group held all of it in an embrace that would never end, even if they separated and never saw each other again. Everything they lived had been forged together; anything was possible. Together they had created the love between Modotti and Weston. Tina grew with Weston. Her spirit, her total being was inflamed by desire. *". . . from my still quivering senses rises an ardent desire to again kiss your eyes and mouth."* She remembered the flavor of wine in her lover's mouth, she drank from his lips, all that existed for her was the possibility of meeting him and the impression of his body on hers.

Robo sat back and observed. "Can I do anything for you? Would you like to go to San Francisco to see your mother and father? Would you like us to go away somewhere?" "No," she said. "I prefer to go alone."

In August 1921, Tina took the train to San Francisco to see her family at their home at 901 Union Street. Perhaps the solidity of the political opinions discussed around the kitchen table or the sound of her father's voice would put a little sense back into her crazed head and her stunned, inflamed heart.

She found her father, Giuseppe, angry and disturbed by recent events. On May 3, 1920, Andrés Salcedo, a Mexican typesetter, had fallen from the fourteenth floor of the Justice Department in New York, where he was being interrogated. He was an anarchist from Massachusetts, a friend of Nicola Sacco and Bartolomeo Vanzetti.

It was also good for Tina to be with her mother, who seemed to read her thoughts, and her little brother, Benvenuto, who was deeply committed to the workers' struggle. How ashamed she suddenly became of her petit bourgeois conflicts! Her parents brought her back to her senses.

When Benvenuto returned in the evening from the print shop, he sat with his sister at the kitchen table until late at night, talking and drinking red wine. "Did you know that the women in the IWW are treated the same as the men? And there are no prohibited words: coitus, abortion, orgasm, sex, birth control, homosexual, lesbian. There is no hypocrisy, no bourgeois power struggle within the new socialism. Senti, sorella, senti; women have control over their own bodies the same as men have over theirs." When Mercedes, her older sister, broke up with her boyfriend, the whole family backed her decision. "Women in a Communist society depend on their work, not on their husbands, and this completely alters the relationship between men and women. They have the exact same rights and both are free, both are comrades and respected friends. Women no longer serve the man of the house. Capisci, sorella, capisci?"

In spite of it all, Tina still thought about Edward. On August 21, she wrote a humble letter to Johan Hagemeyer, Weston's closest friend.

> Mr. Weston gave me your address before leaving (or rather I asked him for it) as I was looking forward to see you. He also told me of the good books and music you have (therefore my impertinence).
>
> I am only going to be here one week more, so any time it

is convenient for you, please call me on the phone and I will come over. My number is: Franklin 9566—about 9 o'clock in the morning is the best time.

Hagemeyer called and she went to his house. He played music for her, served her wine, offered her cigarettes, showed her his books, and spoke about Weston. Tina relished it all. She confided in him that it made her happy and proud to pose for Weston. She wanted to ask him: "Do you think your friend loves me?" but she didn't dare.

Tina was enchanted by the afternoon she spent with him. Later, when she told Weston about it, he became jealous.

Once back in Los Angeles and reunited with her friends, Tina continued to listen to Gómez Robelo's eulogies of Mexico.

"The revolution is the vanguard, and you have it right there on the other side of the border. Why don't you go? I extend invitations to all of you. All the possibilities a revolution has to offer are within your reach," Gómez Robelo said, gesturing with his long thin hands, which were more eloquent than his words.

"The situation in Mexico is perfect for artists," Gómez Robelo insisted, "for an artistic vanguard. North Americans live there peacefully. They feel free. Anarchists, unionists, all philosophies and all ideas have a place in my country. You can even be a Bolshevik if you want! Let's go to Mexico. There is cheap land, and a lot of it. In places like Cuernavaca, the city of eternal spring, they almost give it away. We could live in a commune far away from industrialization and grow our own vegetables. In Mexico City, the ancient canals of Xochimilco, the Venice of America, meander through a land covered with flowers. It will take your breath away. But in Venice there are no flowers, only wet stones. In Xochimilco, even the stones bloom."

Then he announced: "Tomorrow I am leaving. My government has called me back to work in education." The next day he left for Mexico.

Robo was the first to act on Gómez Robelo's inspiring words. He took the train to Mexico in December 1921. After his arrival, he wrote to Tina with even more enthusiasm than his Mexican friend had expressed. In Mexico, he wrote, art was a moral act.

Tina, Edward, everybody: come immediately; it is marvelous. I never thought it possible to find a country made for artists.

José Vasconcelos, Minister of Education, was a giant. Thanks to him, the peasants would soon be reading Plotinus and Socrates. The dialogues of Plato would be sold in bookstalls in Chapultepec Park, available to anyone who happened by. Vasconcelos was a visionary who encouraged the muralists. Robo wrote with noble praise of Mexico's native talent. Mexico's potential was limitless. Nothing he had ever experienced had lifted him to such heights. He lived on the verge of tears. What a model, Mexico, what a great, noble country!

Robo wrote to Edward: *"There is for me more poetry in one lone figure leaning in the door of the pulque shop at twilight or a bronze daughter of the Aztecs nursing her child in a church than could be found in Los Angeles in the next ten years . . . Can you imagine an art school where everything is free for everybody—Mexicans and foreigners alike—tuition, room and board, paint, canvas, models, all free—no entrance exam—if you study, that is the only requirement.*

"Regards to your family and Miss Mather. Please write to me about your photographs and tell me if you are coming. Believe me to be as ever your friend, Robo."

Just as she was about to leave for Mexico to join him, Tina received a cable: Robo had died of smallpox in the British Cowdray Hospital on February 9, 1922.

Poor Robo, my poor dear! Suddenly she felt more love for him than she had in the past year. She gathered together his poems to make a book. She would do for the dead man what she had never done for him while he was alive. She felt deep gratitude toward him when she realized he had never stood in her way.

She went to Mexico with her mother-in-law, Rose Richey. Together they would order a tombstone for the grave. When she crossed the border, Tina thought the humble men and women who approached the train window were singing in sweet Italian voices. In Mexico City, Gómez Robelo himself—even skinnier than before—and his friends graciously welcomed the twenty-five-year-old widow and the mother. Some spoke of Robo's eyes, so full of illusion, how kind he was. Robo had not passed unnoticed through

Mexico. He had left evidence of his work and his human generosity. Even in the hospital, they remembered that he seemed to be hearing voices from beyond and, in spite of the horror of his final days, a soft smile remained on his lips even after he died. Both women were touched when they visited the places Robo had described. Yes, Robo had been right; Mexico had the greatness, the magnificence of a storm.

Tina, excited by the warm welcome and the vitality of the artistic environment, arranged, with Gómez Robelo's help, a showing of Weston's photographs at the Academia de Bellas Artes. Mexican artists and intellectuals such as Federico Marín and Julio Torri and the German Leo M. Matthias enthusiastically applauded Weston's art, and a highly cultured young man, Pepe Quintanilla, wanted to buy a few photographs and offered to speak to his brother, a diplomat, who had excellent connections.

At a banquet for Tina, hosted by Quintanilla, the sweetness and sharpness of the Mexican cuisine suffused her palate: the crunchiness of toasted tortillas, the rich guacamole, the sugary burn of the tequila, the green limes, the hot chocolate that calmed her nerves. She moved constantly, expressing vitality in every gesture. After the meal, Pepe Quintanilla, with the taste of coffee still on his lips, pulled her toward him and boldly kissed her on the mouth. "Don't ever leave. Stay with me forever."

Once the tombstone was in place, Tina and Rose Richey returned to the United States. There, another shock awaited Tina: her father, Giuseppe, had died of stomach cancer in San Francisco, just one month after Robo's death.

Giuseppe Modotti was an artisan, and with the fruits of his labor he had managed to bring his entire family to America. In Udine, those same hands had held the red-and-black flag; his left hand was always clenched in a fist at demonstrations, claiming rights for himself and his comrades. With those hands he had lifted Tina up to see the masses of workers demanding better salaries; they should eat something other than polenta, their children deserved an education. Tina loved those deeply veined hands, the palms of his hands placed softly on the table while he waited for his plate, his steady hands stroking a child's head, the dignified stillness of his working hands at rest on his lap. Oh, Papa, how well you have done. Tina vowed to make her hands as trustworthy as his.

In San Francisco, while Tina and her mother held and comforted each other, Tina confided that she wanted to live in Mexico. She promised she would write often, and that her family would be part of her new life.

But it wasn't until she and Edward went to an exhibition of Mexican folk art in Los Angeles, organized by the young painter, printmaker, and cartoonist Xavier Guerrero, that they both felt that nothing could keep them in Los Angeles any longer.

"I will travel with you only if I can work. Let me be your assistant, Edward, in exchange for room and board. And you will teach me photography."

To ease his guilt at abandoning his family, Weston took with him Chandler, the oldest of his four sons, then thirteen years old. On July 29, 1923, Flora, Weston's wife, took the other children to the pier to see them off. As the SS *Colima* weighed anchor, she called out to Tina: "Take care of my boys."

Tina spent the first days aboard ship leaning over the rail. One of the sailors brought her half a lemon and told her to suck on it hard, get out all the juice and the pulp, and see how much better you'll feel. But the boat kept pitching about, and Weston exclaimed, "Pobrecita," and carried her to her cabin, laid her down, and covered her with a sheet. The air was thick and suffocating, and Tina's stomach could not hold anything down. Finally, the surface of the water turned glassy, and the sound of the sea died away. Once back on deck, Tina could see the small flag hanging limply in the still air; she watched Weston, with his camera, and Chandler, who followed his father around like a shadow. She also watched the disorganized and noisy crew and the loudmouthed Austrian captain, who shouted and swore at them. This same captain regaled Tina with tales about Mexico and the Mexicans, about their filth, their ignorance, and their inefficiency. Despite the captain's expressions of disgust, the world he described sounded to

Tina like a wonderful relief from the American mechanization and efficiency that she had come to despise.

She loved looking at a dark, thin boy in canvas pants as he mopped the deck near her chair three times without rinsing out the rag, then lifted his eyes to her, eyes that burned with the warmth of fire. As soon as the captain began to shout, he scampered away like a squirrel. They all worked without shirts, exposing their dark, hairless chests. This boy's thin, wiry body reflected the light like a panther's shimmering coat.

Her first ocean voyage had been quite different. She would always retain a fearful image of her own tiny figure wrapped in shawls and huddled on the lowest deck next to her miserable belongings: a threadbare mattress, two blouses, a change of underwear, a coat, and a tablecloth. "Mamma, why should I bring that tablecloth?" "You can sell it; it's the finest thing we own." The first few days, Tina was careful not to soil her black skirt, which would have to last the trip and for the first few months in America. She kept her head pressed against the green metal side and spent almost the entire two-week voyage in a fetal position in the belly of this great sea monster. When she found out that the third-class deck was below sea level, she understood why there were no hatches. "The sea is on top of us; I am carrying the sea." She imagined the boat's keel scraping the bottom of the sea, herself separated from the water only by that thin, damp metal that could split open at the slightest impact. The immigrants would be the first to be sucked into the ocean. Only those in first class would be able to escape in the boats hanging off the sides that she had seen from the pier. So when word came that there were hurricane winds, Tina became paralyzed with fear. Suddenly, she heard the shouts of a woman trying to get to the upper deck. The third-class passengers—almost all Italian refugees—had no right to go to second class, let alone on deck. Other than that one woman, who was quickly returned to her place, nobody dared leave the black cavern where men, women, and children were bundled together like rags. They slept one on top of the other, feet on heads, children on adults, the women's heads wrapped in black scarves. When the boat pitched forward, a wave of moans came from the prostrate bodies. The children leaned on their elbows, looking at one another in terror.

Tina stuck to the most removed corner to avoid the stench of the sick. They ate; they vomited. Relief would only come when they reached shore.

Two days before pulling into New York Harbor, a young man with tangled hair touched her shoulder and beckoned to her to follow. Tina could barely stand, but she used the walls of the passageway for support until she reached the spot he had found for her. Light and salt air came in through a hatch. Tina put her head down on her mattress, facing the sea, and fell asleep with the salt spray on her. Thus she arrived in New York and through the ocean fog glimpsed another layer of fog over the city, which was dirty and gray from the smoke of the chimneys. "Look to your left: the Statue of Liberty!" She could only make out the torch. She gathered up her belongings, straightened her skirt, and wrapped her black scarf more tightly around her head. The boat advanced slowly through the mercurial water, and three small black boats came to greet them. Now that they had reached land, the dark, bent shapes were allowed to emerge from the lowest deck. The immigrants were herded into a windowless building where the electric light in the middle of the day added to their desperation. "What happened to the sun?" Another voice was encouraging: "Siamo arrivato, siamo arrivato. Questa è Nuova York."

This is what she remembered on her way to the Pacific port of Manzanillo.

Staged Marriage Portrait of Tina Modotti and Edward Weston, Mexico. Unknown, 1925. Collection J. Paul Getty Museum, Malibu, California. Gelatin silver print, 5 5/8 x 3 15/16 in.

6

$\mathcal{S}$oon after their arrival in Mexico, Tina, Weston, and his son Chandler settled into El Buen Retiro, an old and beautiful ten-room house in Tacubaya, a suburb of Mexico City. One rainy afternoon, Weston suddenly began to take off his clothes, shouting, "Let's go up to the roof. Tina, Chandler, come on," he urged as he raced up the stairs. The boy was first; then came Tina, laughing enthusiastically as she undressed. "We're going to play hide-and-seek. Tina's 'it.' " Weston leapt away. Tina's hair covered her face. "I can't see anything, the rain is blinding me." It rained harder. "Come on, Chandler, come on." Tina's breasts shook as she laughed.

Drops of water slid over her lips, down her neck, and onto her legs as she approached him. Weston sprang up and escaped. As a child, Weston had been a weakling. Determined to overcome this, he trained as a long-distance runner. At thirty-six, ten years Tina's senior, he was proud of his physical condition, his flat stomach, his good muscle tone. When he lived in Glendale, he wrestled naked with his four children, and in Tacubaya, he bathed in cold water every day. But Tina, what a beauty she was! Her perfect, dense triangle shone like a diamond in the rain. Chandler rushed to his father, who happily embraced him. Then, triumphantly joyous to be alive, they ran inside, wrapped themselves in towels, and sat down to read *Moby-Dick*. What wonderful rooftop verandas they have in Mexico! What's on the rooftops in California, anyway? Tina had never bothered to find out. As she read out loud, Weston collected the water that dripped from her hair. Her damp fingers left marks on the pages. "Melville wouldn't have minded." Weston smiled. "I am fiercely happy," Tina said. She shone with well-being. She threw her arms around Edward's neck and kissed him with such force that he felt he had to defend himself: "Enough, enough, your love will kill me."

He had been staring at the sky; when he lowered his eyes, he saw Tina lying naked in the sun. He pointed his camera at her and clicked the shutter. Then he followed her to her room, where she put a robe on over her still warm skin. In the darkroom, he and Tina eagerly examined the negatives. "This is the best series of nudes I have ever done." The pictures had a face and a sex—a rare thing for Weston, who had always hidden one or the other on his previous model, Margrethe Mather.

In the darkroom, beside her master, Tina watched as a new image of herself appeared out of the chemical bath: there it was, her body, which had always been such a stranger to her. Now she could reinvent her relationship to her self, begin to love herself. If her body could communicate such strength, the harmony and rhythm of its design, then she, too, was extraordinary. The body on the paper was working its way into her consciousness. Edward had given her a new way to be Tina, without disguises; showing herself naked was like showing others her most beautiful gown. Edward had placed within her grasp the elements of discovery: the silver plates, the celluloid, the emulsion, and the light, elements that could be turned upon herself or that she could turn upon the world.

• • •

Before daybreak, in the silent house, Weston slipped behind his desk to write in his journal. He rose from each session feeling cleansed, as if his writing had swept the cobwebs out of his heart and mind.

Outside, Mexico was waiting: slow, violent Mexico. The Aztec valley, as Jean Charlot, the French painter, called it: fierce, brilliant Mexico. Inside: silence, penumbra, solitude at the work table at dawn, his space.

Weston lived in a state of revelation, thanks to Tina and the country she had proffered him. "I like everything, I feel part of the people." And he embraced everything within reach. "Tina, look at the color of that wall, that bougainvillea." "Did you notice, Eduardito, that the girls sweep and wash down the sidewalk before the sun rises? Each person cleans his own little piece of the city. Isn't this a fair distribution of beauty? In Mexico, every stone is alive, it speaks. I am going to make a place for myself in this land, I'm going to bring Mamma, my family, they will feel at home here, like in Udine. Do you see the air, Edward, do you see? This high valley is so close to the sky we can touch it. Do you see how delicate the air is? It makes me want to fly. When I was a girl, I dreamed that I could fly, that I left the earth behind, that there was only me and the sky, the sky and me, me and the sky."

One morning, they were awakened by gunfire. They rushed out to the balcony. "Is there a new revolution?" Soon they grew accustomed to the fireworks. Another day, Weston said to Elisa, the maid, "There were more fireworks this morning." The girl answered impassively, "Yes, there was another gun battle in Tacubaya." "What?!" "Don't worry. When the snipers load their machine guns and are ready to shoot, they wave their hats in the air so the passersby can get out of the way." Weston asked Roubicek, the owner of the Aztec Land gallery, if there would be another revolution.

"Not one. Forty."

Weston wrote it down in his diary.

Every time Weston set his Graflex up on the tripod, a crowd gathered around him. The people in the marketplaces didn't like photographers. They suspected he was from the press. "Please don't go away. We mean no harm," Tina begged. "Am I going to be in the newspaper?" they asked. They just couldn't understand the interest these two foreigners took in the black mud of Oaxaca, the baskets, the piles of earthenware. They set up their cameras in the middle of the garbage; they didn't even put a cloth on the ground. Do they want to take pictures of the dirt? They watched the señora cutting open a chirimoya, bringing it to her nose, "what aroma," she says, and bites into it. "I am eating perfume, Edward, taste it." She speaks a strange Spanish, but she's not a gringa, and he doesn't say a word. He goes everywhere with her, so pretty the lady, and so friendly. She claps her hands together in front of the stands and exclaims: "¡Qué lindo, pero qué lindo!" Those foreigners act as if they'd never seen anybody carry water, harvest wheat, open up a gourd, as if they had been born yesterday.

Watching Tina haggle over prices was a spectacle for Weston. She always managed to bring the price down by at least half. Even strangers stopped to listen. Her candor was her weapon. Men looked impudently at her legs and followed her with their eyes as she walked away. They whistled and called out Mamá, Mamacita, and Tina seemed not to hear. Tina's beauty was Weston's passport to Mexico.

He had never seen her so exuberant, so friendly. She attracted others the way light attracts moths. A smile seemed to float between her and the world. When word got out that she had returned to Mexico, Federico Marín, Pepe Quintanilla, and Baltasar Dromundo rushed to El Buen Retiro—for her, not for Weston.

Perhaps it was the combination of gunpowder, the revolution, the state of mind, the climate. In Mexico, everything was extreme. The coffee was as black as hell; the aguardiente brought tears to the eyes; the drizzle rained, the rain poured. Sometimes Tina found her lover in tears and attributed it to the chiles. One evening at dinner, Federico Marín served them anise with their coffee, and cigars wrapped in cinnamon bark. "You like to smoke, don't you, Tina?" How was it possible that everyone knew what she liked? Weston would have enjoyed the evening if it hadn't been for Federico Marín's advances to Tina. Why did he look at her that way?

There was something electric in Tina's relationship with Mexico. She awoke each morning with a new strength she had not felt since she was a girl in Udine. "Edward, I feel as if I have been reborn." She wavered between jubilation and stupor; she felt Mexico as timeless, pernicious, eternal, malignant, a country of savages, a country of wise men. The crickets at night, the chirping of birds after a storm, the shouts of hawkers in the streets, the whistle of the knife sharpener; all these sounds made their way into their house in Tacubaya.

Tina lived in a perpetual state of euphoria; repelled and captivated at the same time. Poverty and all its misery turned her stomach. The pangs of hunger pounded against the walls of their home. Mexico, the cornucopia described in books, did not bestow its plenty on its own people. Then Weston would return from the market with a little straw doll.

"This is incredible. Look!"

How could such crippled, bony hands produce such ecstatic art? These people possessed the spirit of forms. Was it the thin, almost transparent air that had sharpened their visual sense? They had a surprising tendency toward abstraction.

"This country is to be feared," René d'Harnoncourt told them. "It is traitorous."

"They have nothing to betray," Weston said ironically. "They are orphans."

"Mexico belongs to whoever conquers it. I was born for Mexico. Mexico is mine; I am from Mexico," Tina stated emphatically.

"Soon you'll see how your Mexico will stab you in the back. Don't you feel the obsidian knives slicing through the air? A man's word is worth nothing here, nobody believes what is said. Truth has many faces and each person chooses that which is most convenient. Mexicans say one thing and do another. You'll soon see."

Tina feels at home with the Estridentistas, young artists who mock convention, academic painting, and bourgeois taste. She finds their provocative attitudes stimulating. Pepe Quintanilla's older brother Luis—who signs his books of poetry Kin Taniya—asks her to act in his Teatro Mexicano del Murciélago. Manuel Maples Arce and Germán List Arzubide greet her as one of their own at the Café de Nadie—Nobody's Café. They are innovative and playful and share with Weston and Tina an interest in new ways of seeing. Tina takes photographs of electric light, telegraph and telephone wires, and factories for their magazine *El Irradiador*; and for Germán's book of poetry, *El Canto de los hombres*, pictures of laborers, ladders, and tanks.

At the Ministry of Education, Diego Rivera was painting his *Bathers in Tehuantepec*. Four exuberant panels of women and fruit: magnificent, musical women among bunches of bananas and lustrous leaves. Tina took Edward to see them. Pedestrians came and went under the main archway and stopped to watch the painters straddling the scaffold, hanging from the crossbars. Below, in the corridor, the assistants mixed the paints: cobalt blue, sienna, ocher. Rivera waved his palette when he needed more paint, sending Máximo Pacheco clambering like a monkey up the timbers. Along the scaffold, Amado de la Cueva, Jean Charlot, and Fermín Revueltas dipped their brushes in sap and crushed petals, in bloody reds and the blue of a shark's back, in slime and jitomate, in chile ancho and tortoiseshells, and drop by drop they carried the colors to the walls. Art had come out to the street. Everybody had an opinion and made it known. Art belonged to the people. José Vasconcelos, Minister of Education, had decided to take art out of the strongboxes; art would leave the museums, the city would be one huge collective exhibition, music would meander through the streets like the village idiot, and everybody would listen as it drifted up the stairwells and filtered in through the windows; art would embellish the lives of the cart driver and the tortilla maker. General Obregón, President of the Republic, supported Vasconcelos in his fight against illiteracy by exhorting the educated to teach those who could not read. He recruited an army of men and women who became teachers on their days off. Obregón personally gave a diploma to whoever could prove he or she had taught a hundred illiterates to read. Mexico was the most artistic nation on this continent. Art was intrinsic to the culture. The muralists painted in order to know themselves, love themselves; as a result, Mexico, a child born out of a revolution without philosophy, would begin to recognize itself through them.

When Lupe Marín Rivera invited Tina and Weston to Diego's house on Mixcalco Street, she met them at the door with a whisk in her hand. If Mexican chocolate was famous, the chocolate Lupe ordered freshly ground from her house in Guadalajara was the best in Mexico. For Lupe, everything good came from Guadalajara. 73

Weston brought a photograph of Lupe's head he had taken as she shouted from the rooftop of El Buen Retiro. Diego looked at it for a long time, then turned to Tina. "It bothers the painter to see such photographs." Lupe glanced over at it as she rushed back and forth carrying rolls, fresh cheese, tortillas. "I look horrible, look at my hair, such a mess, how dare you, damn you, Weston, it makes me want to pour this chocolate on your head!"

Later, Lupe announced that she was going to get the neighbors and returned with Germán and Lola Cueto. Both were puppet-makers, though by profession Lola was a printmaker and Germán was a sculptor. Diego scolded them, "You are wasting your time."

"That's why I invite them," Lupe interrupted, "because they aren't boring like you, Panzas; all you do is paint and paint and paint." As she spoke, she knocked Diego on the side of his head with the mug.

"Tomorrow, dinner at the Braniffs'," announced El Chango García Cabral, on his way out the door.

At the opulent house of Oscar and Beatriz Braniff, Lupe raised her voice and dominated the gathering with her exclamations. Oscar and Beatriz were trying to create a literary salon where musicians, poets, and painters would meet to listen to a poetry reading or a quartet. Oscar wanted to glow in Diego's reflected light, but Lupe ruined everything with her shouting.

At a table set under the tall poplars in the garden, Diego said that he was on a new diet: "Just strawberries, that's all I eat. In Paris I found the diet quite effective." And he shook some out of a paper bag in a red avalanche onto his plate. Lupe told the white-gloved waiter: "Don't serve this fellow anything; he's an absolute elephant." When they brought out plates of oeufs mousseline on hearts of artichoke, Lupe asked for rice and a fried egg. "Wow, Beatriz, your punch is great!" she cried when they poured the champagne.

After dinner, Jean Charlot spoke of the pyramids. He claimed that the ones in Teotihuacán were older and greater than those of Egypt. Braniff, encouraged at the prospect of elevated conversation, recited what he could recall of the history of the Chinese in Mexico. Lupe, finding it all tremendously boring, decided they could use some help and shouted: "Culture hour is over, boys. Time to liven up the party!" and launched into a chorus of "Borrachita me voy . . ." Even Braniff had to smile.

Lupe kept singing as it grew dark; the waiters leaned against the wall, their napkins draped over their arms. Weston would write later in his diary that Lupe was "barbarically splendid in red and gold with heavy festoons of gold chain and earrings."

One morning, Lupe Marín stormed into Tina and Weston's house.

"Tina, I'm leaving the pots here on the kitchen table. I need a bunch of spices. Did you buy the chicken breasts you were supposed to? In a little while Dalila and María, my sister, will come to debone them. Hey you, muchacha, sweep up here, clear up the breakfast things.

"You told me there was a miller near here who didn't put crap in the flour. You, Edward, go back to your rooftop, climb up to your clouds. Here we are going to make some chiles rellenos, meat ones here, cheese ones over there, enchiladas in that long dish, just the green ones, we'll put the red ones over there, and the mole, make that in the yellow dish over there . . ."

"I don't think you brought enough white cheese," Tina dared to suggest.

"Half a kilo isn't enough? That's because you're Italian . . . But maybe you're right. I'll buy half a kilo of the stale cheese and mix it in."

Waving her large hands in the air, her hair pulled tightly back into a bun, Lupe wrapped her shawl around her flat chest and shouted, "I'll be right back, but while I'm gone, keep those little hands busy over the cutting board . . . Oh no, coriander, I forgot the fresh coriander and the papaloquelite. You'll let the others in, won't you? They always oversleep . . ."

From the roof, Weston watched as Lupe strode away like a panther. The stillness she left in her wake had a gray tone. He could see Tina and Elisa washing radishes in the kitchen. "We'd better hurry," Elisa said.

Lupe returned an hour later, her arms full of packages.

"The others aren't here? What a couple of good-for-nothings! What, do they think I'm going to do everything?"

Dalila and María Orozco Romero arrived at six in the evening, and María whispered to Tina, "I can't stand my sister's shouting."

"You idiots! What do you think? Here the Italian has been sweating for the two of you. Asses! You get here when everything's done and the guests are about to arrive!"

Monna and Rafael Sala and their inseparable Felipe Teixidor came punctually, like good Europeans, as did Jean Charlot. Federico Marín, Lupe's younger brother, arrived with his arms full of herbal teas for Tina. Carlos Mérida and Miguel and Rosa Covarrubias took a special interest in pre-Hispanic remedies: "This one that looks like green cactus is peyote . . . These delicate stems are marijuana."

The tall, elegant figure of Fito Best Maugard, accompanied by two beauties, María Asúnsolo and her cousin, Lolita, caused a stir. Weston ran to get his dictionary so he could talk to the "beautiful señoritas." Tina asked for news of Ricardo Gómez Robelo. It was rumored that he was being consumed by his passion for Tina. Even the Minister of Education, José Vasconcelos, said that Gómez Robelo was wasting away for the Italian.

A recently arrived gringo made his way timidly through the groups. He wanted to be Diego Rivera's assistant. "My name is Pablo O'Higgins." Xavier Guerrero came in after him, accompanied by his sister, Elisa, her hair braided with ribbons that matched the colors in her blouse. The last one to arrive was Rivera, with his dinner of grapes and apples wrapped in a bright red bandanna. "I have the cleanest guts in the world." Weston got involved in a bilingual conversation about intestinal cleanliness. "This country, with its abundance of tropical fruit, is a paradise for vegetarians." Elisa Guerrero only had eyes for Weston, who couldn't tear his eyes away from Rivera. The pistol hanging by Diego's side contrasted sharply with the almost sweet smile on his puffy face. He explained to Lolita Asúnsolo, the future Dolores del Rio, "All Mexican artists are Communists, all the good ones at least. They call me the Lenin of Mexico. We're not the kind that just sit around on our asses. We get our hands dirty." And he stroked his pistol with his small, delicate hands. Weston called Chandler over to him. "Pay attention to that man; he's a genius. Look at his hands; they are the hands of an artist. Look at his forehead; a wide forehead shows the size of the intellect. His is enormous; he has the forehead of a thinker." Diego talked endlessly. When he finally stopped to listen to his interlocutors, he placed his little hands on his huge belly and a placid smile would glow from his face until contagious laughter shook his enormous frame. Chandler couldn't get his eyes off him and his pistol. "Does he use it to protect his paintings?" he asked his father.

When Lupe was around, she and Diego engaged in a sharp and stabbing dialogue that seemed to be conducted mainly for an audience. After her initial "How'd it go today, shorty?" she managed to make everybody laugh. "Hey, fatty, you've got the tits of an old lady, and since I don't have any, we make a good pair." The subject of tits was one of Lupe's favorites. If she got angry at her Panzas, she shouted, "Get out of here and take your tits with you." After dinner, Diego announced that Lupe and Hernández Galván would sing some songs Concha Michel had collected during their pack trip with burros through the countryside. At Charlot's request, Weston showed his photograph of factory smokestacks in Middleton, Ohio, one of his and Monna's favorites.

"Very good, very good," Diego murmured.

At dawn, in the silence of his house, Weston tried to settle accounts with himself in his journal. Mexico is a country on the verge of a firestorm; even the water burned. Tina is in the center of the flames. If Tina had read his journal, she would have been shocked to discover that Weston was jealous. She simply let herself be admired without questioning the motives of those who admired her. On the other hand, Weston, like a good Anglo, had his hormones under control, not like those Mexicans . . .

For her, Edward was the same as in Los Angeles: the revered, the brilliant artist. In Mexico, she had become indispensable to him. They spent most of their time together. Since he spoke no Spanish, he was dependent on her. "You are my Malinche." Their nights seemed better than in Los Angeles. She didn't realize that Weston had begun to possess her with the fury of resentment.

An exhibition of Weston's photographs opened at Aztec Land on October 22 and was nothing less than a triumph. By the afternoon, all the familiar faces had appeared: Lupe and Diego, Charlot, the Salas, Monna and Rafael, Felipe Teixidor, the Quintanillas, and General Manuel Hernández Galván. The visitor book was full of comments such as: "You have taken Mexico by storm." "Weston, how you love and understand our country!" or "You are Latin, not Anglo-Saxon." The heads of Galván, Lupe, Nahui Olín, and Ruth

Stallsmith Quintanilla were much talked about. But the nudes of Tina caused the greatest sensation! "I am so proud of you, Eduardito!" she kept repeating to him. Yes, Tina could be courted by countless other men, but Weston still commanded her unqualified admiration.

Weston particularly enjoyed watching the peasants looking at their art portrayed in his art. Nobody had ever taken pictures of their mud, their straw, their toys; it was as if Weston were giving it back to them, as if he were saying, "Look at the beauty you create." He sincerely hoped that the basket weavers and potters would be able to perceive the homage he was paying to their work, his recognition of the dignity expressed in the small objects they made out of nothing. Roubicek, the owner of Aztec Land, had not expected them to attend in such numbers. They entered so timidly that he decided to keep a respectful distance and avoid speaking to them, for fear of scaring them away.

Diego, his overalls splattered with bits of plaster, responded to the photographs with genuine enthusiasm. He even asserted that he preferred a good photograph any time to a modernist painting. His favorite photograph was the one of the circus tent roof, and he was fascinated by the textures in the photographs of Margrethe Mather's naked torso on the beach. "This is what some of us 'moderns' were trying to do," said Diego, "when we sprinkled real sand on our paintings or stuck on pieces of lace or paper or other bits of realism."

Weston tried to explain: "The camera should be able to record life, give the substance and quintessence of the object itself, whether it be polished metal or throbbing flesh . . . In the new heads I've done of Lupe, Galván, and Tina, I have captured fractions of seconds of emotional intensity that no artist in any other medium can achieve. The most difficult thing is to record this reality."

A few days after his conspicuous absence at the exhibition, Ricardo Gómez Robelo came to visit Tina and Edward at El Buen Retiro. This was the first time they had seen him since their arrival. They found him so changed that Weston barely recognized him. Some people claimed that he was ill with tuberculosis or syphilis; others said that his passion for Tina was devouring him.

With a certain amount of pain, Gómez Robelo spoke about his country, about the many sides of Mexican culture that were in confrontation with one another. The "proper" people hated Rivera's murals, his horrible women and repulsive colors that degraded the classical beauty of a race that deserved to be sculpted in bronze. They believed that the muralists were ridiculing Mexico to the outside world, that Vasconcelos had made a terrible mistake when he gave those walls to rebels who only knew how to distort the human figure, they were making heroes out of those who were on the other side of life: the downtrodden. At the same time, illustrious visitors treated to the hospitality of Mexico's painters, poets, and writers came to believe that the country was leading the Latin American renaissance, that Vasconcelos had freed its soul, allowed art and the written word to realize their full cathartic powers. Mexican artists were educators. They would change the dynamics of society. The era of the cosmic race had arrived. The flames of the fourth race were burning in the melting pot of Hispanic America, and from the ashes, the humanity of the future would be born. Mexico, with its mixture of blood and gold, would ignite the world.

7

*C*an't you get in the taxi any other way?"

Tina was stunned by the grimace on Edward's face.

"Can't you do anything without calling attention to your body? We can't take two steps without being followed by a pack of hounds. What do you think I am, some kind of idiot?"

Tina, wishing to avoid his eyes, pulled her skirt down over her knees and looked out the window.

"Next time, I'm going to get myself an ugly lover."

It was the third time he'd said that. This relegation to the condition of "lover" made her drop her head between her shoulders, like a turtle who crawls into its shell when threatened. Weston was losing his head, forgetting that without her he would have to say goodbye to friends, to parties, to outings to the countryside. He felt like putting his fist through Xavier Guerrero's face, and the same went for that sweet, modest Pablo O'Higgins. Didn't they realize that Tina wasn't the only woman in the world?

Tina belonged to Weston: he possessed her as nobody else could. He mounted her victoriously over the desire of all the others; his possession of her would sweep them all away; out of my bed, you rabid dogs, for here he was alone with her, he alone could do with her whatever he damn well pleased, here, take this, and then leave her alone to show her that nobody possessed him. Tina often begged him: "Don't leave, sleep with me, let's wake up together," but he refused. "I can only sleep alone, I need a good night's sleep, because I have a lot of work to do tomorrow." Even at the beginning of their relationship he had failed to intuit how much this hurt Tina. She wanted to wrap her legs around his, warm her feet between his thighs, curl up in his arms, watch him wake up and open his eyes. "Ever since I was a child, Edward, I had other bodies next to mine, on the floor, and then in the only bed in the house. I could always rest my cheek against somebody else's arm; I am used to waking up and knowing that all I have to do is stretch out my arm to feel another person's skin. My brothers and sisters, Mercedes, Yolanda, Gioconda, Benvenuto, Beppo, and I all slept under the same blanket. Gioconda would tell me to make a little seat, and I'd bend my knees, and she would nestle into them, and we would fall asleep wrapped up in each other. Mercedes was taller than me, so she'd do the same for me." Edward didn't like the proximity of another body; he couldn't express his love after sex was over. Sleep alone. Get out of bed quickly and go to the bathroom. That was his way of starting the day, his only way.

Tina never got up to bathe herself after making love; she preferred to remain within the warm womb of the bed. When Weston first saw her falling asleep like that, he asked, "Aren't you even going to wash yourself?"

"No, I feel good like this."

"It's really better, you know."

"It's better when you are inside me."

Then she would fall into the deep sleep of a satisfied animal, savoring the taste of his milk still on her lips. She would wrap her legs around each other "because I don't want to lose a drop of you, I want it all inside me."

"You are so primitive. I've never known a woman like you."

Once, when they were in Los Angeles, Tina went to Weston's studio at four in the morning and silently curled up under the sheets next to him. When he roused himself from his deep sleep,

Tina felt rejection in his half-closed eyes. She tried to kiss him, but he got up to go to the bathroom, for a glass of water, or to brush his teeth. When he returned, he dutifully performed the act. Edward had often told her that desire kept him awake and blamed her for his sleepless nights. Mistakenly, she took this as encouragement for her to seek him out. Now, in Mexico, when he lay on top of her, Tina could only remember that look in his eyes.

When the party was at Lupe's house, people ate tamales; at María Orozco Romero's house, they had mole; the Salas usually served paella. When Tina was the hostess, she offered spaghetti al dente, red wine, a fresh salad of butter lettuce, watercress, fresh herbs, hard-boiled eggs, olives, and olive oil. Just before dawn, the guests would announce, "We're staying for breakfast."

"Mostly men come to your parties, don't they?" Lupe said insinuatingly.

"Here the men are definitely the ones in heat," said Weston. "That's the one thing you can count on in Mexico."

Xavier Guerrero worried Weston more than any of Tina's other admirers. Perhaps it was Guerrero's silence, the fact that he didn't dance or sing, that so exasperated Weston. One evening, at a costume party at the Salas' house, Weston was struck by the look of disgust on Guerrero's face when he saw him enter in Tina's skirt and blouse. No, he wasn't as virile as Guerrero, God help him, he wouldn't strap a pistol around his waist. These muralists were so ridiculously machista. You'd think they painted with their penises! At one point in the evening, Weston sidled up to Guerrero: "May I have this dance?" Indignation shot out from Guerrero's stone features. He left the party soon thereafter.

"Did you notice, Tina, how impenetrable that man is? He's made of stone, not flesh and blood."

"Yes, but he's well carved."

Tina was drawn to this fierce, taciturn man who never took his eyes off her when they were in the same room. It was uncanny how she attracted such different kinds of men: Robo, Weston, O'Higgins, Quintanilla, and now Guerrero.

•••

Besides all the social activity and the excursions to the countryside, there were quiet days when idleness descended on the house and everybody lay half naked on their beds, catching up on lost sleep with long siestas. Tina sent a note to Edward through the maid, Elisa: "Why not come up here? The light is beautiful at this hour and I am a little sad."

The afternoon was spent in Tina's arms with the doors to the balcony open. Chandler arrived with oranges, chirimoyas, and pulque, and the three of them ate fruit in bed. Only Tina could drink the pulque, the fermented juice of the maguey. She whispered in her lover's ear that it was like drinking semen.

There was "a certain inevitable sadness in the life of a much-sought-for, beautiful woman," Weston wrote in his diary.

Tina had no friends or colleagues; all she had were the men who sought her out. Once, when Edward spoke about an ugly woman they both knew who couldn't find a lover, Tina sadly observed, "But at least she has good friends." Weston wanted to be her friend without making her pay for it the way those Mexicans did. Their relationship would last forever because his love for Tina was exactly what he needed for his art. The question was, how much longer could he tolerate this torture, how much longer could he put aside his jealousy and manage to love Tina and her freedom?

Tina stood just behind her master and focused her Korona (a gift from Edward) on the same object from a different angle. Through Weston's camera, the circus tent became a large cloth spread across the entire frame. Now Tina introduced a solitary spectator under the cloth. "I'm always putting somebody into the frame, aren't I, Edward?" It was vitally important for her that Edward recognize her as a photographer, that he appreciate her work. He once told her that a picture she had taken looked like a postcard, and she immediately destroyed the negative. Primitive art, which comes from the earth, from the artisans, like those marvelous pre-Hispanic pieces, is not descriptive or anecdotal. Her photos likewise would be abstract, essential. They would speak to the intellect and also to the forces in the unconscious; they would exert a power of interiority. Her Korona would capture the treasures she believed to be lurking around every corner, the colonial paintings that could be uncovered with the scrape of a fingernail. Her Korona would record the textures, the flatness of the walls, the airy arches of the convent of Tepotztlán.

In November 1923, shortly after Tina and Weston had taken down the exhibition at Aztec Land, they received an offer from the Ministry of Education to show their photographs at the Palacio de Minería. Tina couldn't believe that she was being included, that a joint exhibition was being proposed. This was a first, and Weston congratulated her. "I am proud of my dear apprentice." They hung their photographs in simple frames. Edward pointed out to her that "your photos lose nothing next to mine, and yet they are distinctly your own." On opening day, the National Anthem rang out, and President Obregón presided over the ceremony. Again, all their friends attended. Luis Quintanilla brought with him a tall, skinny, very reserved Englishman with a thick beard the color of bricks, named D. H. Lawrence. He made only a few terse comments as he looked at the photographs. When he was finished, he asked Weston to make a portrait of him. "But we only know each other superficially," Weston demured.

Quintanilla took Weston aside. "I'll lend you one of his books. He is a very good writer."

"I know his work, that's not the problem. It's just that I am exhausted; sixteen hours a day in the darkroom for the past two weeks has finished me off. I need some fresh air. Tina, Chandler, and I were planning to go to Cuernavaca."

Jean Charlot interrupted. "You complain about working sixteen hours a day for two weeks. Just look at Diego on his murals at the Ministry of Education. He even sleeps there! I don't know how he manages it."

Weston finally agreed to photograph Lawrence. The moment he focused his camera, he knew his heart wasn't in it. Two days later, Tina and Weston watched as Lawrence looked at the prints and smiled with satisfaction. "There is something infantile in that smile," Tina thought, "as if he were carrying Little Red Ridinghood around in his beard."

Tina and Edward loved their house in Tacubaya but were tired of traveling an hour each way to Madero Street to buy their supplies. In September, they moved to 12 Lucerna Street, where they remained until May 1924, when they moved again, to 42 Veracruz Avenue, a street lined with jacaranda trees.

When Tina and Edward went to Diego's birthday party at his and Lupe's home on Mixcalco, Tina headed straight for the kitchen to help. As she was placing the tamales in a deep pot to steam them, Lupe entered; she was in a foul mood.

"Why did you put all of them in? Don't you know that the sweet ones go in later?"

Meanwhile, Elisa Guerrero, Dalila Mérida, and Ella Wolfe prepared the chocolate and strawberry atole and poured it into clay cups.

"As for me," Elisa said flirtatiously, "I've got a whole chain of padlocks on me."

"That's right," shouted Lupe, "but everyone has the keys."

"Carlos carries mine around his neck on a little gold chain," Dalila added.

"And you, Tina?" Ella Wolfe asked.

"She doesn't belong to anyone," Lupe shouted again. "These Italians are allowed to run loose . . ."

Weston had brought Diego a photograph for his birthday. In return, Diego offered them some sketches he had made for the mural at the Ministry of Education and led them to his studio so they could choose from among them. Diego talked while Weston and Tina looked them over slowly and reverently; the decision was difficult: all were equally magnificent. They didn't feel the time passing or hear the house filling with voices. Suddenly, Lupe burst in with her head thrown back and her green eyes popping out of their sockets. "This is why I invited you, so I could see the two love birds together."

Tina went pale; Diego turned his back on his wife and continued to occupy himself with the drawings. As far as Lupe was concerned, Weston wasn't even there. When she went out and slammed the door behind her, the three of them looked at each other in confusion. She returned five minutes later, still in a rage, but now with tears in her eyes.

"So, when are you coming down? You're ruining the party, Gordo. Everyone is asking where you are."

"Calm down, we're on our way."

Weston and Tina walked toward the door. Lupe stopped Tina in the hallway and held two painted gourds out to her as a peace offering.

"It's just that there's a lot of talk about you and Diego," she said, still trembling.

Tina put her hand in Lupe's big hand. Weston looked on. Somebody had once told him that Lupe was "a fury born before the deluge." He assumed that therein lay her charm, though he was incapable of understanding this kind of passion. It was impossible to know when to expect such sudden and unpredictable mood changes, which seemed to come out of the blue. Were they really out of the blue? Weston didn't say a word to Tina the whole way back home.

"Get out," he repeated to himself. "Get out of this hell of jealousy." The time had come. His own people were waiting for him: Ramiel, Johan, Margrethe, people like him, civilized people who knew how to have love affairs without such exaggerated emotions. They begged him to return, they respected him.

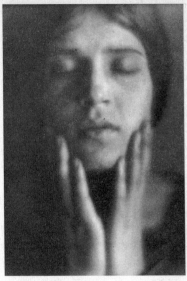

8

𝒯wo days after Christmas, on December 27, 1924, Tina, Jean Charlot, and Elisa silently bid farewell to Weston and Chandler. Elisa was wearing black, and her head was wrapped in a shawl. "She looks like a widow," Charlot thought.

The train departed. Images from the life he was leaving came back to Edward in a rush. He thought he heard the familiar sounds of 42 Veracruz Avenue, the *sssshhhh* of the cane brooms. Elisa's "give me a little something to buy milk, don Eduardito." Tina's face danced in front of his eyes: "Edward, Edward." At Legaria station, a beggar played a tune on a harp. Weston felt like crying but instead wrote in his diary. In Irapuato, a vendor urged him to buy a basket. "For your wife."

"I don't have one."

"You must have a girlfriend, at least," he insisted, his eyes mischievous.

"No, I don't," Weston said gloomily.
And he wrote everything down.

After a brief stop in San Francisco, Weston arrived in Los Angeles and wrote to Tina instead of in his diary. The only good thing he had done, he said, was to dine with the Modotti family at their home at 901 Union Street. From their sunny balcony, he saw the streets of San Francisco hugging the hills up and down. These Mediterranean people: they knew how to live!

> This is the morning after the night before—such a night! of course with your family! Easy enough to say one had a good time. This was a glorious time! I do not—could not exaggerate. Of course we got beautifully borrachito—no—I should not have added the diminutive—at least in regard to the condition of Johan, Benvenuto and myself—and if Mamacita was not, she didn't need to be, for she was quite the gayest person in the room. I made love to her and then to Mercedes with intense fervor and shocking indiscrimination. O she is lovely! Tina mia! I am quite crazy over her. With a few drinks, Johan is always a scream. Last night was no exception. Benvenuto was superb—gave us Grand Opera in the kitchen and acted all over the place. We jazzed—sang—did mock bull-fights. My sides really ache this morning from last night's laughter. I have had little sleep—yet I have no "head" and am still exhilarated. So much for good wine and a good time. And the dinner!— what a feast—with little pigeons so tender one ate bones and all—fresh mushrooms too—and then for emphasis I repeat— the wine!—the Wine!

Tina answered by return mail. His friends in Mexico were urging him to return; a postcard signed by Tina, Nahui, Monna, Felipe, and Rafael made him nostalgic. He imagined them all sitting around the table, talking and drinking mescal and eating nuts from Castile, the room scented with the perfume of the guavas, and he longed to be with them, to take Tina by the arm and walk through the streets filled with the fragrance of heliotrope.

Tina went to work in Guastaroba's bookshop to make a little extra money. After less than a day, she convinced herself that she was useless at selling things and quit. She returned to photography, earning just enough to feed herself and pay the rent.

On one of her excursions to the countryside, Tina photographed the aqueduct of Los Remedios. When she developed the film and saw that the bellows of her camera had cut off the image, she was furious! She swore she'd go back and photograph it again. Her deepest concern was how to live her art without letting life wear her out. Only Edward with his powerful intellect had the capacity to live many moments at once without losing his focus. She, on the other hand . . . She put her emotions even into the act of shelling peas. Then, at night, exhausted, she wondered, "What did I do today? I wasted so much energy! Eduardito, when are you coming? Please come back, without you I fall into dissipation."

July 7th Eve [1925]

. . . I have not been very "creative" Edward as you can see —less than a print a month. That is terrible! And yet it is not lack of interest as much as lack of discipline and power of execution. I am convinced now that as far as creation is concerned (outside the creation of species) women are negative— They are too petty and lack power of concentration and faculty to be wholly absorbed by one thing.

Is this too rash a statement? Perhaps it is, if so I humbly beg women's pardon—I have the unpardonable habit of always generalizing an opinion obtained mainly from an anal[y]-zation of just my personal self— And speaking of my "personal self": I cannot—as you once proposed to me "solve the problem of life by losing myself in the problem of art"— Not only I cannot do that but I even feel that the problem of life hinders my problem of art . . . By art I mean creation of any sort— You might say to me then that since the element of life is stronger in me than the element of art I should just resign to it and make the best of it— But I cannot accept life as it is—it is too chaotic—too unconscious—therefore my resistance to it —my combat with it—I am forever struggling to mould life according to my temperament and needs . . . and consequently I have not much left to give to art—.

Tina did not mention to Weston that she was feeling more and more drawn to Mexico's other face, the one covered with dust and sores, far from downtown, the Mexico of the poor and the hungry who live in shacks no better than dog kennels. Xavier Guerrero took her to Candelaria de los Patos and told her that there were hundreds of ghettos like this one where the police didn't dare enter. It was a side of Mexico Weston had not known. Here was a world where people just barely survived and seemed to expect so little. And yet, behind these people, supporting them perhaps, was an entire world of myths, herbal remedies, and wisdom. Tina began to understand that these Mexicans had two lives: their life of misery on earth and the other one, the true one, their house of sun that would transfigure them.

The Soviet Embassy sent out invitations to a party to celebrate the arrival of the great poet Volodya Mayakovsky. When Tina saw him, she thought he was as magical as his poetry. Every time Mayakovsky opened his mouth, he created poetry, a poetry that was free, innovative, fresh, unpredictable. With his beautiful, resonant voice he recited: *"I will make black pants/of velvet from my voice./A yellow vest with three meters of sunset./I shall walk down Nevsky Avenue of the world/over its slippery stones,/with the steps of an elegant man, a Don Juan."* Mayakovsky improvised his verses after seeing the faces in the crowd. The audience never knew where the poetry ended and the madness began.

Francisco Moreno, a Communist deputy from the state of Veracruz, a thin young man with black straight hair that fell over his forehead, never left the poet's side, and Mayakovsky felt the admiration in the melancholic eyes of his Mexican friend. Cultured Mexicans were charmed by the visit of the eccentric poet and excitedly discussed the fact that although he had a first-class ticket, he rode second class, "in order to know Mexico better." José D. Frias, who interviewed him for *El Universal Ilustrado*, was deeply impressed by him and wrote: "Even the greatest skeptic would perceive in him the powerful will of his people." Mayakovsky despised bullfighting. "I only wish," he wrote, "that it would be possible to hang a machine gun between the bull's horns and teach him to shoot."

On July 20, he wrote the poem entitled "Mexico":

What a country!
Just try
to conquer it!
Instead of Zapata,
a Galván, a Moreno, or a Carrillo
will rise.

At the end of July, sweet, gentle Francisco Moreno was gunned down by hired assassins. Hired by whom? The government? Perhaps a Veracruz chieftain? Everyone knew that Veracruz was run like an independent country. Mayakovsky was right. Moreno had risen from Zapata's ashes. Who would be next?

In his daybooks, Weston defined himself as an individualist by natural law, and believed that putting himself first was the best thing for his children.

In August 1925, after eight months of yearning, he took his son Brett by the hand and boarded the SS *Oaxaca* for Mexico.

During those days at sea, Weston's resolve strengthened; in Mexico, he would submit himself to Spartan discipline and cosmic asceticism: fasting, nudity, sun. He would breathe the air that came down from Popocatepetl and nourish himself on tropical fruits. He would teach Brett order and discipline because art, at its height, can only be reached through order. He had turned Chandler into a strong, sensitive boy, and now he would do the same for Brett. Only people with ugly bodies and dirty minds refuse to sunbathe naked. He looked forward to seeing the expression on Elisa's face as she pretended to shield her eyes from the sight of him undressing on the patio.

Tina waved her arms frantically on the platform at the station in Guadalajara. First she hugged Brett, then held him out at arm's length to get a good look at him. Next she turned to Edward, and they were locked in a long embrace.

José Guadalupe Zuno, the governor of Jalisco, was also at the station to greet Weston. The exhibition of Weston's photographs that Tina had organized was about to open in Guadalajara, and they were to stay at his house. José's hospitality was exuberant: mariachi musicians played until five in the morning, then fireworks were set off and food was served: pozole—a stew made with corn

—chicken wings and drumsticks, refried beans, hot sauce, and beer to nurse along the hangover. Brett was impressed by the long tables laden with delicacies, and asked his father, "Don't these Mexicans ever work?" José Guadalupe Zuno seemed like the king of Guadalajara: if he partied, so did the rest of the city. "We're going to show these gringos a real Mexican celebration." Pink and blue confetti, huge paper flowers, and piñatas seemed to float in the air. They would take a trip to Lake Chapala the next day to rest—from what?—and eat—yet again?

For Carlos and María Orozco Romero's costume party the next evening, Weston dressed as a woman, Tina as a man, and Brett looked exceptionally pretty as a bathing beauty. The press hailed Weston's arrival: "Weston the Emperor of Photography, who, notwithstanding his birth in North America, has a Latin Soul."

The exhibition was an enormous success. The locals flocked to it en masse. Their comments were intense and intelligent, and Weston was splendidly satisfied.

How warmly Mexico has welcomed him back! Now he only wanted to look Rafael Sala, his best friend, in the eyes, watch his wife, Monna, as she looked with appreciation at his photographs, make an excursion to Popocatepetl, and listen to Diego's praise and Lupe's shouts. Mexican hospitality had erased any regrets Weston might have had.

"No, Edward, I'm not getting into that car. I'm traveling to Mexico City second class."

Only eleven days back together, and Tina was already arguing.

"Brett and I bought first-class tickets in Los Angeles."

"I want to travel with the people."

"The seats are so hard."

"If they can stand it, so can I."

She preferred the chicken cages, the vomit, the ragged bundles of clothing, the unbearable odor of urine in the bathrooms.

"Come to our compartment," Weston begged her three hours later.

"I told you I don't want to."

She seemed to be telling him, "You see, you don't belong. You might as well leave again."

Diego Rivera, San Francisco, 1930. Edward Weston, 1930. © 1981 Center for Creative Photography, Arizona Board of Regents. Print courtesy Throckmorton Fine Art, Inc., New York.

9

Weston repossessed his rooftop studio and dusted off his toys—a crimson spotted dog, a couple of viejtos, and pigs with bursting bellies. His room was as white as ever. Tina hadn't touched it during his absence; only the light had swept through.

Elisa prepared a salad of nopalitos with fresh coriander, jito-mate, and onion sprinkled with grated cheese, and soup made from young corn. There was an enormous bowl overflowing with fruit on the table. What a homecoming! Mercedes Modotti, there on a visit, embraced him as warmly as she had in San Francisco. She called him Eduardito just as Tina did.

"Why didn't you tell me you were coming?" she asked him.

"Because I didn't know myself."

In the market, he bought Brett a smiling wood leopard with whiskers along its nose, and several dolls: a bride and groom, a priest, and the bridal party. In the afternoon, Weston took the Tacuba–Tacubaya–Chapultepec bus and got off in front of the

Ministry of Education. Diego flung open his arms from the scaffold. "What a lovely little monkey!" he said about Brett. "He's going to drive the girls here crazy!" Diego opened his portfolio. "Here, Edward, for you, a welcome-home drawing. On Saturday, come eat tamales with us on Mixcalco so you can meet my tadpole; she's so little I can fit her into my shirt pocket."

During Weston's eight-month absence, Tina had made a life for herself in which Weston had no part. "Do you want to come with me?" Tina would ask solicitously as she was about to go out. Weston forced a smile as a lump grew in his throat.

It was Weston who had originally established the game and its rules, and now she seemed to be beating him at it hands down. Why had she written that she missed him? Was it true? How could he make sense of the warmth of her welcome in Guadalajara and her distance now?

Tina had become friends with the Russian ambassador, Stanislav Pestkovsky, and his wife, Maria, and she often visited the Embassy on Rhin Street with Xavier Guerrero. Pestkovsky was a cultured, dynamic man who seemed to love Mexico in a new and thoughtful way. Since he did not have the use of an automobile—the triumph of the October Revolution did not permit such luxuries—he went among the people on the streets and declared that there was no better way to know a country. He even refused to have body guards. Everybody was his brother; two revolutionary countries recognized each other in their good intentions. Tina would have given her life to go to the Soviet Union and shake Stalin's hand. She spoke with José Mancisidor and others in the Communist Party, who repeated the slogans: "All power to the Soviets; all the land to the peasants. Private property must be abolished."

Weston, however, found the parties attended by Communist Party members boring.

"All these Communists think they have the right to interfere in other people's lives!" Weston complained.

"Why do you care?" Tina threw back at him.

"Because they lack imagination."

Edward took refuge in the studio of Carlos Mérida, the painter. Mérida showed him his one-line sketches and his friezes which still exhibited the synthetic quality that had fascinated Weston during his first trip. Mérida had no desire to illustrate the revolution or its violence, nor did he attempt to achieve populist dimensions in his work. He wished only to integrate form and line, and coordinate colors. What was essential in painting? Color, of course; thus Mérida, with one simple symbol, was able to say what others could achieve only through complex explanations. Isn't this what the Mayas and the Toltecs had achieved?

"Look at this stone; the impossibility of getting away from the material establishes its limitations. It obeys its own laws. The stone imposes its own design. The artist must adhere to it and submit himself to its dominion."

Weston looked at Mérida's chiseled face, his features so firm it was as if he had carved them. Therein was expressed exactly what Weston was searching for: the essence.

Early one morning, Weston lay down on the tiled floor of the bathroom to photograph the toilet. The sides of the bowl opened from the base in progressive swellings like wings. Its vigorous movement was the clearest proof that form was determined by function. There wasn't a single flaw in its sensual shape. Modern hygiene had created a new and splendid amphora. Oh, glorious toilet! He could hardly wait to see the developed print.

Every subsequent morning, after ten o'clock, he settled himself in front of the toilet and declared it off limits. Elisa made sure to scrub it until it shone and thoroughly dried the floor for Weston to lie on. At first, jokes were made. Brett offered to sit on it to liven up the shot. Mercedes suggested throwing rose petals into the bowl in case Weston wanted an overhead shot.

Soon, these sessions in the bathroom began to affect the others.

Tina was the first to react. "I'm going to the Guerreros' to take a bath, and I'm taking Mercedes with me. You have pushed us out of the house."

Even Brett complained. "Dad, aren't you ever going to leave the bathroom?"

"I just want all of you to leave me alone."

In his journal, Weston began to express the enthusiasm of his

95

most creative days: *"I have been photographing our toilet, that glossy enameled receptacle of extraordinary beauty . . . Never did the Greeks reach a more significant consummation to their culture . . . It is not an easy thing to do, requiring exquisite care in focussing—and of course in placing—though the latter I am trying to repeat."*

Let's see. Weston looked at his negative. What a pleasure to get back to work after months of sterility!

"It was more simple than I had thought: by placing my camera on the floor without tripod I found exactly what I wanted and made four negatives with no change of viewpoint except that which came from substituting my short focus R.R. . . . Questioned—I could hardly answer which of my loves, the old or the new privy I like best . . ."

Weston wanted to unscrew the wooden toilet seat.

"I don't understand why I didn't think of that sooner."

Jean Charlot's mother dined with them that evening and listened to Weston in awe.

"I have done all these negatives under great stress, fearing every moment that someone being called by nature would wish to use the toilet for other purposes than mine."

Tina looked at him, then went up and put her arms around his neck. "Eduardito, you need a few days' rest; it will be good for your negatives. When you get back, the toilet will be much more of a toilet for you."

Grateful for this show of affection, Edward agreed.

On Sunday afternoon, Weston took Mercedes and Brett to a bullfight. Mercedes was able to enter into its magic, unlike Tina, who detested it. In the evening, they all went to Diego and Lupe's house for supper. Lupe served the meal with little Pico in her arms. Now, when she exploded with laughter, the tremor shook the little one and some of her guests feared its eardrums would burst.

Soon, Germán and Lola Cueto joined the dinner party. Also Ignacio Asúnsolo, another of their neighbors, dropped by for a laugh.

Suddenly Lupe announced, "I'm going to Guadalajara."

"What for?"

"To live there with my daughter. Diego doesn't pay any attention to her anyway."

"She has changed a lot since her daughter was born," Lola Cueto explained to Mercedes. "Everything affects her emotionally;

she doesn't want to travel with Diego or bring him food at the work site anymore. She thinks he's having an affair with your sister."

"Tina? Impossible."

Every time Tina sat for Diego, Lupe strode across the studio, mumbling curses between clenched teeth. Tina was motionless and concentrated on her pose. "Lupe's eyes are like those of the blind," she said to Mercedes.

"You should watch out for her, Tina. She is consumed with jealousy, and you never know when she'll go over the edge."

Lupe finally unclenched her teeth and threw her venom straight at Tina. "Don't think I'm upset because I have any interest in that disgusting, fat, horrible, idiotic, shameless hypocrite, but only because he gave me this child and has to support it. The only thing I'm interested in is the money he makes."

Mercedes made notes in her diary: *"Chapingo by car with Carleton Beals, Brett, Tina. We visited the school of agriculture. Wonderful people. Tasted real Mexican food for the first time. I like it. Continued to Texcoco, where we bought serapes."*

In the chapel in Chapingo, Diego had finished sketching the main figure: Lupe with a still-swollen belly, her breasts enlarged after having given birth, her thick head of hair. Tina, Concha Michel, Luz Martínez, and Graciela Garbalosa would be the other feminine figures. Lupe represented the *Fertile Earth*; Tina, the *Hoarded Earth* and the *Virgin Earth*; Concha Michel, *Water*; Luz Martínez, the women in *The Human Family*; and Graciela Garbalosa, the women of *The Metals within the Bowels of the Earth*. Tina posed nude with her hair over her eyes, her arms in the air, her breasts pushed up and out.

After Mercedes returned to the United States, Tina and Edward grew even more distant. He chose to hide his wounded ego behind sarcasm and increasingly nasty comments. Tina pretended not to hear.

The presence of other people diluted the tension, so Tina avoided being alone with him in the house. Many mornings she dragged Brett out with her to take pictures. She visited the Open Air Art School of Ramos Martínez; she was called on by Gabriel Fernández Ledesma, invited to the Union of Painters and Sculptors. Most important, however, were her meetings with Xavier Guerrero, the serious, humble man who took such an intense interest in her and made her feel chosen. More than Diego, Xavier was Mexico: humble, poor, ineffable Mexico.

When Xavier Guerrero took her hand, his own covered hers completely. In the Villa de Guadalupe they saw a pilgrim making his way on his knees. Tina wanted to intervene, but Guerrero stopped her.

"It has nothing to do with you."

"How can I stand here and do nothing for that man? His knees are bleeding."

"You must try to understand that he wants to be a martyr."

Xavier's strong hand held her back.

"But it is outrageous!"

"Maybe what you do, Tina, seems outrageous to them."

Guerrero's power over Tina was growing. She felt her hand submit to his strong, solid grip.

One night, Xavier, his face beaming with hope, asked simply, "Will you take off your clothes?"

He took her gently, ceremoniously, gazing at her body with the eyes of a painter. When she felt the weight and gravity of his body, she knew that Edward had grown too light for her.

Weston often remained in bed until he heard the door close and could be sure he wouldn't bump into Tina or Brett. There was no relief from the cold, and he felt like running away to Fred Davis's house in Cuernavaca, where he had photographed the trunk of a palm tree in the sun. Any place would do, as long as the sun was shining. He was sick of doing portraits, of using his art to make wrinkles disappear and slim down thick waists; he was fed up with listening to the sound of hail on the thin metal roof of the darkroom, which made him feel as if he was working inside a drum.

Weston's outbursts of desperation coincided with the sky's. Once the storm's onslaught was over, nature would retreat, finally defeated; Weston, also exhausted, would retire early to bed. One night when Tina wasn't home, a telegram arrived from Mercedes. Weston opened it: "Mamma seriously ill." He got out of bed and went to look for Tina. Lupe, back from Guadalajara, slammed the door in his face. Nor was Tina at the Salas' taking care of Rafael —who was very ill—as she had promised Monna. Finally he reached Guerrero's house. No, Tina had gone out with Xavier, and they hadn't returned yet. But Elisa, Xavier's sister, invited him in. They would wait together. Weston declined and returned home.

When he finally heard the door open, then close, he called out to Tina, asking her to please come up to the bedroom. Without a word, he held the telegram out to her. Tina returned it and in a firm voice said, "I'll leave tomorrow."

On December 9, Weston wrote in his daybook: *"Following a telegram with advice of her mother's precarious condition, Tina left for San Francisco this morning! The house is so strangely empty."*

1 0

$\mathcal{M}$amma, your hands are very cold."
The doctor warned that she wouldn't be out of danger until the fever subsided.

Tina couldn't imagine something happening to her mother. Death had no right to touch her. Before Giuseppe had died, his eyes looked aged, but Assunta's still had that spark, that adolescent candor, and Tina was sure she would live until she had used it all up. Assunta gently closed her eyelids, but under them, life was still beating, as if she were saying that this was just a passing exhaustion; the heart, you know, the heart gets tired.

A smile was always on her lips, the same smile Tina remembered seeing every day when her mother opened the front door of their house in Udine for her children. Yolanda, the youngest of the six, would hang on to her skirt, then step away as Tina approached. There were always little brothers and sisters; there was always hunger. Giuseppe sometimes lost hope; Assunta never did. Assunta fought to make ends meet. She sewed all their clothes, became an extraordinary seamstress, and passed on her love of sewing to her daughters.

"Mamma, how do you feel?"

She smiled, she moved her hands, she opened her eyes, and her children saw that she was troubled because she had worried them, ashamed because her illness had taken up their time and energy.

Tina wrote to Weston about her convalescent mother. She also told him that she had sold her Korona and bought a Graflex. She went out, accepting invitations from Consuelo Kanaga, Dorothea Lange, Imogen Cunningham, Roi Partridge, and Ramiel McGehee. Consuelo offered to accompany her to Los Angeles to get the trunks she had left there in 1923. Tina devoted herself to disposing of memories, material things, her past life with Robo. One can become a slave even to a pair of slippers, and she didn't want her possessions to weigh her down, impair her flight. She wanted to travel light, with what she could carry on her back, close the door of her house behind her without worrying about anything disappearing.

> *February 9th, [1926]*
> *. . . I have been all morning looking over old things of mine here in trunks— Destroyed much— It is painful at times but: "Blessed be nothing." From now on all my possessions are to be just in relation to photography—the rest—even things I love, concrete things—I shall lead through a metamorphosis—from the concrete turn them into abstract things . . . and thus I can go on owning them in my heart forever.*

In the same letter, Tina announced that by March she would be at 42 Veracruz Avenue. By then, her mother would be totally recovered.

In Tina's absence Weston's maid, Elisa, sent for her sister Elena to keep her company. The two would peek into his bedroom and ask if there was anything Señor Don Eduardito would like them to bring him. Then they'd run away down the hall in a whirl of giggles and flying braids. Weston found them enchantingly fresh after the discourse of Mexican intellectuals and artists, like a couple of bright-eyed squirrels. When it rained, they would sing: "San Isidro Labrador, turn off the water, turn on the sun."

Elena admired Weston from a timid distance. He smiled at her. She approached his desk softly, and stroked his hair with such devotion that he took her in his arms and kissed her on the mouth. From then on, they embraced frequently, Weston's sentiments as genuine as Elena's; this was an unexpected love, the strangest of his life, which consoled him in Tina's absence.

One day, while getting undressed for bed, Weston heard a whispered voice calling, "Eduardo, Señor Eduardito, come with me." His heart leaped, and without a thought he ran to embrace the figure beckoning to him. What an opportunity, he'd never thought the girl would go so far! He began to caress her with a certain curiosity—what would it be like with her?—but when his caresses became more intimate, Elena held him back. She told him in detail of her affection for him: for weeks she had dreamed about him, she'd never imagined he felt the same. He tried to drown her with kisses, but she continued her monologue. He tried to possess her, but she evaded: "I can't, I can't, Don Eduardito . . ." She crossed her legs and claimed it wouldn't fit into her. Then she cried what would his wife think if she discovered them, what would her sister think if she came in, what if her mother came, and God was surely watching them from heaven, and the dear Virgencita, this can't be! At six in the morning he managed to get her to leave, in tears. What a night. The sisters' ardent coyness drove Weston out of his house to sit on a park bench until they went to sleep. A Mexican would have avoided the situation, understanding the mess that would result from trifling with Mexico's rigid hierarchies, but Weston was innocent of all that. "Oh God, Tina, why have you left me to this?"

Three months later Tina returned to Mexico.

By noon of the day after her return, Tina had organized the itinerary and the money for her trip with Weston to Puebla, Oaxaca, and Jalisco. They had been commissioned by Anita Brenner to take pictures for her new book, *Idols Behind Altars*.

Getting out of the capital was like returning to the good old days. In Amecameca, they spread white geraniums on their pillows. Ixtaccihuatl blew its snowy breath upon them, forcing them to huddle close to each other under their blankets. From their bed, locked in a warm embrace, they watched the form of the Sleeping Woman awaken silently above them. Popocatepetl hovered behind the clouds.

Without Tina, Weston would not have been able to take a single photograph. Earlier, he had viewed the behavior of the Mexicans as the charming result of some kind of pure philosophy; now he found it unbearable. "Mañana," "Tomorrow." "I'll be there soon." "Don't have any." "Maybe yes and maybe no, who knows." He no longer considered a two-hour wait at the train station to be an indispensable cultural experience; now it was simply a torture he was forced to endure.

"Did you come to dig up idols?" "Do you want to buy baskets?" "Do you want to try my tacos?" "Maybe an embroidered belt for the señorita?" The vendors came onto the train with green polished clay items from Patambán, ceramics from Oaxaca; others carried sacks of onions or boxes of jitomate.

Whenever Weston wanted to give up, Tina carried on with the perseverance of a peasant. Her cheerfulness broke down the silence of the most taciturn.

"Do you have any ham?"

"No."

"How about some eggs?"

"No."

"Cucumbers?"

"No."

"Maybe some cheese?"

"No."

"Edward, let me do it." Tina interrupted when she saw the frustration in Weston's face.

"Excuse me, señor, do you think you could do us a big favor and bring us some tortillas?"

"Of course."

"And some beans?"

"Of course."

"And if you could please cut up a little onion, and add a bit of cilantro, and if you have some jitomate, that would be even better."

"Yes, of course."

"How wonderful! Thank you very much, señor, this is going to be a delicious meal. And if you bring it all to us piping hot, I will be infinitely grateful to you."

The villagers opened their doors to them and food appeared on the tables. Their café con leche was ready at five-thirty in the morning, served with bread and fresh cheese. Weston's mood improved. He didn't even feel irritated when he heard, "I'm not from here," whenever he asked for directions. At night, they went back to their old ways: blankets over the windows and towels under the door to keep out the light. They stored their developing chemicals in the chamber pot, put a sign on it—"Do Not Empty"—and hid it in the closet. Weston looked at Tina's pictures and told her he was proud of her. In the morning, they ate in the market and searched for new folk-art pieces.

Tina and Weston returned to Mexico City in November and gave Anita Brenner four hundred negatives. The time they had spent together had been productive, but once they were home, they began to avoid each other in earnest.

As Tina moved further away from Weston, she also lost contact with many of the friends they had in common. The era of wild parties and outlandish costumes had come and gone. By mutual agreement, they would go their separate ways. Weston began to prepare for his departure and openly courted Mary Louis Doherty. He invited her to dinner at Anita's, Monna's, and Fred Davis's house.

Mary, however, remained reticent. "I cannot interfere in the Edward–Tina myth," she protested.

"But it's over."

"I don't believe it. The legend lives on."

On November 13, in the taxi on the way to the train station, Weston looked into Tina's eyes. When he saw what they had to say—he wrote in his daybook—he took her in his arms, their lips met in a kiss, and they pulled apart only after a policeman standing on the street corner blew his whistle. The driver warned them that they could be arrested for immodest behavior. This time it's really goodbye: to Tina, to Mexico, to the policemen, to the stray dogs; this time it is forever.

1 1

The next day, Tina wrote Edward a sad letter. The empty rooms were painful. She looked up Ezra Pound's "Canto LXXXI" that she used to read with Weston, and read it out loud to herself.

> *What thou lovest well remains,*
> *the rest is dross*
> *What thou lov'st well shall not be reft from thee*
> *What thou lov'st well is thy true heritage*
> *Whose world, or mine or theirs*
> *or is it of none?*
> *First came the seen, then thus the palpable*
> *Elysium, though it were in the halls of hell,*
> *What thou lovest well is thy true heritage*

Remembering Edward would be her heritage.

She would not be able to afford the house on Veracruz Avenue. As she packed her things, she was pleased to discover that she had accumulated nothing superfluous. "Travel light," she thought and smiled to herself. She had found an apartment next to Frances Toor's on Abraham González Street. Weston had left her the enlarger and a worktable. She improvised a studio and a darkroom.

Xavier came to her on the third floor.

Making love with Xavier was a rite, an homage to age-old gestures. When she made love with Edward, he would insist that she get on top. He wanted to be her thing, pure submission, do anything you want with me; he was so slender, and his body was firm and tight. He was electric; he leapt like a cat. You could count his ribs, play him like a flute. "All my holes are yours," he said, trembling, offering himself to her.

Then, grimacing like a perverse child, he would say, "That was good, wasn't it?"

Tina would cling to him and say, "Yes, Eduardito, yes, Edward, yes, yes."

But tears of dissatisfaction would roll down her face, and she would curl up on Edward's chest. "Do you love me, Edward? Tell me that you love me."

Making love with Xavier was like leaving the smiling faces of Veracruz to meet the gravity of the Olmeca heads. Tina wanted to dig inside, search, lose herself in that gravity. She was fascinated by his Negroid lips, by areas of his skin that got softer and lost their pigment only to acquire a bluer tint. She buried herself in his chest, his smooth skin. She wanted to penetrate the distance, cross over the silence alone. To love Xavier was to return to a portentous antiquity, to suspended action, to another's essence.

Bursting with newfound enthusiasm, she left early each morning for 54 Mesones Street, the headquarters of the Mexican Communist Party. "What can I do? How can I help?" She felt more and more strongly attracted to the urban world and its inhabitants. She wanted to stop them in the street and say, "I love you. I am yours.

I am at your service." At night, she returned home exhausted and with a feeling of dissatisfaction more ancient than Popocatepetl and Ixtaccihuatl. She felt she had achieved nothing, that her energy had been wasted in running errands, slipping paper into the Underwood, participating in meetings of men, comrades, who were completely immersed in themselves and their theories.

Yet, Tina would wake up the next morning, young and hopeful, brimming over with renewed energy. Today, yes, today she would find what she was searching for. Her commitment would be absolute. She took Mesones by storm, working until well after dark. On her way home, she felt the city grow tired under her steps. "Again," she thought, "again what useless weariness!"

The apartment on Abraham González Street soon lost its nakedness and filled up with Xavier and his work. The first day Xavier was there, he hung his hat over the picture of Weston and blocked the way to the bathroom with a pile of his newspapers. The pamphlets he collected made more piles: the destiny of humanity stacked against the walls. He used the black jar from Oaxaca for his rolls of sketches, and kept a pile of hemp under the bed. His jacket was draped on the back of the chair.

Tina wanted to tell him that it was difficult for her to see her home transformed into a branch office of Mesones. Even the light had changed. She no longer saw the colors of the sun; now she was surrounded by gray, black, brown. The only criterion used by the comrades for choosing a color to wear was its capacity to hide the dirt; this and durability replaced beauty as a standard. The five-year plan: these shoes will last. Her black skirt was her uniform. From all her years with Weston, she had only kept her silk kimono and her Graflex, and inside her, the nostalgia of memories.

Oh, Edward, such a beautiful day and I'm shut up here. Light outside and so much to photograph. You said there were very few people who lived for art and that I was one of them. Just two blocks away, at the cantina, the women peek under the swinging doors to catch a glimpse of their men's legs; they recognize them by their feet, and since they can't get them to leave, they go to the women's section and drink like them until they collapse on the bench. And if I joined those women, would I be able to photograph them? Xavier would scold her. "Foreigners are always attracted to vice, what they see as 'typical' denigrates Mexico. You have wasted a lot of time; if you want to be a militant, you have a lot to learn."

She felt a stab of longing for that man who could go into ecstasy over a woven basket. She remembered how he had one day pulled the leaves off an artichoke until he had reached the white down of the heart: "Look, Tina, look, this is incredible, this is fantastic. Have you ever seen anything like this?"

"This morning I feel so sexy, I can't stand it," she used to say to Edward. If she said it now, Xavier would think she was crazy. Weston searched for beauty from the moment he opened his eyes. Greeting the sky from the rooftop, focusing on the transparent air, the warmth of the light, the clouds: this was his creed. Everything else was rhetoric. The only laws he was willing to obey were those of the developing chemicals and the light meter; this was how he measured his time on earth.

In December, Alexandra Kollontai, the new ambassador from the Soviet Union, arrived in Mexico. Denied permission to go ashore in New York and Havana, she remained on board the *La Fayette* until it reached Veracruz. The Mexicans expected a hard-edged, strident suffragist; instead, they found a soft, round-faced woman wearing a flowered straw hat.

After presenting her credentials in a fashionable black silk suit and exhibiting an excellent knowledge of English and German, Alexandra opened the doors of the Embassy. Party members, including Tina, were eager to meet her. Tina did not recognize the Embassy from the times of Pestkovsky. There were bouquets of wildflowers and pots of begonias all over the room, and tea was served on a table covered with a white cloth.

With supreme graciousness, Ambassador Kollontai stretched out both her hands to Tina. "I have heard so much about you. Everyone loves you, admires you, and considers you a great artist."

Perhaps she was just being diplomatic, but the look in her eyes seemed genuine.

"You are my kind of person," she said as she embraced Tina. "Someone who challenges the world, paves the way for the new order. I congratulate you. Tell me what you are doing now."

"I've been documenting the murals," Tina responded proudly.

"Oh, what a great task, a great task! Mexican mural art is taking the world by storm. Thanks to those painters, art from the new continent is being discussed, and the leader is Mexico, this marvelous country. You are very lucky."

"Yes, it is a unique experience for me to spend my mornings and afternoons in the courtyard of the Ministry of Education. I also take pictures for *El Machete*, the organ of the Mexican Communist Party."

"I've seen your photographs; I read *El Machete*. They are very good and have so much political content."

Alexandra Kollontai continued greeting the comrades, demonstrating time and again her familiarity with their activities. Within a very short time, the ambassador became an important part of the political, social, and cultural life in Mexico. But Tina would not see her again. Six months later, on June 5, 1927, she would return to the Soviet Union. Working ceaselessly with no staff to forge commercial ties in Mexico, she destroyed her health.

The comrades plastered the streets with posters announcing a demonstration "against Fascist terror," to protest the assassination of the laborer Gastone Sozzi in the Perugia prison. Both Enea Sormenti and Tina Modotti were scheduled to speak at the rally. When Tina's turn came, her indignation overcame her natural shyness. She said that the Italy of Mussolini was an enormous jail and a vast cemetery. One hundred people applauded the two Italian speakers. There were other foreigners in the crowd: Mussolini's embassy in Mexico was taking notes. Tina wrote to Edward:

> *July 4th [1927] Evening*
> *. . . Some people—friends of Ella Wolfe here from New York. They wanted to visit the school in "colonia de la Bolsa"—since I also was anxious to know it I offered to take them—Edward when we left the place we all had tears in our eyes—What that Sr. Oropeza (the founder and director) has accomplished is something I will not attempt here to relate—And when we complimented him on his achievement he answered: "I could have done nothing without the children!" They have departments of Carpentering—Baking—Sewing—Printing—Photography—Farming—Shoemaking etc. Everything on the smallest scale it is certain—but serious—each department has*

an expert person as a teacher—I mean: a regular professional baker—shoemaker etc. Everything is run on the basis of syndicates—every department has its delegate—they hold weekly meetings and discuss the problems arising during the week and the way to improve everything—they have a department of justice also elected by the boys and formed by the boys— One case is this: a boy was found stealing a considerable amount of money from the general funds— How do you suppose they punished the boy? By making him their treasurer—.

Besides the manual labor they all have certain hours for general instruction—and some for gymnasium—games etc. I could write on and on about this but I would after all not be able to say all— Sr. Oropeza is writing a book on the founding and developing of this school—John Dewey (one of his greatest admirers) promised to finance the publication—.

I am indeed sorry that we never visited the school while you were here, as we had so often planned—.

Dear one—this is all for to night—.

When Tina received the new batch of Edward's photographs, her first impulse was to go out and buy a pepper, examine its curves and slopes, for never before had she imagined that one could be so suggestive. Weston always searched for the unexpected, and now he had found it. What did it matter how many hours he had worked if this was the result?

Edward's photographs shook the foundations of her renunciation and temporarily released her from the colorless world in which she had immersed herself. As she wrote of her feelings, her reactions to his photos, she knew that she was speaking out of the past as the woman of the world she once was and who now existed only in these brief flashes. He had, after all, taught her to discover beauty.

Edward—nothing before in art has affected me like these photographs—I just cannot look at them a long while without feeling exceedingly perturbed—they disturb me not only mentally but physically—There is something so pure and at the same time so perverse about them.—They contain both the innocence of natural things and the morbidity of a sophisticated

111

distorted mind— They make me think of lilies and of embryos at the same time— They are mystical and erotic.

The seashells, the peppers, Weston's images were still capable of overcoming misery and inoculating her momentarily against anxiety. But could she really choose to shoot roses, lilies, and crystal glasses when Gómez Lorenzo was urging her to photograph the peasants reading *El Machete*? "Tina, we live on a continent of starvation, as horrible as India's." Could she really waste film on the stairway of Tepotzotlán while the streets were exploding with human misery?

"A photograph," Gómez Lorenzo continued, "is an irrefutable document. The pictures you take are a slap in the face of the bourgeois conscience."

"A photograph is also a form . . ."

Misery, on the other hand, had no form, or had all of them. And since that misery did not allow her to breathe, she wanted to transcend it, go beyond it, turn it into art.

Tina took Edward's photos to Diego; he looked at them for a long time. "Has Weston been ill lately?"

Then he added: "Perhaps I am the one who is ill."

She continued to send packages of her own new work to her master and waited for glory or ruin, praise or condemnation by return mail. Maybe he would appreciate the form of the bandolier, guitar, and ear of corn, her synthesis of the Mexican Revolution, even though he would reject it as a symbol.

When she was asked if she wanted to travel to Texcoco to take pictures of a peasant rally, she felt as if she had been offered the keys to life. She would wear her overalls and go wherever she wanted, take pictures from different angles, approach the people, for this was also what *El Machete* wanted her to do: show that a sea of straw hats answered the Party's call. Yes, this was her profession. She spent days on the photo of the bum who hid his despairing face as he sat under the advertisement for a fashionable clothing store: *"We have everything a gentleman needs to dress elegantly from head to toe. Estrada Hermanos, Segunda de Brasil 15, Primera de Tacuba 15."* Of course that one was a montage, and Weston would criticize it. The Mexico that moved her most—

Mexico humble, beaten, profound—that Mexico should be left in peace and not tampered with.

Despite it all, she still spent time on the kind of photograph that was more likely to earn Weston's praise and Xavier's scorn. Two calla lilies—elegant purity of form—had caught her eye, the eye of the artist, not the militant. Developing the negative, she had felt as if she were giving birth. She broke into a cold sweat as she imagined herself with Weston again at her side. "The negatives are going to slip out of my hands; how much time do I leave them in?" Her arms felt stiff. "I must get hold of myself. If it weren't for this excellent equipment you left me . . ." "It's got nothing to do with the equipment: you're a fine photographer." She had to turn the negative every thirty seconds so the liquid would cover it uniformly; Weston himself had prepared the developing fluid, and she repeated the formula like a spell against failure: sodium hyposulfite, two grams; hydroquinone, ninety grams; boric acid crystals, thirty grams. "It's a bit dark," she blamed herself as she held out the finished negative. "You spoiled it," Edward growled. How much longer? My God, what an anguished process! "You don't know how to determine the difference between technique and magic." The shapes outlined in the emulsion seemed the result of a magic spell cast in the darkness; two, three minutes, an eternity. The calla lily was pure and sensual. "Will it retain both its limpid and its carnal quality?" Diego Rivera could retouch his paintings, change colors as he searched for a particular effect, but this wasn't possible in photography. Art was created or lost in the blink of an eye.

Now with the negative in the enlarger, she whispered, "Eduardito, help me." She was going to use the most expensive, fine-grained paper.

Then they appeared, her two dear callas, exactly as she had wanted them in front of the dirt-mottled wall, the shadow on the long spadix culminating in the glaring whiteness of the cups, the sap on the fiber of the petals terminating in that thin black line, a prelude to death. Cruelty is implicit in the beautiful; there is a flaw in nature; death takes the opposite direction from life. The emulsion has repeated its miracle. She hung up a copy to dry, like a small sheet of her imagination.

She wondered why she had been thinking so much about Edward if their last few months together had been so hostile. Hadn't she followed Xavier's lead, forgotten about aesthetics, and turned into a witness, photographing people on the streets, whoever happened by? It wasn't easy for her to forget her formal considerations, think only about portraying the life of the poor, forget what she had been taught by Weston, that photography was also an art form, yes, Xavier, just like painting. And in addition, of course, there was her equipment, her heavy Graflex that made it almost impossible to catch those fleeting moments, the flukes, the urgency. The picture of the flag-bearer on the bridge had been planned in advance. She still wanted her photographs to captivate the viewer's attention by the story they told, by their own value, and for this, she needed to think each one through before she snapped the shutter.

In her ever more encompassing role as a Communist militant, Tina was no longer that creature of endlessly renewed sensuality, but rather a cautious copy of herself. Even so, she couldn't prevent people from looking at her; every one of her movements exuded sexual energy, especially when she walked. Still, she made an effort to be more like Consuelo Uranga, Gachita Amador, María Luisa López. She spoke almost in a whisper: "Excuse me," "Good morning," "I'll be back in a moment." She almost wished Diego had not known her from "before." Her comrades would have judged any of her former activities as extravagant; Weston in drag: a faggot, decadent; Tina, dressed as a man, walking down the street on his arm: degenerate; Brett, wearing her brassiere stuffed with oranges: a pervert; Weston dancing with excited, tremulous Elena the maid: a deviation, a lack of respect for the poor, a nameless malignity; and Weston's attempts at sexual apocalypse that would lead to the intensification of pleasure: an activity for maniacs. What was morality? Was X normal? How did the comrades channel their sexuality? How did Hernán Laborde make love? And Frijolillo? What was the reality of their desires? How did peasants make love with their callused feet covered with mud, their legs and arms scarred by their daily labor, their chests panting like the earth, the flames of their breath? How about the women, wrapped in their shawls, their eyes like timid pools, their hands always hidden? The poor beat each other. The wives, the children, the dogs, the burros, the mules, all received their fair share of beatings. To beat was to educate. "Don't hit me, don't hit me, papa," Tina would hear. "Why shouldn't I hit you if it's for your own good?" According to the code of ethics of the Communist Party, the comrades got up every morning to struggle, not to be creative. They would construct a new society, a Mexico for all the disinherited, and above all, a Mexico for the people, the peasants, the true Mexicans.

When they brought in Comrade Raúl Alvarez—his nails bloodied, his face smashed, his swollen flesh beginning to rot—Tina realized that the Communists were putting their lives on the line.

She had been drawn to Raúl the first time she met him. Regardless of directives from Moscow, he had gone out to the impoverished settlements to be with the squatters and find out what they really needed.

"Specifically, they need toilets, sinks, drinking water, garbage cans."

"Why are they coming to the city?"

"Because they are dying of hunger in the countryside."

The children's cries were sharp and piercing, but the Party had to turn everything into committees, then divide these into subcommittees, and meetings could last for whole days while typhoid infested the settlements. They hadn't finished discussing possible strategies and they were already buying coffins.

Raúl Alvarez told the squatters to arm themselves with stones and sticks, whatever they could find, anything rather than give themselves over to the authorities. They should resist, demand what was rightfully theirs. "What is ours? We don't own anything." They didn't feel they had the right to life, much less to a piece of earth. The poor readily adjusted to their predictably bad luck. "Don't give up. React." He advised them, "Don't urinate or defecate near where you are sleeping; we're going to get shovels and picks to dig holes. In the meantime, here is some cardboard to make yourselves a shelter." They listened to Alvarez distrustfully, as if they were unaware of the degree of their misery.

The comrades disapproved of his activities. "You're wearing yourself out for nothing, and one of these days you're going to pay for it. You must make the government accountable, assign responsibility where it belongs. Write an article for El Machete denouncing the situation. They say that the President has our newspaper on his desk. What do you gain by going over there every day?"

Tina shared Raúl's concerns. How could the comrades abandon those poor people to the elements and the authorities?

Again she was reminded that the Party was not a charity organization, that the Party's work was political.

"But I'm willing to do it myself," Tina said, asserting herself. "I have friends, I can get blankets, cots, whatever is needed."

"Tina, our job is to denounce the problem, not solve it. We simply don't have the means. Next, you and Raúl are going to ask us to build a hospital."

"And why not?" she asked angrily.

"That is not the role of the Party. We must force the government to do it. You want us to turn into a branch of the Red Cross?"

On her own, Tina decided to approach some of her wealthy friends from the past and ask them to support her new cause.

Tita and Tomás Braniff welcomed Tina effusively into their opulent home in Puente de Alvarado, which she remembered from her days with Weston.

She came directly to the point. "I've come to ask for your help."

"By all means. What do you need? I'm sorry you had to wait, but Tomás has taken a great interest in aeronautics. We've just arrived from a test flight in Balbuena."

"We at the Party are committed to helping some families who are about to be evicted."

"Tina, we're leaving for Europe in a few days. Maybe we can help you when we get back. In the meantime, here is one hundred pesos, just to see you through."

"It's not for me," Tina said proudly. "I'm here on behalf of thousands of Mexicans."

On the table, in a silver bowl for visiting cards that stood between the candlesticks, Tina left the one-hundred-peso note. On her way to their house, she had felt the same joy and anticipation she used to feel when she went there with Weston. Now, the Braniffs' response only helped to define even more clearly the distance between Weston's Tina and Guerrero's Tina.

Next, she made her way to the corner of Juárez Avenue and

San Juan de Letrán, to the building where Monna, widow of Rafael Sala and now wife to Felipe Teixidor, had her apartment. Here she would not feel the aversion she had felt at the Braniffs'. The Teixidors' rooms were filled with books; they were intellectuals. How silly she had been to go to the Braniffs. She hugged Monna, who immediately asked about Edward and offered Tina tea. "How well you look, beautiful as always!" They sat on a plush green velvet sofa and Tina told her about the squatters' needs and her commitment to help them. Monna listened with a generous expression in her intelligent eyes, an expression that did not change as she replied.

"We've known each other, Tina, for a long time, so I'm sure you are aware of our way of thinking—Rafael's, may he rest in peace, Felipe's, and mine. You must remember that we have always remained marginal to ideologies. To help you, Tina, would be to betray myself, because I don't share your current beliefs. I don't believe in the dictatorship of the proletariat. This is my response to the militant. Nevertheless, I am willing, and I am sure Felipe would be too, to help you as our friend."

"Your friend is not asking for anything. Your friend doesn't need anything."

Tina hid her disappointment from Xavier. He would have blamed her. "Why did you go? You asked for it. That's the way they are. You should have known." Their rejections confirmed for her that something had been reborn within her that had brought her back to a distant time, to that child on Giuseppe's shoulders at the rallies, the goddaughter of Demetrio Canal, her fist raised in the air. Those arduous days at the offices of *El Machete* on Mesones Street had prepared her for this reencounter with herself. She felt no resentment toward her rich friends from before. She simply knew she would never see them again; the path she was following was different, and she believed it to be sacred. That night she gave herself fully to Xavier, merging with him through all his fibers and his consciousness. The next day, she gratefully became a card-carrying member of the Communist Party.

During the ceremony, Xavier's pride in his comrade was so great that even his stone features betrayed emotion.

Tina was also deeply moved. She received her membership as if she had been knighted, and Xavier Guerrero, a member of the Central Committee and her lover, had armed her. She owed this to him, her commitment unto death. Enea Sormenti told her about cards that had been perforated by bullets and religiously put on display in glass cases by the Russian Communist Party, about the Reds who had gloriously fallen in the struggle, like young girls who died of love. Yes, Tina, like those who die of love.

"I felt very honored," said Enea Sormenti, "when I received my card as a member of the Mexican Communist Party."

"Oh, but you are international."

"You can also be one day, Tina."

"From now on," El Canario joked, "no relaxation, no love affairs, not even a glass of red wine; goodbye to good times, wasted time, to even one single day without serving the cause."

"Here's to one hell of a life you will lead!" toasted Ratón Velasco.

Those were the jokes they told the new members, those who joined the various cells named after Karl Marx, Engels, Zapata, as if each one were a saint of the Church. Soon there would be a Klara Zetkin cell, once she was canonized. Tina felt that in the coming years life would live her, her time would not be her own. Would there be one day a Tina Modotti cell?

When Raúl Alvarez finally obtained authorization to take a brigade to the Bondojo settlement, Tina asked to be included. Raúl refused. Squatting was for the young, the unattached, not for Tina. "I don't want anything to happen to you. Don't take it personally, Tina. In the struggle, obedience is the most important thing. There is no room for pity. The comrades are also poor. They barely make ends meet."

"But I prefer to work in the field, look for a pot, a blanket, anything rather than listen to their interminable speech-making."

"Such individualism! You can't use the Party to resolve your personal conflicts. Don't worry. As soon as this is over, we'll talk again."

And now there he was, lying on the desk, the soles of his shoes torn off, his skin transparent, emptied of blood, his hands clenching his genitals in an impotent gesture to ward off the blows. Dead. Gómez Lorenzo put his arm around her. Tina instinctively moved away. "You see, you see what happens. We warned Raúl again and again. If you had been in that brigade, the same thing would have happened to you."

1 2

Tina soon realized that the main task of the women in the Party was to take care of their men, except for Luz Ardizana, who didn't have a man and didn't seem to want one. María Luisa was always in a hurry because after her work with the Party she had to rush home, her true cell, to serve Rafael Carrillo his dinner. María Velázquez, Juan González's wife, was assigned the task of making coffee and bringing bread for the men at the office. Their work at Mesones was just an additional domestic burden.

What did Tina have in common with these other women? What did they know about her? They were the type of people who never asked for a room with a view of the sea, who had never danced naked on the roof. They couldn't imagine Tina wearing a different skirt or jacket. Anything that symbolized personal freedom, like choosing one's own clothes, was prohibited. One day, Tina arrived at the office with a bougainvillea flower in her hair. Cuca García asked her if she was going to sing in a trio. With

Edward she used to think: "Today, I'll wear the white dress." Or, if it was sunny, "the yellow one." She would dress up the day with colors. It might be: "I'll go out without a hat today, and tomorrow I'll wear that marvelous panama from Chiapas to Diego's party." The embroidered blouse from Oaxaca was a real find; for hours they followed an Indian woman who promised to sell them a shirt just like the one she was wearing. She had it at home, she said, and as she trotted along in front of them, she kept murmuring, "It's right here, just a little farther." Weston had wanted to give up, but Tina insisted. When they finally reached the woman's miserable shack, she showed them a shirt that was even more beautiful than the one she was wearing. Edward admitted it had been worth it. Later, Diego said that it belonged in a museum, and Lupe wanted one for herself. Now she couldn't imagine running after an item of clothing, pursuing anything just because it was beautiful.

Even though Xavier moved in the same social circle as Lupe and Diego, Tina realized that she would never return to their parties. This was a different era. She photographed peasants, greeted them at Mesones, offered them her smile. "Come in, have a seat, please feel at home." Often they didn't have a place to spend the night, or a peso for a taco. The idea for the coffeepot was Tina's, as was the smile that eased the fear and the distrust. From now on, after knocking respectfully at the door, they would ask, "La señorita Tina, please?"

Enea Sormenti invited her to come to the meetings of the Anti-Imperialist League of the Americas and International Red Aid. The meetings began at eight in the evening when the Party offices closed. Ever since she had met Enea at the rally in support of Sacco and Vanzetti, the sight of him put a smile on her face. "Where are you from?" Tina asked. "From Muggia." "My God, I'm from Udine, right next to Trieste! We are friulanos, compatriots!" and she opened her arms to him. And what's more, he knew Sacco and was in correspondence with Vanzetti. "What are they like? Tell me everything you know about both of them." Sacco, a slight man, had been earning twenty-two dollars a day as a shoemaker, more than his modest life required, and his wife, Rosa, accepted his decision to "give half to our comrades." She also understood her husband when he explained that he would not go to war, because he could never take up arms against another laborer like himself, whether German, Russian, Austrian, or Hungarian.

"All of Latin America views Mexico as a beacon of light," Sormenti told Tina. "Here we will organize revolutions." But there was never a peso to be had. Revolutions, plots, conspiracies, uprisings in Cuba, Guatemala, Costa Rica, El Salvador, Peru, even in Bolivia and Ecuador, were planned at all hours of the day and night, in cafés, at the League, at Red Aid. Some young Mexicans went to Nicaragua to fight with the crazy little army of the General of Free Men, Augusto César Sandino. The Mexican Communist Party had six hundred active members who thought they had "the world" in their hands; the comrades believed that *El Machete* was the biggest newspaper in the world. Sormenti smiled when he said, "We're going to tell 'the world' to go to hell."

To be with Sormenti was like returning to her childhood. He asked her personal questions, dug into her private life in a way the other comrades wouldn't have dared.

"What are you doing with that monkey?"

"What monkey?"

"The statue, the sleeping monkey, you know who I'm talking about."

"Xavier?"

He laughed out loud, but Tina couldn't get angry.

"He's got no business with the likes of you. Come on, let's go. Help me organize the rally."

So revolutionaries could have a good time, too? Definitely, the foreigners were more worldly. That's why she got along better with Canario Gómez Lorenzo and Sormenti; they were less solemn, not as touchy. Except Raúl, he had been different, but now Raúl was mulching the grass at the roots, as Giuseppe Modotti would have said.

One evening in August 1927, Xavier suddenly took his suitcase out of the closet.

"I'm going to Moscow, the Party is sending me."

"What?"

"I'm going to the Soviet Union."

Like a robot, he began to pack his things.

122   He was leaving, leaving her behind. What obedience! He owed

no explanation to his comrade, who was, after all, yet another servant of the Party. Anyway, going to the Soviet Union was an honor everyone sought.

In silence, Tina helped him pack his warmest clothes. She wrapped packages of sugar cubes in his handkerchiefs, bought a wool cap and fur-lined gloves. She sat on a low stool by the window to knit him a scarf.

Then, before he left, her head resting on Xavier's chest, she demanded: "And me, what about me? What will happen to me?" Guerrero, the militant, not the man, responded. "I'm going to save the money for your ticket. You'll join me in Moscow, I promise." As Xavier's breathing became steady, Tina had no other choice but to resign herself.

"What an idiot to leave behind a woman like Tina," Sormenti commented. "Two or three years at the Lenin School are an eternity. I would have taken her with me. There are women you forget, but Tina is one who always remains. What a fool! If I were he, I never would have left her."

"¡Viva Cristo Rey!" someone shouted in the street. Tina remembered how Weston had hated the Cristero war. President Calles's harsh laws had created martyrs, and all that young priests dreamed of was dying in the name of Christ, like the first Christians walking toward the lions in the Colosseum. Every day in the papers there was more evidence of fanaticism. The priests in Jalisco, like horsemen of the Apocalypse, their skirts flying in a halo of gunfire, bore aloft the banner of Christ as they attacked trains, yelling, "¡Viva Cristo Rey!" That had been one of the reasons why Weston left Mexico. The extremism of the Cristeros had distressed him almost as much as the recklessness of the taxi drivers.

Xavier left at the beginning of September. The first thing Tina did was set up a daily schedule. After life, the most precious thing is time. She gave herself orders in writing: "Develop negatives," "Prepare emulsion." She made a chart: Activity/Time. Work Plan. Evaluation every weekend. She did her best to keep to her schedule.

Her concept of time used to be different. When she and Weston first arrived in Mexico, there was nothing better than getting together with friends to have a good time. Now, whenever she went to a meeting, it was to get something done: organize a march, write a speech, support a union struggle. Xavier had taught her to punish herself. The image of Tina smiling at parties was lost.

The walls of her studio were covered with quotes from Lenin and reminders of work assignments. She wrote down notes haphazardly in a journal, scribbled on the edges of a notebook in her black, precise handwriting, always rushed.

> *November 23, 1927. Today they executed Father Miguel Pro, his brother Humberto Pro, Luis Segura Vilchis, and Antonio Tirado at the police headquarters fifty yards from the statue of Carlos IV, in the middle of downtown, in the middle of the day, and without a court order. And then they say we live in a lawful land.*
>
> *December 6, 1927. Seven Catholics are strung up and killed in Jalisco in full view of the Guadalajara–Colima train line. Not that I care about the Catholics, much less priests, I just can't stand the way Mexicans carry out justice.*

A few days after the New Year, Tina wrote Weston:

> *You don't know how often the thought comes to me of all I owe to you for having been* the one important *being, at a certain time of my life, when I did not know which way to turn, the one and only vital guidance and influence that initiated me in this work that is not only a means of live[li]hood but a work that I have come to love with real passion and that offers such possibilities of expression . . . I find myself again and again speaking with friends about this precious work which you have made possible for me.*

1 3

Then, just when life was getting dull, Julio burst into her light and time.

Three months later, he was dead. She had taken his photo, dead. By focusing the lens of her black box on his face, she had proven he was dead. The camera could not lie. First Julio had been killed in the street, then she had killed him with her Graflex.

Now that she thought of it, it had taken considerable courage to take that photo, his noble, his beloved head swathed in cotton. At least the cotton was white and not smeared with blood. Raising the Graflex above Julio's dead face had been one of the hardest things she had done in her life. Even strong Luz Ardizana had looked at her in awe behind her thick glasses and asked: "How could you do it?" And Tina repeated her question, trying to find an answer: "How could I do it?" Now she wasn't even able to look at the photograph.

Yet her memory of Julio was vaster than her photographs and

she lived with it. If she had known him as a child, she could have narrated his whole life with photos. As a man he had posed for her seriously, as if he were answering the question: Who am I? What am I? She had taken him looking at her with open eyes, clothed and unclothed, with his hat on and without it, and the only time he hadn't looked at her was on his deathbed, but then there had been the faintest trace of a smile, as if he seemed to guess that she was making his last portrait. By examining that photo, she could relive it all. In her mind, the photo stirred, and she could remember the objects that were on the table that day they went to lunch, the trees in Chapultepec Park, the comrades at the meeting—the images were part of a sequence that she was now the only one to see.

She realized she had never looked at anything longer than at a photograph. Weston also looked more at the photographs he had taken of her than at her. "At least here, I have you under control," he would say. Even when Weston was in love, even when he was in Mexico, his life was the dark box, the darkroom, the black moment of suspense before the picture was developed in his mind.

At first, Tina did not want to see a photograph of Julio; it hurt too much. But for the comrades she pinned him to the wall next to all the slogans, and after a week she realized the picture gave her energy. It gave her life; its intensity had a power of illumination; she could hear his voice in the room. She would always carry his image with her, she would have it on a wall, it was her key to life now that he had gone back through the hole in the black box. Oh, blessed be the black box that had given her such a gift!

A month after Tina's house arrest has been lifted, the letters pile up in Tina's studio. Professionally, she is being sought as never before. Antonieta Rivas Mercado urgently requests a series of photographs of Manuel Rodríguez Lozano's paintings for Mrs. Frances Flynn Payne, a wealthy American patron. From his apartment in New York, José Clemente Orozco, the great muralist, asks for shots of his work and gives instructions on where to position the camera. Gabriel Fernández Ledesma needs specific angles of doors and windows for *Forma*. "Please write to Weston to convince him to continue sending us contributions." Carleton Beals, of *Creative Arts*, and Frances Toor, of *Mexican Folkways*, give weekly orders. She will have a show in the Berkeley Museum in October, and Carleton

Beals compares her *Calla Lilies* to the trumpets of Fra Angelico's angels. Tina's work is being solicited by *Agfa Paper* and the *British Journal of Photography*. From Germany, Willi Münzenberg asks for more photographs. In Brussels they are considering an exhibition of her work. Her photographs that appeared in the International Red Aid magazine, *Puti Mopra*, published in Moscow, denounce the misery in Latin America. Carleton Beals encourages her: "You are in your most creative period. This is your best moment."

What would the Mexican government say about the photograph that appeared in *AIZ*, the one of the drunken beggars? They would surely call her a subversive foreigner. Before he left, Xavier warned her that if she focused her camera on national disgraces like that woman lying on the sidewalk, bloated from alcohol and vomiting, she would offend the Mexicans' sense of pride. Tina also suspects that Weston would dislike her new photographs. He would say they had not been composed with enough care, that they show a lack of respect for the individual. She would answer that poverty is a lack of respect for the individual, that the poor are mistreated, their lands taken away from them, and she would also like to photograph their blood, their shit, their wounds, their faces covered with sores. Tina has decided to distance herself from pure aestheticism, from art for art's sake, but she would also like to raise reality to the level of art.

The phone rings off the hook. Today, for example, one of the Amor sisters whom Weston photographed will come to pose. The Escandóns, the Bringas, the Rules, the Braniffs all ask for an appointment. She has inherited clients from her master. In her portfolio, Tina places the photographs of the worker carrying a beam and the peasants reading *El Machete* next to those of the snow-white, terse, perfectly oval faces of her models.

She also continues to document the work of the muralists at the Ministry of Education and at the National Palace. She worships the murals: they portray the history of Mexico and represent the best work of the artists she admires most. Split between her commitment to the Party and her work as a photographer, she blames herself: "I've wasted so much time, so much time!" She sleeps little; reads a lot. "I must strengthen my character, educate myself."

Her correspondence with people in Europe both stimulates her and causes her anxiety. Just when she wants to get more involved with the Party, her photography is solicited by people all over the world. Tina is unprepared for success and is frightened by it. She is encouraged by the appearance of her photographs in *New Masses* in the United States, and especially by her family's reaction. Mamma sends congratulations to her through her brother Benvenuto. Yolanda also declares herself "very proud" of her militant sister.

When José Pérez Moreno asks Tina for another interview, she refuses. "Three months after Mella's assassination, and they still haven't found the assassin! How is such corruption possible? Yes, that is all I have to say, Pérez Moreno, and you can publish it word for word if you please."

"Be careful, Tina," Gómez Lorenzo warns her. "They still have their eyes on you."

David Alfaro Siqueiros, running his fingers through his hair, gives her the opposite advice. "One should never put a lid on public activity. Our battle must be waged every day and every hour of the day. I'm surprised you are telling Tina to be prudent."

"Julio's spirit pushes me on," Tina says. "I know full well that my public activities can land me in jail."

"You're exposing yourself," says Gachita. "Remember Article 33 of the Mexican Constitution of 1917. It defines the rights of foreigners. If their presence is considered undesirable, they can be expelled from the country."

Benvenuto Modotti arrives in Mexico from San Francisco to support his sister, radiating optimism. He has the same beautiful confidence as Enea Sormenti. His beliefs have given him maturity, confidence, an inner strength that Tina doesn't remember him having before. The moment he arrives, he reassures her: "There's time for everything; don't worry." He accompanies her to meetings of International Red Aid; he converses as an equal with Enea Sormenti. He also finds Sormenti charismatic, but doesn't agree with many of his ideas, or with some of his past activities, such as blowing up bridges and shipyards.

On April 5, 1929, Tina writes to Weston:

> *I cannot afford the luxury of even my sorrows . . . I well know this is no time for tears; the most is expected from us and we must not slacken—nor stop halfway—rest is impossible—nei-*

ther our consciences nor the memory of the dead victims would allow us that—I am living in a different world Edward—strange how this very city and country can seem so utterly different to me than it seemed years ago . . . Benvenuto is here and sends saludos to Eduardito. He is such a fine and wholesome boy, and such a precious camarada! . . . There is something else I have been forgetting to ask you in my last letters—Things are very insecure here for "pernicious foreigners"—I am prepared for the worst—any day they may apply the "33" on us . . . What shall I do with all your negatives?

Sormenti's spirited presence livens up committee meetings and discussions that continue late into the night at the Café Paris. He, Benvenuto, and Tina talk about Trieste and the United States. Sormenti tells them how he left Trieste "like a raging bull." "I am not modest, I have always been a nonconformist, in society, in the Party, an undisciplined member of the opposition. I like to give my opinion; I can't stand not saying what I think." In *El Machete* and *El Libertador*, Sormenti usually has the last word, and he either doesn't realize or doesn't care that many resent him. Confrontations are avoided because he leaves often for long periods of time, because he is "international." Ever since he disembarked from the *Martha Washington* in New York on August 22, 1923, he has been a fearless anti-Fascist activist. He learns English on the waterfront working as a longshoreman; he shaves and washes in subway station bathrooms and sleeps on any bench out of a policeman's sight. "My life is one big train station made up of arrivals and departures. I don't have a home, I don't have a family, I don't have anybody to say goodbye to, all I have is the shirt on my back." He takes everything with a smile; after all, he's young. When he wakes up on park benches, he is full of joy, and he uses all his energy to speak out against Fascism. He gestures as he talks. He entertains. People like him. He stands up to speak to the workers, his speeches are published in *Labor Defender*, he writes for *Il Lavoratore*, the newspaper of the Italian Communist Party in the United States, and ends up as its manager. When Carlo Tresca organizes the Anti-Fascist Alliance of the United States, Sormenti becomes one of his boys. Their motto: "Occhio per occhio, dente per dente, sangue per sangue." He agitates the workers, speaks against the government, and doesn't seem to care that he entered the country illegally.

Finally, of course, he is caught and declared an "undesirable alien." If Sormenti is deported, he will be a dead man in Mussolini's Italy. Whatever happened to Washington's republic and Lincoln's? Sormenti is particularly proud of the fact that Clarence Darrow defends him, and that the Soviet Union welcomes him as a son of the Comintern. Riga is a city of immigrants. The U.S.S.R. is the heroic nation of revolutionaries, and its marvelous people recognize him as one of their own. And even though he looks young, Sormenti has crossed the ocean ten times, always as a stowaway, and wherever he goes, he manages, and manages well.

Tina listens to him with admiration. In Mexico also, Sormenti has made his way, gained respect, his opinion is solicited. Benvenuto holds back. Tina's brother believes in America above all. He agrees with Sormenti that Europe is on the way out, but for him the future of humanity lies in America, not in the U.S.S.R.

Sormenti, Benvenuto, and Tina go to meet Sandino at Adelina Zendejas's house. Tina can hardly believe she is face-to-face with Augusto César Sandino (what pompous names for such a delicate man!), her hero, the hero of Central America. She gazes at the skinny, nervous man with burning eyes that look back at her, and though he has no mustache, she thinks that surely Zapata must have looked like him. Like Zapata, he is a guerrilla fighter, and like him, he wants the poor to own the land. Sitting at his side, Tina asks him in a low voice if she can join the guerrilleros in Nicaragua. In the mountains she could take pictures, be a nurse, help in any way she can. Sandino answers that she is more useful in Mexico, that the Hands Off Nicaragua Committee she works with is a bastion that sustains the guerrillas morally and materially, and she is one of its most valuable members. In Mexico, Tina is indispensable; in Nicaragua, less so.

"What are you planning to do with your life?" Raina asks her one particularly warm night.

Raina, Sormenti's girlfriend, is visiting from the United States, and Enea, always on the run, has asked Tina if she can put her up.

Tina considers telling her of her desire to go to Nicaragua, about her enthusiasm for Sandino's struggle and his way of fighting the Americans with a guerrilla army, but she remains silent.

"Have you thought about a new boyfriend?"

"No."

"There are many who admire you. Whatever it is men want, you've got it."

The night before she is to return to New York, Raina makes a strange request. "Show me your photographs."

Tina places her portfolio on the table in front of her. Raina spreads them out on the floor and looks at them for a long time.

"They are so good! You capture the essence of a place and a moment. You see Mexico from inside, not as an outsider. Just looking at that woman with her child at her breast, one can feel your commitment!"

Raina hugs her. Too bad they hadn't become closer sooner.

The next morning, Raina takes the train back to New York.

"I must go, too," Benvenuto says. "I have to get back to work or I'll lose my job."

They talk about a future meeting. "It's easy for me to go to Havana. Couldn't you meet me there, sorella?"

Vasconcelos had converted Mexico into a time bomb. He accused the men in power, the official party, of corruption. The ruling party is a gang of thieves, highway robbers, the Revolution is worthless. Obregón is a crook. Dwight E. Morrow, the gringo ambassador, is the real president of Mexico, he wants to impose his political system with no awareness of Mexican conditions. "Education, education," Vasconcelos shouted, "or else we're lost." He lashed out against his compatriots. "When God saw that Mexico was so beautiful he said, 'This is unfair to the others, I can't make it that perfect,' so he put in the Mexicans."

After months of severe repression and multiple assassinations, the Mexican Communist Party is declared illegal. *El Machete* is closed down and the printing press is destroyed. The dedicated comrades who continue to meet clandestinely spend their time debating what should be done: Moscow is so far away and orders from the Central Committee take so long to arrive. The cautious ones, the ones with doubts, like young José Revueltas, must be reprimanded or expelled. Hernán Laborde responds to their critiques in no uncertain terms, accusing them of playing into the hands of the capitalists.

"You, as an individual, are the least important consideration.

Your personality should disappear behind your ideas. If not, you become a pawn in the capitalists' game," Laborde tells Revueltas.

Those who arrived from Russia before the repression began, or from Europe, are more open, especially Enea Sormenti because he doesn't wait to follow orders; he gives them. He often needs to be reminded to keep his voice down in public. Everybody, dissenter or not, ends up in jail; that is the destiny of any self-respecting Communist. Moscow is powerless to free them; they are at the mercy of the Mexican authorities.

"The repression here is too severe; nothing can be done, and I can't stand around twiddling my thumbs." Enea Sormenti travels with Siqueiros to Jalisco to join the miners' struggle. Siqueiros arms himself and fights against the White Guard that is defending the interests of the mine owners. Sormenti also likes to hear the bullets whizzing by.

One afternoon in early July, a young man with glasses knocks on Tina's door.

"Excuse me, señora, I got your address from the director of *Forma*. I have been very impressed by your photographs, so I thought I'd come by."

"Please, come in. Where are you from?"

"I just moved here from Oaxaca."

Tina is flattered by the emotion this unassuming young man expresses in his thin, quiet voice, the way he enunciates each word.

"I saw your exhibit and Mr. Weston's at Aztec Land. Even before that, someone pointed you out to me, and I followed you to the Iglesia de la Santísima; you were going there to photograph something, I think."

At the mention of Edward, Tina feels a tightness in her chest. Her guest has not been long in Mexico City, and she realizes that he is completely unaware of the scandals that have swirled around her since Mella's death.

"I hope I am not disturbing you," he says timidly.

"No, not at all."

"I don't want to waste your time," he insists, looking at her shyly. "Your time is very precious."

"On the contrary, I enjoy talking with you."

"You and Mr. Weston," the man continues, "looked at the church for a long time that day, but you didn't take any pictures; you didn't speak, you just looked. I wanted to offer my help, but I didn't dare. I just watched you from the sidewalk."

"Yes, I remember the Santísima," Tina says with growing excitement. "We never took pictures on our first visit to a place. We thought it better to familiarize ourselves with the terrain, then come back and shoot. And you, what do you do?" she asks him.

The young man seems to get smaller as his timidity increases. "I'm a photographer. Well, at least I try to be."

"How wonderful."

"That's why I wanted to meet you and Mr. Weston, show you my work, without imposing on you, of course."

"Do you have something with you now?"

"No," he answers, almost inaudibly. "But if you like, I'll come back with some prints."

He speaks almost in a whisper, and looks at her shyly, like a wounded bird.

"I should tell you that Edward is no longer here. He returned to the United States."

"Oh," he says, his voice dropping to the floor, "I didn't know. Would you be so kind . . ."

"Of course, I would love to see your work."

When he knocks on her door a second time, Tina finds the same insecurity, the same muted enthusiasm in his pale eyes. He has brought an old portfolio. He places his photographs on the table and sits down in a flowered chair near the window, the same one Tina used to sit in when she would wait for Julio to come home. Few other visitors have chosen to sit in that small, low chair.

"I'll just wait here."

His anxiety is palpable as he stares out the window. Tina spends a long time looking at the pictures of straw toys, tombstones, workers in conversation, a sheet hung up to dry, a cross stuck into the earth.

Finally she speaks. "These are very good photographs."

"Excuse me?"

"I said your work is excellent, I like it very much."

He looks at her with the face of a child who just got an A on an exam.

"Are you sure? Don't I make a lot of mistakes?"

His genuine discomfort at her praise makes him even more charming. Tina looks at the pictures again.

"Have you finished looking yet?" he says, his eyes glued to the floor.

"Yes, and I assure you that you are an artist. I am going to show you some of Weston's photographs, but I don't want you to compare yours unfavorably to his. You are very good, and I promise I'll send your photographs to Weston. Can you bring me copies?"

"But which ones, because I don't . . ."

Tina chooses.

"I'm not going to tell Edward whose they are. I'll just send yours along with mine. But you haven't told me your name."

"Manuel."

"Manuel what?"

"Manuel Alvarez Bravo."

"Good, Manuel. Come back soon."

Manuel mumbles a thank you and blushes. "I didn't think anybody blushed anymore," she muses to herself.

The next day, she is surprised to find herself waiting for a visit from the shy Oaxacan who has restored a little of her passion for photography.

Tina takes him aside to show him Edward's and her photographs. Again he finds his way to the small flowered chair, and anxiously sits down to look at them. Manuel returns many times, but rarely finds her alone. He is impressed by some of the people he meets at Tina's house: Carleton Beals, Jean Charlot, Anita Brenner, Fred Davis, Emily Edwards, Pablo O'Higgins; but he seems irritated by the slow discourse of the comrades from the Party.

"Do you like politics, Manuel?"

"Not much."

"Are you interested in what the comrades talk about?"

"Yes, I mean, more or less. It's just that I, you know, never even finished high school."

Tina begins to discuss with Manuel technical problems related to her work photographing Diego's murals at the Ministry of Education.

"I'm just an amateur," Alvarez Bravo says modestly.

"No, you aren't. I want you to come with me to the courtyard and advise me on placing the camera."

"I would be honored."

Tina surrenders herself to his serenity, which is in such contrast to the intensity of the interminable political discussions. One afternoon, Tina gives him a print of *Flor de manita*.

"This is for you, Manuel, a gift."

Once, she asks him to accompany her to the Anti-Imperialist League of the Americas at 55 Bolívar Street. It is a delight to watch her move about, talk to the comrades, speaking in her soft and quiet voice. Tina uses words sparingly. When asked, she graciously accepts the responsibility of taking up a collection. She is also asked to take charge of correspondence and of visitors from abroad.

It isn't until a few months later that Manuel tells Tina that he has a wife and child.

"Why didn't you say so? Bring her to see me."

"It's just that our lives have become so complicated since we came here from Oaxaca. We don't have anybody to take care of the baby."

One night he arrives with a young woman carrying an infant. Her hair is braided with colored ribbons, and she wears a blouse embroidered with flowers. Tina offers her a cigarette and is surprised when the young woman accepts.

"She smokes like a chimney," Manuel interjects by way of apology.

Lola talks, argues, then stops to exhale her cigarette smoke. She seems more open than Manuel, talks more freely about her childhood, about herself, is less afraid to express her originality.

"Her enthusiasm reminds me of Lupe Marín's," Tina thinks. "And she even enjoys talking about politics. She would make the grimmest comrades smile." Tina finds herself hoping to see Lola's animated face every time her doorbell rings in the afternoon.

"You make a good couple," she tells them. "You complement each other."

"Oh, thank you," Lola responds. "But I'm getting ready to pick up the camera myself. I develop, I wash, I hang up his photographs. The other day I even brought the child into the darkroom, and he fell into the sink."

This young woman is so full of joy! Every time she goes out to the street, she has an adventure. "Oh, Lola, those things happen

135

only to you!" Sometimes Lola comes with her baby wrapped in a shawl and without Manuel.

"I had a minute, so I dropped by to bring you this guanábana and guayaba jelly that really turned out good. I made it with lots of sugar."

"You share everything, don't you, Lola?"

Lola never chooses to sit in the low chair as Manuel does. "How can I help you, Tina? I finished my chores early today. How do you manage to keep everything so neat? My house is a mess all the time."

"I have very few things, Lola."

"They say that a house is a reflection of a person's life. In that case, mine is a jungle. Your simplicity can be seen in everything about you, Tina: your dark skirt, your white blouse, and the work schedule you keep."

"My schedule?"

"Yes, the other day when I called, you said, 'Don't come now because I'm going to be in the darkroom from such-and-such a time to such-and-such a time.' "

"That's the only way I can get my work done and fulfill my obligations to the Party."

Certain members of the Party begin to consider Diego Rivera inconsistent and unreliable, and Tina joins the ranks of the accusers. On September 18, 1929, Tina writes to Edward that Diego got married again, to Frida Kahlo.

> Had I not told you Diego had gotten married? I intended to. A lovely nineteen year old girl, of german father and mexican mother; painter herself.
>
> But the most startling news about D[iego] is an other one, which will be spread through all the corners of the world tomorrow, no doubt you will know of it before this letter reaches you: Diego is out of the party. Only last night the decision was taken. Reasons: That his many jobs he has lately accepted from the government—decorating the Nat. Palace, Head of Fine Arts, decorating the new Health Department are incompatible with a militant member of the p[arty]. Still the p[arty] did not ask him to leave his posts, all they asked him was to make

a public statement declaring that the holding of these jobs did not prevent him from fighting the present reactionary government. His whole attitude lately has been a very passive one in regard to the p[arty] and he would not sign the statement, so out he went. There was no alternative. You see there are so many sides to this question, we all know that he is a much greater painter than he is a militant member of the p[arty] so the p[arty] did not ask him to give up painting, no, all they asked him was to make that statement and live up to it. We all know that all these positions were trusted upon him by the gov. precisely to bribe him and to be able to say: The reds say we are reactionaries, but look, we are letting Diego Rivera paint all the hammer and sickles he wants on public buildings! Do you see the ambiguity of his position?

I think his going out of the party will do more harm to him than to the p[arty]. He will be considered, and he is, a traitor. I need not add that I shall look upon him as one too, and from now on all my contact with him will be limited to our photographic transactions. Therefore I will appreciate if you approach him directly concerning his work.

Hasta luego dear.

Sormenti has a strong influence over Tina. "That Rivera is a prima donna; he creates publicity for himself at the expense of the comrades who risk their lives every day. If anyone could be called immoral, it is Diego Rivera."

Since Diego's expulsion, the comrades talk endlessly about the commitment of the artist. Tina adds her voice to Diego's detractors: he is a liar and an opportunist. Tina forgets that, less than a year before, Diego dropped everything to be with her during her time of need, that he got down from his scaffold and attended the hearings every day, that he was Tina's self-appointed defender.

Louis Bunin, an American who had just followed O'Higgins's example and come from Chicago, now works with O'Higgins as an assistant to Rivera. He also makes marionettes and his hands remind Tina of her father's.

O'Higgins and he are always together and O'Higgins comes to see her nearly every day. Bunin is as dark as O'Higgins is fair, and together they make a good contrast. Bunin with his black hair and his pipe is as good-looking as O'Higgins, both the same height, both striking. Because they are shy, women take the first step. Tina chooses among Bunin's puppets and photographs them. But more than the puppets it is Bunin's hands she's after.

Carlos Orozco Romero and Carlos Mérida extend a formal invitation to Tina, in the name of the Organization of Civic Action of the Federal District, to exhibit in the National Library of Mexico under the direction of Enrique Fernández Ledesma, on December 3, 1929. She is also offered the position of official photographer of the National Museum under the direction of Minister Aaron Sáenz.

"How can I accept?" she asks María Orozco Romero. "After the government's handling of Julio Antonio's murder, I feel it would be wrong."

"Considering your position as a foreigner without papers," María advises her, "you should at least accept the exhibition. It's the best thing that could happen to you. Dalila and I will remain by your side with our two Carloses, and you will have the full support of the artists in Mexico."

"But wouldn't it mean that I had sold out to the government?"

"Listen to me, Tina, my husband hasn't sold out to the government, and as far as I know, neither has Carlos Mérida. Anyway, the invitation comes from the rector of the university. What more can you ask for? It's a perfect opportunity for you."

The day of the opening, an uninterrupted flow of people pour through the doors of the National Library. Those who can't get in stand outside, waiting.

"Magnificent exhibition, wonderful, I am deeply moved," the young critic Jorge Juan Crespo de la Serna says as he embraces her. "It is your apotheosis. This is your glory: you have managed to mix high art with the art of the proletariat. All of Mexico is here to celebrate you."

"Yes," says Gachita Amador, "including a good share of pigs. There are more secret agents here than peasants."

"Where are they?" Tina asks.

"Half of those people in overalls are secret police."

Gachita has always had a knack for dampening Tina's spirits.

Federico Marín puts his arm around her and whispers in her ear, "With friends like that, you don't need enemies," and he stays by her side like a bodyguard. Tina can't help thinking that he would be shocked if he knew her current political opinions. Aurora Reyes, the only woman muralist, makes her way through the crowd, dressed in overalls. "I got down from my scaffold to be here with you." Aurora confides in her that it is very difficult for the men in the Party to recognize the value of a female comrade. "I am a Communist, and I would rather die than renounce it, but if the Party ever takes power, I'll commit suicide, because I know every single one of them, and I know what they are capable of." For a moment, Tina wishes Edward were there. Strange that she doesn't think of Julio Antonio, though she used for her brochure the Trotsky quote her camera had spotted in Mella's typewriter. Groups of people continue to arrive. Even Lupe Marín appears in the company of a tall, thin man with heavy eyelids who follows her around like a lapdog. "I am Jorge Cuesta," he says because Lupe does not bother to introduce him. Tina suddenly remembers Gómez Robelo's devotion and that of others who once courted her. How many have come and gone! "I'm going to write something about you," a man with straight black hair says to her, taking her arm as if he'd known her all his life. He stops in front of a group of photographs. "This one," Gustavo Ortiz Hernán says, "is a perfect synthesis of a great social ideology: the guitar, bandolier, and the ear of corn; the crystal glasses are stupendous, too: they have rhythm and musicality."

Tina thanks him. "When I developed it, I was afraid it had nothing to say, just like the roses."

"No, it says a lot."

"But it doesn't have a message."

"So what? You are creating a new kind of still life; you have a fantastic sense of the plastic. These scenes of daily life, the buildings under construction, the stairways, the stadiums, they acquire a kind of exotic prestige and personality thanks to your camera."

Siqueiros, listening over the man's shoulder, agrees. "I want to give a talk about your work."

Tina's exhibition is also attended by hundreds of workers who are clearly impressed by the depiction of their conditions; the comrades from the Party and the delegations of peasants enter slowly, hat in hand, and follow the photographic route laid out by Tina.

Ortiz Rubio is named President by the Chamber of Deputies, and four days later Vasconcelos, who has lost, crosses the border to the United States. On Saturday, December 14, 1929, at the close of Tina's exhibition, Siqueiros speaks about the "first revolutionary photographic exhibition in Mexico," and Baltasar Dromundo adds his own words of praise. Tina writes to Edward: *I wish you had heard Siqueiros's speech. It was stupendous. He has such profound knowledge of the history of art and his point of view is so vital and meaningful.*

On January 13, 1930, Mexico breaks off diplomatic relations with the U.S.S.R. and recalls its Embassy in Moscow. Makar, the Russian ambassador, is expelled. One week later, fourteen Vasconcelos supporters are arrested and accused of conspiring to kill Calles, Ortiz Rubio, and Portes Gil. On January 25, another twenty-one people are arrested. On February 5, Ortiz Rubio, while walking to his car with his wife and niece after taking his oath of office, is shot five times by Daniel Flores and is wounded in the jaw. Those accompanying him are also slightly wounded. Flores is arrested but refuses to talk. Some say he is a Vasconcelos supporter and a student; others say he is a Communist.

From Los Angeles, Vasconcelos makes this statement: "There will be no peace in Mexico until free elections are held."

He has crossed the frontier to come to the very people he had fought against. He who affirmed Mexicanness and spoke of a new race in the universe, who dreamed of a Mexico that would make itself known in the world precisely for its racial mixture, who believed Mexicans would surpass the Greeks and recover lost lands in North America—he now takes refuge among his enemies. He would never be President of Mexico, yet his supporters have been persecuted and jailed, and one of his lovers, Antonieta Rivas Mercado, with a sharper sense of loss than his, would shoot herself in the head with his pistol, one year later, in Notre Dame, in Paris.

1 4

On February 6, 1930, Tina, Enea Sormenti, and Farabundo Martí go to the country to walk through the pine forest. When they return, Enea and Farabundo accompany her to the corner of Abraham González Street. "I'll call you later," Sormenti says to her. Tina opens the door to her apartment and finds the police waiting for her. Again, the house has been searched. Tina immediately wonders what has happened to Sormenti and Martí. Were they arrested at the corner?

Sormenti calls Tina as he said he would. A man answers the phone.

"Who are you?"

"The police."

"May I talk to Tina Modotti?"

"She has been arrested."

That same night, Sormenti goes into hiding.

Although Tina is first placed in solitary confinement, she soon finds out that many other men and women from the Party have been arrested. David Alfaro Siqueiros is being held virtually incommunicado.

"Mexico is a sinister place," Tina thinks with a shudder. "What would José Pérez Moreno write now?" She is being kept in a holding cell on Victoria Street. She has good reason to believe that she, Isaac Rosenblum, and Johann Windisch will be deported. A while ago, Julio Rosovski was deported. Whatever happened to Enea Sormenti and Farabundo Martí?

After almost a week, Tina is moved to the women's section of the prison. They give her a cup and a pewter plate; the tortilla will serve as her spoon; she receives a ration of coffee, beans, and a soup in which hairs and slivers of bone are floating.

"You've had nothing but water for three days. Are you going on a hunger strike?" the guard asks Tina. "Wouldn't you rather stay alive?"

"I would appreciate a lemon, if you could get me one. They haven't even told me yet what I'm accused of. It's illegal to hold someone without charges."

"So is Communism."

"It didn't used to be. Now they persecute us because the gringos tell them to."

The guard is a dark girl with a mole on her upper lip. Tina wins her over, telling her stories and talking to her about the political situation. She brings Tina paper and a pen and promises to smuggle her messages out.

The first letter she writes is to Mary Louis Doherty, at 42 Minerva Street. Tina remembers Mary exactly as Edward photographed her, with her lace collar, her cameo, the intensity of her eyes, her wrinkled brow.

Dear Mary:

I find myself in a real jail since Thursday afternoon. It is much worse here, a cell of iron and stone, and the food, well, you can imagine. I think something needs to be done, if not, I don't know how long I'll be kept here. Please talk to somebody, perhaps Mendizabal, but don't say I mentioned him. Maybe we need to talk to a lawyer? Tell him I have about four hundred pesos that I had been saving for my trip, but I can get more. Ask him what he can do. This jail is used to serve out sentences, so this is completely arbitrary. Please don't tell anybody how you heard from me: it is forbidden to send messages. Thank you for everything and please receive a big hug.

Luz Ardizana talks the guard into letting her in to see Tina, but the guard warns her that she may only stay for a few minutes.

Luz gives Tina a hug. "I've been in contact with your friend, Mary Doherty. She came here twice, but they wouldn't let her see you. Don't worry, we're going to get you out."

"And Sormenti?" Tina interrupts her.

"He's in hiding; we're going to take him to a ranch in Tampico."

"Carrillo is looking into your case, as well as Johann Windisch's and Isaac Rosenblum's. We should consider ourselves lucky, because more than sixty Vasconcelos supporters have disappeared and nobody knows where they are."

"What are they going to do with us?"

"I don't know. Listen, the guard told me you aren't eating. You must; you're going to need as much strength as possible."

Tina ignores her advice. "What has Diego Rivera done?"

"Nothing, he hasn't said a word in support of the comrades, that miserable fat pig. Just a year ago he lived in the court, and now no sight nor sound of him! That's how artists are."

One morning at six o'clock, Tina, Johann Windisch, and Isaac Abramovich Rosenblum are released from jail and given forty-eight hours to leave the country.

Luz Ardizana meets her with a glass of orange juice, "the best thing after a fast."

"Where are we going, Luz?"

"To Abraham González Street to pack your things. We'll be accompanied by guards. Dwight Morrow, Diego's friend, said that the United States Embassy considers you an American citizen, and that if you renounce all political activity they will give you a passport."

"That's blackmail. I refuse. I'd rather go to Europe than stop fighting. I have opportunities to work in Germany and in France."

"Ratón Velasco already went to the Italian Embassy and they offered you a passport that is good only if you return to Italy. They're just waiting to get their hands on anti-Fascists like you."

"I don't care. I'd rather leave Mexico on my Italian passport."

Mary Doherty arrives just as they are walking away from the prison gates. She speaks in a low voice. "I have talked to everyone, written letters everywhere."

"We're being watched," Luz warns.

"Mary, you should be careful, you're a foreigner, too. Tell Katherine Anne Porter about all this. Let as many people in New York know about my deportation as you can."

Just like the year before, two policemen stand guard in front of her door; two more are sitting in a car outside.

"Will you help me sell a few things?" she asks Luz, then turns to the policemen. "May I use the telephone?"

"Make yourself right at home," the policeman answers, looking at her legs.

Tina calls Manuel and Lola Alvarez Bravo. "Lola, I have to leave the country, and I want to sell one of my cameras. Do you want it?"

"Thank God they let you go. We'll be right over."

Tina takes her suitcase out from under the bed. She doesn't want to think. She tries to focus on the tasks at hand. The policemen never take their eyes off her.

Manuel and Lola arrive. They buy Tina's large camera, the one she used to photograph the murals.

"It was Weston's." She smiles sadly. "The two of you can finish the job of photographing the murals. I only managed about half."

"What about this pile of photographs, are you taking them?" Luz asks.

"I can't take much, whatever I can fit into this one suitcase. But I'm taking my Graflex."

Manuel blushes. "Maybe I can keep some of the photos for you."

"Yes, Manuel." Tina smiles again. "I would love you to have them."

He looks at her sadly. Tina stifles a sob, then smiles when she sees with what reverence Manuel and Lola treat her photographs.

"Such good friends you are!"

"I'm sure Diego would be interested in the ones of the murals."

"Yes, but he'll have to pay for them."

"And the tripod?"

"You can sell that, too, and those boxes of photographic paper. They're too heavy. Also the bottles of developing fluid."

"Take one with you," Luz urges. "You might need it there."

"There? Where, Luz?"

"Well, there, wherever they're sending you," she says sadly. "I don't know." Luz begins to cry.

"Don't cry, Luz, I won't be able to go on if you do."

"I'm not crying," Luz cries.

"Those clothes, Luz, give them to people who need them. Take the kitchen things to your house. And the furniture, too, give it away to whoever needs it most. I haven't paid the electric bill or the telephone. I owe half the rent. Can you return the keys?"

"And the quilt?"

"Do whatever you want with the quilt, and the curtains, and the towels. There's really not much. I'd like to take a few books with me, but they're also too heavy."

"Let me help you pack."

"Right now I'd like to be alone. I have two letters to write."

She gives Lola and Manuel a big hug.

At the door, she turns around and looks at the small flowered chair.

"You always liked that chair, Manuel, and it's not heavy. Do you want to take it?"

"Tina, I'm staying," Luz says. "I promise I won't bother you."

Luz helps her pack without saying a word.

Tina looks over her correspondence, whatever remains, that is, after the police search. Curiously, Edward's letters are all there. She finds a passport picture of Julio at the bottom of a drawer and puts it in her purse.

Ever since Julio was murdered, Tina has been aware of the precariousness of her situation and has taken certain precautions. She sent Edward his negatives, very carefully wrapped. She writes a letter to Benvenuto. Since Mella died, Mexico has rejected her. 145

Weston would not recognize the Mexico she is now leaving, a world without art, without beauty. And would he recognize in this anguished militant his former disciple and partner?

Tina places the last papers in a cardboard box and gives them to Luz.

"I want to spend the night here," Luz says.

Luz goes to talk to the guards and returns to Tina in tears. "They won't let me. I'll come tomorrow morning first thing."

"I'd rather you look for Sormenti. Find out what happened to him."

"I'll meet you at the station."

"Okay, Luz, but now I need all my strength for myself. I beg you to leave now."

Exhausted, Tina lays her head down on the pillow and thinks, "This is the last night I will spend in Mexico." Then she allows the tears to flow.

At the Buenavista train station on February 21, 1930, the morning fog has settled like an old blanket over the tracks. Tina walks with Manuel, Lola, Manuelito, and Luz. The guards remain close behind them.

Tina takes a window seat; Manuel silently sits down beside her. A guard sits down across from Tina, and Isaac Rosenblum stands on the train steps. Tina keeps her eyes down. When the whistle blows, Manuel looks at her and in a soft voice says, "Adiós, Tina." When she doesn't respond, he gets up to go. A second whistle rouses Tina. She looks out the window and sees the small, desolate group on the platform. She runs to the steps and calls out to them. The guard follows her. Luz is no longer there. Lola and Manuel hold Manuelito up to Tina, and she kisses the child on his head. "I hope I'll see you again, but in a better Mexico and under less bitter circumstances." She begins to choke on her tears.

She doesn't appear at the window again. For a long time the others remain on the platform, Manuel waving his hand for nobody to see.

In Veracruz, Tina is handcuffed as she boards the Dutch ship *Edam*. Captain Jochems orders her confined to her cabin. When Tina hears that, she feels as if she has been punched in the stomach.

It doesn't take long, however, for the captain to fall under the spell of her beauty and her modest demeanor. Soon he allows her to walk freely around the deck and enjoy the sun and fresh air. Once again, her elegance wins out. The passengers begin to vie for her attentions.

Tampico, Feb. the 25th [1930]
On board the "EDAM"

My dear Edward:

I suppose by now you know all that has happened to me, that I have been in jail 13 days and then expelled. And now I am on my way to Europe and to a new life, at least a different life from Mexico.

No doubt you also know the pretext used by the government in order to arrest me. Nothing less than "my participation in the last attempt to kill the newly elected President." I am sure that no matter how hard you try, you will not be able to picture me as a "terrorist," as "the chief of a secret society of bomb throwers" and what not. . . . But if I put myself in the place of the government I realize how clever they have been; they knew that had they tried to expel me at any other time the protests would have been very strong, so they waited the moment, when, psychologically speaking, the public opinion was so upset with the shooting that they were ready to believe anything they read or were told. According to the vile yellow press, all kinds of proofs, documents, arms, and what not, were found in my house; in other words everything was ready to shoot Ortiz Rubio and unfortunately, I did not calculate very well and the other guy got ahead of me . . . this is the story which the mexican public has swallowed with their morning coffee, so can you blame their sighs of relief in knowing that the fierce and bloody Tina Modotti has at last left forever the mexican shores?

Dear Edward, in all these tribulations of this last month, I often thought of that phrase of Nietzsche, which you quoted to me once: "What doesn't kill me, strengthens me," and that is how I feel about myself these days. Only thanks to an enormous amount of will power have I kept from going crazy at times, as for instance when they moved me around from one

147

*jail to another and when they made me enter a jail for the
first time and I heard the slamming of the iron door and lock
behind me and found myself in a small iron cell with a little
barred skylight, too high to look out from. An iron cot without
mattress, an ill smelling toilet in the corner of the cell and I in
the middle of the cell wondering if it was all a bad dream.*

*Well it would be impossible for me to go into details about
all the impressions and experiences of these past weeks, some
time I hope to relate them verbally.*

*Now I am on my way to Germany. Please drop me a few
lines to this address: Chotopatoya, Friedrich Strasse 24-IV, Berlin S.W. 48 Germany. But don't put my name on the outside
address; use two envelopes and put my name on the inside one.*

While they are in Tampico harbor, Tina, Johann Windisch,
and Rosenblum are confined to a cabin next to the captain's quarters. Luckily, the ship weighs anchor, and Tina is again allowed on
deck. As the new passengers are processed, she notices that one
man is holding up the line in front of the immigration control
station. Tina asks Rosenblum who he is.

"What business is that of yours, señora?" says Sormenti, turning
to Tina.

Her mouth drops open when she recognizes him. She restrains
herself from blurting out his name.

She hears the immigration agent congratulate Sormenti for de-
voting his life to the teaching profession.

Enea turns to Tina. "You see how well the authorities treat me,
señora."

Tina can't believe her eyes. Sormenti's audacity has no limits.
He is a hunted man in Mexico, Italy, and the United States. If he
is caught, it will be the end of him. Nevertheless, he announces
that when the *Edam* stops in New Orleans, he plans to go to Mardi
Gras.

Enea Sormenti found out the name of the ship on which Tina
would be deported and decided to board it in Tampico. A friend
of his—anarchist, typesetter, and printer—falsified his documents.
148   He asked Jacobo Hurwitz for his passport.

"What are you going to do with it?"

"I'm going to chop off your head, Jacobito. Then, so I resemble you, I'm going to make myself look just a little foolish, and a little like an intellectual, and I'm going to go by the name of Jacobo Hurwitz Zender, Peruvian professor. When the persecution ends, you can have your identity back."

Two weeks later, when they reach New Orleans, Tina is handcuffed and taken to the immigration holding area and locked in a cell. She isn't alone long before the guard announces that a journalist has come to interview her.

"I'll bet this is the first time you've heard Spanish since you left Mexico."

Startled, Tina raises her eyes from the letter she is writing to Edward and sees Sormenti standing in front of her.

"Could you please say, in a few words, how you see the future of socialism in America?"

Sormenti, dear Sormenti, capable of making her smile and giving her hope even under the direst circumstances. Throughout the interview, he manages to tell her a number of times that the situation is favorable. Then he smiles, winks, and as he leaves her, he gives her a warm, significant handshake.

In writing to Edward, Tina forces herself to impart a serenity she doesn't feel.

New Orleans, March the 9th [1930]
U.S. Immigration Station

My dear Edward—
   . . . The place I am in now is a strange mixture between a jail and a hospital—a huge room with many empty beds in disorder which give me the strange feeling that corpses have laid on them—heavy barred windows and door, constantly locked this last one. The worst of this forced idleness is, not to know what to do with one's time—I read—I write—I smoke —I look out of the window into a very proper and immaculate american lawn with a high pole in the center of it from which top the Stars and Stripes wave with the wind—a sight which should—were I not such a hopeless rebel—remind me

149

constantly of the empire of "law and order" and other inspir-
ing thoughts of that kind—.

The newspapers have followed me, and at times preceded
me—with wolf like greediness—Here in the U.S. everything is
seen from the "beauty" angle—a daily here spoke of my trip
and refer[r]ed to me as to a "woman of striking beauty"—
other reporters to whom I refused an interview, tried to con-
vince me by saying they would just speak "of how pretty I was"
—to which I answered that I could not possibly see what
"prettiness" had to do with the revolutionary movement nor
with the expulsion of communists—evidently women here are
measured by a motion picture star standard—.

Sormenti is so used to dodging the police and living outside the law that he cannot possibly realize how desolate Tina feels even now, out of jail and back on the ship. It is difficult for him to imagine that a militant can be demoralized. Life, what an adventure! There will be exciting challenges in Moscow, you'll see, Tina, everything awaits us. With her newly found wings, Tina will soar. Then, like a pelican, she'll swoop down upon her prey: her new life.

Nor can Sormenti imagine the hell of Tina's nights, the moments when her anxiety is so overwhelming she must put her hand over her mouth to stifle her shouts, then splash cold water on her face. She is haunted by visions of her past; she blames herself for all the wasted years, all the wasted life. She spends her nights wondering how she will survive. Grateful for the dawn, she joins the other seven passengers, drinking coffee, and tries to lose herself in something other than her fears, doubts, and regrets.

Enea often finds her on the deck of the *Edam*, her eyes on the horizon, completely absorbed in her thoughts. At other times he surprises her while she writes a letter or in her journal. As he approaches, she quickly closes the notebook.

Sormenti hears her speaking German to another passenger. "You never told me you spoke German."

"I speak it very poorly. Most people from Friuli learn it because they work across the border in Austria, but I was never happy there, and I always try to forget it."

Her accomplishments are much greater than she ever let on in Mexico. She speaks and writes Italian, English, Spanish, and has a good working knowledge of French as well as German.

Sormenti respects her solitude and doesn't interrupt her when he finds her busy writing.

1 5

The he SS *Edam* is an old cargo ship that has long since ceased to be truly seaworthy. No matter how hard the crew works, the rust eats it up, and the rats infest its hold.

Hot, humid air currents waft the oily smell of coconuts and the dank smell of swamps onto the ship as it approaches land. Soon, palm trees, sand dunes, and coral reefs appear. The *Edam* puts down anchor in Havana, and Tina feels suffocated by the heat and the heavy scent of spices. "It's the combination of coffee, tobacco, vanilla, and sugarcane," Sormenti tells her. Sormenti goes ashore while the ship is being loaded with sugar. Insects swarm around the longshoremen, and Tina, confined to the ship, wipes the sweat off her forehead and tries to control the nausea produced by the thickness of the air. It feels as if sticky syrup were dripping out of a huge pot in the sky and oozing through the hatches.

Sormenti spreads the word through Havana that Julio Antonio Mella's comrade, Tina Modotti, is on board the *Edam* as a refugee.

Sormenti recounts the Italian comrade's stoic behavior in the aftermath of Mella's death. An article is published in *Diario de la Marina*.

Tina would always remember that when the *Edam* was ready to weigh anchor, a number of small boats approached in the darkness. Leaning over the rail, she saw their lights dancing over the water and heard a shout ring out in the Cuban night: "Comrade Tina, we send all our affection and respect to you." For a moment she imagined that Julio was in one of those boats and was rowing toward her.

Three nights later, a storm comes up. The *Edam* creaks and groans as if it were about to split apart, and Captain Jochems advises his passengers to remain in their quarters as much as possible. When Tina does not appear at mealtime, Sormenti knocks on her door. "Tina, come out for a moment."

Sormenti urges her to take deep breaths. "The only thing that matters is for your mind to gain some control over this packaging we call the body."

Tina is surprised when the slow, deliberate breathing eases the nausea.

"I thought that someone like me, so prone to being seasick, could never overcome it. Ma lei, Enea, where did you learn all these things?"

"I am a man of the sea, Tina, or rather, a boy of the sea; all of us from around Trieste are. I left Trieste as a stowaway in the ship's coal bin; when they found me, they almost tossed me into the sea."

An avalanche of memories carries them back to Trieste and their youth and forges a bond between them. "One wind blew me out of my house, another took me to Algeria, and another pushed me onward to New York; a North Wind carried me to Mexico, but the strongest wind of all is the one that is now taking us to Russia."

"I'm not going to Russia, Enea," Tina reminds him.

"Soon you will. The sea did everything for me. It cleansed me, it allowed me to dream. Didn't you long to travel when you were a girl in Udine?"

"When I was thirteen years old, I began to wait for my father   153 to send me the ticket to the United States. It arrived when I was sixteen. Until then, I had never been on a steamboat."

"When I was very young, I swore to myself that I would leave that horseshoe where Muggia is imprisoned by the Adriatic. From the Piazza Grande and Via Candia I could see Istria, Carso, the gulf and the sea. I went to Venice as a stowaway. You've been there, of course."

"No," Tina admits, feeling ashamed.

"I'll take you there one day."

He tells her about Captain Giacomo from Muggia, who taught him to sail.

"He was the first dead man I ever saw. I was with my brother, Humberto. The captain's white beard was spread over the mortician's sheet. Humberto was younger, and he didn't understand, so I explained it to him. 'To die,' I said, 'means not to see, not to hear, not to eat or drink, not to breathe, not to move. Once you're dead, you can't do anything, they throw you in a grave or toss you into the sea.'

"When I was young, I wanted to be a pirate, a Roman gladiator. I swore to myself that Vittorio Vidali would be a leader."

"Vidali? So Sormenti isn't your real name?"

"We revolutionaries change our names. I have others as well. You also will change your name."

"I like Vittorio better than Enea. Victory!"

Tina enjoys listening to him, and after a few days she wonders how she would have gotten through the voyage without him.

"When I was a girl," says Tina, "the only thing I wanted was for my fingers not to hurt. They were always red and aching from the spinning, and I was ashamed of my hunger. We were so poor."

"I was a grown man before I first tasted real wine. At home, we drank water with a little vinegar."

Tina tells him about St. Ruprecht, in Austria, where her father went in search of work; about her godfather, Demetrio Canal; about Gioconda, one of her younger sisters, who got pregnant by a soldier and couldn't come with them to the United States.

"I understand why you feel drawn to Russia, Vittorio, but I think my future is in Europe, in Germany. I have contacts at the Union Bild and I think they'll give me work. My photographs have already been published in Berlin, in *AIZ*, and I can go see Willi Münzenberg, who is very well known and well connected. Italian citizens don't need a visa to travel to Berlin. Mamma and Mercedes could join me in Germany, as I once hoped they would in Mexico."

After the storm, the passengers come together to play games, drink Rhine wine, and eat ham, Dutch and German cheeses, and apple strudel. Vittorio talks to everybody, and continues to give Isaac Rosenblum and Tina daily doses of encouragement. "What good does it do to dwell on your problems?" People take turns entertaining the others after meals. Tina and Vittorio sing Italian and American melodies. Vittorio sings a Wobbly song:

> *Oh, why don't you work*
> *like other men do?*
> *How in hell can I work*
> *When there's no work to do?*
> *Hallelujah, I'm a bum,*
> *Hallelujah, bum again,*
> *Hallelujah, give us a handout*
> *To revive us again.*

One afternoon, Vittorio sees Tina leaning over the prow of the *Edam*, and for a moment he fears she will fall. He runs to her, breathless. When Tina turns her head, the look in her eyes is so full of rejection that he stops dead in his tracks. She stares as if into a void, as if he were invisible.

Standing on the deck at night, Tina is enveloped in darkness and salt air. How easy it would be to give herself over to the black inky water, through which her black sex would plow like a slow, mysterious ship, like a clam that shuts down upon itself, shutting out everything around it, an enormous body with water crashing against its hull, the air, the motor that reaches inside and up to the propeller, spreading it open, overflowing.

When she sits on the tiny iron toilet she fulfills a certain function. Whatever is happening to her body happens far away, outside herself, to someone else, since she, Tina Modotti, no longer has a place on this earth. The stifling heat that invades the ship reminds her of an orgasm she once had that lasted so long she rose from the bed and felt the final spasms while standing, until Julio gathered her in his arms so that her trembling flesh would not be so isolated. The white lake of the sheet, the desire that rose to wound her, the sigh that came from so deep within, only to be left inert, nobody touch me now, don't touch me after he has touched me.

If only she could erase herself when she closed her eyes and thereby manage to rest. To disappear, to be swallowed up by the sea, enveloped in water, what a relief! Nothing would perish because the "I" no longer has any life, the "I, Tina" has already been killed, transformed into complete submission, into a vehicle for others. I am a hole, a cavity: the currents swirl around me, the fish enter through my sex and leave through my mouth.

But the pain tightens around her. Outside, nothing, except the liquid beckoning of the sea.

During the day, as the sun's rays dance over the surface of the water, Tina stands on deck and watches the wake of the boat. Behind her is Julio's body, his image lost in the transparency of the air. She sees the water as an immense blanket spread over the earth and thinks: "I am barely a tiny spot the size of the head of a pin, far from everything, separate, suspended between the immensity of the sky and the profundity of the sea. Why worry so much, just let go, Tina." She listens to Enea, or Vittorio; she sees how exultant he is to be at sea, to breathe in the salt air, how euphoric he is simply to be alive.

"Come here, Tina. Take a picture of me at the stern of the boat."

"Only if you take off that black hat. You look like a condottiere."

Tina shoots him gazing at the ocean.

"Now I'll take one of you."

"No, nobody touches the Graflex. Anyway, I don't want a picture of me."

Vittorio senses her inaccessibility. "You are like a castle with all the drawbridges up."

She smiles and pushes back the locks of hair that have fallen out of her bun.

There's no doubt about it; the sea has curative properties. And if not the sea, then perhaps Vittorio. When he looks at his past, he doesn't torture himself as she does. "What if I had gone to live with Julio as soon as I met him? What if I had gone with Xavier to Moscow?"

"You'd be better off thinking that if you could live again, you would do it even worse." And Tina laughs at his advice. "What matters is the here and now, Tina, this sun, this sea, this boat that creaks and is full of rats, our conversation, you with me without anybody interrupting us, our destiny that does not simply come to us but that we can direct. Life is always bigger than we are. In a few months, you will blame yourself for not having enjoyed everything you possibly could today. When we disembark, you will be a new woman; don't give up."

Vittorio's destination is Moscow; Tina's is Berlin. But Vittorio speaks as if he will never abandon her. How good he makes her feel! By now, the *Edam* has become a refuge, a little taste of heaven.

It's a desert of sand, my pain . . .

"You know, Vittorio, I'd like to be a passenger forever, and never land."

"Not me, I already miss the struggle . . ."

They travel through the English Channel and at dawn enter the port of Rotterdam. The other passengers prepare to disembark: they carry their luggage to the deck and hold their travel documents in hand. Tina remains in her cabin and Vittorio comes to reassure her.

Pale and trembling, Tina asks him to embrace her.

"Who knows . . . Anything can happen, maybe we'll never see each other again." She presses herself against him.

Vittorio disembarks, alerts Dutch Red Aid, then returns to the ship. When the immigration and customs agents come on board, they are accompanied by three people who ask to talk to him.

"Moscow informed us of your arrival, Vidali. I am the secretary of Dutch Red Aid. I have authorization for your two friends to disembark and remain on Dutch soil for forty-eight hours. These two gentlemen with me are lawyers."

Captain Jochems approaches with another official. "I am the Consul General of Italy. I've come for the deportee, Tina Modotti, who will continue her trip in an Italian ship that leaves today."

The Dutch immigration agent turns to the consul. "Do you have permission from the Minister of the Interior? I have no authorization to turn any passenger over to you without an order of extradition."

"Miss Modotti is an Italian citizen, and she is traveling on an Italian passport."

"She cannot be taken out of Holland without the proper documentation."

"We are talking about a dangerous terrorist. Just look at her documents. My government claims her; I represent Il Duce."

"That may well be, but these two gentlemen are lawyers from Red Aid. Miss Modotti and Mr. Isaac Abramovich Rosenblum enjoy the protection of the Dutch government for the next forty-eight hours."

A few minutes later, Tina and Isaac leave the *Edam* escorted by the secretary of Red Aid and the two lawyers. Vittorio goes on ahead to clear the way. They get train tickets and safe-conduct passes to leave Holland. The comrades have reserved rooms in a small hotel.

The next day, as they are dining, Vittorio hands Tina a bouquet of the first narcissus of spring. "You see how a new life can begin?"

When they emerge late at night into the humid Rotterdam air, Tina presses the flowers to her heart.

On April 4, they take the train to Berlin. At the train station, well-dressed people walk by quickly in their thick coats and fine shoes. In the train compartments, each passenger places his luggage in the overhead rack, sits in his assigned seat, and unfolds his newspaper. Through the window one can see the same order reflected in the rectangular snow-covered fields. As they approach Berlin, they see little shoots of green grass poking up through the snow.

"Look, the new is being born." Tina smiles.

Vittorio realizes that she is unaware that the threat from the Italian government still hangs over her, that real dangers lie ahead.

When they reach Berlin, they see women in felt hats and fur wraps walking quickly down the street, their cheeks flushed from the cold air. Tina's cheeks are also flushed: she is trying to get in step with the European rhythm, the quick pace of those who always have something to do and know exactly where they are going.

"You don't have a hat," Vittorio tells her, "but you look very good."

It's true. She looks younger. In spite of the fact that her hair is parted severely down the middle and pulled tightly back, her face expresses a desire to live. Until she gets settled, she hopes to stay with the Wittes, friends from Mexico and admirers of her photography and Weston's. They wrote to her that they would always have a room ready for her. When Tina knocks on their door, Frau Witte greets her with open arms, and shows her to a charming room with its own bath—a rare luxury in Europe.

"I'll only stay a few days . . ."

"You must promise to stay here whenever you come to visit. For a long time we have been calling this 'Tina's room.'"

After a few meetings with the comrades, Vittorio, Isaac, and Tina realize that the situation of the Communists in Germany is worse than they had thought. Their polemic with the National Socialists has weakened and isolated them. The police pursue them through the streets with rubber truncheons and guns. Whenever there is a workers' march, the police shoot at the protesters, who are armed only with sticks and stones. Hunger haunts the streets. Even the rich are feeling the pinch, and it is impossible for a foreigner to obtain a work permit. Tina's spirits, however, remain high.

"The cafés and bars, the stores and bakeries are all full."

"It's always like that during a crisis. People live in the streets and empty their wallets."

"Somehow I'll get a work permit. The Union Bild will come through. Willi Münzenberg wields a lot of power."

Willi Münzenberg is very influential; he's in touch with Louis Aragon, Romain Rolland, Henri Barbusse, Arthur Koestler. He travels all over Europe, America, and Asia. Modern and eloquent, he is de facto in charge of the political and cultural diffusion of international Communism. His magazine, *AIZ*, has a circulation of one million, and he has published Tina's photographs. All her hopes rest with him.

On Friedrichstrasse, Tina and Vittorio stop in front of a store window filled with cameras, lenses, and other photographic accessories. When they enter the store, Tina is stunned by the activity inside. Amateurs bring their rolls of film here to have them developed. How can it be so easy to do something that has cost her so much effort? Her Graflex looks prehistoric next to these cameras. She watches a man open and load his camera the way one sticks a stamp on an envelope.

Vittorio perceives Tina's dismay. "It takes a while to get used to a new country; be patient, technology can never take the place of talent."

"I know, but I never imagined that technology would have come so far. In Mexico, I've been completely cut off from all these changes."

Vidali invites her to accompany him to the Anti-Imperialist Center; he wants to give them an update on the struggle in Nicaragua and solicit help for Sandino. He suggests that they may need a translator.

"Oh, no, I don't want to translate, not now!"

Smera, the director of the Anti-Imperialist League, receives them warmly. Chattopadhyaya, the representative from India, and his companion, Lotte Schultz, are particularly friendly. Lotte and Tina immediately strike up a friendship.

Isaac Rosenblum leaves for the Soviet Union alone. It wouldn't have been safe for him and Vittorio to travel together.

Tina's burst of optimism seems to be wearing out, and she is becoming depressed. She speaks now in monosyllables, as if overwhelmed by the difficulties of starting all over again.

Vittorio begins to worry about her. "Tina, if you want, you can come to the Soviet Union with me. I'm sure I can find you work there."

"No, I want to try to stay here in Germany. I promise I'll write you if things don't work out."

She accompanies him to the door and steps outside. The sky is gray, and Tina looks very pale.

He takes her arm. "Come to the Soviet Union."

"No," she insists.

The look in her eyes remains with Vittorio throughout his journey.

Hands resting on tool. Tina Modotti, 1927. Collection of the J. Paul Getty Museum, Malibu, California. Platinum print, 7 1/2 x 8 1/2 in.

16

*B*erlin in April 1930 brings back the sounds of her childhood. At any moment the factory siren will awaken her. Rows of dark, dreary houses are drenched in water and snow. When the rain stops, clothes are quickly hung out to dry over narrow balconies where they catch a sliver of sun between the window and the railing. How different from the rooftops in Mexico! On the street she walks by organ-grinders turning the heavy cranks of their Hohners. The little monkey in his red suit is more appealing than the music. A Strauss waltz accompanies the children as they dance around the monkey and try to pet him. The gray streets smell of malt but Tina avoids the beer halls. They exude the same warm, fermented odor as the breath of the men who shout obscenities at her when she passes too close.

Compared to Mexico, Berlin lacks modesty. The streets swarm with people who rush past shop windows and restaurants that look like stores: from the street, diners can be seen gobbling large pieces of white sausage and washing them down with beer. They don't care if people watch them eat. They chew the meat and bang their mugs on the table when they want another round. There is a shoemaker's shop next to the inn, then a movie house, a tailor's shop, a millinery shop, a beer hall, and another shoemaker's. Women pull up their skirts and expose their thighs when they try on shoes.

Several days after she arrives, Tina writes to Weston:

Berlin, April the 14th [1930]

My dear Edward;

Berlin at last! In fact I have been here ten days already but the first days have been taken up looking for a room and other matters of immediate attendance. Now I have found a room, very convenient and private where I can live as cheaply as can be expected in a foreign country. For a while it will do.

I cannot yet say whether I will remain in Germany or not, so many things have to be taken in consideration: first I want to be where I can be most useful to the movement and then where I can make a living. The idea of portraiture in Berlin rather frightens me; there are so many really excellent photographers here, and such an abundance of them, both professional and amateur, and even the average work is excellent; I mean even the work one sees in the windows along the streets. Besides there are so many restrictions and taxes, enormous taxes, for one in business. (If my landlady here wants to buy an egg, for instance, she must pay a tax, and if afterward I want to buy that egg from her, I must pay a tax to her, and so on . . .) All this is caused of course by the terrific war loans exacted from this country; and only thanks to the admirable teutonic stubborn[n]ess and self pride can this nation keep from going under. But the strain shows on the people; they never laugh, they walk the streets very gravely, always in a hurry and seem to be constantly conscious of the heavy burden which weighs on their shoulders.

But going back to photography, I have been wondering if I could work out a scheme by which to get a sort of income from the blessed U.S. Perhaps by contributing to periodicals, magazines, etc. I feel that if Frau Goldschmidt gets around one hundred marks for articles in the New York Times I should be able to do the same. What do you think?

163

Speaking of Frau G: last evening I was invited to their house. I needed to see Prof. G who is a member of the International Anti-imperialist League and there was no way to avoid the wife, but oh Edward, how horrible she is! Such a poseur and such a bourgeois at heart, posing as a grand lady and as an intellectual. Poor professor, always the same, accepting matrimony very philosophically as an inevitable evil (at least in the case of Frau G for a wife, matrimony can be justly called an evil; I am sure you agree with me, knowing the certain wife in question.) Here in Berlin she is even worse since she naturally considers herself in her dominion. It is plain that her effort is to transform her drawing room in a "salon" in the french sense of the word, but it is all so shallow and forced, really unbearable to me.

But oh, on the other hand, how can I praise sufficiently that exquisite and heavenly creature called Lady Witte! Of course they were the first people I looked up in Berlin. In all her letters to me in Mexico she had told me of having a room all ready waiting for me and she was also waiting for me with her arms opened! I love her so much, there is such an understanding in her and Mr. Witte, and she emanates such a spiritual beauty that the best of one is stimulated in her presence. Of course I could not accept her invitation and live at her home, but at least I had to promise to sleep there whenever I called on them. She will not listen to any reasonable reasons and insists in calling that charming room: Tina's room.

Now I want to tell you of something which happened to them, really a tragedy and they feel terribly about it. They were even reluctant in telling me of this and only accidentally I learned of it, but I am going to disobey them because I want you to please if you can in some little way mitigate their loss: It happens that on their way from America to Europe, they lost among other things, all the beautiful photographs they secured from you. They will never get over this loss, I could see how heart broken they are over it. I asked if you knew of it, th[at] is when they said they don't even want you to know of it, and it seems they cannot afford to reorder the same pictures over, for otherwise I know they would do it. (They live well but carefully, that much I could see myself, and his health is not very good just now.) Now Edward dear, I know that this news will sadden you also very much, to hear that your valuable work has been lost, and yet I felt the impulse to tell you because I wondered if you by chance happen to have a print that you could send these dear people, whether one of the same they had chosen or not it does not matter, though of course they did speak of the print of me with special tenderness. But I could give them one of the many you were so gracious to give me and send them instead something else. Dear Edward, I know it is asking a lot from you, and I would never do it if it was not concerned with such dear and lovely friends.

Now I must close, much to my regret, for I could go on for hours writing about so many things; Berlin is a very beautiful city, even though I have not yet seen the sun once during my ten days here; and for one coming from Mexico the change is rather cruel. But I know that the wisest thing is just to forget sun, blue skies, and other delights of Mexico and adapt myself to this new reality, and start, once more, life all over . . .

Do you by chance know some photographers in Berlin? If so will you please give me a note to them. I well know of course that it is not good policy to look up photographers if one is also a photographer, but all I would want from them is practical advice as to purchasing materials, and find a place to do some printing, etc. If possible I never again want to go to the trouble of fixing up a dark room, and I hope to be able to work in some dark room. If I was in the U.S. I would become a member of the Photographers Association and make use of their work rooms; perhaps something like that exists here, I shall see.

My affectionate thoughts to Sonia [Noskowiak], and to the two boys, always my devotion to you dear.

Tina

My love to Tilly [Pollak]. I shall write to her very soon! The address you already have is always good even if I should leave Berlin, only I must correct it a little:

CHATTOPADHYAYA

BERLIN S.W. *48*

FRIEDRICHSTR. *24* IV GERMANY

And please do not *put my name on the outside envelope.*

Two days later, on April 16, 1930, the newspapers are full of the details of Mayakovsky's suicide. Tina agrees with his critics: he was a coward, a petit bourgeois, a nihilist, a weakling. She loses all respect for him. Yet, at night, in her dreams, she sees the brave round little face of the eight-year-old Francisca Moreno, the daughter of the murdered deputy of Veracruz; Mayakovsky had liked her as much as her father, and Tina feels tenderness for them both.

Still without work, Tina attends meetings at Party headquarters. The only people she knows in Berlin are Smera, Chattopadhyaya, Lotte Schultz, and the Wittes. She has not been able to arrange a meeting with Willi Münzenberg, who always seems to be away on a trip. Neither does she manage to see Eugen Heilig, the head of the Union Bild photographic agency. She sees a ray of hope when she reads in *Der Arbeiter-Fotograf* that "only Mexican and Japanese photographers have achieved the same excellence as German photographers." Mexican photographers! That's her they are talking about.

The political scene in Berlin is as discouraging as her professional predicament. She had thought that in Germany one could struggle openly against Fascism; as it turns out, Fascism is rapidly taking over Berlin, Chemnitz, Dresden, and Leipzig. Vittorio had warned her before he left: "Be very careful. You are probably being watched by the police."

As the pressures mount, it is some comfort for Tina to know that the Wittes also feel a deep nostalgia for Mexico. They speak often about everything they have given up by returning to Germany. They also miss Mexico's clouds sweeping the wide blue sky and dislike the Berlin they have found. And they are Germans!

In Mexico, Tina's life was so full of commitments that she had no time to reflect, consider, doubt. Now every gesture has become a monumental act, a subject for deliberation. Her desire to meet Käthe Kollwitz and George Grosz has faded away. She was told that it was too difficult, that there is too much fear, that "they don't receive anybody." In Mexico she would have said with a smile, "I'm not just anybody," but in Berlin she no longer knows who she is. She wants more than anything else to cross Austria and get to Italy to see her mother and sister. But she doesn't even know if they have arrived from the United States. Tina has never smoked so much: she spends all her pfennigs on German cigarettes; she fills her mouth with smoke that caresses her palate and stimulates pleasure. She exhales slowly and stares at the smoke as it lingers in the cold, damp air.

Tina finds a room in a working-class neighborhood, in one of the many two- or three-story houses with one toilet per floor (which everyone helps keep clean). She wants to live among these people, among people who eat boiled potatoes and consider thick black bread with marmalade a special treat. She hears children singing for pfennigs on the street corners:

> *Das schönste Land das ich auf Erde weiss*
> *das ist mein Vaterland.*

"The most beautiful nation on earth is my fatherland."

She had forgotten how damp Europe was. The Mexican sun warms even the poor, doing away with poverty and bad odors. Here the expression in people's eyes terrifies her. Hard, drab, hard, brazen, hard. Mexicans do not have those aggressive jaws, those heavy brows that scowl. In Berlin's poor neighborhoods, the grumble of discontent is audible. In Mexico, the poor stretch themselves out meekly in the sun to heal their wounds. There is no meekness here. They snarl at her when she asks for directions.

Near Unter den Linden, stacks of bread and chocolate and colorfully wrapped candies glisten in the shop windows: plentiful but costly. In Berlin, people are paid once in the morning and once in the afternoon. They rush out to buy sweets with bills so devalued they could be used to paper the walls.

The cold rises from the wet, sooty asphalt up her legs and darkens the spirit. Tina remembers the streets of Mexico, the poor people who hug the walls to keep out of your way, who smile mischievously with their eyes, and she compares them to these beefy Germans wallowing in the mediocrity of their routines, unhappiness written all over their faces, weighing down their steps. The indifference lies heavy on her heart. Oh, Europe, how worn out you are, fattened up with tripe and chestnuts, chopped liver and hard, black bread, but now facing times of bitter want.

Nobody to turn to, nobody to speak with, nobody who will knock at her door as on Abraham González Street when Frances Toor peeked in with her hang-dog expression and asked, "How about a cup of coffee?" Suddenly she hears angry shouts. She alone

167

stops to look. A fat German woman scolds her dachshund, who is the same brown color as her hat and coat.

At first, Tina is unaware of the pervasive atmosphere of mistrust. She is so preoccupied with her immediate problems that she doesn't realize that Berlin has become a nest of spies. Chattopadhyaya and Lotte warn her: "Be careful, don't trust anyone, don't talk to strangers." But here everyone is a stranger. She is so anonymous she could die of hunger and nobody would know.

Once she is settled into the Schulz boardinghouse, at 5 Tauentzienstrasse, she must repeat to herself each painful effort she makes to get through the day, to stay alive: "Now I get up, now I wash, now I get dressed, now I heat up the coffee and force myself to chew a piece of bread, now I tie my hair into a bun." Her life is no longer divided into activities that give meaning to each hour. She has no obligations. Nobody will come to pose at noon. There are no photographs to develop and print. She rationalizes: "When I begin to work, things will return to normal."

She has never spent so many months without people who love her, without people she loves. She has never lived without earning at least a subsistence income. The five hundred dollars she brought from Mexico have gone on rent, an enlarger, potatoes, sauerkraut, cigarettes. At night, she sits on the edge of her bed and asks herself: "What did I do today?" She can't remember. She repeats to herself: "My money is running out, and I haven't achieved anything." Her work has never been worth so little, perhaps nothing at all. For the first time in her life, she feels inadequate. In Udine, when she was eleven, she earned money working the loom. In Mexico, she was paid for her photographs. Orders came in from the United States and Germany. How could she have guessed that in Germany her Graflex and her technique would be so out of date?

What can a photographer do in a city with 550 photography studios? Tina forces herself. "I'll go to the zoo." She doesn't feel like taking pictures of anything or anybody. At last, she sees a fat German couple. They stand in front of each cage so long it is easy to capture them. She feels nothing as she sets up the shot. Then she places the camera next to a statue of a naked woman. Some nuns walk by. She shoots, with no illusion that the photograph will say anything to her. It's just one more picture—a picture of Europe that anyone could take. She tries to encourage herself: "Come on, you have everything going for you: skill, experience, a trained eye. Let the picture grow inside of you, it can be dramatic, even profound if you want." Click. Her head says yes, click, there it is, her fingers respond, click, but it isn't what she wanted. The moment she shoots, Tina knows it isn't worth it. Taking a picture is not just pressing the shutter. It is not just a question of agility.

In the past, the shot would develop within her like a symphony: first the allegro, then a deep, melodic urgency, until the sound of the click. "What's happening to me?" she asks in anguish. "What am I going to do with myself?" Not one face, not one gesture, no quality of light, not even a crack in the wall attracts her gaze. Cold and empty.

When she opens her eyes in the morning, the simple act of rising from the bed is a challenge. "Why am I getting up?" Only some remnant of self-respect propels her toward the bathroom and gets her into the tub with its gray ring that no scrubbing can eliminate. A pathetic stream trickles out of the shower hose: as she wets one part of her body, the other parts get cold. Berlin, is like this trickle, is also pathetic, even though there is more order here than in Mexico, more libraries, more monuments, more paved roads, people without age-old hunger in their eyes, people who have mustard, pastry cream, and butter flowing through their veins, people who walk robustly through the drab days.

On a scrap of paper which hangs on the wall she has written:

CURRENT BALANCE
Alone
Broke
Exiled
Depressed

Under that list she hangs another scrap of paper:

a. I have no children. Nobody misses me.
b. I have no work; I don't support myself.
c. I don't know what to take pictures of.
d. Mexico deported me; if I go to Italy, they'll put me in jail. Where is my homeland?
e. Edward doesn't write. Nobody in Mexico has written. Well, Edward has written, but his letter was no reply. He is too far away to understand. Frances Toor also wrote and

I would like her to get Antonieta Rivas Mercado to pay me. How is it that the rich manage never to pay? Is that why they are rich?

Tina decides to take her portfolio to Union Foto GmbH, an agency for proletarian photographers that represents their work in the Soviet Union. After meeting there with several people, she is approached by Heinz Aldrecht, a photographer from the Black Forest. He says he would like to come to her house to see her work.

Carefully looking over her photographs, he addresses her with great audacity. "You claim to want to put your photography at the service of the people, but you haven't shown any vocation for service. Photojournalists are in demand; but maybe you don't want to disappear into the crowd."

She is shocked by the degree of professional aggressiveness she finds in him. She is not used to such an openly competitive and critical attitude.

"On the contrary, that's just what I want: to disappear," Tina says. "But I don't want to talk about me. I want to talk only about photography and what we can accomplish with the camera. I want to photograph what I see, honestly, directly, without tricks. That would be my contribution to a better world, a socialist world."

"The picture of the hands of the day laborer, *Hands resting on tool*, for instance. It's no different from the photograph of your hands on the robe that Weston did ten or twelve years ago. Taking pictures of poor people in itself is not necessarily a political act."

"I've been told," Tina murmurs humbly, "that *Hands resting on tool* is a social document."

"Photos can be whatever you say they are, but you, you who stand behind the camera, who are you? It seems to me that the real concern of Tina Modotti is aesthetic. You'll do anything for a beautiful composition! In that respect, you still haven't stepped out of Weston's shadow. War correspondents put their lives on the line; the person behind the camera takes the same risks as those who fight. What are you willing to risk?"

"How can you say that when you know I have been expelled from Mexico and I cannot even go to Italy?"

"Your personal life and your travel documents don't interest me. What matters is what I see in your photographs."

Tina wants to tell him that he has hurt her and that she wishes to be alone. Yet, despite the fact that he is so wrong, he is the first person in Germany to take her seriously. She makes him some coffee. He smiles at her, and from that moment on, she feels he cannot be her enemy, that she is the one who is wrong.

"Tomorrow the Union will lend you a Leica to use instead of your clumsy Graflex. Go out and shoot a whole roll."

Eight pictures in one day! She always mulled over each shot, even visited the scene and studied the light at different times of day before shooting; she waited for the exact moment, the click ringing out in the sacred silence. Now he is telling her to press the shutter without thinking about the results, like the unconscious blink of an eye. That is journalism.

That night, she goes to see Lotte Jacobi at her house at 5 Joachimsthalerstrasse. Lotte is also a photographer, and the daughter of photographers. Unlike Tina, who identifies with the poor and the forgotten, she searches out celebrities and would love to see her walls covered with portraits of Lotte Lenya, László Moholy-Nagy, Bertolt Brecht, Kurt Weill, and Thomas Mann. The dim light in her studio is velvety and the tea Lotte brings her on the maroon sofa is soothing. The shelves are full of art books that speak of the love of beauty. She has an amphora found in the Adriatic with shells stuck on it like barnacles on a whale, a bronze statue from Mycenae, a Roman buckle, four daguerreotypes of a young Juliet in a winter garden.

"Is Heinz Aldrecht a good photographer?" Tina asks Lotte.

"Excellent."

"And, as a person?"

"Neurotic, but indispensable to Union Photo."

She returns home, unable to dispel the image of herself as a wild bull, click, click with the Leica, click, click, shooting here, there, anywhere. The idea turns her stomach. Click, click, the roll is finished. Eight wasted shots. She remembers the way she and Weston would hang the photographs on the museum walls, how they spent hours debating how to exhibit them, grouping them thematically, imposing some order for the public. "Don't put the puppet master's hands next to Dolores del Rio. Better to put Modesta there with her child in her arms." So many years, so much dedication, so much commitment, just so the photographs can pile up in an editor's drawer, waiting to be rummaged through at a whim. She is repelled by the way Heinz picks them up and looks at them. The point isn't one's attitude toward art; it's the reflection of one's attitude toward life. She did not photograph a mother nursing her child so that someone like him could finger the print; she did it because she needed to capture the emotion the scene produced in her. But, as Heinz Aldrecht told her, "Technical progress has changed the concept of photography."

No German photographer is going to spend a whole morning in front of a construction site waiting for the carpenter to cross the scaffold carrying a beam on his shoulder; nobody is going to wait at the corner of Londres and Aldama in Coyoacán for the sun to rise. "Those were other times, Miss Modotti; today, the instant is what matters." The photographs that in Mexico were considered engagé and political are considered purist in Germany: art for art's sake. Photojournalism is the only acceptable mode for a political militant: soldiers on the front line.

"Maybe you should go see Walter Ditbender," Lotte Jacobi suggests. "He is the mentor of political exiles here in Germany. He could probably find you work as a typist or something. He lives at 77–78 Dorotheenstrasse."

At home, Tina sits down and writes to Edward, trying to sort out her thoughts and feelings.

Berlin, May the 23d, 1930

My dear Edward:

I wonder why this silence from you? Did you receive my letter of the 14th of April? It seems I have written you since then also, though I am not sure, I keep track of the letters I send and only the 14th of April is annoted; perhaps the feeling that I have written to you more is due to the many times I have thought of you, during all my photographic troubles here. Have I told you of my surprise on arriving here to discover that throughout all Europe different sizes are used altogether for films, papers, cameras, etc. That was my first trouble. I kept awake at nights wondering what to do; either I should have sold my graflex or order films from the U.S. I decided to do the last of these two things since nobody would have interest in my graflex on account of its format. Naturally I could not afford to buy another camera unless I could first sell this one. Then came problem of all my negatives 8 by 10. I brought absolutely nothing from Mexico outside the graflex. I needed a

printing frame 8 by 10 and have had to have it made to or-
der. Paper that size I have had to order in larger quantities
than I wished to, otherwise the factory here would not cut it
special. You would be surprised perhaps to know that most
photographers here still use glass plates. Then there is the trou-
ble of different standards of measurement: you know, not
grains, but grammes. A hell of a mixed up affair. And on top
of it all, the difficulty of the language! I tell you I have almost
gone crazy.

I had the hope, on arriving here that I would be able to
make arrangements with some other photographer, or photogra-
phers' association, where I could go to do my work; I even
went to see the manager of the Eastman Co. but nothing came
out of it. So I had to buy an enlarging apparatus and enough
"tools" to work with. I did this unwillingly, since I wanted to
feel that I could pick up and go whenever I felt like it (or
whenever I was forced to . . .). Now I feel in a way tied down
to my dark room, (which by the way is not ready yet, that has
been an other hellish problem) I needed to find a furnished
room (since I absolutely refused to invest in furniture also)
with an other smaller room next to it, with water. *I under-*
lined the water part, because one ought to be in Berlin to real-
ize the difficulty of finding rooms with water. At last I have
what I needed; of course, the furnished room is not fit for a
studio, but since I am going to try getting along without mak-
ing portraits, I don't need a studio.

Oh Edward dear, how I longed for you to help me out
during these past weeks! Just to talk to you and discuss these
nasty affairs with you would have helped me; I have felt like
giving up photography altogether, but what else can I do? Even
in photography, I don't yet know just what to do. I said a mo-
ment ago that I am going to try getting along without making
portraits; partly because I prefer not to, and partly because
competition here is so great, and the prices so cheap that I do
not feel valiant enough to step in and compete. Of course I am
talking about really excellent portrait work; were it just the
trash turned out in Mexico by the photographers we both
know, I would not even give them a thought and just go
ahead, but this is really excellent work and I don't see how
and why they almost give it away.

I have been offered to do "reportage" or newspaper work, but I feel not fitted for such work. I still think it is a man's work in spite that here many women do it; perhaps they can, I am not aggressive enough.

Even the type of propaganda pictures I began to do in Mexico is already being done here; there is an association of "workers-photographers" (here everybody uses a camera) and the workers themselves make those pictures and have indeed better opportunities than I could ever have, since it is their own life and problems they photograph. Of course their results are far from the standard I am struggling to keep up in photography, but their end is reached just the same.

I feel there must be something for me but I have not found it yet. And in the meantime the days go by and I spend sleepless nights wondering wondering which way to turn and where to begin. I have begun to go out with the camera but, nada. *Everybody here has been telling me the graflex is too conspicuous and bulky; everybody here uses much more compact cameras. I realize the advantage of course; one does not attract so much attention; I have even tried a wonderful little camera, property of a friend, but I don't like to work with it as I do with the graflex; one cannot see the picture in its finished size; perhaps I could get used to it, but anyway buying a camera now is out of a question since I have to invest in the enlarging apparatus. Besides a smaller camera would only be useful if I intended to work on the streets, and I am not so sure that I will. I know the material found on the streets is rich and wonderful, but my experience is that the way I am accustomed to work, slowly planning my composition etc. is not suited for such work. By the time I have the composition or expression right, the picture is gone. I guess I want to do the impossible and therefore I do nothing. And yet I shall have to decide soon what to do, for although I can still afford to "take it easy" for a while, this cannot go on for ever. Besides, my mental state is not a very pleasant one. If only I had somebody with whom to tell all my troubles, I mean somebody who could understand them, like you could Edward.*

I was advised not to give an exhibit till fall, that being the better time; by then I ought to have something of Germany to include, which would all be very good, if only I begin to work soon. Otherwise all I will have is "merda."

The weather has been so nasty, cold, grey miserable; the sun only appears at moments; one cannot really rely on it, you can imagine how I feel after the weather I am accustomed to, both in California and Mexico. Well, there is nothing to do but go ahead; I recall often that wonderful line from Nietzsche you told me: What does not kill me strengthens me. But I assure you this present period is very near killing me.

I see the Wittes once in a while. They are wonderful friends to have and their kindness to me is like a ray of sunshine. And yet I don't tell even them all my troubles, I am terribly scrupulous being a new comer here. I feel constantly that I must solve my own problems and not bother friends too much. And yet I have done nothing in this letter but tell you all my problems, but you are far away and certain things nobody but you can understand; besides you must not worry about me; I will find a way out somehow and perhaps by the time this reaches you I will be in a more settled state of mind. So please dear don't let this interfere with your own problems and worries; but do drop me, if only a line, for I am hungry for your words.

If you have not yet but intend sending the Wittes one of your photographs, please do not mention their lost ones; I am afraid they will resent my having told you.

Always my devotion to you.

Tina

and best regards to Brett and Sonya!

Tina finally gets a letter from Weston and she responds immediately:

Berlin May the 28th [1930]

Dear "grandfather"!

How I laughed over the information regarding Chandler's matrimonial progresses! Well, your being a grandfather sounds wors[e] than it really is, for I am sure if you had the little imp near you you would just play with him, or her, with the same precious youthfulness which belongs to you.

Your letter reached me yesterday; oh how happy I was to hear from you! A few days ago I wrote you again but now I almost regret having sent it; I was in such a despondent state of mind and weak enough to not just keep it to myself, and made you the victim of my weakness. Please forgive me, and do not worry about me; I will fight my way and the last word has not been said yet. And all these trials will bear some fruit, I am sure; in other words, I have enough self confidence and realize I must not undervalue my capacities. Only there are moments, who doesn't have them?, when everything appears black (perhaps they are black and those are the moments of most lucidity) but maybe next day the sun shines and the little birds sing, and the panorama changes as if by magic!

Dear one; about the Wittes pictures; I did not mean that you should replace all the pictures they lost (I don't even know how many they were) but just to send one, and of course I cannot ask them which one, as they would never permit me to make it known to you their loss. That is why in my last letter I begged you to not mention to them their loss. They are very sensitive people and feel terrible about their loss and would feel even more terrible and mortified if you knew of it. The idea is just that they should have an Edward Weston *print; so send anyone you can spare. Of myself I made them choose among the many exquisite heads you made of me. They did not want to do it and to convince them I had to show them the negative (the one with both hands on chin) and only then did they accept it because I could reprint it for myself. When you send the print for them just say you wanted them to have it and never mention the loss, please!*

I wish I could see Sonia's work. Frances [Toor] has written me so beautifully of Sonia and it just seems as if I know her. Does she think I am a crazy nut? Please give her my very best wishes and all my tenderness!

I was interested in your decision about the glossy paper. Yes, I can just picture the "pictorialists" lifting their arms in horror at this new "outrage" by this terrible terrible iconoclast Edward Weston! *Do you mind telling me what paper you now use? Is it american or foreign?*

So far I have undertimed everything I began to make; this

damned light after Mexico! And yet I had accounted for it; but I will know better in the future.

A big abrazote to you, Sonia, and the boys from

Tina

When Tina receives a letter from Vittorio announcing that he's back in Berlin, she feels that the sky is opening up for her. When he knocks at her door, she runs down the stairs and throws herself in his arms.

"Vittorio, help me get to Italy."

"Tu sei matta. They'll arrest you. Come with me to Moscow."

Tina looks at him without responding.

"Do you have other plans?"

"No. The situation will be the same in every country. I don't know how to be a photographer or a militant."

"Bene, bene," he says as he caresses her back. "Then why not accompany me to Moscow, to the center of anti-imperialism?"

Vittorio revives her with his confident, earnest voice. At that moment, she hopes he will never let go of her hand.

He takes her to a café, where she eats heartily for the first time in weeks. "Just taste this cheese, and have a glass of Rhine wine. It will do you good." He isn't bothered by the Germans, who come out of the cabarets bursting with laughter, or by the frivolity of drinking from crystal glasses. But when they overhear a conversation at a nearby table in which Ernst Thaelmann, Secretary of the Communist Party, is being ridiculed, Vidali interrupts, and they almost come to blows. The police arrive, grab him by the collar, and take him to the nearest police station. Tina goes with him.

"Your documents, please."

"Here. I am a Peruvian journalist."

The inspector hands back his passport and advises him to be more careful, especially in the company of a German lady. Tina does not open her mouth. As he escorts them out, he lets them know that he is a Social Democrat and that the situation is very difficult for anybody who is not a Nazi. Hitler is gaining power all over Germany.

Vittorio tells Tina that in 1922 he was in the Borlitz prison and was expelled from Berlin and put in a detention camp in Cottbus, from which he escaped with the help of another Social Democrat. The German police have his fingerprints and it is probable they will find Vittorio Vidali in the Peruvian Jacobo Hurwitz Zender.

She stares at Vidali. "He is a barbarian, a braggart, and has no concept of danger, or maybe for him death is a joke as it is for the Mexicans, but he is my only connection to life."

Every night her head is filled with memories of Mexico, but gradually her friends, even loyal Luz Ardizana, fade into shadows. Perhaps she will derive strength from not needing anybody.

1 7

ina's one desire as she gets off the train at Moscow's Alex-
androvsky station on October 2, 1930, is to find Xavier Guerrero; she wants to explain in person the letter she wrote from
Mexico. She is sure that Guerrero will understand, as he always
did, and she dreams about going to museums with him, examining
up close the icons of the Novgorod school. Tina owes him so
much; he is such a noble man, so dedicated to the cause. On the
platform Vittorio's cheery face beneath a Basque beret greets her
in spite of her wish.

Moscow's Red Square spreads out like a vast gray sea. The
stones rise to Tina's eyes in slow waves. Standing next to Vittorio,
Tina glances up at the round, colored onions crowning St. Basil's
Cathedral. The inside of the cathedral is like an icebox.

"I can't wait to see Moscow, I can't wait to see Petrovka Street,"
Tina says, suddenly feeling like a carefree tourist.

"Tina, members of the anti-Fascist community are used to accounting for themselves. As guests of Red Aid, we are obliged to keep those who welcome us, dress us, feed us, and pay us informed of our whereabouts."

Tina blushes. "I am planning to go to the Lux Hotel to see Xavier Guerrero. Comrade Nadezhda told me that all the members of the Communist International are staying there. I have a map of the city and I think I can find it, it's not far from Tverskaya."

"Is he expecting you?"

"I think so, I wrote to him from Berlin."

When Tina returns to the Soyuznaya Hotel, her meeting with Guerrero is written all over her face.

She speaks quickly and indignantly. "He just stood there listening to me, as cold as a stone. When I was finished, he didn't even look at me; he just said, 'For me, you are dead.'"

They drink tea, and Vittorio tries to soothe her. "Forget about him. Once you begin to work, you will be so busy your personal problems will fade away. In a few days you will meet with the head of International Red Aid, Yelena Stasova. She is a great revolutionary. She was secretary to both Lenin and Stalin."

"Stasova will probably realize that I'm not a true militant, that I don't know anything. How can I help? In Mexico, I wanted to take pictures of everything. In Berlin, I was paralyzed. And here I still don't know."

"If you don't want to be a photographer, you can do summaries of the foreign press, write articles, do translations. Your knowledge of languages is very useful."

"I'm homesick, Vittorio."

"A useless emotion. You mustn't have regrets. Look at me, I try to push away my memories."

When she returns to her room, Tina remembers the cold expression on Xavier's face. She tries to follow Vittorio's advice, but her memories are more stubborn than his. She calls up her mother's face, superimposes it over Guerrero's. Mamma, why aren't you with me? Vittorio's perennial good mood suddenly irritates her. Perhaps he can hear her pacing back and forth all night on the floor above his room. In many ways he is completely insensitive. In the early hours of the morning, sleep finally comes, and Tina dreams about a smiling Xavier who beckons to her.

A few days later Tina, arm in arm with Vittorio, returns to Red Square. Beyond the sea of paving stones stands the walled Kremlin, a palace as secretive as a monastery. "Everything in the Soviet Union is immense." They have walked there from the Soyuznaya Hotel down Ilynka Street, to the Central Committee building, Staraya Ploshchad, then to Lubyanka Street. "Look, this is where Stalin works; the walls in his office are bare except for two portraits: Lenin and Marx. We just might see him one day with his bodyguards on his way from the Kremlin. There is always light in Stalin's window because he works until dawn. He was used to staying up all night when he was underground. He makes all the decisions; he doesn't delegate authority to anybody. Come, we need to eat something. Did you bring the coupons?"

Tina smiles. "They even gave me rubles for personal expenses." "These Russians are so warm and generous," she thinks.

On the afternoon of October 19, Vittorio and Tina go to Stasova's office for their appointment.

She sits behind her desk, her hair pulled straight back into a bun. She wears a man's shirt with a high collar. A pince-nez rests on her long nose, making her look like a heron ready to pounce on a fish. Stasova stares at Tina as she interrogates her. Vittorio interrupts from time to time like a father who has brought his daughter to the headmistress on her first day of school. Yes, she knows French, he has heard her speak; yes, she speaks English like a native; yes, she is an excellent typist, and he can personally testify to how quickly she takes dictation. Tina's hands are crossed on her black skirt.

"She also can take pictures."

"Are you very interested in photography?"

Tina raises her eyes and says, "I submit myself to the needs of the Party."

Her response seems to please Stasova, who holds out her large hand as a sign that the interview is over.

They return, arm in arm, to the hotel. Two days later, Stasova calls for Vittorio. She looks him up and down without offering him a seat.

"According to my information, you are a polygamist."

"What?"

"Po-lyg-a-mist. How many women do you live with?"

"I live alone."

181

"Is it true that Paolina Hafkina is pregnant with your child?"

"I found her in my hotel room one night when I got home."

"What about Tina Modotti?"

"There's nothing."

"What do you mean, nothing? You bring her from Berlin. You make a big effort to find her work. Clearly, you are interested in her."

"Because I believe she can serve the Party."

"When will your child be born?"

"Soon, I'm not sure. I don't live with the mother. I live at the Soyuznaya Hotel."

"Will you give it your name?"

"Yes, I promised Paolina's father."

Next, in a commanding voice, Yelena Stasova informs him that Modotti has made a good impression. "I think we can use her. Tell her to come see me."

The next morning, Tina is given a chair and a desk in an office already occupied by five other members of Red Aid. It is in a building on a dead-end street with narrow windows that face an interior courtyard paved with red bricks. Tina notices a lone tree in the courtyard with only a few leaves left on it. There is a photograph of Lenin on one office wall; on another, a photograph of Stalin. Compared to Lenin's, Stalin's features are almost gross, and his eyes focus on nothing in particular; even from far away, one can see that he has no audience. Tina feels privileged to be part of Red Aid. Those who work here are anonymous heroes building the new Soviet Union. No other country in the world has managed, in only ten years, to give refuge to so many persecuted people from other countries and transform them into giants, saints, new men and women with four hands, two heads, and fire in their hearts.

During her first days at Red Aid, Tina is feverish with excitement. The strong woman she once was is reborn within her. At night, she lies in bed thinking about the moment when she will get up to be the first to get to the office, sit down to take notes, translate, all with such enthusiasm and dedication that she soon stands out among her comrades. She loves to hear their names: Alexander Davidovich, Yelena Petrovna, Yekaterina, Vasili, Galina, Ilya, Kostya, and the little messenger boy, Andrei, with his wise eyes: he settles down on the floor in front of Stasova's door and jumps up the second he is needed.

Tina watches how Stasova leaves her office, always in a hurry, striding by as she pins her felt hat on her hair. Tina never sees her wear anything other than this gray hat that has survived many a Moscow snowstorm.

On the street, the men are dressed in thick, rough, khaki-colored garments and worn-out boots. Those with astrakhan hats stand next to peasants in woolen caps and wait for hours in line for a kilo of beets and then in another line for a kilo of potatoes.

But there's tea in abundance, and during tea time, everyone pours himself a glass from the heavy samovar. "Aren't you going to have your tea, Comrade Modotti?" The first time Tina hears herself being addressed as Comrade Modotti, she feels a warmth filling her throat and belly: the golden liquid of belonging. She is part of a group that will not easily give her up.

Still, compared to America, Europe is very old. "Maybe that is why my father went away, because everything here has already been done." Here in Russia, for some reason, everyone seems to be living in hiding and to distrust one another. The Mexican "Come in, my humble house is yours" is totally improbable in Moscow.

1 8

On the night of November 7, people carrying red flags, banners, and effigies of Lenin, Marx, Engels, and Stalin gather under the sharp clear spotlights. Tina has never witnessed so much enthusiasm. It's freezing outside but everyone seems to be burning from within. The people near her hug and kiss one another with tears in their eyes. Asians with faces like full moons, Siberians with flat noses, the wide foreheads of the Tatars, the old people's sunken mouths. Everyone drinks from the same bottle, and when it is finished, another appears and is passed from hand to hand. In Mexico, the masses are Indian; here each individual is distinct and yet like the others. Thousands and thousands of marvelous human beings march down the middle of the street. "Look," Vittorio says as he points to the high rostrum presided over by Stalin. The atmosphere is liturgical: the masses of the faithful fill Red Square, turning it into a living cathedral. Vittorio looks at Tina's face and senses some deep emotion, as if she were struggling with an inner demon.

"What's the matter?"

"It frightens me to be alive."

When they reach the hotel, she is still agitated.

"Do you need more air?"

"What I need is more clarity."

"Why do you say that?"

"I don't know what I have lived for until now, how I have used my time. I'm ashamed of myself. Why didn't I know about all this before? It would have given my life the meaning it never had. I wonder how I could have been so frivolous, so selfish."

Tina sheds her first tears since Julio Antonio Mella's death.

"Don't cry, or you'll make me cry, too."

In the midst of her tears, Tina looks up in surprise. That a fighter like Vittorio Vidali should say such a thing makes her wonder about his real nature. In utter exhaustion, Tina lets herself be held tightly. She realizes then that she is holding him, too. This sturdy, balding man is an anchor. By remaining near him, she may keep from drowning. Fate has thrown him into her sea so she can stay afloat, for the time being at least.

The following night, Tina and Vittorio give up room 207, and she moves into room 107. For a long time now, they have kept each other company, exorcised their problems together, each one complementing the other. When Vittorio reflects on himself, he comes up with concrete answers. Tina, however, is vulnerable to criticism, and filled with confusion and self-doubt. She cannot help feeling that even now, if she disappeared, Vittorio would pick up where he left off and carry on. "That's life," he would say. He would find another woman around the corner. Tina needs him much more than he needs her.

Of all the men she has had, he is the most familiar, the one closest to her because their language unites them and they carry the land in their flesh. Making love to him is like being with her mother, her father, herself, the poverty of her childhood. That first night he came naturally into her and she knew instinctively that she could love him like family. This was bound to be. He gave

Italy back to her. And yet Vittorio was often rough, always in a hurry, never tender. She would never love him as she had Julio Antonio, but she would nest in him the way a house nestles in the hills.

Together they sang. Vittorio loved to sing like her father, Giuseppe. In Mexico, at the Mesones fund-raising parties, they had sung with the others the Mexican corridos and rancheras. Tina's "Tipsy, tipsy I go" was always cheered. Now there would be more reasons to sing together, not only because they knew the same songs, but also because they sang into each other.

Trieste is what unites Tina and Vittorio most, because it was their childhood home. Trieste is more than just a port; it is one of the prized crossroads of Europe. It is a great Adriatic city with a plaza as large as the Piazza d'Unita d'Italia, and it is open to the salty gray sea. Its solid neoclassical buildings stand up to the bora. That is what Vittorio and Tina like best, to talk about the bora of their childhood, that pummeling wind they faced and withstood along with the other child centurions.

Tina is grateful for the companionship of two families from Trieste, the Marabinis and the Regents. She also treasures her relationship with Leocadia Prestes, the mother of Luis Carlos Prestes, Brazil's knight in shining armor who fought against the dictatorship of Getulio Vargas under the direction of the Comintern. He marched 26,000 kilometers, leading his guerrilleros across the immeasurable expanse of Brazil, and was captured by the dictator and locked in a cement cell built especially for him. In Moscow, the Comintern takes care of his mother because, in more than one way, they are responsible for her son's defeat. In Mexico, Tina would certainly have criticized the Moscow politicians who interfere in Latin America without the faintest idea of its real situation, but in the Soviet Union she bows her head devoutly. For her, Russians are saviors no matter what they order her to do. She pays a visit to Klara Zetkin, who is almost blind, and to Ada Wright, Tom Mooney's mother. These older women, revered by the Russian leaders, are models for Tina: their integrity speaks to her more directly than a hundred speeches.

Klara Zetkin insists on the link between the needs of the Communist program and women's personal needs, which, she believes, should be taken into account by the Revolution. She says: "If we don't have millions of women on our side, we can never exercise the dictatorship of the proletariat."

She appreciates the friendship of Ivan and Malka Regent, who have been Vittorio's friends since 1919. Malka, called Amalia, is a short, sturdy woman who works in a doll factory. One would think that their daughter, Mara, would have a doll, but she doesn't. Tina knows she has a lot to learn from her, because Vittorio has told her so. Amalia is optimistic. She loves her life and is so efficient she will probably become a Soviet deputy for her neighborhood. She is a wonderful companion for Ivan, and he is lucky to have her. Is Vittorio lucky to have Tina?

Tina depends heavily on Vidali and his friends to restore a sense of order and optimism to her life. Something in the general atmosphere distresses her. In the capitalist world, everything is based on individual good humor, goodwill, good nature. Under socialism, individuals are swallowed in the grandeur of the enterprise. Tina keeps fighting against the sensation that everything in Europe is old, worn out and that she is also. When she buys herself a fur cap, she realizes that under it her tired face looks older and has grown larger, fleshier, her eyes have become smaller behind her swollen eyelids, and her teeth are no longer white, thanks to the Belomor-Kanals, Russian cigarettes.

And rewards do not come in the intimate form Tina loves most. Rewards come from the Party, and only rarely, certainly not when you are a beginner. Punishment is the one thing people can count on in Moscow. The atmosphere is one of persecution. Space and breath are rare privileges that Russians must learn to appreciate.

In Moscow, everyday life is a terrible chore. With winter coming, the streets will soon turn into rivers of mud and snow; just the thought of taking off coats and putting them on again makes Tina weary. She has the hardest time with the galoshes, the "galochs" as Vittorio calls them, that are worn over felt shoes and boots. Even walking exhausts her; the sidewalks in Moscow are gray and narrow. While waiting in line outside the shops to buy butter, Tina feels she is becoming part of a long human cord that gets tighter and tighter, while the cold slowly freezes her feet and legs. Fruit is scarce, but there are expensive bakeries and pastry shops with all kinds of cakes smothered in meringue and whipped cream. The toy-shop windows are radiant, filled with beautifully carved toys. Children and adults stop, smile, and cry out in joy. It would be lovely if all Moscow could sport the colors of its toy shops. Even mineral water is expensive. A small apartment of one's own is an impossible dream. Vittorio and Tina can only afford the cut-rate Soyuznaya Hotel.

"Oh sun, sun, why have you forsaken this half of the world?" Tina is more strongly affected than Vittorio by the lack of sun. Another dreary day under the same gray sky.

It starts to snow. There are only a few cars on the streets, and rushing crowds bundled in gray coats emerge from the Metro only to stop in front of closed food shops. They stand patiently in long lines. At some point the shops will have to open. When one finally does, its shelves are desolate, with a single item—usually potatoes or beets—offered for sale. Huge posters of Marx, Stalin, and Lenin preside over the Russians' grim lives.

Whenever Tina looks out the window—in her office, in her hotel room, at the Regents' house—she sees the snow falling. When she dares to open a window, she is blasted by frozen air that penetrates to her very bones and takes her breath away. It is more than fifty degrees below zero.

Vittorio likes best to engage in discussion or, better yet, to hear himself speak. She could never take him to the Meyerhold Theater or talk him into going to a ballet or a concert, yet only Vittorio can provide the anchor, the stability that Tina needs. One evening she goes with Pablo O'Higgins, in Moscow on a visit, to meet his artist friends. They dance and play the violin, the accordion, and the piano, and a party surges out of nothing. Tina drinks a glass of Armenian cognac and holds hands with the others in an almost childish circle dance. Sweet moments.

On another afternoon she and O'Higgins go to Sergei Eisenstein's for tea. Tina had met Eisenstein once in Mexico, but the man she now sees in Moscow is unrecognizable. There, he was overflowing with humor and joy and couldn't stop drawing. Here, Eisenstein's hands shake as he talks, and he interjects French words into his soliloquies. In his spacious Moscow apartment there is a candelabra with seven arms, some Mexican straw donkeys, and an idol with a carved stone head: reminders of Mexico, where he was admired for his sense of humor and astute comments. Now he nervously repeats that life's goal is to "make known the high ideals of our era."

"They have called me a cosmopolite," and it is true that he feels more comfortable in Paris or Mexico than in Moscow, where they do not leave him alone. He has been awarded a Doctor of Arts degree by the University of Moscow and is Professor of Directing at the Institute of Cinematic Science, but he is still not satisfied. He is a man of the world: he knows Gertrude Stein, Tristan Tzara, Otto Frank, and Colette. He likes to walk in the Bois de Boulogne and is sympathetic to certain forms of social decadence.

Eisenstein's good mood returns as he remembers Mexico. What a treasure, what light in Mexico. Then he speaks about Mayakovsky, and he shows Van Gogh reproductions to Pablo and Tina.

"What a wonderful afternoon!" Pablo sighs as they leave three hours later.

"Doesn't our friend seem just a little decadent to you, Pablo?"

"Decadent?"

"Yes, as if he weren't grateful for the privilege of living the Revolution."

"He lives it in his own way. We each live it as we can."

Vittorio attends the plenary session of the Central Committee in which Stalin analyzes the achievements of the first five-year plan. Between bouts of prolonged applause, Stalin reviews the situation of industry and agriculture, the living conditions of workers and peasants, and the struggle against the industrialists, the private sector, the landed aristocracy, the kulaks, the former White officials and their lackeys, all kinds of chauvinistic bourgeois intellectuals and other anti-Soviet elements. Comrade Stalin never forgets to quote Lenin.

"We have not only been victorious; we have done much more than we ever expected, more than the most fertile imagination could have hoped. Not even our enemies can deny our achievements.

"We had no metallurgic industry, the backbone of industrialization. Now we do.

"We had no automotive industry. Now we do.

"We had no industry for the production of machinery. Now we do.

"We had no modern chemical industry. Now we do.

"We had no dependable industry to produce modern agricultural equipment. Now we do.

"We had no aeronautics industry. Now we do."

At the end of the speech, Vittorio is bursting with pride. When they get home, he tells Tina that the U.S.S.R. has gone from last place to one of the first places in the world in the production of electric energy, in the extraction of petroleum and coal, in metallurgy; in the same period, the industrial capacity of the United States has decreased. The Party has transformed the Soviet Union into the largest agricultural producer in the world. Collectivization hasn't failed. On the contrary, instead of suffering the catastrophic unemployment plaguing the capitalist countries, the U.S.S.R. has dramatically improved living conditions for the workers in only four years, one year less than had been proposed. Vittorio repeats Stalin's words reverently. Tina listens in awe.

"Tina, tomorrow I am leaving on a mission to liberate a German comrade. It is a delicate operation; I must take him from Germany to Czechoslovakia, then bring him to Moscow."

Tina turns pale, remembering Stasova's words: "The important thing is to be of service."

At the station, giving him a kiss that may be the last, Tina presses her cold cheek against Vittorio's. "Toio, Toietto, be careful."

As the train pulls out, Vittorio's Basque beret disappears from sight. Tina makes her way back to the red brick office and the imprisoned tree.

Tina's primary job is to welcome refugees and help them get settled; the work is exhausting, but she prefers men and women of flesh and blood to the endless paperwork and bureaucracy. She even goes out to buy milk for the children, searching everywhere for this scarce commodity. Stasova has also asked her to write articles about the struggle in Latin America, under a pseudonym, of course: "The important thing is to tell what you saw and experienced with the peasants in Mexico. Also write about Italy, the garment workers, your childhood memories, the revolutionaries you knew from Central America, Sandino, don't keep everything you know to yourself. Share it."

Tina feels a terrible anxiety. Until now she has only written personal letters and two articles, one about photography for *Mexican Folkways* and another for the Peruvian periodical *Amauta* headed by José Carlos Mariátegui. Stasova doesn't realize what she is asking, doesn't know that Tina is not capable of it, that she is very insecure. How could she take on the assignments usually given to Vittorio, who writes as easily as he talks?

This business of writing, what torture! Translating, yes, but writing? In her office, while she attends to the refugees, she thinks anxiously about the blank page. When she gets home, she lies down and reads and makes notes in her notebook. She starts, then crosses out, then begins again. Finally she decides to write the article as if it were a letter she was sending to an imaginary Weston, a Russian Weston who wants to know, for example, how the Mexican workers lived.

In Vittorio's absence, she struggles with the dullness of the routine, the sticky slowness of bureaucracy. How many times has she heard things like: "Comrade Modotti, finish the translation so it can be distributed as a preliminary report on the adoption of decisions applicable to our situation before they are up for a vote." Is this where the Revolution is headed? The novelty of the first few weeks sours like cabbage in the tiny apartments, like the unavoidable vigil outside a shop just to buy that kilo of potatoes and another of beets. "When did the line begin?" "An hour ago." And the cold, especially the cold, freezes her good intentions. "We struggle, we give our lives, death will be our compensation," she repeats to herself.

January 12—1931
Moscow

My dear Edward:
    I have been living in a regular whirlpool ever since I came here in October, so much that I cannot even remember whether I have written to you or not since my arrival. But at any rate, today I received the announcement of your exhibit.

191

(just about three months later due to carelessness of the person who forwards my mail in Berlin) and I cannot wait one day longer to send you my saludos with the same feeling of always!

Is she telling Weston the truth in this, her last letter to him? Why doesn't she say that she thinks of him less and less every day, that she doesn't have time for him because her time belongs to the Party, that she is a different person living a life he could never even dream of? They share nothing anymore, not even photography. The decision has been made: the Revolution is difficult and inevitable; everything that is happening here would seem to him like bureaucracy gone mad. Weston pays attention only to the demands of his own body, his own sensibility, his own art; he knows nothing about fighting for a cause; his only cause is himself, and photography is his mirror.

On January 13, 1931, Yelena Dmitrievna Stasova calls Tina to her office.

"Close the door, comrade. We have chosen you to take some passports to Berlin. This will be your first mission. Your contact speaks German and English. You will leave tomorrow. Comrade Abramov will give you your money and the passports."

"I would have liked to go with Vittorio."

"Agents do not share their missions, comrade."

Stasova stands up and holds out her large, bony hand. "I don't think I need tell you that any mistake you make puts you and Red Aid at risk. It will be very dangerous if they stop you with three passports and a large sum of money. Your name is Hedwig Flieg. In Berlin you must go to the café on Friedrichstrasse where the comrades of Red Aid meet. There you will meet your contact. You must not carry even one written address."

"I know, I know," Tina says, trying to sound experienced, confident. "How will I recognize my contact?"

"He will recognize you. He will say: 'A bird in the hand is worth two in the bush.' "

That night, Tina sews the passports into her underwear: two in front over her belly, and one behind. She hides the money in her brassiere. At dawn, she places Hedwig Flieg's passport and some family pictures in her handbag. Who are these children and that man gazing at her out of those little oval frames? A handkerchief, a lipstick, a compact, a comb, three packs of cigarettes, keys, and a ticket for the Berlin Metro that she has kept all this time, give the appearance of normality.

When the conductor slides open the door to her compartment, Tina lifts her eyes from the magazine she bought at the station, opens her bag, and shows him her passport. "Danke schön, Frau Flieg." She never thought it would be so easy.

Tina waits an hour and a half in a nearly empty café on Friedrichstrasse. Two women at a table on the other side of the room talk constantly and never look at her. Obviously, this is not the right place, or perhaps something has gone wrong. Tina asks for the bill, pays, and leaves. Two blocks away, she stops at a bookstore and buys a fashion magazine, thinking that a woman with a fashion magazine would attract less attention. She enters another café and takes a quick look around: the tables are clean and white, there are many customers; the atmosphere is very different. A man and a woman at one of the tables are speaking in low voices. At another table, Tina thinks she recognizes an agent from International Red Aid; he looks at her, then turns back to one of his companions. A half hour later, they pay and leave. (Years later, Comrade Fritz Karger would explain to her that two policemen took him to the café that day to attract other comrades and that many were caught when they came up to speak to him. "My instinct not to show any sign of recognition saved me," Tina would say.)

Tina continues to wait. Nobody looks at her over a newspaper; nobody acknowledges her. Now she will need to look for a room for the night. She knows the Berlin of the poor. She remembers a tiny inn she used to pass on her way to Lotte Jacobi's house. As she leaves the café, she is sure she is being followed. She walks more quickly and senses that somebody is trying to catch up with her.

"Comrade, comrade, it is I."

Paralyzed with fear, Tina turns around. The man has only one arm. "A bird in the hand is worth two in the bush." And then he adds, "Comrade, we have been waiting for you since yesterday."

He places in her hand a tiny piece of paper and walks away. She thinks she hears him say, "Hurry," but she is not sure.

An address is scribbled on the piece of paper. As the taxi she rides in approaches a building with long, narrow windows like slits, she sees the one-armed man waiting. She follows him up many flights of stairs until he stops in front of a dirty door and knocks briefly. The door opens immediately.

Two men and a woman sit around a table in a room dimly lit by a small lamp. They offer Tina a cup of coffee. They keep glancing fearfully at the door; at every noise, every sound of distant steps, they stop talking and look at one another.

"Do you have the documents, comrade?"

"Yes. I'll need a pair of scissors and a little privacy to get them."

"Come with me to the other room."

Tina's hands are trembling as the woman sits and watches her perform the operation.

Once Tina hands over the documents, she must figure out how to leave inconspicuously. All public transportation after midnight has been halted, and starting at eleven o'clock, all passengers are checked.

"I'll take a taxi," Tina suggests.

"That can also be dangerous. Be careful."

They inform her quickly and in low voices about a confidential memo in which the Berlin police give the Nazis a free hand in dealing summarily with anybody caught printing or putting up Communist propaganda. The one-armed man tells her about the nightly executions, how they meet in cellars and change their hiding places every day. Thanks to the passports, a few will be saved.

Tina says goodbye. Nobody offers to accompany her. She won't need to spend the night now, so she heads directly to the station to catch a train back to Moscow. She keeps looking behind her to make sure she isn't being followed. In the foggy street she sees a cleaning truck. Two workers approach her.

"Fräulein, fräulein, come with us."

Tina begins to run; they run after her, shouting obscenities. Then they turn around and walk away.

At the station there are huge crowds waiting on the platforms and in front of the ticket windows. A conductor shows her to her compartment. Tina begins to lift her large handbag onto the overhead rack and a bearded man with red eyes taps her on the arm and offers to help. "Did he notice how light it was?" Tina takes out her magazine and begins to memorize it; she tries to drown out the sharp, tiny voice inside her that feeds off thoughts of defeat. "What if they catch me? What if they kill me?" The thought of her own death is almost liberating. At least she would no longer have to suffer the pounding in her temples. Suddenly, the bearded man offers her a cookie, and Tina jumps as if he had placed a pistol to her head. Then he speaks to her in German. Tina answers in monosyllables, and he, after telling her that he is a traveling salesman, falls asleep with his mouth open. Maybe he is sleeping peacefully because he knows they will arrest her at the next station. She must escape, get off the train. While she decides on a plan of escape, she goes out to the corridor, stares out the window, and smokes a Belomor-Kanal. She looks back into the compartment and sees the word *Bayer* written on the briefcase under the man's legs. Maybe that, too, is just a clever ruse, an agent's disguise, and she becomes even more agitated. She looks out the window again and removes another cigarette. The conductor walks by and offers to light it for her. Tina suddenly realizes that she is smoking Russian cigarettes. The only thing she can think of doing is to look straight into the conductor's eyes. She must get rid of the last pack without anybody seeing her. She smoked in the first train, in both cafés, at the station, and now on this train. How stupid of her!

She decides to go to the bathroom. There, she throws away the pack and rinses her face and mouth. As she combs her hair, she decides to move to the second-class car; it is full of women with their children, peasants, animals in cages, bags of seed and beets and potatoes and a leg of lamb wrapped in bloodied newspaper. Are they going to market or coming from market? Tina feels more comfortable here. She leans her head against the bundle next to her and finally feels able to rest. A child begins to cry: blessed child. Only then does she realize that she hasn't had a bite to eat since she had tea and apple pie in Berlin. She asks someone for a cigarette and inhales deeply. Two heavy-set women with children clinging to their skirts pull out some bars of chocolate. Where did they buy them? She wants one.

When the inspector comes, Tina takes out her passport and Hedwig Flieg flashes a charming smile. "Everything in order, Fräulein. Have a good evening."

"I congratulate you, comrade. You have increased the prestige of Red Aid."

The bony hand presses her own. The old woman's voice is very intense; her eyes glow.

"And Vittorio?"

"You'll be returning to your desk now, Comrade Modotti, although I don't think you'll be there for very long. Those who have had a taste of danger often become addicted to it."

A few days later, Vittorio returns to the Soyuznaya Hotel; despite his perpetual smile, Tina can see that he is upset. As it turns out, they were in Berlin at the same time, but Stasova hadn't told either of them. How reassuring it would have been for Tina to have seen Vittorio, even from a distance! Stasova, the system, the Supreme Soviet: how harsh and unyielding they are. "My mission was to get W.B. out of jail, but I found him sitting at a table in a tavern in Reichenbach, a few feet from the border, a free man, completely relaxed, with his arms around a woman. I had very strict orders to take him across the border, so I did."

Vittorio expresses his doubts about W.B. to Stasova, who does not seem at all surprised. Adjusting the pince-nez on her long nose, she responds, "Time will tell. You have carried out your mission by bringing him to Moscow." Then she turns to Tina and says, "We have two new missions for you, Comrade Modotti, one in Rumania and one in Hungary. You will be taking gifts to prisoners. We are certain that you will be successful."

Tina is not fully aware of all the changes she has undergone, of how natural conspiracy and obedience now seem to her and how confident she is of success. She feels such awe for the Soviets' ability to reorganize their huge, semi-feudal nation. Hadn't they built a factory for sulfuric acid in Voskresensk, near Moscow, in only six months? Hadn't they found gigantic oil deposits in the Caucasus? Elated by their progress, the comrades execute saboteurs without remorse. How could the workers steal sacks of cement, or the peasants filch grain? Why would the farmers prefer to kill their animals than turn them over to the collectives? Who are the people who hide their animals' feed? Why do they refuse to rotate virgin lands, and why doesn't anyone volunteer to go to the land north of Kazakhstan and begin cultivating grain? Don't they realize they are creating a society under the critical eyes of the entire world? Once, Vittorio traveled on rutted roads in deep snow to find out what parts were needed to repair the kolkhoz's tractor and why the collective let an entire harvest of wheat rot, with the pretext that they lacked the manpower. The men of the steppes in gray smocks, caps pulled down over their ears, looked at him in silence. Vittorio did such a song and dance to make himself understood that they laughed and asked him if he was an opera singer.

Vittorio is always on one mission or another: Helsinki, Prague, Budapest, Warsaw. Tina finds out where he has been only when he returns.

Tina has her own missions to the Ukraine and Armenia.

"A telegram for you, comrade," Boris says as he hands Tina an envelope.

Tina opens it. *"Pepe died in Davos. Stop. His last words. Stop. Tell Tina Modotti. Stop. Quintanilla family."*

Tina closes her eyes and sees Pepe gazing at her. She hears his words.

"I kiss the ground you walk on. I worship you, I venerate you, I pray to you; you are my sanctuary; don't ever leave me, Tina, I want you never to leave my sight." And her own: "Pepe, you should fear me, I am a dangerous woman." "Yes," he says, laughing, "yes, you are *redoutable*," he adds in French and laughs again. "I've been lost for a long time, Tina. This isn't a joke for me, I love you." "Between suffering and pleasure, how long will you wait, child?" says Tina.

Tina made him wait, and wait, and wait. Pepe Quintanilla came often to El Buen Retiro. Monna Teixidor, sitting next to him during their get-togethers, observed him. "I have never seen such a cultured young man. He speaks English and taught himself German." The Quintanillas were an exceptional family. Such handsome men with deep voices, strong jaws, and well-shaped chins, their aristocratic breeding visible from miles away. The Quintanillas enjoyed life and approved of those who live it well. They never rejected, never judged, never criticized.

And the most remarkable one of all was that pale young man who made the room shake with his laughter.

Rafael Sala and Felipe Teixidor admired him. "An extraordinary young man," they used to say.

Even Weston fell under his spell. He was so attractive, so refined! He spoke about his photographs knowledgeably and with sensitivity. Weston was grateful that he spoke English. Pepe lived life quickly, as if speed were a kind of defense against loneliness.

"I am going to escort my family to New York," he announced at a party one evening.

"We will all miss you, Pepe," Tina said.

"I don't know how they manage to travel," Monna commented later. "They lost their entire fortune and still they go sightseeing with the children and the nursemaids."

When Pepe Quintanilla returned, he brought gifts for everybody, especially for Tina.

"Mexico is simply splendid," he said, gazing at the sky. "The air here is so good. The skyscrapers in New York don't let air circulate. Je suis un des habitués du Buen Retiro."

"Is the air in El Buen Retiro kind to you?" Tina asked flirtatiously.

"Oh yes, the kindest thing that has ever happened to me in my entire life."

Tina went to Fred Davis's house in Cuernavaca; Edward and Chandler would join her there the next day. That night, Pepe entered Tina's bedroom barefoot, as thin as a boy in his pajamas. He just lay down by her side, a strangely pure and quiet presence. She made the first move by taking him in her arms.

"Come to me."

They saw each other at El Buen Retiro, and at the homes of their friends. Charlot was the only one who looked at them with suspicion. Monna, usually so perceptive, detected nothing. Pepe sang Tina serenades that Weston, thinking they were meant for the neighbors, would hum the next morning. Tina and Pepe were very cautious. When Weston closed himself in the darkroom, Pepe flew to Tina's bedroom, fear oozing from every pore.

Pepe had an indefinable quality that excited Tina.

"You are the most romantic person I have ever known; you are a boy, a child. You are a messenger of grace."

No man had ever treated her with so much admiration while demanding nothing of her in return. Pepe could sit contemplating her for hours, running his long, delicate hands over her thighs, her hips, her breasts until she could bear it no longer.

"Not just your hands. You."

She wanted to possess him, make him hers, feel him tremble.

His concern for her was infinite. "Did I hurt you? Do you like that?"

There was no battle here. "I love you, Tina, I have never, will never love anybody as I love you."

He remained inside her for a long time; thus he prolonged the afternoon, the summer, thus he forestalled death. Then he sank, clinging to her body. She held him and they closed their eyes.

Powys said the body is like a flowering branch, the essence of life. Tina took large bites of Pepe's flesh; she was giddy as she mounted this white youth, and sank, sank to the very bottom.

"Nobody knows you better than I do. You are mine, Pepe, my lover, my son. You are me."

In an unfolding of wings, they wrapped themselves around each other without ever weighing the other down. Even in bed, all was lightness. Then, in a flapping of those same wings, they separated. Pepe left for Switzerland, but he promised to come back to the great whirlwind, to the heat that set their cheeks aflame in the quiet afternoons. "Tina, I shall return. You can be sure of that. I shall always return."

"I won't let you forget me."

The next news Tina had of Pepe was the telegram.

1 9

During collectivization, the kulaks kill hundreds of thousands of heads of cattle in defiance of the government's agricultural program. Horses, sheep, and goats go to the slaughterhouse; anything rather than support the kolkhoz, the communal farm. Meat becomes a fond and distant memory. Throughout the country, the radio and newspapers extoll the virtues of rabbit meat. A manual is published describing methods of raising and preparing rabbit. The Soviet Union consumes rabbit for breakfast, lunch, and dinner: rabbit au jus, roast rabbit, fried rabbit, marinated rabbit, stewed rabbit, ground rabbit.

The authorities soon realize that the fur is being wasted, and suddenly there are rabbit-skin hats, mittens, scarves, and blankets. The daily sacrifice of the rabbit is a direct order from the Supreme Soviet. Only a monument is needed to complete the canonization of the rabbit.

In the field next to the building where Vittorio works, the

comrades begin with two hundred and fifty rabbits, which, given their natural fertility, quickly multiply. One Sunday, Vittorio and his comrades go out to the country to cut grass for the rabbits. It takes two hours for the old truck to travel a distance that should have taken one hour. They return in good spirits, seated festively on piles of feed, while Vittorio sings and passes a bottle of vodka around.

When Monday comes, Vittorio goes to work as usual, but he finds the offices deserted. His comrades are clustered around the rabbit cages, looking at hundreds of rabbits lying on their backs with their legs in the air. As they dig the mass grave, Vittorio cannot refrain from making a joke. "Thank God for that miraculous grass, at least we won't have to eat rabbit for a while!"

Dashkova, the administrative director, looks at him with hatred. "This is sabotage, and you are responsible."

"What?"

"You organized the outing, and you chose the grass."

Vittorio is about to throw a dead rabbit at her head, but he decides instead to keep digging. Besides having no sense of humor, the tall, fat Dashkova is easily roused to anger. After the burial, she calls an emergency meeting.

The rabbit hutch remains empty until Vittorio offers to dismantle it. This arouses renewed suspicions. Dashkova looks at him as if he had the plague, and every time she walks past him in the corridors of the Comintern, she turns the other way as if to avoid infection.

Vittorio is a member of the Comintern (along with two other Italians, Palmiro Togliatti and Luigi Longo), but he gets angry and says and does things that nobody else dared. "That can't be tolerated!" he would exclaim, pounding his fist on the table. He's been like that since he was a child: rough, exuberant, incorrigible; as a schoolboy he was considered a delinquent. He'd never accepted authority. He went swimming in the Gulf of Muggia when he was supposed to be in school, and skipped barefoot over the rocks of Carso. He showed his prowess by going out into the bora, a wind which would carry off houses, but which the boy withstood heaven only knew how, looking straight into it, his little face a steel mask, his body as immovable as stone. He was like a gang leader, and other rebellious children followed him. At the age of seventeen he did not hesitate to storm into the Trieste government palace, pistol in hand, to raise the red flag and proclaim that the free territory of Trieste was at war with the Austrians. As a boy, Vittorio stole fruit, but he felt completely justified when the three anarchist Curet brothers in Muggia explained to him that "private property is theft," that anarchists expropriate from the bosses and don't take orders from anyone, not even God. As a professional agitator he found it exciting to be wanted by police forces around the world: the U.S. police, the Mexican police, the Cuban police, the French police. He was indignant at the violence perpetrated by Latin American governments against their own starving peasants, at the outcast condition of the indigenous people uprooted from their pre-Hispanic past, and the extreme poverty of the miners in the copper, mercury, lead, silver, and zinc mines, condemned to extract the wealth of the earth for the vulgar, cruel tyrants supported by Wall Street: the Somozas, the Vicente Gomezes, the Trujillos, the Ubicos. His goal was to get the people to rise up in arms and squash individuals like Gerardo Machado as if they were cockroaches. Here in Moscow he fought ferociously against bureaucracy, and since he talked in a loud voice and offered his opinion without paying attention to whom he was giving it to, many people detested him.

Vittorio and Tina still don't suspect how many complaints and accusations have been lodged against Vidali to the Central Committee.

Vittorio is better off doing work as an agent on one of his many missions abroad than he is in Moscow. Except for his trip to Germany, his missions are always successful. He comes back charged with enthusiasm.

He has traveled often to Barcelona, Madrid, and Asturias to encourage uprisings and protests. He speaks about Marx, Engels, Lenin, and Stalin; he lectures to the workers about the evils of finance capital, industrial capital, the Church, and the army. No mission has fascinated him as much as Spain. He returns to Moscow pleased with the progress of the workers' movements, especially among the miners. But he also warns Yelena Stasova that the Spanish right is the strongest in all of Europe.

Europe is terrified of the Bolsheviks and their Revolution. In Germany, the Krupps, Thyssens, Daimlers, and other magnates finance Hitler and Mussolini and begin to send money to the party of the Spanish Falangists, founded on October 9, 1933, by José Antonio Primo de Rivera. Primo de Rivera vigorously opposes Republican parliamentarism and any move toward socialism. In reality, there is only one unified European regime, that of the bankers, clerics, the military, and the feudal rural structures supported by the courts of the landowning aristocracy. In Spain, the clerics and monarchists unite against the Republic. Anti-clericalists attack convents and burn churches. In Barcelona, Vittorio watches a man desecrate a statue of the Virgin with a pickaxe. The aristocracy is shocked at the Republic and fears the expropriation of lands and the dismantling of the entire social system which serves them so well.

For most of 1931 and 1932, the majority of Tina's missions take her to Czechoslovakia, Hungary, Sweden, and the Baltic countries. Between missions Tina visits factories, addresses the men and women of Red Aid, speaks in a German sprinkled with a few words of Russian about the need to liquidate the kulaks, and repeats Stalin's words with fervor: within her bosom shines a red star. She discounts the imperialist attacks she reads about in the foreign press with a vehemence that surprises even herself. So much passion in such a small body attracts the workers. "The Party is the superior form of the proletarian class." "Nothing outside the Party." "Destroy the old and build the new." "We must move from the individual exploitation of the peasant to the collective exploitation of agriculture." "Victory will be achieved by any means necessary, by doing away with those who do not work and who get rich off of others' labor." Like Stalin, she condemns the bourgeoisie and the petite bourgeoisie.

When a French delegation arrives, she wins them over to Moscow and the Soviet Union: her power of persuasion is enormous. Tina sees how impressed the capitalist bank presidents are by the paved streets, the newly planted trees, the recently built houses, the nursery schools and child-care centers. Tina listens to their exclamations and is filled with adoration for Joseph Stalin. There is no doubt about it: this is a great country, a country blessed with soul and idealism and full of hopeful youth.

Yelena Stasova has come to trust Tina more than any other

agent. At the end of 1932, after having proved her competence, Tina is given a mission to take funds to the comrades in Spain.

"Irún, Comrade Modotti, Irún is your destination."

Tina does not come back when expected. Vittorio is worried as he waits for her in Moscow. Though she departed in high spirits, she finally returns demoralized and angry at herself. She was arrested and spent two days in jail in Irún, refusing to undress for fear that the jailers would discover her unusual girdle. She showed her Guatemalan passport and pretended to be a tourist.

"If you are a tourist, why didn't you visit the museums instead of knocking on the door of Party headquarters?"

"I was lost. Anyway, one doesn't travel only to visit museums. If you must know, I saw a very good-looking man go in there. It was purely feminine curiosity."

"You were also seen with Serrano, a known Communist."

"How would I know who he was?"

Tina, by now a professional revolutionary, used all the ploys she had learned on her other missions. She was released from jail after two days for lack of evidence. Her excellent Spanish and her sweetness saved her.

"You sing when you speak, señorita," the judge said admiringly.

"That's how we talk in Central America," she said, flashing her best smile. "You really must visit the Mayan ruins. I extend a personal invitation to you."

Irún, with its plaza surrounded by iron benches and its neatly pruned trees, reminded her of the small towns in Mexico. Even the loudspeakers hung on corner lampposts were familiar: here as in Mexico, the radio was God. Tina felt at home. Spaniards made a commotion, turned a conversation into a shouting match at the slightest pretext.

Taking extra precautions, she changed her return route to Moscow. From Irún, on the border with France, she took a bus, then trains instead of a plane. Thus, her delayed return.

Back at the offices of Red Aid, Stasova is understanding. She says to Tina, "The Party would approve if you want to do some photography, comrade."

"I don't think I can, it's been so long," Tina says and smiles sadly.

"You have been living under constant pressure since you came to us. I think you need a rest. I am going to make sure you get some time off as soon as your workload lightens."

In Germany, especially Berlin, the military forces goose-step for hours in endless parades and the population comes out en masse to cheer them. After dark, the Nazis continue their triumphal marching by torchlight. "Heil Hitler!" The German Communists have gone into hiding. Tina wonders what has happened to Chatto and Thaelmann and her other friends.

On February 27, 1933, the Reichstag goes up in flames. A twenty-five-year-old Dutch worker, Van der Lubbe, confesses that he acted on his own when he set the fire. The Nazis use the fire as an excuse for unleashing a fierce attack against Communists. Ernst Thaelmann is arrested. The Nazis also arrest the Bulgarian Georgi Dimitrov, a distinguished member of the Comintern.

The burning of the Reichstag ultimately results in a Nazi victory in the elections, and on March 5, 1933, Hitler receives forty-four percent of the German vote. Four days later, the trial against Dimitrov begins in Leipzig.

Word of Tina's and Vittorio's successful missions reaches the IV Section of the Red Army, the Secret Service. General Kliment Y. Voroshilov, in command of the border with China, proposes that they leave International Red Aid for a year and join the Soviet espionage service in China. In Beijing, they would reinforce a group led by Richard Sorge. The Secret Service particularly needs someone like Tina: photographer, polyglot, and translator.

Vittorio says they will give their answer in a few days.

Once they are alone, he explains to Tina, "If we join up with Richard Sorge, we will be agents of international espionage."

"We already are, but the counterespionage front is the most dangerous. I'm interested. We have a lot to learn from Sorge."

"So you think we should accept, Tina?"

"I'd do anything not to sit in an office between Red Aid missions."

"And you think you are qualified?"

"I meet all the requirements, and to tell you the truth, I like the idea."

How far his woman has come! If he had been more observant, he would have noticed the fanaticism in her eyes. He realizes that Tina speaks with absolute conviction about the dictatorship of the proletariat, the class struggle, the authority of the Party, internal contradictions, and the triumph of socialism, and constantly repeats that one must always be on guard because the Soviet Union is surrounded by enemies. During hours of loneliness and struggle Tina has fought against the petit bourgeois in herself, eliminating Weston's Tina as well as she could. Now her devotion is to the Party. Expulsion or disapproval would have been the end of her life. "I have to force myself to believe," she would repeat during that first year. She was incapable of listening to any kind of criticism; she wanted to be an extraordinary Communist. Vittorio himself was surprised to hear her say: "I am convinced that the saying 'The Party is always right' is correct and necessary."

In light of Tina's enthusiasm, Vittorio lets Voroshilov know that they both agree to go to China. Before leaving, they will go to Foros, a resort town on the edge of the Black Sea, for a vacation ordered by Yelena Stasova and will maintain the discretion that Voroshilov demands.

Sebastopol rises before Tina under a glossy sky embraced by the deep blue sea. The sun shines down on the enormous square filled with people taking a stroll. Vittorio and Tina walk arm in arm. Vittorio forgets that he has not slept for weeks and that he is suffering from lumbago; the sea spreads out before him and soothes his spirit. All afternoon, he shows Tina the sights. From the bay, they climb up the hill overlooking the port and enter the enormous dome of the planetarium, on whose walls is depicted the Battle of Sebastopol, an exhaustive miniaturized reconstruction of the armies and their respective positions on land and at sea. Tina smiles.

"It looks like a huge Mexican ex voto, and just as naïve."

Foros brings them peace and repose. The sea, always the sea: the sea of her infancy, the sea of her obsession, the sea of Julio's death. They walk along the promenade with their faces turned toward the salt air. They visit Maxim Gorky's house. Vittorio has never read Gorky, but Tina has, and she remembers him well: "If the enemy will not give up, he must be destroyed."

In the mornings, Tina and Vittorio go for a walk or sit in their canvas chairs and watch the waves breaking on the beach. Vittorio reads *Izvestia* and sometimes translates for Tina. He also looks through *Krasnaya zvezda* and the magazine *Proletarskaya revolyutsiya*. They return to the promenade after lunch and again before dinner. In the dining room on the second night there, Vittorio points out a small man dressed like a peasant, his austere face surrounded by red hair.

"That is Lev Kamenev, one of the heroes of the October Revolution."

Vittorio introduces himself to the old Bolshevik. From then on they sit together whenever they meet in the dining room. Kamenev's face lights up when he sees Tina, and he offers her a seat next to him. Kamenev is modest; he thinks out loud, expresses his opinions clearly, and is very curious to hear those of others. He speaks with Tina in French about Mexican mural art; he asks questions and listens to her answers attentively. "He knows a lot, he is very cultured," Tina remarks. However, Kamenev evades Vittorio's questions and refuses to comment on the dissensions within the Party. Afterwards, Vittorio tells Tina that Stalin always remained silent whenever Kamenev spoke. Next to him, Stalin had nothing memorable to say.

Stella Blagoeva makes a fourth at the table. She is more open than Kamenev; she is disgusted with the Nazis and obsessed with Hitler's rise to power. "How is it possible that the Germans idolize him?"

Blagoeva's vehemence contrasts sharply with Kamenev's reserve. He seems to resent Vittorio's and Stella's voices and does not mention the burning of the Reichstag or the Bulgarian leader Georgi Dimitrov, now a prisoner in Germany. He stares at his plate and waits to resume his conversation with Tina. She asks herself if it could be true that Kamenev led the Revolution alongside Lenin and Stalin, if a man who was once a guiding light of the masses can turn into a shadow who asks her questions about Mexican murals. He invites her to join him for coffee on the terrace where they can look out at the sea.

In the middle of March, Vittorio receives a summons to leave Foros immediately and return to Moscow: Dimitrov's trial has begun, and he is urgently needed. "You see, I told you," Stella says proudly. That last night in Foros, they drink a toast with Georgian wine, to the liberation of Dimitrov and his comrades, Popov and Tannev.

Before leaving the Crimea, she has an argument with Kamenev. "The purges are good," she affirms with blind faith. "The hypocrites, the enemies of the people, the moral delinquents, the bourgeois degenerates must be eliminated. The trials must continue. The Revolution is more important than any individual."

Even Kamenev is taken aback. Tina insists. "During a revolutionary process, traitors deserve to be hanged." Kamenev's face shuts down completely. Later, Tina wonders if it was right of her to speak with him every evening. "I should not have responded to his attentions. Even in 1915, Lenin said that his behavior was not fitting for a Social Democratic revolutionary." She forgets Kamenev's warm face gazing at her, his finesse, his gift of conversation around the samovar, the glasses of tea served with doses of refined intelligence. She must rid herself of any internal counterrevolution. Conversing with Kamenev was an error; the proof is in her sadness.

Tina and Vittorio arrive in Moscow a few days later; it is a white night, so luminous that one can read in the middle of the street. "I have never seen Red Square look so beautiful," comments Tina, "and perhaps I shall never see it like this again."

"Stasova is furious," Vittorio says. "She has summoned us."

Without any preliminaries, her voice and expression as cold as ice, Stasova announces: "Your little trip to Shanghai has been cancelled."

They look at her in shock.

"There's no need to pretend. I know that before you left for Foros you received an offer from Voroshilov and you agreed to work in China, without telling anybody, not even your old friend, Yelena Dmitrievna Stasova.

"I am not going to reprimand you for what you have done," Stasova continues. "When I found out, I wrote to Voroshilov in the Crimea. He cabled back that you were both released from your commitment."

She holds the cable in her hand. They are silent. Vittorio is clearly ashamed.

"But I have another proposal," she continues. "In Paris, Marcel

Villard is organizing a group of lawyers. An 'alternative trial' has begun in London to prove the innocence of Dimitrov and the other Bulgarians and the guilt of the Nazis in the burning of the Reichstag. You, Vidali, will be in charge of the Paris branch of Red Aid, and Tina will help you lead the campaign on behalf of Georgi Dimitrov."

Vittorio gives Stasova a hug.

"Good, now go see Abramov; you will leave early tomorrow morning."

Vittorio gets the shivers every time he sees Abramov—the man in charge of false documentation. Bald, pale as a corpse, he has white puffy hands like dead fish, and bad breath. He stares at Vittorio and barely moves his lips as he speaks.

"I hope you are aware of the enormous organizational responsibility it will entail to transform this section of International Red Aid into a true political body. Don't forget that all major decisions will be made in Moscow. We will also set up another department, a clandestine operation, to help the persecuted and undocumented."

"Bene, bene," Vittorio agrees.

"Since when have you two known Comrade Lev Kamenev?"

"We met him two weeks ago."

"And Citizen Blagoeva?"

"I've known her for a few years. Comrade Modotti had never seen her before. Why do you ask, Comrade Abramov?"

"The two of you had numerous conversations with them. I must warn you that on this new mission you must be very cautious. Paris is a den of espionage and counterespionage, provocateurs, informers, double agents trained to infiltrate our organization, professional saboteurs. They are so efficient that some have already made it to Moscow. We have, of course, identified them."

Tina listens approvingly.

"We need some new photographs of Comrade Modotti; you will receive your passports tonight."

He offers them his puffy hand and looks over their heads while saying goodbye.

"I hope we never have to see Abramov again," Tina admits to Vittorio.

When the two of them reach the street, Tina instinctively turns her head: they are being followed. Not even in the Crimea did they go unnoticed. All their conversations with Kamenev have been reported. She recalls the shrewd and sensitive look in his eyes. Is it possible that a man like that could be a traitor?

That evening, Vittorio returns to the Soyuznaya with two passports: one from Costa Rica for Tina; the other one, from Spain, for him. "It's so badly done I should return it," he says.

The prospect of shaking that hand again is even more repulsive to him than the passport; anyway, Vittorio can work miracles with any document.

They travel separately and by different routes. Tina goes via Prague to drop off urgent documents at the offices of Red Aid, and Vittorio takes a direct flight so he can immediately legalize his residence in France.

Once her mission in Prague is over, Tina feels extraordinarily confident. She loves traveling alone, her sole companions on her missions her black jacket and her little bag.

While Tina is delighting in her newfound sense of mastery, Vittorio has to deal with the mountains of paperwork to which the French government subjects foreigners. After leaving his luggage in the Le Bihans' apartment on the outskirts of Paris, Vittorio makes his way to the police station. Through the window of the train that connects Paris to the suburbs, he can see many houses with blinds drawn, like closed eyes on dead faces. There are no leaves on the black branches of the trees. One gray wall after another, one sidewalk after another; the train platforms, like the tracks, go on forever. People get on and off the train without raising their eyes. In the police station the foreigners also keep their eyes lowered. Men and women stand in line, hoping to receive their residence visas, permis de séjour.

"It is written here," the typist points out, "that your name is Julio Enrique and that you were born in Guadalfara. Please tell me which is your first name, which your last, and where in Spain is Guadalfara."

"My first name, mademoiselle, is Julio and my last name is Enrique. You're not the first one who doesn't understand that Enrique is my last name. But everyone has the right to be as ignorant as they wish and doubt things even if they are printed on official documents and stamped by the authorities. As to my birthplace, it is Guadalajara, not Guadalfara. Some worker in Madrid replaced the 'j' with an 'f' and left out the 'a.' "

The secretary copies faithfully. Vittorio curses Abramov to himself. "Imbecille, disgraziato, cretino di merda, what, you want them to shoot me?"

But the policeman who also looks over the documents is not so easily convinced. "What is this ridiculous name? And what do you want to do here in France anyway?"

"Look," Vittorio responds with the same haughty tone, "this is not the first time I have been in France, and nobody has ever made fun of my first or last name before. I am a history professor, and I like Paris. Are you satisfied?"

The secretary is giggling. "I have a friend who is called Liliana Felipe, and she is very pretty. She sings and plays a twelve-string guitar."

"You just do your work," the policeman growls at her. "Who asked you to count strings?"

Vittorio receives his permis de séjour thanks to Odette, the typist. When Tina arrives later that day, Vittorio acts out for her the scene at the police station. When he imitates Odette's giggles, Tina laughs. He realizes that he hasn't heard her laugh in a long time. He takes her by the hand. "Come on, let's go to Montmartre. We have a free afternoon."

Hands with Marionette (Mildred from "The Hairy Ape"). Tina Modotti, 1929. Courtesy the Museum of Modern Art, New York. Gelatin silver print, 9 1/2 x 5 3/8 in.

2 0

In Paris, despite the heavy demands of her job, Tina rediscovers some long-forgotten pleasures. The most beautiful thing about Tina is her body, still a fresh sprout, a flower in the breeze. When Vittorio sees her naked, he says, "After they made you, they threw away the mold." Tina laughs. "What do you know? You know nothing about art." "You are still as lovely as ever," he asserts. "Hey, listen, I'm only thirty-six, just four years older than you." Vittorio doesn't know the Song of Songs, but Pepe Quintanilla used to quote from it when he spoke about her belly, "like a heap of wheat set about with lilies"; about her two breasts, "like two young roes that are twins." Tina holds Vittorio's shoulders, encircles his wide torso, and tells him, reciting by heart, "My beloved is white and ruddy, the chiefest among ten thousand, his locks are bushy and black as a raven; his cheeks are as a bed of spices; his belly is bright ivory overlaid with sapphires."

Vittorio would silence her. "Ma tu sei matta?"

To have a child, to let her body be the vehicle for another's existence—Tina had never thought about it before, not with Robo, not with Weston, who already had his own. She never mentioned the possibility to Xavier. The only topic between them was Lenin, Stalin, the Party, the mechanism of the struggle. Julio Antonio didn't get her pregnant, either. But Vittorio, in his playful and carefree way, talks about pushing their bambino in a baby carriage through the streets under the noses of the secret police, about hiding propaganda in its diapers and meeting up with other agents and their bambinos in the Luxembourg Gardens. Vittorio already has one child. In Moscow, Paolina Hafkina gave birth to his daughter and named her Bianca, for Vittorio's mother.

In Mexico, God's generosity is measured by the children He gives. All children are children of the sun. For María, Tina's neighbor in Tacubaya, her kids were the prolongation of her self, a mixture of entreaty and pride. From the moment of conception, the gods had transferred to María their powers. It is said in Mexico that a woman kneads her offspring inside her like the gods creating the first man out of cornmeal. Tina remembers the bundle in María's belly, then the bundle in the tiny coffin. "Don't cry, Señorita Tina, don't take the glory away from my little girl, my little queen, Reina." When she died, Reina invigorated the cosmos, giving a different meaning to the sky and the earth. "It's so easy to have a child. You'll see, Tina, they simply start to grow inside of you."

Of all Tina's sisters, only Gioconda is a mother, and she stayed in Udine to wait for the father of her child to return, a passing soldier who probably did not even know what he left behind.

The first thing to do was ask Germaine Le Bihan to recommend a gynecologist. She would even stop smoking during her pregnancy.

"Is something wrong? Why do you want a doctor?" Germaine asks.

"Well, just for a checkup."

"We Communists are so poor that when we're sick we go to the Hôtel-Dieu. If you want, I'll go with you."

"No, no, I'm a big girl."

At the Hôtel-Dieu, Tina has a gynecological exam.

"Your uterus is undeveloped, almost like a little girl's."

"But I menstruate, Doctor."

"That is not conclusive. A womb like yours cannot carry a child. It could be a genetic condition."

213

"Genetic?"

"If you have sisters, they may have the same problem."

"So, I cannot carry a child?"

"No, it is physically impossible."

Germaine sees her sadness when she returns.

Tina reassures her. "I'll feel better in a few days."

When she tells Vittorio, he doesn't flinch. "If you want, we can adopt a little black baby when we're old. Or a Chinese or Japanese baby. We'll order one from Sorge; he'll get us one."

Vittorio is immersed in the Committee for the Defense of Dimitrov and travels regularly to London in support of the "counter-trial." In Paris, he reports to Marcel Villard, Jacques Duclos, and his team of liberal lawyers. Vittorio never flinches and finally, in July, the counter-trial in London establishes Dimitrov's innocence.

On December 28, 1933, the trial of Dimitrov and his two comrades concludes in Leipzig with a not-guilty verdict. Dimitrov insists that Goering is responsible for the burning of the Reichstag. Democratic forces all over the world watch the encounter between Dimitrov and his judges with excitement. Absolved! This victory livens up the New Year's party at the Le Bihans' house. Henri hugs Vittorio. "You helped rescue him from the claws of the Nazis."

Conspiratorial life is oppressive. Some comrades irritate Tina with their "Is everything ready, comrade?" as they rub their hands together, waiting for the international revolution to explode any minute. Tina is silent, but it is a great effort for her to be prudent while observing other agents who distrust everybody and are sensitive to the point of hysteria. To the rigidity of their conduct, they add the enigma of their lives. They lay traps for one another, then watch each other fall. Their authoritarianism comes from the Soviet Union. All sins of bourgeois morality must be denounced. Drinking one extra glass of wine is a crime.

One afternoon, Tina becomes the object of criticism. "Why do you have that vice, comrade?"

"Which?" Tina asks, surprised.

"Smoking. You smoke like a chimney."

From that day on, Tina tries not to smoke in public. But she can't do it: smoking is second nature to her. When she is in bed with Vittorio, she lights her last cigarette of the day and then her first in the morning before even going to the bathroom. She wonders how other Communists accept the heavy liturgy of conspiracy, adapt, set an example, forget their petit bourgeois egos.

In spite of the limitations, life in Paris is stimulating. "Babel, oh Babel." Vittorio smiles as he listens to four or five languages and watches someone else communicating with signs. Tina is no longer moved by tales of persecution. She has heard too many. As she listens, another voice makes itself heard inside her. She does not grow impatient, but her eyes betray a lack of trust as she attends to yet another political comrade exiled for his anti-Fascist activities.

Tina visits the headquarters of the French Communist Party at 120 rue de La Fayette with Germaine and Henri Le Bihan. She likes going to the Secours Populaire and never dreams that she may be commiting an indiscretion. She helps serve a meal to the workers of the CGT, their faces full of frustration. Factories have closed; many are unemployed. Those who work earn less than their parents earned in the twenties.

On February 12, 1934, Tina accompanies Germaine to a Communist-organized march of the Republican Association of War Veterans. Vittorio warns her that, in spite of the crowds, she may be noticed. "Don't do it again," he advises. Tina is disappointed; this is the Paris that makes her feel alive. She has no idea that the newspaper *La Défense* will have a record two years from now of her participation as Comrade Carmen Ruiz Sánchez:

Let us listen with eager attention to a brief and energetic speech by Comrade Carmen Ruiz Sánchez, just arrived from Madrid, who spoke about the 30,000 people arrested because of the Asturian uprising of 1934. "Until the time of their liberation by the Popular Front," she said, "we have fought on their behalf, not just out of a sense of humanity, but also because they have been the best sons and daughters of the Spanish people: José Manzo, González Peña, and all those who are now in the front lines of the fight for a free Spain. In the midst of the storms of this horrible war which it has been our lot to experience, our thoughts go out to Thaelmann and all our German brothers and sisters whom Hitler wants to kill, having first deprived them of their liberty. Long live the struggle of Thaelmann and all the anti-

Fascist prisoners in Germany." An emotional ovation greets the representative of the heroic Spanish combatants.

Tina takes charge of the underground activities of Red Aid in Paris. Orders come from Moscow, but Vittorio is her boss. While the official Red Aid headed by Vittorio negotiates their permis de séjour with the government, Tina hides the political refugees who arrive daily from Rumania, Hungary, Turkey. One has only the shirt on his back, another is having a nervous breakdown, a third is wounded, a fourth wants to rent a cellar and amass weapons. Finding doctors, getting false documents, food, clothes, housing, and listening to tragic stories—this is Tina's daily bread. She protects, comforts, heals. Tina often carries a baby in her arms while she accompanies the family to its quarters.

One day, not knowing what else to do, Tina rents a hotel room for a pregnant Turkish woman.

Vittorio is indignant.

"Who's going to pay for it? You? Out of your own pocket? You cannot make personal decisions in this struggle. You must consult your superiors. Discipline, Tina, remember. Because I am going to have to answer to Moscow for you."

"Did you want me to put her in our bed?" Tina retorts.

"The woman took advantage of your kindness; if she managed to get from Istanbul to Paris, she could just as well have found herself a place to stay. Naïveté and good faith have no place in this work."

"But how could I ask your advice if you're never around? Your absences are growing harder and harder for me. And what am I supposed to think about all these Mimis and Paulettes and Lulus who come around looking for you almost every day?" Tina's eyes flash with anger.

Vittorio returns fire with fire. "Oh, really. Well, you know what your friends used to say about you in Mexico? That you're an expensive whore!"

Tina is paralyzed by a blast of fear. She should not cry, but she feels huge waves crash against her chest. Vittorio has crossed over into poisonous territory. Vittorio contaminates her existence, repulses her. If only she could destroy him with a word, but her tears get in the way.

"Forgive me, Tina, forgive me, I was beside myself. It's this tension we live under, always being hunted—Paris, I don't know. Please forgive me, you know I love you."

Tina rejects his overture.

Vittorio insists.

"No, you're torturing me, Vittorio."

"I lost my head, I'll never say anything like that again."

"Just leave me alone."

That night, Vittorio does not come home to sleep.

Nor the next.

The third day he returns with his head down.

Tina realizes that she has no strength to stand up to him. Two days ago she cried from rage; today she cries because she is unable to reject this rough man. Stasova would understand. They have spoken about patriarchal society. But she and Vittorio are now united in their mission, and Stasova would definitely not accept failure.

On February 26, 1934, Tina receives an order from Moscow: "Go to Vienna immediately to organize the escape of Schutzbund members who are in hiding." The recent workers' uprising in Vienna against Chancellor Dollfuss has been heroic. For four days, they fought defiantly, but when the government ordered artillery to be used indiscriminately against the inhabitants, they retreated. One thousand eight hundred dead, thousands wounded, and thousands of the Schutzbund—the socialist Red Guard—imprisoned. Dollfuss's police continue to search for the instigators.

The next day, on the train to Vienna, Tina reads in the paper that Dimitrov has flown to the Soviet Union and been offered Russian citizenship. The Supreme Soviet prepares a great welcoming celebration. On the other hand, the Dutch arsonist, Van der Lubbe, who had no support, no defense committees, was hanged two weeks after sentencing, on January 10. "Poor boy," Tina thinks. "So alone, so foolish."

Her contact, a man with white hair, will be sitting on a bench at the station and will recognize her. For two hours she searches for him among the rushing travelers until, dead tired, she decides to look for a hotel and come back in the morning.

Tina throws herself on a dusty bed in the Viennese pension.

Her room is long, narrow, not much bigger than a pantry, and cold. Through a tiny window she can see a sign illuminated by the streetlight: Four Seasons Hotel. There are no curtains, no towels, nothing except the drab bed. She tries to cover herself with her raincoat; her eyes close, but her anxiety keeps her awake. "Mamma, I could die here tonight and nobody would find me." A cold shiver passes through her body. She scolds herself: "You are a peasant; you have known hunger, solitude, this is not your first mission. What's gotten into you?" Hot tears stream down her cheeks. In the Party, her capacity to keep her cool under adverse conditions is a subject of admiration. Yelena Dmitrievna Stasova once said: "Tina, we give you the difficult missions because we know you can keep a firm grip on yourself."

What would she say now to her firm grip? Tina goes to the window and looks out. In spite of her exhaustion, some unfathomable excitement keeps her alert. Never, not even as a child, has she believed that the afterlife, if there is one, could offer more than this life. She remembers the faces in Mexico raised toward the Virgin: that terrible faith in the upturned eyes. She turns toward the streetlight. "You are a realistic woman," she reminds herself. "You were always a realistic child. You never thought heaven would protect you. Did you ever even wonder about heaven when you sat in front of your piece of fabric with the clanking of other machines in your ears, shutting you off from any world beyond the factory?"

She feels a dampness between her legs, leaves the room, and walks to the end of the corridor. In the slimy bathroom she realizes that it is blood and she smiles. As she flushes the toilet, her courage returns. "No wonder I feel so depressed," she thinks.

The room no longer seems cold. She stretches her legs out confidently on the gray sheet. Tomorrow she will look for her contact in the Vienna train station. The only clue: a man with white hair sitting on a bench.

In the morning, a number of white-haired men are waiting for the train, but not one is sitting on a bench. She will return the next day. She must not make a mistake.

Tina's days in Vienna are a nightmare, not only because she never finds the Communist Party member she was to see but because she has the very clear feeling that Hitler's power is increasing in Austria as well as in Germany. She returns to Paris, shaken by the strength of the Austrians' anti-socialist sentiment. A worse shock awaits her in Paris. Germaine and Henri Le Bihan tell her Vittorio has been arrested and jailed, then deported to Brussels and summoned from there to Moscow, where he will certainly be subject to severe sanctions. It is unclear whether he is still in Brussels, or already on his way to the Soviet Union, thanks to the intervention of well-known leftists Marcel Villard and Jacques Duclos. France's Deuxième Bureau figured out that Raymond, Julio Enrique, Carlos J. Contreras, and Vittorio Vidali were one and the same Soviet spy.

Tina runs to her office. She locks the doors and windows and begins stuffing the contents of files into the iron wastebasket. She sets it on fire, knowing that if the papers ever fall into the hands of the French secret police, hundreds will be arrested. When Willy Koska unexpectedly arrives, he sees smoke billowing out from under her door. He breaks it down and drags Tina out, who is on the verge of suffocation. Koska puts out the fire and takes her back to Germaine's.

The order comes from Moscow that Tina is to be solely responsible for both the official and the clandestine operations of the Paris office. She is also charged with organizing the International Women's Congress against War and Fascism in August 1934, which will be attended by more than a thousand international delegates. There she meets Dolores Ibarruri, La Pasionaria, for the first time.

Yelena Stasova herself attends the meeting and congratulates Tina. She tells her that in a few months she will be able to return to Russia. She also informs Tina that Vittorio is considered a suspect by the GPU, the Russian secret police, and is under surveillance.

When Tina arrives in Moscow, she finds that a cloud of suspicion hovers over Vittorio: even his friends keep their distance. Before, everybody sought out his company, but now he walks alone. Luigi Longo has accused him of having had "terrorist tendencies" in the past. "I'm walking through a dark tunnel with no exit," he tells her. There is no room for his humor, his antics, his imitations of

219

the peculiarities of the Russian soul when he would tear at his shirt and pull at his hair. There is nobody left to laugh with him.

Lore Pieck, the daughter of the Secretary General of the German Communist Party, Wilhem Pieck, lets Vittorio know that, on top of the Paris failure, Dashkova has again made the absurd accusation that "the Italian Vidali poisoned the rabbits." Nanetti, an Italian comrade and member of the secret police, confides that he has orders to follow him and report his movements to the GPU.

"In order to get your membership renewed, you have to go from hell to heaven, if you ever get to heaven," he tells Tina. "Criticism is abolished. You have no personal opinions. The Party is well informed and has the final word. Next to Stalin, God is nothing." Public sessions of self-criticism and denigrating interrogations are held nearly every day; political immigrants are subjected to the worst kind of bureaucracy and insensitivity.

Tina is sympathetic, yet she repeats what she once said at a Party discussion: "I am convinced that the saying, 'The Party is always right,' is correct and necessary."

On December 1, 1934, Sergei Kirov is shot in the neck in his office in Leningrad.

"One of our own killed him. Nikolaev is the murderer; he was one of his collaborators; he is a Communist," Vittorio says incredulously.

Everybody knew that Kirov was one of the people closest to Stalin: he even spent summers with him on his dacha. The trial is held throughout December behind closed doors. Stalin himself interrogates the suspects. Nikolaev is executed.

Stalin orders a monumental funeral. Tina watches him walk next to the coffin and kiss the cadaver on the cheek. As a result of the assassination, the persecution of Trotskyists, Zinovievites, revisionists, and other enemies of the people has intensified. Zinoviev, Kamenev, and seventeen dissidents are put on trial. Zinoviev is condemned to ten years in prison and Lev Kamenev to five. As it turns out, Lev Kamenev is a Jew. His wife, Olga, is Trotsky's sister.

At the first assembly she and Vittorio attend, Tina is struck by the hostile atmosphere. Everyone is potentially a traitor. Everyone knows deep in his soul that he has been weak, and weakness fills you with secret remorse. Certainly, everyone has something to hide.

The huge hall has become a confessional where a mass of guilty people await their punishment. Repentance is never enough. Comrades repent that they did not correctly understand the theory of permanent revolution; that they abstained from voting or voted for the opposition in 1923; that they underestimated the achievements of the first five-year plan; that they knew somebody who had been accused of Trotskyism. To hold any idea that may be considered suspicious by the Party is reprehensible. Anything that reduces the stature of the leaders is considered a crime against humanity.

Andras Biro, a Hungarian political exile, appears before the commission for his self-criticism session. When they hear the story of his militancy, they praise him. Of course they will renew his membership and will even award him special honors. The audience applauds enthusiastically.

"I renounce my membership."

Silence falls upon the hall. After a few tense minutes, the president of the commission asks him to explain.

"I no longer recognize myself in this party. Any criticism is immediately silenced. The two or three people in power fiercely hold on to their positions and make all the important decisions. Nothing is discussed and nobody knows what really goes on on the inside. This decision has not been an easy one for me to make; I have given it much thought. I am over fifty years old. I have been a revolutionary since I was fourteen. I am sorry, but I believe I will be a better Bolshevik without a membership."

"Members do not leave our party; they are expelled. From this moment on, you will be considered a deserter, an enemy of socialism."

"I will continue to do the same work I have been doing until now; the only difference is that you will not recognize it. I love my country." When he finishes speaking, he makes a bow and walks out slowly.

Tina does not agree with him—he is an individualist—but she admires his courage.

In their room at the Soyuznaya Hotel, Vittorio expresses his concern and Tina comforts him as best she can. The truth is, she is also terrified.

"Request another meeting with Stasova. She loves us; she won't abandon us now."

Stasova agrees to see him. She greets him with a severe expression on her face. Vittorio declares, "Either I go to Stalin or I should be arrested, once and for all, by the GPU."

"What are you saying, you fool?"

"That, if necessary, I will take this all the way to Stalin."

"You foreigners are very different from us Russians."

"Why, because I take things a little less solemnly, because I dare make a joke now and then?"

"I believe you are not aware of the serious nature of recent events."

Vittorio seethes. "I cannot accept being treated as a traitor."

"Go to your hotel and take a cold bath," Stasova tells him.

She sends for him a few days later and, placing her hand gently on his arm, says, "The Comintern, the Profintern, Wilhelm Pieck, André Marty, and Fritz Heckert have all examined your case. The best thing for you to do is leave. Politically," she adds in a friendly voice, "you have done good work in Spain. The Central Committee believes that you are the right person to help the miners in Asturias, which is to become the first Soviet republic in Spain. We wish to assure them of our moral, economic, and legal support; Red Aid has collected money to aid the victims of repression. If you succeed in your mission, you will be exonerated."

Monsieur Charles Duval, a half-Canadian businessman from Quebec, bids farewell to Tina and boards the train with a profound sense of relief.

On December 20, 1934, Tina walks alone through the cold streets of Moscow on the eve of her own self-criticism session. Her boots are as muddy as the streets. Water has frozen in translucent spirals around bare twigs. "That is the closest I'll ever get to diamonds," Tina thinks, enjoying their beauty. The red sun gives no warmth. "It looks like a rotten orange." She suddenly yearns to be on her Mexican rooftop, under the Mexican sun, deadheading her geraniums, catching a whiff of the peppery scent that remains on her fingers.

"It will not be a public session, comrade," Stasova reassures her. "You will only need to prove that you are useful to the Party."

Kamenev had said, "Not having known how to serve the revolution with my life, I am willing to serve it with my death."

At the sessions, a terrible feeling of guilt seems to suffuse the comrades. Self-criticism turns into flagellation. "My crimes against the nation and the revolution are immense." "I kneel down before my country, my party, my people." If terror is the only way to govern, sooner or later, each will have his turn to be interrogated and sentenced.

"Why do they do it?" Tina had asked Vittorio before his own ordeal.

"That's how these Russians are," Vittorio said half jokingly when the purges began. "It runs in their blood. They're always tearing at their souls. Just think about the Romanovs and Rasputin. They seek out the illuminated to whip them. Fanatics, they torture themselves with guilt. But in their own way they are right."

Vittorio then made a gesture as if he were cutting off his head. "That's how to create socialism. You give your miserable ego over to the cause, beat it, blame it until it is utterly degraded, then forget that you ever belonged to yourself. Stalin owns you now. You have donated your amour propre to the Revolution and, more specifically, to the Soviet Union. But Stalin is still right. Life in Russia made no sense before him."

Tina believes just as firmly in authoritarianism. "The people need to be led, corrected, their resistance needs to be overcome, they long to be taught that they will receive compensation for their sacrifices in the future. Collectivization is the only way to build a new world. If the people don't understand, they must be made to understand. Spare the rod and spoil the child." This creed is now Tina's reason for living. She has lost the capacity for joy, even the ability to laugh at herself. Vittorio's jokes seem foolish. One day he teased, "How quickly you have learned the lesson of Bolshevism." She responded with anger: "One does not argue in the Soviet Union."

On her way from the Comintern to the Soyuznaya Hotel, she is obsessed by only one thought: what to say and how to say it. "Never lose your critical sense," Edward used to tell her, but she fears that she has. And, worse, she feels herself at the mercy of an indefensible past.

A message from the Central Committee is waiting for her at the hotel. "Interrogation tomorrow at eight."

" 'Comrades, before becoming a tool at the service of the

masses . . .' No, that sounds too presumptuous. 'I would like to bring up all the evidence against myself.' No, it sounds false. Better would be 'I have experienced a radical change,' no, worse, because my change is yet to be proven. 'There is nobody more aware than I of my errors.' Yes, that is a good beginning, because it is the truth." She clings desperately to the Party. Where would she be without the Party? What would she do with herself if she were not a member of Red Aid? Who would she be?

The next morning, when she walks into the somber courtroom, she sees a secretary with a notebook in her hand and twenty comrades sitting with grave faces; one is the High Commissar and another is the prosecutor assigned to her case. Nobody gives her even a look of recognition. Stasova stares at her own bony hands. The hatred Tina feels is almost palpable. The door closes without a sound: in this section of the Comintern—where Tina has never been before—the doors close silently and the sounds of footsteps are absorbed in the padded funereal atmosphere.

"So, comrade," says a voice in Russian, with measured politeness.

"Comrade Modotti will speak in German," says Stasova.

The faces of her judges look so much alike that they soon blend into one face.

"Comrade, we are listening."

She recalls a different courtroom, in Mexico, where the public, the lawyers, the bureaucrats all bustled about as if in a marketplace. She still blushes when she remembers the impudence of the stenographers who looked her up and down as they wrote. Here, the judges are blind—all violence is blind—and even Stasova, who stares at her hands as if seeing them for the first time, refuses to give her the support of a friendly nod. Tina feels as if she is suffocating. "What should I say?"

"Comrade Modotti, we are waiting."

"May I light a cigarette?"

A bailiff points to an ashtray.

"I was born in Udine and we were always poor; more than poor, miserable," Tina pauses to exhale and takes another puff of the cigarette. "Polenta is what the poor eat in Italy. We ate polenta on holidays. Most days we had only bread and warm water. When my father got home, he would say he had already eaten, so as not to take food from his children."

She tries to swallow but her mouth is parched; she takes a deep breath. Even smoking fails to restore her confidence.

"Udine, which is in the Friuli region, is close to Austria and the factories in Lombardy, a region of social conflict. As a child I used to hear about the exploitation of workers. My father was a mechanic and always worked with his hands. He was also a militant who dreamed about a nation where everybody would have the same opportunities. I remember that my godfather, Demetrio Canal, used to carry me on his shoulders in the May Day parades. He was one of the central figures of socialism in Friuli, and I was proud to be his goddaughter. In Austria they needed cheap labor, and many poor Friulians went there to work. When I was eight years old, my father took us to Klagenfurt, then to St. Ruprecht. We returned to Udine as poor as when we left. We grew up, though I still haven't figured out how children can grow without eating. One brother died at birth: I don't know when. One day my mother simply mentioned that his name was Ernesto, and then never spoke of him again. The day laborers always talked about America, about golden California. Those who had already gone sent back enthusiastic letters and money. My uncle convinced my father, Giuseppe, and he left with my older sister, Mercedes. One by one we followed him. I left in 1913. When I got to America, I worked in a garment factory. I am a machine operator," Tina explains, her voice growing firmer. "I can operate a loom."

There is no response from the hall. Deaf, dumb, blind. What do they want from me? she asks herself. Without thinking, she lights another cigarette.

"Continue, comrade."

She inhales deeply before going on.

"The noise in the factory in San Francisco was not as loud as I remembered it being in Udine; our food at noon was good and plentiful, and I got used to eating meat and apple pie and vanilla ice cream, things I had never even tasted as a child.

"I met an American, Ruby Richey, at the Pan-Pacific International Exposition in San Francisco in 1915. He changed his name to Roubaix de l'Abrie Richey for artistic purposes. I felt an affinity with his aspirations: he painted, wrote poetry, he seemed shy and sensitive. I decided I wanted to marry a man like that. After the wedding, I left the factory. I sewed at home, designed clothes, made batiks, and that's when my first deviations began. I wanted to buy things I saw in shop windows, things like dresses and gloves. I passionately loved the softness of silk kimonos. I performed with a theater group, and one night a talent scout from Hollywood came to see us and said to me: 'You are exactly what we are looking for.' I guess we all like to feel that we are needed."

She looks at her listeners. She must hurry, skip over certain stages. Stasova continues staring at her hands.

"In 1920, I appeared in a number of movies. I was always the harem girl, the villain, the gypsy. I was not seeking commercial success, but I was strongly attracted to a different world, a world less flat and monotonous than the rest of Los Angeles, a world of men and women striving for an alternative to everyday life. They sought it in good music, in different systems of belief, in esoteric traditions from India, Tibet, China. All of us bohemians were trying to be original, different, and the atmosphere in Robo's studio —excuse me, l'Abrie Richey, my husband—was one of freedom. Our friends used to say that our house was like a beacon of light in the middle of the disaster of American modernization."

Her words echo off the cold walls and are thrown back in her face. What can she do to cool off her burning cheeks, calm her trembling lips?

"I wish to confess that when we met at Diego Rivera's house in Mexico, we smoked marijuana. I smoked marijuana, it was natural, everybody did it. Rivera used to say that it gave him the strength to stay on the scaffold for so long."

As she speaks, a series of images flash before her eyes. She sees herself with a dagger between her lips advancing on a set in Hollywood. "Make cat-like movements," the director ordered. She remembers sitting through the long makeup sessions. Now she feels disgusted by bohemians like Margrethe Mather, who does whatever she feels like; Ramiel McGehee, who lives at the mercy of his depression; Johan Hagemeyer, or even Weston: neurotic individualists, self-centered because they live in a country without history, where individualism is encouraged. They could never compare to the rugged comrades who rise each day ready to carry out their duty.

Even Ricardo Gómez Robelo, who came from an impoverished country and devoted his life to encouraging artisans and indigenous culture by rendering homage to Mexico's past, even he could not see beyond his own nose and was consumed by desires. What she wouldn't give to have been a soldier of the glorious Russian Revolution since she was a teenager! She is repelled by her former life. How many hours she wasted in self-regard and voluptuousness!

Her narrative, which seems to fall flat on the judges' ears, unleashes within her a silent phantasmagoria. Images of Edward, Julio Antonio, Xavier, the Chapingo Chapel, Diego painting slowly, as if caressing her with his brush; the men in the streets who followed her; all the men she has had and all she has desired. Yes, she confused her feminine condition with narcissism, delighting in her own body in a way that so fascinated Edward. He helped her discover her sexuality, her dark nipples that would suddenly swell and become erect; she walked with him on the edge of perversion, one foot in what she now considers the abyss. Because it was abysmal that he loved to dress up as a woman to go to parties; kiss her feet, and suck each toe as she recited, "This little piggy went to market . . ." After covering his face with makeup, he would ask her to call him a doll, wanting her to nibble his lips as if they were cherries. It was abysmal that she was excited by her possession of him, that she liked licking the paint off his lips, spitting all over his face, tearing off the skirt he wore that was her skirt, taking off his stockings, shouting out her desire. How could she possibly have lain naked in the sun until she was soaking with sweat, then enter the house and take her man, "Make love to me, Edward, right now, in the middle of the day," without being ashamed that Elisa in the kitchen would hear her groans of pleasure? Edward loved life and loved Tina; he knew how to direct her thoughts, always a bit too scattered. To Edward, sadness was bad for the health. Would the judges understand their cold-water baths on the rooftops, the games, the chasing, biting each other like puppies, licking each other, sniffing each other, outbursts of laughter, Brett at thirteen, Brett and Chandler far from their mother, electrified by the lover, accomplices of their father? Oh, the smell of the earth that rose from the garden, the juice of the zapotes dripping through her young fingers, the guava that imbued the whole house with its aroma.

She would like to tell the High Commissar that she belongs to only one man, that nobody, nothing could console her for Julio's death, that the fact that she did not die when Julio died, that she has not died in thirty-eight years, is enough for her to deserve the Order of Lenin, the red flag, the medal of heroism, any medal they have. What should she say to all these judges, so greedy for her life, perhaps for her body? What would save her? Her pain for Mella's death? What is the key to her redemption? She could imagine them talking among themselves. What love for Mella if they lived together only five months? What love for Guerrero if her life is a rehashing of promiscuities? "Oh, if only a woman could live forever clinging to her lover's hand, allowing him to shield her, to live forever in his shadow!"

Weston would consider this trial outrageous. "What the hell are you doing? These people are insane. No one has any right over you. This is against art, against creation." He would protect her from herself, he would lead her through the streets past all the men who turned their eyes to look at her.

"Comrade Modotti, please be more concrete. It would be better if you answered our questions."

What has she said? Was she thinking aloud? Was she delirious? Now everybody, even Stasova, is staring at her. If she could only behave like Vera Figner, Olga Lyubatovich, or Yelizaveta Kovalskaya, the women who struggled against the Czars, if she could say, like Sofya Perovskaya, the first woman executed for a political crime in Russia, "I feel no sadness for my fate . . . I have lived according to my beliefs; I could not have done otherwise . . . I shall face it calmly."

"When did you begin to participate in the acts of solidarity for Sacco and Vanzetti?" the High Commissar asks.

"I was living in Mexico when they were arrested; it was there that I became involved in activities to support them."

"What exactly was your assignment?"

"Propaganda."

"Do you consider your work satisfactory?"

"Not enough. They were executed on August 23, 1927."

"Did you have any contact with Russian comrades?"

"No. I admired Lenin's and Stalin's party, and I am now proud to live and serve the Revolution . . . to follow the greatest leader of all, Joseph Stalin."

"Continue with your story, Comrade Modotti. Tell us about your expulsion from Mexico. We know that you were accused of attempting to assassinate the newly elected President of Mexico. Did you have any connection with terrorist groups?"

"Never."

"And here in the Soviet Union, have you had any contact with terrorists?"

"No."

"Did you know that Vidali has a terrorist background? Did he ever speak to you about his past activities?"

"He told me only that in Trieste, when he was still a child, he placed a bomb in a shipyard."

"You are not aware of other acts of sabotage he committed?"

"No."

"Have you seen Comrade Vidali armed on any occasion?"

"In Mexico, but everyone is armed in Mexico."

"And now, does he carry a gun?"

"Yes, we keep a gun in the hotel."

Where is this leading? What are they trying to find through her?

"Do you receive letters from abroad?"

"My mother and sisters write me from Italy, and I receive a few letters from friends in the United States."

"That's all?"

"Yes."

"You carry on no correspondence with other militants?"

"I have no activities other than those the Party assigns me; at night, in my room, I prepare my task for the following day."

"Do you talk with foreign militants? You have been working for Red Aid abroad."

"In Mexico, and later with Vittorio in Paris, we had contact with militants from other countries. In Moscow, I meet people only through my work for the Party."

"In your opinion, do the Trotskyites have any hope of taking power?"

"Where?"

"Taking power here, in the Soviet Union, Comrade Modotti."

"Only if they defeat the Soviet Union."

"Does this seem plausible, comrade?"

"No."

"Are you aware of the fact that Trotskyite organizations have reverted to ultra-terrorist methods in their struggle?"

"No, I have never had contact with Trotskyites."

"Are you sure?"

"Yes."

"Comrade Vidali is very familiar with ultra-terrorist methods. He has not taught you any, citizen?"

"No."

"For the moment," the prosecutor says to his comrades at the table, "I have no further questions for Comrade Modotti."

"Would you please tell us in detail about your activities from the time you set foot on German soil in 1930?" asks the High Commissar in a harsh voice.

Tina again sees herself on the black, rainy streets of Berlin. She remembers her militant friends: Smera, Lotte, Chattopadhyaya. Before Tina can answer, the Commissar interrupts her. "Are you aware that Trotsky's defenders have now allied themselves with Germany? Is Trotsky defensible, Comrade Modotti?"

"No. I consider him a traitor."

Tina continues, her voice now so vehement and full of emotion that she fills the chamber with life.

"Tell us about your first missions for Red Aid. Did you know your responsibilities?"

"I knew that to be arrested meant years in jail or death, but I was the right person for the job. Nobody suspected me and with a good passport I could cross borders."

"Who were your contacts?"

"I have no idea. I have never seen any of them again."

"Do you know that Trotsky was planning a coup d'état?"

"No."

"You never talked to comrades who wished to meet Trotsky?"

"Never."

"Are you telling the absolute truth?"

"Absolute. But I don't think any comrades would have said in public that they wished to make contact with Trotsky."

"Do not answer with subtleties, we want only the truth from you. Do you know that the question of sabotage is very important to Trotsky?"

"No."

"Do you know about Trotsky's orders to organize terrorist activities?"

"No."

"Do you know that there is already a terrorist organization in the Soviet Union?"

"No."

"Do you know about Trotsky's ties with Japan and Germany?"

"No."

"What do you think about the achievements of the five-year plan, comrade?"

"They are enormous. The rich peasants have had to back down in the face of overwhelming evidence; heavy industry has been created in this country; in a few years we will have light industry as in the rest of Europe."

At that moment, the prosecutor mentions Vidali's name again. "Don't you believe that the consequences of his carelessness are now obvious? Vidali's arrest in Paris is a result of his personality. Do you believe that he takes necessary precautions?"

"Of course."

"Considering his rather volatile nature, do you think Vidali is imprudent?"

"No."

"I will repeat the question. Does he commit errors, of a day-to-day nature, as a result of his particular character, his way of talking, his need to be noticed?"

"No."

"Don't you believe that he lacks a larger perspective, and that, as an activist, he loses sight of his ultimate goals?"

"On the contrary. I have always heard him give clear instructions, precise analyses."

"Do you think he is capable of determining the real consequences of a particular action?"

"Of course."

"Do you believe in the way Vidali directed the Russian section of Red Aid in Paris?"

"Yes. Everybody has faith in him."

"Faith?"

"Trust, they trust him. He is a born leader."

"Is Vidali afraid of popular movements, general strikes and such things?"

"No, he has always shown signs of political clairvoyance. He does believe that a badly planned strike only frustrates the workers; he says that the specific conditions in a country are decisive for mobilizing the workers."

"Do you believe that there are forces determined to destroy what we have built?"

231

"You are telling me that there are."

For the first time, Stasova interrupts the prosecutor and says politely, "Comrade: Comrade Modotti works exclusively for Red Aid. Her job is to welcome political emigrants, take care of them, and improve their living conditions, find them housing and work."

"Yes, but acts of sabotage are carried out through contacts with other countries. Agents often collaborate with internal traitors."

Tina's bones ache, not so much because of the tension of the interrogation, so harsh and repetitive, but because of her own feelings of guilt. She does not even hear the High Commissar when he says, "That will be all, Comrade Modotti. You may leave."

When she doesn't move, he repeats in a louder voice, "Comrade, the interrogation is finished."

Tina walks to the door with her head down. In the corridor, it seems that everyone is rushing past her. They have so thoroughly emptied her she cannot even savor her suffering. The only thing real is the exhaustion centered somewhere in her belly that makes her stoop as she walks. She has smoked all her cigarettes. The moment she reaches the street, she is struck by the certainty that nothing that is happening to her has any importance whatever; in fact, she is not important. Her ideas, now almost ten years old, exercise some kind of hypnotic control over her: she does not even recognize them as her own. She believes out of inertia. All she wants is to throw herself on her bed.

All night, between dreams, she hears someone screaming. Now, when she awakes at dawn, she realizes that it is she who has been screaming.

Within a week, Tina learns the outcome. They have raised her in the hierarchy; now she is not only a militant but in some way also a leader.

When Vittorio finally comes back to Moscow and goes to the Comintern to report on his mission, Stasova praises him. "Wilhem Pieck, Fritz Heckert, Dimitrov, everyone is satisfied. You will leave again for Spain. Palmiro Togliatti has insisted on your going because you did such good work. Your comrade will join you there later."

In the privacy of the empty street, the only place where she has no fear of being overheard, Tina leans her head against Vittorio's and confides in a low voice, "I'm glad we're leaving."

2 1

Soon after Vittorio leaves for Spain, the VII International Communist Congress opens in Moscow, on June 1, 1935. Miguel Angel Velasco, Hernán Laborde, and José Revueltas arrive from Mexico. Tina greets them affectionately. It's like a dream to hear about Mexico after five long years.

They hold a private meeting with Manuilsky to discuss the situation back home. The atmosphere is charged with enthusiasm. When the heroic leaders of the miners' strike in Asturias arrive, they become the center of attention. Tina inquires about Comrade Carlos Contreras, sent by the Soviet Union. The miners smile. "He's working hard, don't worry, comrade, nothing's happened to him, that man will last a hundred years." In the corridors of the Comintern, delegates from Austria, Germany, France, Spain, and Mexico come and go. Dimitrov's triumphal crossing from Leipzig to Moscow has filled them with hope. The anti-Fascist alliance is proclaimed and the Bulgarian hero is the principal speaker. Georgi

Dimitrov with his clear eyes and his broad forehead dedicates his speech to his comrade, Ernst Thaelmann, imprisoned by Hitler. He defines Fascism as "a terrorist dictatorship of the most reactionary, most nationalistic, most imperialistic elements of financial capitalism; the most reactionary variety of Fascism is German Fascism." Tina applauds furiously.

Throughout June, July, and August, the congress helps Tina forget about Vittorio's absence. She spends her free time with the Mexicans. They love Vittorio and hope to see him later in Moscow. With them she remembers the Mexican miners in Pachuca and Guanajuato. Once she went down into a tunnel with Edward. They saw the Mexicans, all ill with silicosis, sweating in the narrow spaces. They called silver "the white excrement of the gods." In Asturias the miners did not give themselves up to divine providence before going down into the hole. They cursed their bosses, the government, the army, God, the Communion wafer, and exploded with anger, while in Mexico 300,000 men died of hunger without a single complaint. For the Soviets, the burgeoning struggle in Spain is fascinating. They look at Spain as if it is their child being fashioned in their own image; it could well end up as another Soviet republic. Many Russian officials travel to Madrid pretending to be delegates of Red Aid; they promise weapons, technical and ideological assistance, and supplies. Great things are expected of Vittorio Vidali. Tina waits through September, the Congress ends, and she again begins to worry about Vittorio and wonders what would happen to her without him. Stasova says to Tina, "Don't get upset; he's invaluable to us. If anything serious happens to him, we will be the first to know."

Tina tries to be strong and repeats to herself what Dimitrov once said to Vittorio:

> *If you lose your house, you've lost nothing.*
> *If you lose your honor, you've lost a lot.*
> *If you lose your courage, you've lost everything.*

In Spain the repression of the Asturian miners unifies the left and helps the Popular Front, a coalition of Republicans, Communists, socialists, and two labor unions, win the elections. The day after, the peasants occupy lands owned by the aristocracy. In Yeste, near Alicante, the Civil Guards stop the peasants from chopping down "the master's trees." The peasants, armed with stones, pitchforks, and sticks, face the guns. Eighteen die. In Oviedo and in Valencia, the jails are opened and worker-prisoners are set free. The miners are also released from prison.

Spain is ripe for revolution. The peasants seize more and more land and begin to cultivate it with the help of Communist advisors. In the town of Mansalbas, in the province of Toledo, two thousand hungry men take over the El Robledo ranch which the Romanones had seized years ago without giving anything back to the people. The same thing happens with 1,317 hectares in Encinar de la Parra. The workers in eight villages in Salamanca—eighty thousand peasants from the provinces of Cáceres and Badajoz—reclaim the land, yearning to create a future, a new life.

Tina feels that what has been happening in Spain is Vittorio's triumph, so when Yelena Stasova tells her Spain is her next mission, she rejoices. "There will be an International Red Aid Congress in Madrid in July. We will send a message to Vittorio telling him about your arrival. Before the Congress, you are to do propaganda work for Red Aid and distribute the newspaper *Ayuda* in other cities. This mission will be longer than the others. Take your belongings with you. The situation in Spain is unpredictable," advises Stasova as she says goodbye.

In Tina's closet are two skirts, one black jacket, three blouses, and a pair of summer shoes. Her possessions have become fewer and fewer over the past years. She would feel ashamed to be attached to superfluous things.

Her only luxury is the pile of photographs she brought from Mexico. They are carefully wrapped and stored away in the back of the closet. They include the stairway of Tepotzotlán, the sickle, bandolier and ear of corn, the hands of the puppet master, Louis Bunin. She hasn't looked at them since she was in Lotte Jacobi's studio in Berlin, when she organized her show six years before. With whom should she leave them during her absence? The Regents, that's it. They will take good care of the camera and the package. "How easy it is to dispense with a part of my life that I have held on to for six years," she admits.

Tina boards the twin-engine plane bound for Paris. When the plane hits air pockets and suddenly loses altitude, she feels no fear. Perhaps she doesn't care if she dies. For some time she has been watching herself live with a growing degree of indifference. She brings the spoon filled with borscht to her mouth and continues to nourish the body she carries around, which remains strangely detached from herself. The Party is the only thing that keeps her going: each one of her cells obeys, willing to give of itself, even the ultimate sacrifice. "Good work, comrade," Stasova and the High Commissar tell her. "Mission accomplished," and they smile at her. "All the missions assigned to you turn out positively." Even Abramov changed his attitude toward her after the missions in Rumania, Poland, and Czechoslovakia. "Excellent contact element." "Of all our agents, she is the only one who understands right away." "She doesn't make problems." "She is always willing."

She sits next to a window and watches the propeller. She feels almost ashamed of her comfortable, privileged position: others are being interrogated and registered by the border police, while she, flush against the sky, lights a cigarette and leans back in her seat.

In Paris, she will stay with Germaine and Henri Le Bihan at 8 rue Louis Ganne. From there she will take a train to Bordeaux, then to Bayonne, where she will find some way of getting to Gethary, between Biarritz and St.-Jean-de-Luz, near San Sebastián. She will meet her contact in Alfajarín at noon. The code—No encontré llave para esa cerradura—sounds so funny. Spanish. How familiar it is, how warm it feels. She has an Argentine passport: Estela Arretche from Buenos Aires. How does Abramov pick his countries and his names? How does he forge passports? Who is this Estela Arretche whose face looks exactly like her own? Tina sighs. A new life. Her hands rest on her thighs. They, too, are merely servants of the cause, the source of so many of her experiences.

"Here are your new documents," Henri Le Bihan says as he hands her a small package in her room in Paris. Tina sees that she has been turned into an American citizen, a professional photographer born in Madison, Wisconsin. Her name is Rose Smith (how strange, she called herself Rose Smith in Mexico the first time she was arrested). She bids farewell to Germaine and Henri and their little girl, Cecile. Her mail will arrive at their house, which has been a home for her also.

2 2

ina has been to Andalusia, Cordoba, and Granada. On
July 17, 1936, while she is in Granada distributing Red Aid's
newspaper *Ayuda* and collecting information on political prisoners,
she receives a message from Vittorio. "The military rebellion has
taken place in Melilla. I don't think they will be able to cross the
Straits of Gibraltar, we will have time to get mobilized. Francisco
Franco, the general responsible for the massacre in Asturias, is in
command. You should come to Madrid through Jaen, then to La
Mancha, Ciudad Real, Toledo, Illescas."

There is a stillness under the July sun, an air of expectation.
The bus bounces along, going over potholes and shaking up the
passengers, who doze on each other's shoulders. Rows of olive trees
line the highway. "The trees are walking," Tina thinks. Under
tightly pulled scarves, the severe faces of the women traveling with
her are as closed as the mountains that form the horizon. Their
lips and eyes are sunken into their faces like the tiny whitewashed

villages in the landscape. "Spain is so old, and the winds that sweep the plains are so hot!" One of the women opens her eyes: the expression in them is as hard as her features. Tina wonders if she will also go all the way to Madrid. The sound of the motor breaks up the vastness of the landscape. A grenade goes off in the distance.

"How quickly the days pass in wartime; everything happens at the same time, and then, without anyone's feeling it, comes death," thinks Tina.

When they finally reach Madrid, Tina gets off the bus carrying the same small bag she has taken on all her assignments. She has no trouble finding the address Vittorio gave her. She stops in front of a mansion. "The Ganivet house is enormous," Vittorio wrote. He also said that Matilde Landa and Paco Ganivet were devoted to the cause and to him. Their daughter, Carmen, comes down to open the door, and from the balcony a woman shouts to her as if she had known her all her life. "Come on in, the men will be arriving soon for dinner."

The events of the past few days demand quick decisions and immediate action, leaving little time for sentimental exchanges or other pleasantries. Vittorio brings Tina up to date by telling her that the International Red Aid conference has been suspended so the delegates can return to their cities to organize the resistance. Even as Vittorio speaks, the sound of gunfire comes through the window, but nobody pays much attention.

Each person is summarily assigned a task. Paco Ganivet will go to Somosierra with Galán's column; Vittorio will return to the barracks of the Fifth Regiment on Francos Rodríguez Street, where he and Enrique Lister have been creating a fighting force; Tina and Matilde will work at the Hospital Obrero, a private tuberculosis clinic taken over by the Fifth Regiment a few days before, now under the aegis of International Red Aid.

"What will we do there?" asks Matilde Landa.

"Win," Vittorio responds with a smile. "That's what we're going to do: win."

"But, Toietto, what are we going to do, specifically?" Tina insists.

"Nursing, or whatever is necessary. Some of the old patients are still there, but it must be set up to receive the wounded. As of today, you are also members of the female battalion of the Fifth

Regiment. We will teach you to use firearms and pistols, and throw grenades. You may also be asked to carry out special assignments. Tina will certainly continue traveling for International Red Aid." Then he laughs, pulls at Tina's cheek, and whispers in her ear, "And my name is no longer Vidali or Toietto or Vittorio; here I am Comandante Carlos Contreras."

"How quickly he decides everyone's destiny," she thinks. After so many days of slow traveling, her life is resolved in a flash.

"And you and I, where will we live?"

"I will come to the hospital to see you, and you will come to me on Francos Rodríguez."

Tina watches Matilde cover the furniture and draw the blinds to prepare her beautiful home for a long absence. "Who knows if we shall ever return," Matilde says as she takes her daughter's hand. Tina feels light and free, though her heart is beating fast. She is living these moments with her entire being. She will be a nurse, and soon she will find out what that means.

When Carlos Contreras takes Tina to the headquarters of the Fifth Regiment for the first time, she is struck by the atmosphere of euphoria. People don't talk, they shout. Carlos pushes his way through the crowds waiting impatiently at the doors.

Amid the clamor of voices in the barracks, Tina recognizes a familiar Cuban accent and feels a surge of joy. She meets María Luisa Lafita and her husband, Roberto Vizcaíno, and invites them into Comandante Carlos's office.

"How did all of you get here? When did you get here?"

"In May 1935. We left the island when the persecution against the Communists intensified. Now there are twenty-three thousand Communists in Spain."

As she listens to María Luisa speaking excitedly and swallowing her sibilants, Tina thinks, "Julio, Julio, you are with me, you sent me your comrades."

Tina feels as if she has known them all her life. They bring a festive atmosphere to the struggle, as if they have filled the air with pineapples. How is it possible that the war could have given me such a gift! "Chica, here in Madrid there are almost a thousand Cubans fighting for the Republic," says María Luisa, who speaks with her hands and throws her beautiful strong arms in the air. Tina tells them about *Ayuda*, which she distributed in Granada. "You'll see, chica, the director of *Ayuda* is María Teresa León, a wonderful comrade. Her husband is a poet, but he's so good-looking he's a little conceited."

From now on, Tina's life will revolve around four points: the Hospital Obrero in the neighborhood of Cuatro Caminos, the headquarters of the Fifth Regiment on Francos Rodríguez, the International Red Aid office on the Gran Vía, and the Regional Red Aid office on Abascal Street.

Vittorio describes to her the difficulty they had seizing the Hospital Obrero. The nuns stood their ground. "If we have to, we'll shoot our way in," warned the militiamen. They waited, and when there was no response, they shot off the locks. By the time they entered, most of the nuns had fled through the back door, but not before they emptied the medicine cabinets and locked up the medical instruments, taking their keys with them. Nobody has yet managed to break the doors open. A few old consumptives, who watch everything from their beds, were left behind.

When Tina arrives at the hospital for the first time, an old revolutionary and a member of Red Aid, Isidoro Acevedo, advises her to change her name.

"What should I call myself?"

The old man looks through lists of volunteers.

"How about María? It's a common name and easy to remember."

"I like María. In Mexico they call the women who beg on the streets Marías."

"You are registered here as María Sánchez, then. What do you think?"

"Good. Sánchez is also a common name."

When Tina first hears someone addressing her as "María," it is pleasing to her ears, and she responds immediately and quite naturally. María on the stair and in the corridors; María in the operating room; María in front of the large dusty gray windows that need to be washed; María in the midst of this chaos of a hospital. Everyone knows that an operating room has to be sterile. So where are the buckets and mops, where are the medicines, the cots, the linens, the X-ray equipment, where, you cursed nuns, where? The wards are numbered 1 to 10, and each one has twenty-five beds. What a relief not to be Tina anymore!

On the walls of the consulting room are two pictures: a photograph of a nun with a shadow on her upper lip, and an image of St. Francis de Paul. Matilde Landa walks in and turns them toward the wall. She also removes the crucifixes from the wards.

"To the trash."

"There aren't going to be enough beds," Matilde warns. "We're going to have to fit more in here."

"I'm going to find some soap and rags."

"Leave that to the others, María; the girls who have no experience can begin with the cleaning."

"I don't have any experience either, and I want to be useful."

"Listen, don't underestimate yourself," María Luisa adds. "You'll have plenty of opportunities to wear yourself out."

The dispensary, the X-ray room, and the treatment room look very dirty.

"And just think: all the single women in Spain are nuns! More than sixty thousand women have taken vows."

"So how do the Spanish reproduce if everyone's a nun?"

Matilde ignores the question and looks out the window. She sees a garden and some huts in the corner.

"What are those for?" Matilde asks.

"For contagious diseases. Down there is the washing machine, the most modern one in Madrid. The hydrotherapy department, which has never been used, and the radiology department are also there. This hospital costs eight million pesetas and is one of the biggest in all of Europe. Look at the size of the wards. This leads to the main chapel; the sewing rooms and the nuns' rooms surround the chapel, connected by a circular corridor," answers Juan Planelles, director of the hospital.

María Luisa Lafita cannot stifle an exclamation of astonishment when she enters the chapel, which is as large as a church and sumptuously adorned.

"It's all going to have to go," says Planelles. "We need this area for the wounded. In the cellar, there is a cart on wheels that takes the dead to the morgue. The kitchen is also in the main building. The operating room is so large that three operations can be performed at once. And have you seen the size of the sterilizer?"

The following evening, Juan Planelles designates Matilde Landa as the political commissar of the hospital.

Mari Valero, another volunteer, asks pertly, "Why do we need a political director? This is a hospital."

"We must maintain vigilance and control over the patients and the nurses. She will also be taking charge of special missions."

The old men watch everything from their beds. Some cry. The wards fill up with new nurses who run around in alpargatas, talking and laughing; war is a party, and they hold hands and dance in a circle. The experienced nurses are not Spanish. Blanca and Anita Muller are Belgian; Carla van der Rijs is a tall, strong Dutch woman always ready to smile. They are the ones who make lists of basic necessities. María Luisa Planelles, the wife of the director and an experienced researcher, settles down in front of the microscope; Angelines and Pedro Dorronsoro take charge of the administration and the budget; María Postigo is the seamstress and is in charge of linens. Encarnita Fuyola offers to carry messages to the barracks or do anything else they need. The other girls are peasants accustomed to working from sunup to sundown: for them, these large white rooms are a vacation. Pilarica Espinasa, Candelaria, Remedios, Lola, Angustias, Inmaculada, and Mercedes all have smiles on their lips. "One must communicate to the sick a desire to live." So they sing while they give the old men their sponge baths.

Matilde Landa is the one who has undergone a curious change, or perhaps Tina simply cannot associate her with the housewife she met when she arrived. A few weeks after becoming the political commissar, she also becomes Dr. Planelles's indispensable assistant; he consults her about everything. With her calm face, she inspires confidence. It becomes natural for them all to say, "Let's ask Matilde." Her job is to settle all the conflicts that come up in the hospital. She not only takes care of the sick but also recruits nurses, searches for food, is the first one to get the bad news, and she has complete political responsibility for the hospital.

When the others refused to wear the long bothersome robes the nuns had left behind, claiming they brought bad luck, Matilde put one on and told them not to be superstitious. She parts her hair down the middle and pulls it back into a tight bun. Thin and small, she walks through the corridors as if she were a nun. Mari

Valero, an actress, imitates her and has begun to call her the lay nun. "Individualism and Fascism coincide," Matilde Landa repeats. She criticized Mari Valero for being too flirtatious; she made Tina feel ashamed when she complained that she had left her comb in the bathroom and couldn't find it when she returned. Matilde berated her: "Why do you care about your comb, your stupid little comb, María, when there is war and death?"

In response to the military uprising, the people of Madrid pour into the streets to take over buildings; in their anger they loot shops, break windows, rob houses, and terrorize. The priests run like rabbits, and the militiamen fire at them. They confiscate fuel refineries, electric companies, textile factories, pharmacies, beer factories, printing presses, movie theaters; armed vigilance committees are set up all over. The revenge of the poor is exhilarating to Tina. Splendid old walls are painted over in red: "Seized by the CNT," "Seized by Red Aid," "Seized by the Communist Party." "This is my new home," shouts a youngster, an ax in his hand. Tina takes his arm, not noticing the ax—though if she had one, she'd hold it aloft. When squatters enter the Palace of Liria, which belonged to the Duke of Alba, they are paralyzed by its beauty. Any museum would be proud to own such Goyas, Velázquezes, El Grecos; such tapestries, sculptures, jewelry, rare books, incunabula, the likes of which no national library in Spain has ever seen. "Victory is in our hands!" posters announce in big red letters, along with countless other slogans from countless political parties: there isn't a wall in Madrid that is not plastered with somebody's propaganda.

The leaflets still smell of ink. Buses and streetcars are covered with graffiti, and even benches have been "confiscated" by one or another of the unions or political parties. People run through the streets with no fixed destination, rushing past burned-out churches, and whenever the noise lessens for a moment, the sound of distant machine-gun fire can be heard. Tina joins a group of men and women pulling up cobblestones to build barricades. Sandbags slowly begin to surround the city.

Men and women are recruited in the courtyard of the Francos Rodríguez barracks. The immediate goal is to arm the people and create a united front of Communists, socialists, progressives; anybody who is anti-Fascist can join. About five hundred men receive their marine-blue fatigues, which remind Tina of her Mexican overalls. The biggest problem is weapons. Where are they? What are they waiting for to distribute them? The slow pace of the Republican government is frustrating. In Comandante Carlos Contreras's opinion, Manuel Azaña, the President, is a little rich boy; he has no idea what to do. Some say that Azaña claims that the uprising in Morocco is nothing more than a protest and we must wait. Doesn't he know the military? Are any officers going to be loyal to the Republic? Anyway, why didn't he get rid of the generals he knew would be disloyal? Tina considers Azaña to be deluded, inept, like all the others who want to stop halfway. He doesn't know that the military class is reactionary by definition and must be gotten rid of.

Fifteen- and sixteen-year-old boys, bursting with revolutionary ardor, march around the barracks. Right, left, about-face, halt. The instructor makes them march in columns. He doesn't show them how to load a gun or how to shoot. Rosy-cheeked children demand arms.

Suddenly word goes out: "The chief of police sent rifles to the Casa del Pueblo." The volunteers run down Castellana, then to the Gran Vía, and into the Plaza de España. In the great square Tina watches joyous and combative people, men and women, workers and peasants, beg to be recruited. "When are we going to fight?" "Arms for the Republic." Any other kind of work is rejected. "To the front, to the front, we want to go to the front."

On July 20, 1936, the sound of cannon fire awakens the city. A handful of men and women dragged an old cannon to the walls of the Montaña army barracks. They placed another one near the Plaza de España, aimed it at the fort, and blasted through the wall. A shout of triumph explodes when the white flag is seen.

When the crowds rush in, they are received by machine-gun fire. Enraged by this deception, they push through the doors, tripping over bodies. Some regular army officers throw themselves out windows, preferring to save their honor by committing suicide. The courtyard of the Montaña barracks is strewn with the dead and the wounded. The people of Madrid have taken the Montaña barracks. They pass out magazines for the rifles.

That same night, the inspiring voice of a woman is heard on Radio Madrid: "Anti-Fascists, fellow Spaniards, everyone must rise and defend the Republic and the democratic victories of the people! Communists, socialists, anarchists, Republicans, soldiers, and military forces loyal to the Republic, the first defeats have been inflicted on the Fascists, who are disgracing the tradition of military honor of which they themselves have so often boasted . . . But they shall not pass! I, La Pasionaria, tell you this."

This initial victory encourages the popular army. Vittorio, euphoric, communicates his optimism to Tina. "More than half of Spain is with us. If with five thousand bad rifles and an old cannon we managed this glorious victory, can you imagine what awaits us? In Carabanchel, in Leganes, in Getafe, the people have gone out to the streets and they are winning. Madrid is the heart of the Republican victory. Spain is ours!" Tina, walking beside him, is sure he's right.

Comandante Carlos Contreras's ambition, like that of Enrique Líster, knows no bounds. The armed forces have joined the rebels, the enemy. To oppose them, Contreras and Líster set up the Compañía de Acero, most of whose members are metallurgy workers. Contreras and Líster impose rigid military discipline. "Improvisation is our worst enemy. It's not enough to be willing. We must develop military foresight." The Spanish are brave but they are not good at following orders.

The enthusiasm in the streets is contagious; Tina feels it. The volunteers in their blue fatigues are ready to face death. Khaki and blue are the two predominant colors on the Gran Vía. "Anyone wearing a tie will surely be shot," Tina thinks. The Republican militiamen are so young they look like gangs of schoolchildren playing hooky. "Salud, compañero." "Salud." Everybody talks to everybody else. Everybody is a comrade. People she has never seen before call out to her, "¡Salud, compañerita!" One shouts "¡Guapa!" reminding Tina that she is still a young woman. The soldiers address their officers informally and if they don't like an order, they question it. Most of the soldiers are laborers. Strangers embrace one another, and share cigarettes, bottles of wine, food. Madrid has become a proletarian city.

How different all this is from Paris, where well-dressed people are served by haughty waiters in a world of cafés and sparkling shop windows. Where did all those people go, where are their children who used to be pushed around in prams by nursemaids in uniform? Maybe they have gone off to summer homes in the Costa Brava or San Sebastián. Only the gypsies still beg. Waiters and office boys turn down tips. There is no coal. "What will happen in December when the first snow falls," Tina wonders. "We'll win before winter comes," Comandante Carlos reassures her. "The Republic will triumph in two months. The people are with us, and wherever the people are, so is victory."

When Tina sees the red-faced children on the streets screaming threats at the Fascists and spouting revolutionary slogans, she turns to Vittorio. "They are children. They should be in school. They probably don't even know what the word Fascism means."

"The problem isn't that they are children; it's that there are no weapons," Vittorio says.

"They have no idea what war is about; they don't know what they are getting themselves into," Tina insists.

"They'll learn soon enough," he says.

"And it will cost them their lives. How much are they paid?"

"Ten pesetas a day. Some take food home, and we have to punish them for stealing."

The news on Radio Madrid is very optimistic. In Galicia, popular resistance is enormous; the people of the wheat-growing areas of Castile, Levante, parts of Aragón, Extremadura, Asturias, and Catalonia are on the side of the Republic.

Almonds, oranges, olives, figs. Andalusia, with its cattle and its vineyards, is also Republican. For centuries the land has been cultivated in the same way. Peasants take water from the well, light their way with tapers, carry wood to make fires. They have always led difficult, hard-working lives. Their children have never gone to school and were the first to die during epidemics. Cruel, deaf Spain turned its back on the peasants. Now they are ready to bring their pitchforks down on the head of anyone who defies them. Revolutionary fervor gives them the courage to take revenge on the landowners and their lackeys, the Civil Guard.

Every few minutes, radio programs are interrupted, and a voice is heard giving instructions. "Union members must report immediately to the headquarters of their respective organizations." Nothing better than being recruited by the unions and being issued a weapon. The CNT and the UGT enlist thousands and send them off to victory.

Women, children, and the elderly are digging trenches to fortify Madrid and prevent access by the Nationalists led by Franco. Later the Republicans will complain: "They are too narrow!" "Where are the men going to hide from the bombs? Where are the dugouts?" "When it rains, soldiers will drown in these trenches. You forgot all about drainage."

Photographers and journalists have arrived, especially from France, and they walk through the streets armed with cameras and pens. They complain about the slow, crowded trains. They complain about the state of the streets. At first they settle into the Gaylor Hotel and send their dispatches from there. Not even the telegraph works well in Spain. Spain is still in the Middle Ages.

Mikhail Koltsov, chief editor of *Pravda*, admires the power of Carlos Contreras's optimistic presence, how easily he moves about, how he manages to be everywhere, from the munitions factory to the bakery. He takes care of the food and the schooling; the young volunteers need to learn to read and write, and they have time to do this in the trenches. In the Soviet Union, anti-Fascist reading primers on the front gave good results. Tina sees how Contreras gains authority each day. His gestures become increasingly incisive. He begins to speak Spanish like a Spaniard, and peppers his speech with expletives. "It is the people who fight, the people who form the first units of combat. Their models are their own political and union leaders," he explains. "Are you a shoemaker?" Carlos asks a man bent over in a corner of the courtyard, fixing the sole of his shoe. "You will open a shoe workshop next to the uniform factory."

"This Italian wants to impress the Russians who sent him," Enrique Castro Delgado says. "He's collecting merit points."

"Whatever he's doing, he knows how to command," Vicente González responds.

"The one in command here is the Central Committee of the Communist Party," Castro Delgado continues. "If you're on good terms with it, you'll be a leader; if not, nothing. Carlos Contreras learned firsthand that the strength of Communism rests on discipline; he is a born organizer, even though he is a brute and a womanizer. But his woman, that María, what sadness she carries around! What sweetness! That woman is pure honey. Contreras doesn't deserve her."

Of all the Republicans in command, Tina prefers sweet Manuel Tagueña, who is fighting in the Sierra de Guadarrama, and Juan Modesto. The most popular leader, however, is Buenaventura Durruti, who is scorned by the Communists. He has no military experience and is suicidal in combat, but the people adore him. Tina had heard of him in Mexico because he left his hotel without paying, claiming that private property didn't exist.

Comandante Carlos, hoarse from shouting at those standing at attention in the courtyard on Francos Rodríguez, asserts: "The best army, with the best discipline, the best equipment, and the best weapons, always wins. We shall be that army, thanks to our training and the support from the Soviet Union."

The anarchists and the anarcho-syndicalists don't want armies: they want popular militias. Militarism brutalizes man, turns him into a puppet. Federica Montseny of the Iberian Anarchist Federation, the FAI, declares that the revolt of the army that began in Melilla has sped up the collectivization of the land. When Tina shouts "¡Tierra y libertad!" she is thinking of Mexico's General Zapata, who said the land is for those who cultivate it.

At night, La Pasionaria speaks on Radio Madrid, demanding arms for the workers and telling the women to fight with knives, boiling oil, whatever they have on hand, to defend their dignity. "It is better to die on your feet than to live on your knees. Better to be the widow of a hero than the wife of a coward." Nobody turns off the radio: Radio Madrid will tell everybody what to do; Radio Madrid is the only clear light in the midst of so much confusion.

It's amazing but true: Madrid is still a city with night life. Nobody sleeps. The cafés on the Gran Vía, Alcalá Street, and Puerta del Sol are full of customers despite the bombing raids. People shout from one table to the other. Pietro Nenni is seen with André Malraux and his wife, Clara; across from them are Rafael Alberti and María Teresa León, José Bergamin, Koltsov, Soria, Corpus Barga, discussing the revolution as they sip their wine. It is like one big street party. Cars with red flags honk their way through the crowds. One night, even Comandante Carlos stops at the Hospital Obrero and asks María and Matilde if they would like to go have a glass of wine on the Gran Vía.

In Extremadura, the Monarchists, who are fighting alongside Franco, capture the Republicans of Badajoz, put them in the bull ring, and execute them: one thousand in a day.

The correspondents of *Paris Soir*, the *New York Herald*, and *Le Temps* find bodies in the atrium and at the foot of the altar of the Badajoz Cathedral. The sidewalks are covered with blood and hats. Those who are still alive and manage to escape are turned back at the Portuguese border; when they return to Badajoz, they, too, are slaughtered. The reign of terror has begun.

The only positive outcome of the massacre is the resulting fury of the peasants. The terror has sharpened their anger. They want to avenge their dead daughter, their murdered brother, the body at the foot of the altar, the sister raped by the Moor, because the first thing the enemy does is abuse the women. Tina identifies so strongly with their cause that she feels they are avenging the deaths she has suffered, too.

Queipo de Llano, the Nationalist head of Andalusia, reports on Radio Seville on July 23 that "the Red women have learned that our soldiers are real men, not militiamen; kicking and screaming will do them no good." Listening to the radio on August 18, Tina hears him warn: "Eighty percent of the families in Andalusia are in mourning, and we will not hesitate to implement even more drastic measures."

Franco states to a journalist from *News Chronicle* that he is ready, if necessary, to "shoot half of Spain."

Colonel Barato assures a correspondent from the *Toronto Star*: "We will have established order when we have executed two million Marxists."

The Metro tunnels can hold only one hundred thousand people in case of an aerial bombardment, Carlos warns. "But don't worry. Soon we will have antiaircraft defenses; Russian aid is on the way."

Madrid is full of Falangists hiding in their houses, waiting for the Nationalists to arrive. In the meantime, they are working under General Mola of the Fifth Column. At night, they shoot at the

Republican guards with pistols that make a dry sound like a bottle being uncorked.

In the morning, bodies litter the streets.

Nobody has seen anything.

Tina lies awake.

"That's just the Pacos, the Fascist snipers, the traitors left behind in Madrid," Vittorio reassures her. "We will soon finish them off. They shoot from the rooftops. We know who they are."

War's rhythm imposes itself, the pulse of war in the wrist of the wounded, between Tina's thumb and forefinger: "What can I do for you, comrade, what more can I do?" Her feet take her quickly from one ward to another, then to Francos Rodríguez. "My God, why are there so many people here? Madrid has become a magnet for refugees." Fords and Pontiacs taken from their owners pass by sporting banners with large white lettering: "Militiamen of the Francos Rodríguez barracks."

María Luisa Lafita warned Tina about establishing personal relationships with the patients. "If they die, it hurts too much." Yet Tina stops at each patient's bedside when she makes her morning rounds. Lafita wonders how she manages to communicate so well. "Why didn't you ever have children?" she asks.

Tina pauses, then answers obligingly. "I'm glad I don't have any now. Just look at Matilde Landa, separated from Carmen. She runs to see her at every opportunity."

2 3

Every night, volunteers from around the world cross the Pyrenees to fight for the Republic. Local peasants, loyal to the
Republic, guide them along the mountain paths, fastened one to
the other on a long rope, so they won't get lost in the dark. Luigi
Longo, otherwise known as Gallo, takes care of them once they
arrive. He has requested that Comandante Carlos send María Sánchez to the border to help register them.

Tina goes to Albacete. Most volunteers come through Perpignan; others wait in Pau. Few speak Spanish. Those who know
something about war show up with boots, canteens, overcoats, salt
and sugar. Longo is pleasantly surprised by a worker who comes
on his motorcycle, having heard of the shortage of transport. Four
carpenters cling proudly to their bicycles. Two Hungarians carry
pistols; three Poles bring small revolvers with ammunition; a Czech
arrives with a pair of binoculars. A prince of Polish origin crosses
the icy Pyrenees carrying a backpack full of cans of pâté de foie

gras, truffles, and other delicacies from Fauchon. Longo suggests that he stuff newspaper into his suede shoes before they disintegrate altogether. Tina looks at him in surprise when he offers her a pack of Gauloises.

Longo wonders what he is going to do with all these people and their often misguided enthusiasm. Will Spain be turned into a nursery school for these children who offer so little besides good-will? They are required to show some identification to prove they are of age. Few can produce such proof.

"You can't stay here."

Tina tries to soften the rejection when she sees the youth's despair.

"Does your family know you have come to Spain?"

"I'll write to my mother later."

All they want is guns, but guns are in short supply.

The men and women who come through Paris have already filled out forms giving their name, age, education, military experience, political allegiances, job history, and a person to be contacted in case of death. They are the easy ones for Tina to register.

"These women," Longo tells Tina, "are Communists and want to go to the front. You must convince them that the war is also being fought behind the lines."

A Cuban shouts a protest. "I didn't cross the ocean to be in the rearguard."

"You see," says Longo, "they won't listen."

While waiting her turn, a large woman cleans her nails with the tip of a knife. She pulls a loaf of French bread out of her bag. Suddenly she shouts, "I came to fight; I want to die fighting."

"We don't come here to die."

"Everybody here is going to die, you'll see."

"Who are you, señora?"

"They killed my son. I came to fight."

Nobody can talk her out of her obsession: "I came to fight." Revenge is in the air. Luigi Longo takes her aside and puts his arm around her. A few minutes later he leaves her in tears and returns.

"May I speak with her for a moment?" Tina asks.

She places her hand on the woman's hunched shoulder. "What is your name?"

"Sanda Dumitrescu."

After a few minutes with Tina, Sanda stops crying. Whatever

Tina said to her has the desired effect: she is now willing to follow orders. Tina, however, finds it momentarily difficult to return to being María with her pen and pad and list of vital statistics after such a personal encounter.

"Communist?"

"I am an idealist."

In line are some Albanians from the military academy in Turin, and two Germans.

"Your name? Your profession?"

"Sam Master. Tailor. English."

"I am a tailor, too. My name is Nat Cohen. We met in the South of France, competing in a bicycle race. We left the race and here we are with our bicycles."

"Benjamin Balboa from Morocco."

"I am opposed to the criminal Fascist intervention in Spain," exclaims an old woman.

"We can use you as a nurse."

"I want to fight."

"I'm sure you do, but the first duty of a soldier is to obey."

"I am a trained Citroën mechanic, specializing in small transmission parts."

"Your skills will be most valuable."

"These aren't rifles; these are harquebuses," someone shouts in fury.

Longo is an expert at spotting the provocateurs, those who will later make up Franco's Fifth Column.

Tina notices a very thin woman standing in line wearing thick eyeglasses and a Basque beret. "Your name, please?"

"Simone Weil."

"Your reason for coming to Spain?"

"I have never liked war, but those who remain in the rearguard are the worst. Paris is the rearguard."

Simone Weil has no reason to give so many explanations, but she says even more in response to the second question. "I have worked at Renault. I can type if necessary. I know some militiamen. I also have press credentials."

Tina would remember the seriousness of her words, the intensity and weight she gave to each.

Months later, she hears that a half-blind and very clumsy Frenchwoman had put her foot into a pot of boiling oil and had been sent back to Paris despite her protests. Her name: Simone Weil.

The incident amuses the troops. "Just imagine, an intellectual!"

Tina remembers her sympathetically, but Vittorio corrects her. "That Frenchwoman is an anarchist. She came here to meet Julian Gorkin. They oppose the Popular Front, and all they talk about is land expropriation."

By the end of October, Albacete, in southeast Spain, has become a tower of Babel. A ship from Marseilles has brought five hundred volunteers and another five hundred are due to arrive in Alicante. Supply trucks, however, do not arrive. The Germans want beer, the Italians want spaghetti, the French want pommes frites; there is plenty of wine, but not enough of anything else. The Germans march in perfect order; the Italians march in perfect disorder. The French, Belgians, English, and Germans brag about their fighting experience in the war of 1914. They look down on the others who are untrained, who don't know which end of a gun is the barrel. The Communists are the most politicized; the rest have assorted ideologies, and many are anarchists. "Uniting them is going to be my trial by fire. What am I going to do with them?" says Longo as he walks through the camp. The Communists fight the socialists, the anarchists fight the pacifists (who nonetheless ask for rifles); everything must be discussed and voted upon. Surely these volunteers from fifty-three countries, including Indians, Algerians, Arabs, South Africans, and Latin Americans, expected something else, but what can Luigi Longo give them if he doesn't have equipment and supplies? What can he offer these "liberty volunteers"? "Patience, for the moment, I beg you to have patience. Our first job is to dig trenches." "No, we're here to fight." "You're here to obey orders and to dig the trenches of European freedom in the Spanish soil."

The Nationalist radio station, Radio Salamanca, calls them Communists (the greatest insult), atheists, adventurers, flea-bitten devils, drunkards, bastards, criminals; the prisons of Europe have flung open their doors and all the inmates have rushed to Spain. Radio Salamanca rants and raves against the international Communist hordes who are spilling their black bile into Spain. Tina is outraged because she hears that the Nationalists are receiving help from the regular army in Hitler's Germany and Mussolini's Italy. "Those are the bad ones," says Tina. "Most Italians aren't like that"—forgetting that she's supposed to be a Spanish woman named María Sánchez.

More than two thousand Russians have come to Spain, most of them technicians; they have sent arms, many of which are left over from the Crimean War and are completely useless. As a political commissar, Vittorio has surprising mobility: he travels to Paris, to London, and even into occupied territory. The secret police of the U.S.S.R., the GPU, has set up operations everywhere, with headquarters at the Gaylor Hotel on Alfonso XIII Street. Vittorio goes there constantly. They need interpreters, and Vittorio leaves for Albacete to tell Tina that her help would be greatly appreciated.

"I don't want to be an interpreter anymore. I'd rather go back to the Hospital Obrero and to my duties at Red Aid. I'm needed there and I'd rather work with the people than with a bureaucracy."

When Tina returns a few weeks later by train from Albacete to Madrid, she gets off at the Chamartin station and runs to the Francos Rodríguez barracks. There she is told that Vittorio has recently left for Paris with Matilde Landa.

Who is this woman leaning against the wall? Who is she, standing here assailed by the news that Vittorio has gone away with another woman? An enormous weight presses on her chest, then turns into sharp, stabbing pain. Her left arm aches, and she can't move it. "I am immune," she repeats to herself. But it isn't true. Jealousy takes up a huge space in her heart. Calm down, Comrade María, calm down. Aren't you as free a spirit as he is? Suddenly Edward appears before her, pale and ghostly in memory. Who was I to laugh at his fits of jealousy? Tina now feels the workings of the poison for the first time and realizes that there is no antidote.

She stumbles along like a drunk or an old lady as she makes her way to the hospital.

24

*D*r. Juan Planelles announces to Tina and the other nurses that Mary Bingham Urquidi, wife of a Mexican diplomat and a professional nurse, has asked to join them as a volunteer at the Hospital Obrero.

"She is a highly trained nurse from Mt. Sinai Hospital in New York, and speaks Spanish perfectly."

Fifteen days later, Mary Urquidi becomes head nurse and asks to talk to Tina. "Can you help in the operating room?"

Tina agrees and immediately gets to work. Dr. Nafría washes his hands and holds them out to Tina for his rubber gloves. She hears him mumbling: "They bring them to me half dead and expect me to revive them. I can't perform miracles."

As the front line moves closer, the hospital receives more and more wounded.

"And on top of that, our supply of medicines and disinfectants is dwindling. Soon, we'll just have to ask the nuns to pray for us."

The anesthesiologist places the mask over a wounded man's face. He carefully measures out four ounces of ether, enough to keep him unconscious for two hours. "Breathe in . . . Exhale . . . Inhale, slowly, slowly . . . One . . . Two . . ." Suddenly Tina feels a wave of terror as the wounded man loses consciousness.

The inanimate body floats without anchor, belonging to no other space than this operating table, at the mercy of the shadows surrounding him. She suddenly remembers Julio Antonio, alone in the operating room, at the hands of those who cut up bodies. Tina doesn't dare take her eyes off the unconscious man. She is paralyzed with anxiety. "I want to go with him, I'm going with him."

Nafría moves rapidly and energetically. First he scours the abdomen with a soap solution. He stretches out his hand, and Mary Urquidi places the scalpel in his palm. Nafría traces a line across the entire abdomen. A thin line of fresh blood appears. Such long incisions are not normal medical practice, they leave big scars, but in Madrid the only consideration is to save lives and move on to the next case as quickly as possible.

Doctor Nafría carefully explores the internal damage with his hand. Mary gives him one instrument after another. Tina admires her skill and confidence. Nafría's hands fly as he cuts and holds and sews and seems to stay just ahead of the threat of hemorrhage. When he finishes, his voice sounds muffled through the mask. "The damage is not irreparable."

Tina's relief is obvious. He holds his hands out so Tina can remove his gloves. "This is the last one for today," he says decisively, and heads for his office.

While Mary Urquidi sips her tea after the operation—she is the only one who doesn't drink coffee—she says to Tina, "The doctors here are excellent, but if I didn't watch them carefully, they wouldn't even wash up before operating." And then, in English, she says, "You are very competent, María."

"Why do you speak to me in English?"

"They told me you were American."

"Yes, I am."

"But you have a slight accent in English. I'd guess Italian."

"I lived for many years in Brooklyn, maybe that's why."

"Why did you come to work in this hospital?"

"Because I am a Communist. And you?"

"God help me, no. I am a nurse."

This refined and educated woman tells her about a young man, just twenty-three, who arrived with his stomach blown open. She describes how Dr. Bolea took out his intestines, washed them in a strong stream of water, and stuffed them back into the abdominal cavity. He sewed him up and the wounded man's heart began to beat normally. "He's a wonderful surgeon, wonderful," Mary Urquidi comments. "The patients, though, don't deserve him. Yesterday afternoon, they found out that in Ward 9 there was a casualty from the other side, a Nationalist, and if I hadn't gotten there in time, they would have thrown him out the window. Can you imagine? Nobody can come to me with stories about how magnanimous the Republicans are; they are as cruel as the Nationalists. Or worse. They are all Spaniards. Don't people realize that this is a war of brother against brother?"

Why does she say these things to Tina? To enrage her? To test her? María Luisa Planelles joins them for coffee and Mary Urquidi asks her, "What's the point of having a big laboratory without a blood bank? All I've seen since I've been here are the wounded who end up dying from lack of blood. The situation is desperate," she continues. "A few months ago I visited the Santa Adela Hospital, and Dr. Elosegui showed me his blood and plasma bank. He even showed me an article from a Mexican newspaper about some experiments being done there to use the blood of those who had just died. There must be blood at the Santa Adela Hospital."

"Dr. Elosegui was a Fascist; they killed him and destroyed his laboratory," María Luisa Planelles states coldly.

"How can they kill someone who could have saved so many lives? It's pure vandalism to destroy a blood bank!"

The atmosphere in the hospital is even more tense because of all the shortages. Yet Tina refrains from answering, because she admires Mary Urquidi's courage despite her political views. Just yesterday, Mary burned her arm on the flame of the sterilizer yet continued next to the doctor in the operating room for two hours, holding the instrument tray. She was sweating, with knitted brows, but not a sigh escaped her mask. When the operation was over, she spread toothpaste on the burn and continued until three in the morning sterilizing instruments and assisting in operations, always the first to get to work the next day.

On November 4, 1936, the systematic bombing of Madrid begins. The city is burning. Nationalist airplanes fly low and the crews watch as the people of Madrid run through the streets. Women, children, and old people seek shelter in burned-out buildings. On November 14, Buenaventura Durruti and three thousand men reach the Aragón front and the crowds welcome them. Durruti defends the Casa de Campo in front of the Ciudad Universitaria, the most dangerous place on the front line, and there he dies, the most beloved, charismatic leader. Five hundred people attend his funeral. It is an impressive show of anti-Fascist unity. To the surprise of the world and the outrage of the Nationalists, Madrid resists. The Asturian dynamiters are everywhere, hurling their explosives at the Nationalists from the Casa de Campo.

A young woman comes to the hospital to ask for work. Her name is Agueda Serna Morales. She belongs to the Young Communist League and has been a committed militant since she was twelve. Tina is attracted to this beautiful woman who experiences life as a cataclysm. She repeats in an urgent voice: "I want to do more, I want to do more than pick up basins under hospital beds. I want to kill the enemy." For her this war is the end of the world. "The day of the Last Judgment has come for the priests, for the landowners, for wicked Spaniards," and when Tina asks her, "Why do you burn churches?" she answers, "To free God. A new Spain will be born if we win, Spaniards will live as people do in Russia, where everyone has enough to eat."

Finally, the Ratas and Katyushkas fly over, and when Agueda Serna Morales sees them in the sky tracing a hammer and sickle, she cannot control her rapture. "We have airplanes, we are no longer alone!"

"Agueda, Agueda, get inside, it's dangerous."

"I don't care if they kill me. The Russians have arrived!"

Agueda confides to Tina that, besides doing volunteer work at the hospital, she is learning to blow up bridges. After the first air raid, when she saw that the Junkers attacked the entrances to the Metro, the poor neighborhoods, and the lines of people waiting to buy bread and milk, she decides to join a group of young men and women in the mountains who are specially trained as guerrillas. Her name will be Mura. She promises to come back to see María if she can. But Tina never sees her again.

Mary Urquidi remains the only dissident voice among the nurses in the Hospital Obrero, and when she takes tea with the others, she provokes them with her views. But they, like Tina, listen because she is training a number of nurses and has earned everyone's respect.

"The Republicans are not angels and the Nationalists are not devils. This is not a war of good against evil. Things are not black and white."

Mari Valero interrupts, making the others laugh. "Of course they are. The Moors are black, and they are on the side of evil."

"Well, let me tell you what they told me at the Mexican Embassy, so you'll see that horrors are committed on both sides. Miguel Martínez, who according to *Pravda*'s Koltsov, is a Soviet official and according to others is a Mexican general who fought in their Revolution, gave an order to release the most important Nationalist prisoners from the Model Prison. That very day, the prisoners were murdered by their guards on the road to Arganda. Two days later, four hundred more officers died the same way. So you tell me which side has clean hands.

"This war is not what I thought it was at first, a confrontation of peasants and landlords and priests. It is a confrontation of the European powers: Russia, Germany, and Italy."

Every afternoon at the Hospital Obrero, the staff listens to the news on Union Radio. "Augusto is on!" The Communist radio station broadcasts from the Convent of the Apostolic Ladies of Chamartin, on Mexico Street. Augusto Fernández reads the war news in such a way that even the most desolate reports sound encouraging.

"Our forces are resisting bravely, holding their positions at the front." "Our forces have excellent morale." "The enemy has been badly defeated."

Tina, Matilde, Mari Valero, and María Luisa Lafita huddle around the radio to listen to Augusto's voice. Only Mary Urquidi stays in the operating room watching over the needles as they boil and prepares bandages with the help of a new volunteer. "Tell me about it later; if I sit down now, I'll fall asleep."

"Please, Mary, come hear this. He is even more inspiring than Dr. Planelles." And Mari Valero laughs.

Ambulatory patients also congregate in front of the radio. Rumors circulate through the hospital, but Augusto has the final word. If Augusto says so, it must be true; and if he doesn't mention it, it never happened. Even the sound of cannon fire just beyond the hospital walls doesn't shake their faith; Augusto has told them that everything will be okay.

One morning Dr. Planelles calls Tina and María Luisa Lafita to his office. He tells them that La Pasionaria is going to be admitted to their hospital for the treatment of a liver ailment which has pained her for years. "The utmost discretion is called for." Three hours later, Mary Urquidi feels a current of emotion running through the hospital.

"Three of us just recognized La Pasionaria as she came in the front door," Flor Cernuda says with a wide smile.

"How?"

"Even the walls whisper it."

Matilde Landa, Tina, and María Luisa Lafita take her to her room; Dr. Planelles welcomes her in the name of the Hospital Obrero. Tina is deeply impressed by the way she speaks, her warm voice, the way she calls everyone, even Dr. Planelles, "my child." It is the same voice she has heard on the radio. Nurses and orderlies fight to be assigned to her, and her presence lifts everyone's spirit.

An explosion rocks the Hospital Obrero; people run, doors slam, shouts are heard. "It's a raid!" "Is there anyone in the operating room?" The authoritative voice of Dr. Planelles announces over the megaphone: "The first priority is to evacuate the patients." Some panic and run down the hall toward the doors. Where do they get their strength? More explosions follow. Tina hears cries from Ward 7. She sees an old man with white hair holding his head, but he is not the one crying out; it is his neighbor, who has fallen to the floor wrapped in a sheet.

"We're going to get you out of here, don't worry; the orderlies are coming to take you to the shelters."

In the middle of the shocked silence, she hears laughter, vulgar chuckles coming from the women's ward.

A man runs down the hall holding up his pants. Is he the one who laughed? She tries to catch up to him, but another explosion stops her. Dr. Planelles carries a wounded man on his shoulders and comes back for another one. Tina stays with the patient with the white hair.

Tina goes into the hall and grabs Pilarica by the arm. "Before saving your own skin, think about the others." The young woman tries to get away.

"Go to the second floor and help with the evacuation."

"Let go of me, María, let go."

Since Tina doesn't let go, she punches her in the stomach and runs off.

Tina takes a few steps toward the window to regain her breath. She tries to find excuses for Pilarica: "she was in a state of panic, she really is a good nurse." Tina watches people run out into the streets, their guns in their hands, screaming, "Long Live the Republic!" "Fascist traitors!"

Suddenly La Pasionaria comes out of her room. Her presence stops the torrent of people rushing toward the exit, who seem to freeze in place. "My sons, my daughters, don't lose your calm. Our lives have been a constant learning how to suffer, a constant suffering. Starting today, our lives must be a constant learning how to fight, a constant learning how to overcome."

She is like a pale statue blocking their way. "Listen, my children, don't run. I am your mirror, look at yourselves in me: a mirror must not have cracks. You, my children, are the rearguard, but this does not mean you will suffer any less. The front line is terrible, but our militias there are dreaming of victory. Here we see only the aftermath of the battle, the wounded and mutilated bodies, the destruction of war, the pain. Don't run away, my dear sons and daughters. Let us fight together."

When she finishes, Mari Valero shouts, her fist in the air: "¡Que viva la Pasionaria!"

Everyone joins in: "Long live La Pasionaria!"

A few days later, La Pasionaria, cured, leaves the Hospital Obrero.

"Planelles just told me that Mary Bingham Urquidi is going to leave to join her family," Mari Valero announces. "She is trying to get a safe-conduct pass into France. Planelles says we should be looking for somebody to replace her in the operating room."

"She has trained a number of nurses," Tina notes. "Asunción is very good, and so is María Luisa Lafita. And what about Flor Cernuda?"

Flor Cernuda is one of the youngest.

Planelles calls an emergency staff meeting. "The most urgent issue now is the kitchen. The hospital is full and nobody is supervising the kitchen."

"I volunteer."

Juan Planelles stares at Tina. "Are you sure, Comrade María? The kitchen is more difficult than nursing."

"If you accept me, I am willing."

"If you accept me," she repeats, as if they might not. Tina is too modest. Matilde Landa intervenes. "María is a great comrade with a magnificent spirit; she could run any of the wards."

"If Comrade María wishes to take charge of the kitchen, and this is what we need, we can do nothing more than thank her," Dr. Julio Recatero says.

After the meeting, Dr. Planelles approaches Tina. "If everyone were like you, María, we would win the war tomorrow."

"We are going to win." Tina smiles.

There is still some food left. There are fruits, vegetables, a sack of potatoes, and the doctors, orderlies, and nurses receive their ration of wine. It's amazing how much energy a glass of wine can give you. Since she lived in France, Tina is used to drinking wine, and in the hospital Dr. Martínez Riesgo asserts that it is medicinal. From time to time, the doctors and nurses come down to the kitchen for a cup of coffee that Comrade María serves them graciously.

Soon Tina notices that her legs are swollen, but this bothers her less than the steam from the pots. "It's good for the skin," Mari Valero tell her. "It moisturizes. All of us are going to be wrinkled before you." Sometimes, when she wipes her face, she wonders if she is not, in fact, crying. Her feet are tired and the numbness rises from the ankles to the knees. She goes to take off her stockings, which seem to be cutting off the circulation. As she turns the corner, she sees Vittorio standing next to a woman dressed in white. She thinks she sees him embracing her, or maybe he has just put his arm around her waist to help her up the stairs. Tina stops and watches them walk toward the door. She forces herself over to the window. When the woman and Vidali go out to the street, Vittorio does not touch her; they simply walk side by side in the cold air. Tina, her heart turning over, feels pain in every rib. "Something in me is going to break, not only my legs, but my heart," she thinks as she watches them drive away in a Studebaker, on their way to the front. Tina cannot repress a moan from the very depth of her being, a hoarse, guttural moan. She returns to the kitchen, opens the door, drags her legs over to the stove, and gets a blast of steam in the face.

She and Vittorio rarely see each other these days. He goes from front line to front line in his Studebaker, nicknamed "The Front." In Mexico the mistress was called the "second front." And she, Tina, what is she? She goes to the Francos Rodríguez barracks twice without finding him. The kitchen is destroying her health; now she understands why nobody else volunteered. Once, Vittorio comments, "You look very tired. What's wrong with your ankles?" But usually he is out of the city, off on his missions.

Finally Planelles advises her to lie down and keep her legs up. Instead, Tina goes up to the wards to change sheets. That evening, Matilde Landa tells her she doesn't have to come up during her time off. "Your legs look very bad; don't overdo it." Later that same night, Matilde removes her from kitchen duty.

Tina moves slowly, painfully.

"When Carlos returns from the front with the second batallion of Talavera, I'll tell him you aren't taking care of yourself," Matilde reproaches her.

Tina answers angrily. "I'm sure you will see him before I do. What the hell is going on, Matilde?"

"What do you mean?"

"Since when do you know more about him than I do?"

After a week of forced rest, Tina takes charge of Ward 9. The following day, the patients begin to have convulsions. The hospital workers run from ward to ward but can do nothing to alleviate the suffering. The patients turn themselves inside out, spewing up their souls with endless vomiting.

Within two days, there are a hundred dead. At an emergency staff meeting, María Luisa Planelles announces that cyanide was found in the stomachs of the dead.

Planelles asks, "Did anyone see anything unusual in the kitchen?"

"Nothing out of the ordinary. Meals have been served as usual by the same comrades."

"I never should have left the kitchen," Tina blames herself. "I was on guard there twenty-four hours a day."

"Comrade," Juan Planelles interrupts her, "we are all on our guard and nobody saw anything unusual."

"Whoever did it deserves to die," María Luisa Lafita shouts.

"All of us are responsible for finding the criminal," Planelles admonishes. "This was an act of Fascist sabotage."

"I'd like to return to kitchen duty," Tina states.

"Please, comrade, we don't need another death."

"I'm not blaming anybody," María Luisa Lafita says, "but maybe we should keep a closer watch on Amalia."

Amalia García came after Mary Urquidi left, and she made an excellent impression. She was smart and efficient and knew exactly what to do.

Amalia sings while she works, and all the patients gather around to listen to her. Her voice cheers up even the most depressed.

"Amalia?" Planelles asks. "Why Amalia?"

"I don't know. Instinct."

That night, Planelles looks for Amalia's file. He cannot find it; either somebody removed it or nobody bothered checking her documents. Tina Modotti, alias María, political exile; María Luisa Lafita, Cuban activist; Mari Valero, actress; Flor Cernuda, activist; Encarnita Fuyola, recommended by Carlos Contreras; Pilar Espinasa, philosopher; he finds everybody's file except Amalia's.

Summoned to Planelles's office, Amalia maintains a desperate silence. That same night, the high command summarily passes judgment and sentences her. The order comes from the political commissar, Carlos Contreras: "The execution will take place in the central courtyard of the Hospital Obrero at six in the morning."

All hospital personnel and any patient able to get out of bed crowd around the windows.

Amalia sheds no tears. The head of the firing squad warns her in a respectful voice that this is her last opportunity to divulge the name of the person who sent her to the hospital and gave her the cyanide.

Amalia asks for a priest. "Before I die, I wish to state that I will fight with my last drop of blood to eradicate from Spain the plague of Communism that is responsible for the deaths of priests and nuns."

At 6:03 a.m. the firing squad takes aim.

In December, Tina enters Vittorio's office, a crumpled piece of paper in her hand.

She silently hands him the note from Mercedes. Mamma is dead.

"To think that I was here and my mother was alone, without her children, so many years alone, without us, and her children all over the world."

"She wasn't alone. Mercedes was with her."

"But she was dead all that time, and here I was, alive. Writing letters to her, without even suspecting. She was already dead."

Tina begins to cry. "Three months, for three months I haven't suspected anything. Do you understand? I worked, I made war, I lived, ate, slept, made love with you, bathed, laughed, and she was dead, my mother was dead. Do you realize what that means?"

She keeps repeating, "She died three months ago."

Vittorio holds her in his arms for a long time; her tears moisten his shirt, his shoulder, and he presses her to his chest until someone calls at the door, "Comandante Carlos?"

"Stai qui, torno subito."

Tina is overcome by the brutal realization that she will never see her again. "Mamma. I need your strength, your solidness, Mamma." The pain digs into her gut. "Mamma. Here I am, alone, alone with this piece of paper in my hand. Mamma. You were buried three months ago, in the ground, the earth covering your face." The pain crushes her chest, her ribs, her belly; it smashes like waves against her throat. The pain rings in her ears, flashes in her eyes. "It can't be true; it didn't happen."

She has been with many as death approached. In the hospital, she places a compassionate hand over their eyes. Quickly, before Matilde comes, "Change the sheets, here comes another one," she will say. She then makes the bed with rapid, efficient gestures, without thinking, fluffing up the pillow to receive a new head. Death on the wing. Death, always in a hurry.

She hears a woman's voice shouting something about food for the soldiers. "This is the world I live in," Tina says to herself. "This is the war I must continue to fight. Why fill their bellies if their bodies are just going to be collected from the battlefield and brought to me with their brains oozing from their skulls, their eyes shut tight in panic, the locked jaw, the cells still burning with fear, the mouth trying to shout?" Tina's legs are numb. She wants to get up but can't; an invisible weight pins her to the floor. She remembers that they found the remains of a meal in Julio Antonio's stomach, garbanzos, yes, garbanzos . . . When Vittorio returns, he finds her asleep on the floor. Her face is swollen from crying, tired, old, worn out; not a trace left of the Tina of Berlin, with her elegant tailored suit; not a bit of the seductive Tina of Mexico. He watches her sleep, her mouth partly open; lines run from her nose to the edges of her mouth. She wakes up and continues crying, choking on her tears.

"Lie down on the bed at least."

"Why should I?" she shouts. "All these months I saw her in my heart, cooking, laughing, hugging me."

"Do you want to stay here with me?"

"No, Planelles is waiting for me."

"You can't go in this state."

"I have guard duty."

"Remember, tomorrow I'm going to Valencia to prepare for the government's departure. The whole government will soon be leaving Madrid. You should go, too."

"No, I'll stay with you. I don't want to live apart from you, even if I hardly see you. I don't want to leave Madrid."

"Bene, bene."

For a week now, no shots have been fired, and things won't start up again until after New Year's. Even during a war, there is a Christmas season. But Madrid looks sad, its streets emptied by the cold. The unfinished pavilions of the university are deserted, the clouds low and dreary, the earth scarred by the bloody battles between the Republicans and the Moors hired by the Nationalists. The Republican resistance has been surprisingly tenacious; the militiamen have reason to feel proud.

The headquarters of the Fifth Regiment takes on a homey, intimate feeling; Cruz Díaz, Flor Cernuda, Encarnita, María Luisa Lafita, Mari Valero, and Tina hang paper garlands to celebrate the victories and the quiet on the fronts. On a wall, they write: "Welcome, 1937."

Comrade María offers to make a hot punch with wine and fruit.

"We don't have any fruit, María," says Mari Valero.

When Tina leaves the room, María Luisa Lafita scolds Mari Valero. "Couldn't you see that was the first time in I don't know how long that she has expressed any kind of enthusiasm? Why did you have to spoil it for her?"

Some of the most important political and military leaders of the anti-Fascist alliance come to the party, including La Pasionaria. María Luisa Lafita and Roberto Vizcaíno bring an old grammophone, and Alberto Sánchez, the Cuban, still upset over the death of Pablo de la Torriente Brau in Majadahonda on December 19, makes an effort to smile. María Luisa Lafita speculates: "If Mella had lived, he would have been here with Pablo and would have died by his side, fighting."

Pepe Díaz pulls La Pasionaria onto the dance floor. Everybody claps as she spins around; she looks stunning in a dark dress, and Vittorio shouts "¡Guapa!" Francisco Antón takes her hand, cutting in on Pepe Díaz. Vittorio offers Tina his arm.

"I don't know how to dance pasodoble, Toio," she says uncomfortably.

"Don't worry, just follow me."

Vittorio feels like reminding her of their parties in Mexico, but he holds his tongue. It is not the right moment.

"Let's go slowly."

She moves back and forth, always the same step, keeping her head down. Vittorio jokes, "You see, it's not so difficult. Come on, now, don't be shy. Lift your head and let's pick it up."

"No, no, please no."

How strange. War has taken her self-confidence. What's wrong with her? Vittorio feels like asking, "Didn't you dance with the others?" But the expression in her eyes stops him. For the first time, he sees the tragedy in Tina's face.

Tina excuses herself and goes to get something to drink. Vittorio calls to Matilde Landa, "Come on, let's finish the dance."

Pepe Díaz steps in to dance with Mari Valero, who is a real show girl. Vittorio gestures to Tina, "Come on, let's go."

"It's almost midnight. Can't we wait?"

"So what's with her now?" Vittorio wonders with irritation.

Earlier, when they were alone together in his room on the top floor of the barracks, Vittorio had come to her. "Love conquers death, come on, you'll see, we'll defeat it." But Tina did not respond. Perhaps she did not want to exorcise death.

Now, after midnight, when Vittorio finally lies down next to her, Tina has her face to the wall. "No, Toietto, I can't."

He whispers to her, "Maybe we'll never see each other again."

Tina turns to him with unexpected vehemence; an expression of panic distorts her features. She responds to his embrace, clutching his body, which has been her anchor since Moscow. Her lips swell, and she trembles as she clings to him.

Afterwards, he tucks a blanket around her as if she were a newborn baby.

"Sleep now, I have to go downstairs; I'll be right back."

He picks up the pistol he always carries with him.

When Tina wakes up, many hours have passed, but Vittorio is still not back. She gets dressed quickly; she sees through the window that he is deep in conversation with Luigi Longo.

Vittorio turns to her as she approaches. "Go back upstairs, we're almost done."

When he returns to the room, he finds her sitting in the chair. Without a word, he carries her in his arms to bed. He undresses her and takes her again with the same ardor of their days in Moscow.

But it's not the same.

Their meetings at headquarters become more and more infrequent. Vittorio practically lives on the battlefield and Tina at the hospital.

Then Tina is assigned to the battlefield with the Sanitary Services. Alberto Sánchez and Esteban Larrea are stretcher-bearers, and María Luisa Lafita gives them cover.

"You collect them, and I'll cover you. The enemy shoots where they know others have fallen."

María Luisa Lafita says they must first pick up the officers because they carry documents that might be useful to the enemy.

Tina was also trained to use a gun at Francos Rodríguez, but she is a bad shot and doesn't like to carry one. María Luisa offers to teach her. She is excited about being on the battlefield with the ambulances and her husband, Roberto Vizcaíno. Tina dodges bullets to pick up the wounded on the front lines. Once, María Luisa pushed her down when she stood up in a trench. "When you make yourself a target, you put others in danger as well." María Luisa stayed by her, and Tina realized why members of the Sanitary Services prefer to be on duty with her: on the front line, in the middle of combat, María Luisa stands out because of her courage and her good aim; she knows how to defend her comrades. She berates Tina for not being more careful. "If not for yourself, then do it for the hospital."

At night they return to the hospital, where there's not a moment's rest. Only the laundry workers are able to listen to the radio, and they report the latest news. Some nurses have left and nobody has been found to replace them. Tina is amazed at how passionately the wounded hold on to their desire to live, even when they are on the verge of death. Some have lost a leg or an arm. They try to walk, and when they fall, they pick themselves up and, like children, insist on trying again. They boast to Tina about the progress they have made. "I shaved with my left hand." "I can go downstairs without help, Comrade María. Come, let me show you." They go on living their lives, such as they are, in the corridors.

"Do I love life that much," Tina wonders. She marvels at the strength a human being can possess. "That boy, Miguel, with parted lips parched from fever, clings so tenaciously to life." "I'm getting better, aren't I?" he asks, shivering. Matilde assures him that he is, yet nothing in the world can save him.

26

Mañana dejo mi casa,
dejo los bueyes y el pueblo.
¡Salud! ¿Adónde vas, dime?
—Voy al Quinto Regimiento.

Con Líster y Campesino
Con Galán y con Modesto
Con el comandante Carlos
No hay miliciano con miedo.

Tomorrow I leave my home
I leave the oxen and the village
¡Salud! Where are you going, tell me?
—To the Fifth Regiment.

With Líster and Campesino
With Galán and with Modesto

The flat, open terrain of Castile makes an easy target for Nationalist bombers. The least experienced pilot could hit a lizard from the sky. The stretcher-bearers are right in the line of fire as they run for miles to collect the wounded.

Under a field tent, the doctors give orders to the nurses: chloroform, syringe, please boil that, a tourniquet, bandage his head but don't cover his ears, quick, he's all cut up, wash his chest well, what do you mean there is no more alcohol? María, we need more masks. Cruz, how's his pulse? Take a look at that one who's in so much pain. Why that one? Because suffering is a sign of life. This one, on the other hand, so pale, hollow cheeks, half-closed eyes, what is he, about sixteen years old, he's finished, he's lost too much blood. In the medical-aid stations the doctors use insulin, camphor, anti-tetanus shots, anti-gangrene. They wash wounds with soap and water, and administer first aid. It's the best they can do.

One of the biggest problems is getting blood to the front. Norman Bethune, a Canadian doctor, offers to take blood to the aid stations in a mobile unit.

"But how would you keep the blood fresh?"

"With sodium citrate."

When he returns to Madrid, Bethune proposes to María and Comandante Carlos that they do blood transfusions in the trenches.

"I can request funds from Canada," says Bethune.

"When can you start?"

An hour later, Bethune cables Toronto: "Need sterilizing equipment, instrument trays, microscopes. Many new ideas. Send all the money you can."

Upon receipt of ten thousand dollars from the Canadian Committee for Aid to Spain, Bethune goes to Paris to buy equipment and rouse more support. He makes speeches condemning France, England, and America for refusing to sell arms to Republican Spain. "We will all suffer the consequences if the Fascists win. The war in Spain is a war for democracy."

In London, he attacks the British government. Hazen Sise is in the audience. He is so impressed he offers to join Bethune as a volunteer.

On February 6, Bethune returns to Madrid with Sise and a truckful of medical supplies.

Contreras smiles from ear to ear. "Red Aid, recognizing the importance of your project, has designated a special location for the blood-transfusion unit."

Tina, Vittorio, and Bethune arrive at an eleven-room villa on Príncipe de Vergara Avenue, one of the most luxurious streets in Madrid. Don Isidoro Acevedo, head of Red Aid, comments without irony, "You won't be bothered by bombs here. Franco is very careful not to hit the property of the wealthy."

Three bedrooms are used as sleeping quarters and the rest are turned into laboratories. Two young Spanish doctors, two laboratory technicians, three nurses, a cook, a housekeeper, a secretary, and a doorman make up the rest of the team. Isidoro Acevedo reassures Bethune, "We guarantee as many blood donors as you need."

For three days, the newspapers and radio stations broadcast appeals for donors.

Bethune hears the announcements on the radio. He wonders what he will do with his huge laboratory, his brand-new equipment, and his transfusion room with three beds if only a few bums arrive. At five in the morning, Tina wakes him. "Comandante Bethune, please look out your window."

More than two thousand people—men and women, young and old, civilians and soldiers—wait patiently in line. Bethune gives orders, the doors swing open, and the first donors are ushered in. Tina calls Red Aid to send militiamen to help. They empty out ice chests in the kitchen to make room for plasma.

From the balcony, Tina announces that they are unable to accept more donations for the moment. A wave of protest surges from the crowd. Tina tries to explain that they have no more room to store the blood.

"The secretary will take down your names. We'll process as many as we can today; in a few days we will call you."

Bethune cables the Committee for Aid to Spain in Toronto. "Excellent response from the people of Madrid. The first transfusions on the front last night were successful."

• • •

When Bethune asks for a battlefield assistant, Tina raises her hand, and Matilde nods in agreement.

"María is first-rate; she is fearless."

"Are you sure you want to come?"

"Yes, I'm sure," Tina says calmly.

"I have to tell you my last assistant was killed by a stray bullet."

"I know, everyone in the hospital knows."

"Are you strong enough?"

"Yes."

"Can you keep calm in the face of danger?"

"Yes."

"Just remember: tanks are faster than you."

Bethune, his strong features surrounded by a mass of streaked gray hair, radiates confidence. They call him Comandante because on the pockets of his marine-blue overalls he sports the insignias of the Republican Army; he also wears a Canadian maple leaf on each shoulder.

Bethune and his team receive orders to go to Málaga, which has been bombed and taken by the Nationalists. The people of Málaga are fleeing to Almería along the coastal road, the only route available. Thousands of men and women are making their way on foot. Almería is more than two hundred kilometers away. Even at a good pace, it will take them six days. Some have horses, donkeys, and mules to carry their belongings. Even the old people and the children are on foot. Dogs run through the crowd. A few lambs and goats are herded along. The flapping of a hen can be heard. At night, the temperature drops.

Riding in Bethune's truck, which accompanies the exodus, Tina lifts her eyes from time to time to search for bombers. There is no longer any such thing as a starry night sky. The stark beauty of the landscape is marred by the possibility of finding a tank at the end of each valley. The thundering cannons tear the hills apart, shake the earth, drive people out of their homes, shooing them away like insects. Out, out, get out of here. Spain is no longer yours, go find some other place.

Bethune states: "A strong, young person can walk between forty and fifty kilometers a day. But what about the women, children, and old people? There is no food in the towns they pass through, no transport, no trains, no buses, nothing. They have to walk—or die."

Tina watches as the exodus become denser and more painful. Thousands of children go barefoot, clothed in only one garment, leaning against their mothers' legs and hanging on to their arms.

Eighty-five kilometers from Almería, the people rush toward the truck. "The Fascists are right behind us," they say.

Mothers and grandparents lift their children up to the truck. "Mercy, comrades, for the love of God . . ."

Pressed into a rushing river of humanity, Tina must help the doctors choose between this child who is dying of dysentery and that mother looking at them with her newborn at her breast. Next to her, an old woman who can't take another step says, "Please, comrades, I'll stay, but take the child . . ."

Many other old people simply sit down on the side of the road.

For the first time since the war began, Tina remembers something she had forgotten long ago: the hunger of her childhood, the nights without even a supper of polenta.

When the refugees reach Almería, they find no food at all.

They sleep in the main street, huddled together, unable to take another step.

For forty-eight hours, Ted Allan sits behind the wheel while Bethune and Tina stand at the side of the truck, collecting the next group to go to Almería. Desperate from lack of sleep, they lose all sense of time or direction or hope; they are consumed by anxiety for the ones they have to leave behind. They also know that each trip could be their last. In Almería, Allan goes to the government house to demand gasoline and any vehicle that can be used to help the evacuation.

"There's nothing left in Almería," he explains on his return, "not even a cart. The governor and all the civilian authorities have run off. The criminals from the prisons have ransacked the stores. There's no gas, no water, no electricity."

On one of their many trips, some oranges miraculously appear along the road. Ted Allan gives one to Tina. Despite the horror around her, she sinks her teeth into the juicy pulp. Tina will never forget the taste of that orange.

Comandante Carlos, Matilde Landa, and Mari Valero head a

convoy that meets Bethune in Almería. Behind them come María Luisa Lafita and Flor Cernuda.

Vittorio greets Tina with a hug. The Comandante dictates a telegram to Largo Caballero: "Send medicine, food, a train and soldiers immediately." The response: "Route is impassable. Can't get to you."

Mari Valero describes it later as "an Old Testament exodus: a river of people, like ants, leading their donkeys along the rocky road that followed the curving edge of the sea, and the children, the children . . . I think there must have been five thousand children, at least."

That same night, Comandante Carlos makes a radio broadcast to reassure the population. He asks them to be brave and says that reinforcements will arrive, that they will have food soon, and that ultimately they will win. Just the sound of his voice calms them.

But before he finishes his speech, he is drowned out by the buzzing of airplanes. The bombing of Almería has begun. Buildings crumble to dust; the cries are unbearable. German planes, ten huge bombs. The Fascist target is not the Republican warship anchored in the harbor; it is the people. They want to exterminate the 150,000 men, women, and children they expelled from Málaga.

"They're aiming at civilians, unarmed civilians," Bethune cries in disbelief. Hazen Sise runs toward a group of people standing in line for a cup of condensed milk, the only food available. "Get down on the ground!" he shouts. When they don't respond, he throws himself on top of them. "On the ground, this is an air raid." Bethune picks up three dead children. "There are more than fifty dead and twice as many wounded," Thomas Worsley reports, sifting through the wreckage. Bethune is beside himself with indignation. What did they do that they should be massacred in this way? He sees a bomber slipping smoothly away in the moonlight, taking its sweet time as it drops more bombs, the occasional bursts from antiaircraft lighting up the sky like harmless fireworks.

Tina's ears hurt, and she wishes she had no eyes. My God, how many children! Some older children are taking care of the little ones, and they are all looking for their mothers. In the middle of this chaos, Tina tries to look after them, to help them find their parents. She doesn't stop moving. She promises to get the children milk, and takes them to find a mattress to sleep on. They follow her, and then they don't want to leave her. Tina is surrounded by children.

Bethune works tirelessly and with the utmost calm. Tina keeps up with him and does not flinch. Suddenly they hear a cry from a collapsed house and run to find a three-year-old girl screaming under a pile of rubble. Tina and Bethune pull her out and carry her to an ambulance.

When Tina returns to Madrid, she is too exhausted to resume her duties at the hospital. Reluctantly, she agrees to go to Valencia, where an office is waiting for her at International Red Aid headquarters. There she sees her good friend, Constancia de la Mora, nearly every evening after work. Constancia, an aristocrat who has rejected her Nationalist family, is married to General Ignacio Hidalgo de Cisneros, the head of the Republican Air Force. Her father was Prime Minister Antonio Maura. She is now a Communist, in charge of the foreign correspondents in Spain. She issues battlefield passes to Ernest Hemingway and Herbert Matthews.

At International Red Aid, Tina distributes the donations received from International Labor Defense, making sure that the shipments of food and clothing actually reach the militiamen.

Next she goes to Barcelona, where she finds the Red Aid office full of volunteers from the Women's Auxiliary of Barcelona. Another of her friends, Cruz Díaz, wife of General Azcárate, is in charge. Each of the younger women has an adopted soldier at the front to whom she sends packages as regularly as the war permits. They fuss over their packages; their hearts and minds are full of romantic illusions about their adopted soldiers. They ask them for photographs of themselves in the trenches and put their own in an envelope along with an affectionate letter. Some have adopted soldiers on different fronts, and they write letters to all of them, telling them about their lives and warning them to be careful, so they can meet after the war has been won.

It is here that Tina first hears the cheerful voice of Eladia Lozano. Eladia is putting together a treasure box of cigarettes, razor blades, a small bar of bath soap, and some laundry soap. She is barely sixteen years old, lively, cheerful, and charming in spite of everything; she seems like a ray of sunshine to Tina. Once, long ago, Tina was like that, a dynamic young woman who made people smile, someone whom everybody liked. War or no war, Eladia loves life, and young men love her.

There is no better medicine for Tina than Eladia. But morbid thoughts still pursue her at night: What would happen if a bomb fell on the Red Aid building and she found Eladia with her eyes staring at the ceiling, her hair matted with blood?

The Women's Auxiliary of Barcelona organizes a party for a group of American Marines who have risked their lives to break the blockade and bring in food. Eladia is surprised to hear Tina speak English with them, and she is even more impressed when she hears her chatting in French, Italian, and even Russian at a party for the International Brigades.

"María, how is it that you speak so many languages? Where did you learn them? Have you traveled a lot?"

Tina smiles and changes the subject. She feels good among these girls. "How quickly the human body recuperates, how little it needs to start up again!" It's enough for Tina to hear the girls' energetic voices to make her forget the war, the wounded, the rows of beds, the dead. For a moment she even believes there will be no more bombings, no more convoys of wounded soldiers.

On the corner of San Juan and Corcega, Tina runs into Gerda Taro, Robert Capa's companion and a photographer in her own right. She has been traveling back and forth between Spain and France, where she and Capa publish photos in all the international magazines. Dressed in shorts even though the weather is cold, she makes a dramatic contrast to Tina in her modest black suit. "María, let's go to the Ramblas and have a cup of coffee," she says, smiling as usual.

Tina is about to refuse.

"It will be good for you."

"And your boyfriend?"

"Bob? He stayed in Paris, but we're finished; he's too frivolous. My only passion now is photography."

Tina once watched Robert Capa and Gerda Taro at the front,

how they spent a whole day with their faces behind the lens, first with an Eyemo, which they shared. Then he switched to a Leica and she used a Rolleiflex. "What a beautiful couple!" she thought. But now it's finished, kaput, fini.

As they sit in the café, Gerda opens her heart. Tina thinks, "How immodest!" but listens out of curiosity.

"You see, he wants to share everything. Then he signs his name alone to the photographs we both take. He doesn't give me credit, or only once in a while. He takes everything I have. In all the newspapers and magazines—*Vu, Regards, The Illustrated London News, Berliner Illustrierte*—they never give me credit, and I'm just as good as he is, maybe better. He's good, though, there's no doubt about that. Do you remember his first photos of Spain? Do you know the Vallecas neighborhood? Did you see how miserable those people were who were sleeping in the Metro? Bob took pictures of those poor starving devils the first time he came to Spain.

"I want my independence," she continues. "I want to make a name for myself; I don't want to be Capa's shadow. I'm going to be more respected and famous than he. Relations between men and women will always be about power; that's why I'll never get married. Least of all to Bob. Hey, do you know Gisèle Freund?"

"No, but I know who she is."

"She is fantastic, a great photographer, generous with her time and her knowledge. And have you met Germaine Krull? She's Joris Ivens's wife, she took pictures of factories, pipes, things like that, architecture and industry. How did you get a visa to Russia? I want to go, but I'm also interested in China; I'd go there tomorrow if I could. What do you think of Frank Borkenau? Oh, María, you should have seen Haile Selassie in Geneva at the League of Nations. If anybody looks like a fly in soup, it's him. Can you imagine having such an emperor? Poor Ethiopians. The first time I came to Barcelona, I took pictures of fallen Christs, upside-down sacred hearts, beheaded Virgin Marys. I'd love to show you my photographs. I have the feeling you have a good eye. Don't you think there are too many divisions in the militias? It seems as if they dislike each other, that they fight among themselves."

Gerda talks endlessly, jumping from subject to subject like an enthusiastic child. Her joy is contagious. The coffee tastes terrible, it must be chicory, but the conversation is heartwarming. So why, Tina wonders, does she judge this woman so severely? She runs the same risks as the rest of them, and wasn't Tina just like her at that age? Wasn't she also ambitious? Didn't she also want people to stand in line behind her? Weston never took credit for her photographs. She also wanted to exhibit, to be known. "Gerda's ambition is more vehement than mine was; mine was gentler, but it propelled me forward. Now I think I have no ambition at all. Something inside me has gone dark," she concludes.

All the convoys go through Barcelona. If they are fighters, they sing loud; if they are men and women on the run, they pass by in silence. The girls are afraid most of the Moorish mercenaries that Franco brought from Africa. Even Eladia says, "I would prefer a Catalonian anarchist to one of those filthy Moors." The debates over divisions within the fragile Republican coalition are endless.

"But the anarchists are thugs, they are undisciplined, crazy, they have no idea how to stop Franco," Tina says.

"But they have always fought for Spain," Eladia argues.

"Long live social revolution!" shouts someone in Catalan.

"It's sickening that it should end like this, with Communists, anarchists, and Trotskyites shooting at one another in the streets instead of fighting Franco, Comrade María," Eladia cries out.

Tina doesn't agree, but she likes the girl and doesn't have the heart to argue.

The National Confederation of Labor (CNT) and the Workers' Party of Marxist Unity (POUM) think social revolution is what is most important, whereas the Communist Party wants to take charge of the battle and win the war begun in Melilla and defeat the Nationalists. Barcelona on one side; Madrid on the other. Pepe Díaz is furious: "The enemies of the people are the Fascists and the Trotskyites, who are out of control. Trotskyism is not a political party: it is a band of counterrevolutionary elements."

In Barcelona, the POUM and the FAI—Trotskyists and anarchists, respectively—decided to start the social revolution and take power. Communists and Trotskyists raised barricades and shot at each other in the streets. From Valencia and the sea, twelve thousand soldiers were sent by Juan Negrín, the Minister of Finance, to put down the revolt in Barcelona. They met no resistance.

Now that the Communists have defeated the anarchist thesis of "Make the revolution to win the war" and continue to advance

281

their own strategy of "Win the war to make the revolution," Comrade María feels better.

The power of the anarcho-syndicalists in Catalonia has been broken.

Tina returns to Madrid. She receives visitors, answers letters, and clarifies questions about aid sent by U.S. sympathizers to Republican Spain. She is in good health again, her spirits much higher.

Woman with Flag. Tina Modotti, 1928. Courtesy the Museum of Modern Art, New York. Palladium print. 9 3/4 x 7 11/16 in.

2 7

$\mathcal{E}$ ver since Matilde Landa, as Political Commissar for the Hospital Obrero, and Comandante Carlos, Moscow's appointed Political Commissar for Spain, decided that she should not return to the hospital, Tina has surprising mobility. She is such an efficient administrator, in her own quiet way, that she is sent to Red Aid offices in other Spanish cities. She also goes to France to visit sister organizations and foreign solidarity groups, which tend to mistake Red Aid for the Spanish Red Cross. With Tina's help, food and money are properly distributed.

On June 27, Comandante Carlos sends her to meet the delegates to a writers' conference when they arrive in Barcelona. Tina is to accompany them to Valencia, where the meeting will be held. María Luisa Lafita will go with her. Many of the delegates to the Congress for Cultural Freedom stay at the Hotel Majestic. Barcelona is full to overflowing. Vacationers turn their faces to the sun at the beach. The sidewalks are crowded, the Ramblas is bustling, the cafés are packed with people living normal lives, drinking, dancing.

She approaches Juan de la Cabada.

"Juanito," she says timidly.

He smiles because Spain has touched him, and he is always smiling, but he doesn't recognize the woman who addresses him. He's about to walk away with María Luisa Vera when the woman insists, "Juanito."

"Excuse me, are you from Campeche?"

"It's me, Tina, Tina Modotti."

"Heavens, Tina! It's been such a long time. What a wonderful surprise!"

"I was sent here to look after all of you. If you need anything, just ask me."

When they part, Juan says to María Luisa Vera, another delegate from Mexico, "She was the most attractive woman in Mexico in the twenties, the most tantalizing."

"She still walks very gracefully and her dark suit is well cut," María Luisa says.

"But she's not the same. I didn't even recognize her."

He follows her with his eyes; Juan feels a deep sadness.

Despite her recent improvement, Tina is still a shadow of the woman Juan knew in Mexico. Her hair is graying around the temples and there is a resigned expression to her face. How exhausting war is, how it drains us. Even he, a young man of twenty-nine, has aged since he came to Spain.

A French delegate, André Champson, complains, "Madame, we were woken up at six in the morning only to wait three hours in the lobby. When are we going to Valencia?"

"There's a shortage of transport. We'll have to wait."

Lack of punctuality is intolerable to the Europeans; the Latin Americans couldn't care less.

"That's the way it always is," Stephen Spender says in a conciliatory tone. "They round us up before they move us on."

"It's the war," Ralph Bates explains.

"No, it's not," Mari Valero chimes in. "It's just the Spanish way. You'd better get used to it. No matter where you want to go, you lose a few hours."

"Or gain them." Ludwig Renn smiles.

Alexei Tolstoy takes advantage of the delay to rush out to the street with his camera. He returns late, flushed, sweaty, carrying his big belly in front of him; he's happy with what he has seen.

There are two fat men among the delegates: Tolstoy and Silvestre Revueltas. Of the two, Silvestre is more interesting. Tina goes for a walk with him toward the Ramblas. "Did you bring any Mexican cigarettes? What's going on with the Party? Tell me about Luz Ardizana, El Ratón Velasco, Laborde. And Concha Michel, I saw her in Moscow. Will Mexico be sending us more arms and cartridges? David Alfaro Siqueiros often visits the Francos Rodríguez barracks."

"I saw Siqueiros. Tell me the latest about Contreras," says Silvestre.

"On the Guadalajara front, he took a megaphone and addressed his compatriots across the trenches. 'Tutti siamo italiani, tutti siamo italiani.' He fought the battle with words. 'Comrades, fellow Italians, why have you come here to kill your brothers?' The Italians asked about the Russians, the Russian enemy. 'What Russians?' 'They sent us here to kill Russians and Reds.' 'Well, we are Republicans, Garibaldians.' And that time he managed to convince them, though it doesn't always work." She asks Silvestre if he heard about Guernica, then lowers her eyes as if praying. "It was a market day and hundreds of peasants were crowded around the stalls. At four in the afternoon, all the church bells started ringing: this was the signal for the raid. There were six large explosions. By eight in the evening, the city was a great torch that could be seen from twenty kilometers away; Guernica was a pile of rubble. Sixteen hundred people dead and nine hundred wounded. Only the two ash trees in the square remained standing. It was the work of Hitler and his Condor Legion."

"The whole world is shocked. But Nin's disappearance is shocking, too."

Andrés Nin, director of the POUM and an outspoken anti-Stalinist, disappeared ten days earlier. Vittorio Codovilla confirmed that the Russians had interrogated him, that he had been arrested by the GPU. The executions of Trotskyists had begun in the Soviet Union and were continuing in Spain. The POUM said that the Russian police had no right to arrest and interrogate Spanish citizens. They claimed that the Russians were sending not only arms but also secret agents, who acted with impunity. The Communists termed Nin a Fascist. But where is he? Is he in Salamanca or in Berlin?

Tina suspects that Vittorio knows the answer, but she doesn't say this to Silvestre. Instead, she warns him, "It's better not to talk to Trotskyites. You should tell Elena Garo and Octavio Paz."

The Congress impresses everybody in the midst of war. In Valencia the assemblies are held in the partially destroyed city hall. Delegates separate into national groups and carry on their conversations in French, German, English, and Spanish. Paradoxically, their exhaustion and their concern make them more receptive; fatigue breaks down their defenses.

Tina looks at the names of the dead written in gold lettering: Federico García Lorca, Ramón del Valle-Inclán, Ralph Fox. María Luisa Lafita is overjoyed to see her fellow Cubans, Juan Marinello and Nicolás Guillén. The foreign delegates try to speak Spanish. Cesar Vallejo wants to avoid Pablo Neruda, while María Luisa Vera, an admirer of poetry, pursues Vallejo. Tina moves from group to group, facilitating communication between those who cannot understand each other.

"Another government, during wartime, would have hesitated before offering hospitality to eighty extra consumers of electricity, water, food, gas, hotel accommodations, and vehicles. But Spain has opened its arms to us," Anna Seghers says gratefully.

When Tina isn't sitting on a bench listening intensely to every word being said, she is walking around, checking her list, asking, "Do you need anything? Can I help with something? Did you get some rest? Did you find your luggage?" Though many have already arrived from Barcelona, others are still expected. Some are still in Port Bou, the Catalonian port. Others will go on to the Soviet Union or to Paris. Some complain that it is cowardly to sit there listening to useless speeches when the battle should be waged in the trenches. "A gun, I want a gun, now." Octavio Paz asks to be a political commissar. They sit around in cafés and discuss strategies. Life continues: people go to work, the theater, the symphony. At four in the afternoon, the restaurants run out of food, but those who arrive on time get their soup, bread, meat, salad, dessert, and wine, all the wine they want.

A request has arrived from the militiamen on the front: they would like the writers in Valencia to send them a shipment of books. The news electrifies the meeting. "The same thing is happening in Spain as in Russia," Tina explains. "Portable libraries are being set up in each city, and even the most isolated villages are requesting educational materials."

Large numbers of university students, factory workers, and militiamen ask Tina if they can come to listen and talk to the writers. The delegates are especially impressed by the presence of soldiers straight from the front, covered in dust, exhausted, yet ready and willing to go back. "Thank you so much for your help, comrades," they say as they leave.

The delegates talk a lot about the preservation of works of art. They accuse the anarchists and the Republicans of burning churches, but according to María Teresa León, Spain's national treasures are safe in cellars and warehouses. "Rafael and I helped rescue them. The Committee for the Preservation of Artistic Treasures in Madrid has catalogued every object." This information pleases Stephen Spender. Julian Zugazagoitia tells how some laborers saved three El Grecos in Illescas; the Nationalists, on the other hand, bomb everything and then blame the Republican loyalists and their leaders, calling them "ignorant peasants."

The Soviet delegates have only one objective at the Congress: to condemn André Gide and his book, *Retour de l'U.R.S.S.*

"I thought we came here to talk about Spain, not Russia; that isn't the point now," says Jef Last. "Eugène Dabit and I traveled with him; we saw his reactions, and we shared them. It was very painful for him to write all this."

"Would you have written it?"

"No, but I would like to ask the Russian delegation right now why they didn't include on their list of the persecuted, along with Mussam and Ossietzky, the names of those persecuted in the Soviet Union, like Tarasov, Mandelstam, Bezimensky, Gronsky, Tretyakov."

"It's more important to condemn Adolf Hitler's Germany and Benito Mussolini's Italy; the real danger to culture comes from those countries," asserts Arturo Serrano.

"Don't forget that Gide was a leader of the anti-Fascist movement. He headed the International Congress for the Defense of Culture in June 1935," Jef Last says, seconded by André Malraux.

"All the more reason to expose him: he is a traitor to the cause."

Pepe Bergamín moves to condemn André Gide. The delegates

second the motion. "That's good," Tina thinks. "Books like that only weaken the anti-Fascist democracies."

After the congress has been in session for five days, Gerda Taro exclaims, "What am I doing here? I like action." She decides to leave for the front with some other foreign correspondents: Claud Cockburn, the English Communist who writes for *The Daily Worker*; Egon Erwin Kisch, the German-Czech; and Ted Allan, Norman Bethune's political commissar, who is in love with Gerda.

When Tina looks at Gerda—twenty-six years old, sought-after, funny, a smile on her lips—she remembers Mexico and all her admirers, from Gómez Robelo to Pepe Quintanilla, everybody following her around and worshipping the ground she walked on. She remembers Weston, pale with jealousy, opening the door and finding her in Xavier Guerrero's arms. Poor Gerda, so close to the world and its vanities. Perhaps she reminds Tina too much of what she once tried to be: the center of attention, the heroine, a woman of action, an adventuress.

At four in the morning, the delegates are shaken out of their beds by the sound of sirens. The sky turns red with explosions. Tina feels a certain satisfaction that the intellectuals will experience the rigors of war firsthand.

The explosions sound muffled. "They're a long way off." "Yes, far enough away so that we don't have to run," says Max Aub.

At ten in the morning on the day after the conference ends, a caravan of cars leaves Valencia for Madrid. Exhausted from staying up all night and from all the tension, the delegates drink a respectable amount of wine. That night, Madrid is illuminated by the red splendor of grenades. The writers go up on the rooftops as if to watch fireworks. How quickly they have gotten used to it!

"You know, María, that red-haired woman, that photographer who was always looking for you, was killed near the American camp hospital close to the Escorial," says Flor Cernuda.

"Gerda Taro?"

"Yes, she was run over on the Brunete front by one of our tanks. It charged the car she was riding in with Ted Allan and General Walter. Allan was badly wounded; they say he'll never walk again. Walter wasn't hurt. I told Gerda twice: 'Put on a beret or they'll shoot you from above.' She died before they could operate."

"Why wasn't it me?" is Tina's first thought. Then she feels angry. "Gerda was careless, always on the lookout for the hottest spot."

Now Tina realizes that she never told Gerda that she was a photographer, too. Once, Tina took the camera and held it up to her eye, and Gerda said: "I'm sure you could take good photographs, María, come with me."

Tina returned the camera, saying, "I'm more useful at the hospital."

Gerda was like a flame in the trenches. The International Brigades, the Germans, the Poles, the Czechs, the volunteers from the Balkans and Central Europe would invite her to join them for a sip from their wineskins. Salud, compañera. Her Venetian-red hair could be seen from a distance, glowing in the sun like the gold on an altar.

"María, do you think that my photographs look like they were taken by a woman?" she had asked Tina.

"I don't think so. But I do think you're risking your life."

Tina goes with Flor Cernuda to the chapel at the palace of the Marquis de Bella Espina, the headquarters of the Alliance of Anti-Fascist Writers. Rafael Alberti and María Teresa León have organized a memorial service. Nobody can find Robert Capa. Louis Aragon will pick the coffin up at the border.

When Tina sees Gerda lying in her lead coffin, surrounded by flowers, her youth buried under so many lilies, she cannot help thinking that if she had gone on as a photographer she might have ended up the same way: achieving fame in death rather than in life. Gerda would be considered a heroine, the first female war correspondent killed in action, the Joan of Arc of graphic journalism. Tina understands that Gerda's fearless pursuit of glory has also been her defeat.

2 8

The International Brigades arrive in Barcelona on the dark, dreary morning of October 28, 1938. They will parade for the last time past their commanders along the Avenida del 14 de abril. The walls are still painted with their slogans in many languages: "Workers of the World: Unite!"

When they arrived almost three years before, the brigade members had read an open letter from José Díaz: "This is not only about the liberation of Spain; it is a problem shared by all progressive human beings." Now, they are being forced out by political pressures beyond their control. They look tired, weather-beaten, toughened, immortal: fighters from many countries offered their lives to the struggle and would be united forever.

On Spanish soil, among the furrows, two hundred thousand bodies have been left behind; of those, one hundred thousand were volunteers. Those who died on the battlefield might later be located by their families; each was buried with a stone marker engraved with his or her name. Those who were executed were thrown into common graves.

"You came speaking different languages, but you understood one another. You can march with your heads high. You are history. You are legend. Long live the heroes! Long live the International Brigades! Long Live the Republic!" shouts La Pasionaria.

The Spanish brigadists sing the "Internationale" in Spanish; the others sing it in their respective languages, with tears in their eyes. The streets are carpeted with petals, the tanks are covered with flowers.

Girls break through the crowds and run to embrace the soldiers and give them bouquets. Everybody is crying; some soldiers carry children on their shoulders; others limp along on crutches or smile under their bandaged heads. All leave friends buried in Spanish soil and walk with pride in spite of their injuries. The Abraham Lincoln Brigade passes by: out of thirty-two thousand North Americans, only fifteen thousand will return; of two thousand Englishmen, only fifteen remain. Then come the Canadians, the Cubans, the Mexicans, the Latin Americans; all suffered great losses. Scandinavians, Germans, Austrians, Dutch, Polish, Hungarian, Czechs, Yugoslavs, French.

Standing next to Tina, Mari Valero begins to cry. Tina puts her arm around her.

Comandante Carlos approaches the two women. "Pull yourself together, Mari."

"It's just that we're all alone now. Forgive me, I'll be okay in a minute."

"Look at La Pasionaria, Mari. We should be like her and not cry."

"I don't want to be like La Pasionaria. She scares me."

Beside Valero's tear-stained face, Tina's is frozen in bitterness; a deep furrow runs across her brow.

"Non e giusto, Toio. It's not fair for it to end like this. For almost two years we've watched them fight and now they leave, mutilated and wounded. Why? It's ridiculous to compare the Italian and German Fascist invaders with a popular army; they aren't the same at all."

"They're leaving covered with flowers. They're leaving their second families behind in Spain. They'll come back someday. But the war goes on, and we can still win. Soon we'll hold the Red Aid Congress. We have sympathizers all over the world."

"And what are we going to give them to eat?" asks Mari Valero, her voice stifled by sobs.

"The Eastern Zone has promised to get us supplies. A lot of soldiers from the front will come for a few days. It's going to be a great congress of the masses. You'll see how much unity there is between the front and the rearguard."

"How do you manage to be so optimistic?" Tina asks him. "All I ever think about are the dead."

"I think about them, too, but my work is for the living."

Perhaps even Vittorio doesn't believe what he is saying. A few days later he leaves Tina in Barcelona and goes to Paris to organize the retreat. Before, he went to plead for arms. Now he is asking for shelter for countless refugees.

Barcelona is defenseless, and the Nationalists drop bombs every day. Valencia is cut off, the highway has been taken by Franco. Tina feels it is urgent for her to go to Valencia to help those who are leaving. When Vittorio returns, Tina tells him she's going to Valencia with Red Aid to bring desperately needed medical equipment. The only way to get there is by boat.

"By boat?"

"Yes, a steamboat. We'll travel by night."

"Ma tu sei matta. The coast is being watched. You'll be caught for sure, if you don't drown first."

"I'm not going to abandon our comrades."

Vittorio is unable to dissuade Tina. She knows the risks are enormous, though she doesn't share this knowledge with Encarnita Fuyola, who is going with her. At night, the sea is threatening under a moonless sky. They navigate through the darkness, the cold penetrating their bones. Miraculously, they avoid the Falangist patrols. The ink-black sea is all around their small boat. "Don't worry, we'll get there soon," says Tina, to reassure Encarnita. Then she hears the motor stop. Deep silence. "Nothing to do but go ashore into enemy territory," says the navigator. Tina looks up at the sky: it is a damp cavern echoing guttural moans. Encarnita takes her hand. She is in a cold sweat. They drift. The waves break soddenly against the hull. An eternity passes. "We can't go back," says the sailor, "and we can't go forward." Tina would like to take her hand out of Encarnita's. Tina is calm; she is thinking that perhaps the time has come. Julio Antonio waits for her beneath the waves. Suddenly, the motor coughs, sputters, recovers some power; the boat furrows slowly, very slowly through the water. Tina lets go of Encarnita's icy hand, and the stuttering engine carries them to their destination.

The National Congress of Solidarity is held in Madrid at the beginning of November 1938, in the middle of heavy artillery fire.

Representatives arrive from all over Spain: 1,200 Communists, socialists, anarchists, determined to show their friends in France, England, Holland, and Poland that the popular resistance is still alive and well. In spite of the terrible situation, there is a hopeful atmosphere at the sessions. Tina, Matilde Landa, María Luisa Lafita, and Roberto Vizcaíno listen optimistically to the brave delegates who try to keep their spirits up in spite of the bombings.

On the last night of the Congress, enemy planes and artillery pound Madrid, but the sessions continue uninterrupted. The militiamen wish to show at all cost that Madrid is not lost.

That night, Contreras summons a few select delegates for a private meeting. He is accompanied by Melchiore Vanni, an old friend of Tina's who, under the name of Bonnet, directed the Paris branch of the International Committee for Aid to Spain. In the middle of the meeting, a bomb falls on the table they are sitting around. A number of the participants are killed instantly. Melchiore Vanni is seriously wounded; Vittorio loses consciousness, but not before he feels an avalanche of glass and rubble fall on him and a sharp stab of pain in his right side.

When Tina hears the news, she rushes to the building and finds it surrounded by people and ambulances as the dead and wounded are evacuated. She is unable to locate Vittorio or Melchiore Vanni and nobody knows what has happened to them.

Tina searches one clinic after another. She looks at the faces of cadavers stretched out on cots; every time she lifts a sheet, she chokes on the fear that she will see Vittorio's face. "More than five thousand," they murmur in the corridors, repeating estimates of casualties of the latest bombings. "Mamma mia, help me find him.

If I don't find him in Madrid, I'm going to look for him in the camp hospitals. Don't let him die, please, don't let him die, he's all I have."

When he wakes up from the anesthesia, Vittorio finds Tina asleep at his feet, her head resting on the bed.

"What happened? Where are we?"

"At a clinic on the outskirts of Madrid. Your right arm is broken and you lost your thumb. You're alive, Toietto; many others aren't."

"That means I can get up. I'm not staying here because of a stupid thumb."

"You're not moving, Toio, not until they release you. You're going to need some kind of therapy. How are you going to hold a pen?"

"For God's sake, woman, you're worried about how I'll write? I'll write the way I've always written: with my fists."

In the morning the doctors come and stand around his bed. "We came to see how the hero of the Fifth Regiment feels this morning."

"How are you, Carlos?" asks the head doctor.

"Very well."

"Really. 'Very well'?"

"Well, I know that my arm will never be the same, I won't be able to lift it as I used to, or shoot without my thumb. I guess I'll have to learn to shoot with my left."

"Yes, that's right. Unfortunately, the glass and rubble that fell on you damaged some nerves."

That night Tina returns to the foot of Vittorio's bed. At dawn, after assuring herself that he is better, she runs to the Hospital Obrero. She walks through a wounded city, one crippled like Vittorio. Traffic is held up by barricades; many houses are only half-standing, their guts exposed, beams and bricks strewn over the sidewalks.

A new bombing raid shakes Madrid; people race madly into the streets. At the clinic where Vittorio is convalescing, the wounded pull out their IVs and run naked through the corridors, with the nurses chasing after them.

The doctors stand at the door of the room where the Comandante lies: how will he react?

"Carlos, there is more bombing."

"Okay."

"The clinic might be bombed, too."

"Okay."

When the raid is over, one of the doctors asks him, "Now you can tell us how you managed not to run like a scared rabbit."

"Actually, I was terrified. My legs were shaking under the sheets; I'm sure you noticed. My first impulse was to get up and run, but you were watching me, and I thought, 'Okay, they're bombing the city again. How many times have they bombed the city, and this hospital has never been hit? If a bomb falls on us tonight, that's fate.' And I don't believe in fate. I'm a materialist. I don't believe in destiny, so I didn't believe a bomb would fall here. I looked at my watch and counted thirty seconds, one minute, two minutes, three minutes, and as I counted, my legs began to relax."

"How could you muster so much control?"

"You did the same thing. You stood there watching me from the door. On the battlefield, when there is a bombing run or artillery or both at once, people start running. But the best thing is to hide. If you can't get to a shelter, it's not worth running. I just start walking back and forth, and then the soldiers say, 'If Comandante Carlos is standing here, watching us, how can we run?' "

"Bravo, Comandante."

Tina doesn't dare tell him how poorly Melchiore Vanni is doing. When he asks, she just says, "Recuperating." Nor does she tell him about the five delegates who died. She'll tell him when he leaves the hospital. When he talks about the bombing, Tina pats his hand as if he were a little boy. When he looks at her closely, he is struck by how distant she has grown. "How strange, as if I didn't know this woman," he says to himself. He realizes that she never confides in him anymore. "What do I know about her?" There's never time for them to be together except when they scour the battlefield for wounded, as they did in Málaga and Almería.

Two weeks later, Comandante Carlos is discharged from the hospital and Tina accompanies him to Albacete. There they meet Mari Valero and Encarnita Fuyola, who has come from Barcelona to the American Hospital to collect medical supplies. At dinner, the desperate situation of the Republicans dominates their subdued conversation. "It's all over," Valero blurts out. "We haven't got a chance. Only the Russians can save us now."

Vittorio and Tina take a plane to Barcelona. Half an hour after takeoff, they are forced to return to the airport because the radio doesn't work. After a few hours on the ground, they take off again, but an enemy Fiat pursues them throughout the trip. They finally land on the outskirts of Barcelona, in the midst of furious shelling. The crew praises Tina's calm during the ordeal, and she smiles the way she used to, young, innocent.

Vittorio arrives at the barracks with a turban of bandages on his head and his right arm in a cast from shoulder to hand, sticking out in front of him as if in a Fascist salute. When La Pasionaria and Enrique Líster see him come in, they break out laughing.

Ignacio Hidalgo de Cisneros tells him that not only does the Popular Army lack arms, it is also low on food.

"All we have left is lentils."

Since there are no streetlamps, it is almost impossible to walk through the cratered streets at night. Still, two and a half million people go out every night looking for food. The nights and days are clear, perfect for bombing raids. Whenever the people sitting at cafés hear the buzz of engines, they run to the bunkers; after the raid is over, they go back and sit down at the same table. One, maybe two hours pass, they sip their orangeade, then vanish again when they hear an engine. The people of Barcelona stay out late at night waiting for the sirens; they feel safer on the street.

This year there is no Christmas truce. Franco has refused. On December 23, Franco attacks Catalonia. On December 31, the Fascists march on Barcelona. Franco's troops advance from the north and the east. Airplanes take off from the Baleares Islands to bomb Barcelona, sometimes as many as twenty raids in one day. Thousands die in less than twenty-four hours. The Italian Air Force is bent on destroying every industrialized Catalonian city; the Nationalists control Spain's ports; the Republicans have no ports left in Spain, and the French have refused to help. No one celebrates the New Year.

Vittorio travels to Madrid, where the atmosphere of defeat is inescapable. Nobody thinks about fighting anymore. He hears a young blond man say in broken Spanish, "It's all the fault of the Communists."

Vittorio checks an impulse to strike him.

"This is the last winter of the Republic," says another young man.

"Are you in the brigades?" Vidali asks.

"Yes," the first one says, shaking his head sadly.

Vittorio feels like telling him that his defeatist attitude is to blame, that attitudes like his are losing the war for them, but instead he asks if he belongs to the Party.

"No," says the young man. "I mean, not really." A flash of fear shows in his eyes.

"Damn it," Vittorio exclaims, "Franco's Fifth Columnists are more and more visible. The Communist Party is about the only group that doesn't allow itself to be swallowed up." He remembers that he is not among his men and wonders where they are. In the field? Freezing to death? On the road?

He returns to Barcelona by car and finds the city in ruins. Occasional shots break the silence.

He can no longer counter Tina's pessimism. The Catalan government, like the Spanish government, has taken refuge in Figueras. The civilian leaders watch helplessly as hundreds of thousands of refugees leave for the north.

Through the auspices of Red Aid, Tina organizes the removal of Melchiore Vanni, whose wounds have still not healed, and Isidoro Acevedo. Vanni, posing as Acevedo's son, will cross the border wrapped in a large khaki overcoat. They will say that he is going to be hospitalized for tuberculosis in the foothills of the French Pyrenees. Inspectors always keep their distance from people with TB.

Before she leaves, she begs Vittorio to find Antonio Machado, the great Spanish poet, and his family to try to help them. Vittorio and his driver, Emilio, search through silent streets, past darkened windows. There is not a single light anywhere, no voices from the shadows.

"Even the dogs have left," says Emilio.

Finally they locate Machado's house, abandoned. The Comandante cannot help worrying about the poet lost in the river of desperate refugees. He imagines an old, sad, gentle man leaning on his stick as he leaves his native land.

29

Only a few comrades remain in Barcelona to watch over Party headquarters. In a candlelit room, Palmiro Togliatti studies a map. He raises his head when Tina and Vittorio enter and asks, "What are you doing here? Why haven't you left?"

"Because Barcelona needs to be defended," says Vittorio.

Looking at Vidali's arm in its absurd salute, Togliatti begins to laugh, and his laughter spreads to the others, even to Pedro Fernández Checa, the Fifth Regiment's Secretary of Organization.

"Do we still have the means to defend Barcelona?" Togliatti asks.

"I'm sure that all is not lost," Fernández Checa replies. "Many Internationalists have remained. We still have battalions capable of holding back the Fascists. We must make a stand to the bitter end."

"But enemy artillery is pounding the city."

"Carrillo is organizing our defense," Fernández Checa says.

"You're endangering yourself by staying behind, Pedro, and you are indispensable to the Party. And you? What are you doing here, Vidali? You should go with Longo and Marty," says Togliatti.

"I'm staying to defend the city," says Vidali.

"I'm not leaving until Vittorio goes," says Tina staunchly.

"The movement needs you," Fernández Checa adds to their protests, "and you should leave, too, Palmiro."

Togliatti shakes his head and with a surge of pride says, "I am the representative of the Communist International."

No mercy is shown to those who fall into Fascist hands. They are summarily executed. The Internationalists are treated even more harshly than Spanish Communists for intervening in the domestic affairs of Spain, attempting to take over a country that doesn't belong to them. Palmiro Togliatti, a key man in the Republic, is in danger. So is Contreras.

Tina returns from the border and continues to assist those who have remained in Barcelona. Most of them are children and old people, unaware of the danger or unable to leave before. She wears a scarf on her head like the Spanish women, and often carries a child in her arms. She moves mattresses, improvises seats in carts, applies bandages where necessary, assists the weakest, wrapping their feet in newspaper if nothing else is available. "You should be as prepared as possible for the journey. You can't make it in rope sandals." She finds boots among the equipment left behind by the International Brigades. "It's okay if they're tight, Don Cipriano; anything is better than having your feet freeze." She discusses the most insignificant details, convincing them to take olive oil because it's more important than tobacco. She gives advice, picks up chickens, dogs, puts the cat in a basket, shuts the canary cage. Tina won't leave until her people are on their way. "Lock the door and give me the key," an old man instructs her as if his return were imminent. "The house has to be locked, so nobody can get in."

While Vittorio comes and goes with Emilio from Figueras to Gerona, from Gerona to Barcelona, Tina partakes of the anguish of those who are leaving. Red Aid has fewer and fewer resources. "I don't even have bandages," she tells Vittorio when she next sees him. "I'm wrapping them in newspaper. There's nothing, nothing to take care of them with. I can't give them food. If they aren't killed outright, how will they survive?"

Tina watches the oxen pulling heavily laden carts; the peasants carry their children in their arms. Defeat is slow, so slow. But one must not give up; one must go on walking. When the children sit down to rest, an angry voice says, "Come on, come on, don't stop." But where are they going? To Gerona, to Figueras, to the Bay of Rosas, to Port Bou, to France, to salvation. On the cold, snowy trail, the elderly drop their belongings along the way, until they leave behind everything that was their life. And when they cannot continue any farther, they themselves drop by the side of the road.

Sometimes someone picks them up; sometimes the others must simply carry on.

So that they will not die, too.

"Leave me be. This is my land." The line is long. Behind the carts, there are some Buicks, a few Fords. "We're almost out of gas." Everybody slows down the march in turn: the oxen hold back the cars, the old people hold back the young, the children cling to their mothers' legs. A sign on a tree says, "Negrín, we are tired of resisting." It has not yet been washed away by the rain. Another asks, "Negrín, what have you done with Nin?"

The gray sky hangs above the muddy earth. Suddenly, something hisses overhead.

"Planes!"

They run to the side of the road and throw themselves on the ground with their arms over their heads.

The planes drop their bombs on the fleeing population.

Then they vanish.

Vittorio meets Togliatti in Gerona. "The situation is bad but not catastrophic. We can still put up a fight. Come with me to the Figueras castle for a meeting of the Republican parliament. Negrín, Lamoneda, and others will be there."

"This will be the last time," Vidali says.

Few attend this meeting, but Negrín speaks noble words. "Republican Spain will never surrender." His efforts to find grounds for negotiation to end the hostilities get nowhere. During the session, the parliament proclaims three principles that the winning side must comply with. First, Spain must remain independent from any foreign nation. Second, the right of the Spanish people to choose their destiny through a referendum must be respected. Third, there must be no reprisals or persecutions once the war is over.

This is the last time the deputies will meet on Spanish soil. They salute the army of the sea, the land, and the air. They affirm their belief in the glorious future of Spain, their native land. They say they have been battered, but not defeated. They want freedom, they want an independent, Republican Spain.

Togliatti orders Vidali to go to France and help the refugees.

The bombing continues. Vidali and Emilio leave Gerona a few hours before the Fascists occupy it. Tina left just hours before with Red Aid.

On January 26, Franco enters Barcelona. The fifteen thousand refugees fleeing from Catalonia must contend with the cold, the rain, then snow, lack of provisions, and merciless bombing. Thousands of civilians on their way to the border are protected by divisions of the Republican army: the casualties are enormous.

Matilde is one of those who insists on staying until the bitter end. "I'm not leaving, Carlos, I'm not leaving Spain. I'm going to stay here and fight."

"What about your daughter, Carmen?"

"She'll be fine in Russia. I'll get her when we win."

"And Paco?"

"I don't know. He'll do what he wants."

"Matilde, you're not thinking straight. You have to stay alive for your daughter's sake: you have a duty to her."

"You and María aren't Spanish, you don't understand." Matilde Landa stares at him with hatred. "The war will continue. The Madrid–Alicante–Valencia triangle is still controlled by the Republic. We don't need those who have decided to go to France. You are all cowards."

Matilde is beside herself. She reaches out as if to hit Vittorio.

He tries to embrace her. "Oh, Matilde, poor Matilde."

Then she throws herself on him. "Don't poor Matilde me, poor you and María, you're a couple of idiots, a couple of—"

Vittorio no longer hears her. He turns to leave, murmuring: "Poveretta, poveretta donna, poveretta."

On February 6, 1939, the Nationalists occupy Figueras. Franco has won the war. In Burgos, he refuses to even listen to Negrín's proposals. He demands unconditional surrender. Azaña, Aguirre, Companys, and Martinez Barrio have gone to France, leaving their people behind.

"Leaders like that deserve nothing but contempt," Franco says. "How do they dare speak about the freedom of the Spanish people?"

Tina, whose passport shows that she has been in France a few days before, has no problem crossing the border. Rivers of human beings descend from the mountains and approach the border, believing that they will encounter the friendship of the French. Trust and faith glow in their faces.

Fifteen thousand Spanish citizens have crossed the Pyrenees and reached the border posts manned by French police. The police see endless lines of soldiers, women, children, many sick, some wounded, and attempt to legalize the exodus.

"Vos papiers s'il vous plaît."

Vittorio finds Marty and Longo standing next to a flag in front of a mountain of guns and rifles. They shake hands with each Republican soldier after he tosses his weapon on the pile. This will be the last time the militiamen march before their generals. In spite of their exhaustion, with their uniforms covered in blood and mud, they hold their heads high and pride shines from their faces. Some are on crutches; some have bandaged heads, others have their arms in slings. If all is lost, we may as well sing, right, comrades? Singing lightens the heaviness in their hearts.

Vittorio still has not decided to cross the border, that invisible line between worlds. He stays in the car beside his driver without speaking, watching the others pass by through the frosted window. Images run through his head like a movie reel: a dead girl on her mother's belly; a young soldier smiling at the sky; Juan Negrín in his office, the look of desperation on his face. And there sit the Comandante and his driver, Emilio, together every moment of this interminable tragedy.

Comandante Carlos, the political commissar of the glorious Fifth Regiment, crosses the border in a miserable state, unshaven, dirty, hungry. Now he is the one immersed in a terrible silence, the one with muddy shoes. Far off, there is an explosion, a muffled shout. His cast is wet and coming apart in places; his arm hangs like a piece of dead meat; his wounds are reopening. He throws his gun on the enormous pile and continues walking without looking back.

Each man is searched by the French police. They are asked if they are carrying arms, if they were in the hospital, about infections. They make them empty their bags. Their belongings spill on the ground. While he empties the contents of a paper bag on the snow, a French policeman asks, "What's this shit?"

"It's Spanish earth," Carlos replies.

General Francisco Durán is the last one to cross. At the very moment he says goodbye to his soldiers, his voice cracking with emotion, he sees that they are laughing.

His mare, her legs spread, is pissing.

Argelès-sur-mer, St.-Cyprien, La Lozère, Las Haras, Aude, Agde, St.-Etienne, Le Vernet, Gurs, Barcères, Sept Fonts, Bram, Arles-sur-tech, Château de Collioure, La Reynarde, Château de Montgrand, Le Perthus, Hérault, Haute-Garonne, Mazères, Le Boulou, Prats de Molio, St.-Laurent-de-Cerdans, La Tour de Carol, Bourg-Madame, Mont Louis, all concentration camps.

Most of the Catalonians are sent to Hérault.

Two of the largest concentration camps for the Spanish refugees are on the beach: St.-Cyprien and Argelès. Four hundred thousand refugees have been put behind barbed wire. The guards are not deliberately cruel; they simply don't know what to do. Nothing is provided. If the Spaniards do not build their own barracks, they will have to sleep in the sand. They relieve themselves on the sand; on the sand they leave their few belongings. The sand has become their only home. They walk on the sand, sit on the sand, they eat sand. Sand sticks to their hair; they are blinded by the sad, black, muddy sand of the Mediterranean. Not a tree, not a patch of green, only these faces, these shoulders, these necks bowed by defeat and by the weight of the sand.

In St.-Cyprien many have taken off their shoes to wash their feet in the salty water, shivering under the gray sky.

The children still have the energy to run on the beach, but they do not dare get their feet wet in the chilly water.

Mexico has offered refuge to eighty thousand families. They will be granted Mexican citizenship.

The *Mexique* sets sail with three thousand families on board, then sails through the Strait of Gibraltar, and out into the ocean, out into the solitary Atlantic.

3 0

*O*n the Grand Hotel in Perpignan, Herbert Matthews, the *New York Times* correspondent, and Gustav Regler confirm Vidali's worst fears: France and England will recognize Franco's government; only Alicante, Valencia, and Madrid still resist. Regler says the Quakers have sent supplies of milk and chocolate up to the mountains to the many women and children.

"The Republican troops are received at the French border as if they were outlaws. They come to Perpignan in good faith, unaware of what awaits them. They still believe in the Popular Front. Matthews and I watch them arrive with their rifles on their shoulders while they are still on Spanish soil; once they cross the border and throw away their rifles, they are nobody."

Vittorio is shocked by the indifference in the air. The French don't seem to care about the condition of the defeated Republicans. They look at them with scorn and treat them like cattle.

Tina and Vittorio meet at the Secretariat of the French Communist Party. He is in very bad shape, though no worse than a lot of other soldiers. Their fellow exiles continue to arrive: Ignacio Hidalgo de Cisneros and his wife, Constancia de la Mora, come with Juan Modesto. The discussion grows more and more heated, voices are raised.

"It's inconceivable that Azaña resigned without thinking about what would happen to his fighters and militants," says Hidalgo de Cisneros.

"Prieto might be brave, but intellectually he's a coward," adds Constancia. "He was so sure that we were going to lose the war, he spent all his time convincing others instead of fighting to win. He did a lot of damage to the Republic with his disastrous war policy."

They are all shouting when Antonio Cordón comes in, exhausted, his wife Rosa holding on to his hand. They embrace him and continue their discussion.

"It's a disgrace! Negrín wanted to talk to Franco, and the only thing Franco wanted was to kill him."

"Defeatism is the worst kind of poison; it settles in the blood and ends up contaminating even the healthiest organism," Hidalgo de Cisneros says sadly.

"It's one toxin I've never imbibed. Let's not fall into defeatism now," says Vidali.

"But we lost," Constancia de la Mora insists.

"Yes, we lost, but we have been part of Spain's heroic stand against Fascism," Cordón says. "This has been the most decisive and important experience of my life."

"And one page of history follows another. The confrontation between the proletariat and the bourgeoisie doesn't stop here," Vittorio continues as if talking to himself. "When I threw down my pistol before crossing the French border yesterday, February 9, 1939, I realized that I'm not even thirty-nine and I fought my first political battles more than twenty years ago. Now I'm sick, and wounded; I gave everything during these nine hundred days of war. I'm as tired as you are, comrades, but I'm not giving up. I have a strong, brave woman by my side. We'll begin again somewhere else in the world. There's other work to be done."

"The problem is the destiny of a whole people, Carlos, not just your own," says Hidalgo de Cisneros.

Vittorio turns on Ignacio Hidalgo de Cisneros. "I speak this way only because here I know I am among friends. We're all worried about our futures, whether we say so or not. When I talk about myself, I'm talking about all of us."

Benigno Morilla, Luis Cabo Giorla, Giorla Manso, Juan Vicens, and Del Val appear at the door. After greetings are exchanged, the exiles take comfort in a bottle of cognac a sympathetic French official has given one of them. They even try to smile and look beyond the catastrophe. Del Val offers a toast: "To our return!" In a corner, Tina is barely breathing. The only words she spoke at the table were, "Look, silverware." She caressed the white napkin and lifted the fork and knife in her hand, repeating: "Silverware."

Then Vittorio turns to her. "What about you, Tina?"

"If it were up to me, I'd go back to Spain. If that's impossible, I'll go to Italy. We can get work there. Togliatti and Nenni will help us. Let's go home."

Tina's eyes always say more than her mouth, expressing an infinite sadness. She has fought the war from the first day to the last, and now she is being pursued by voices: "María, a bandage." "María, I can't find my son." "María, help me cross the border with my children, so they won't kill me." "María, save us, don't forget us, don't let us fall into enemy hands." Now, through a whole night of arguments, recriminations, and criticism, with the bitter finality of defeat weighing down on all her comrades, Tina continues to listen to the inner voices.

In the morning, they bathe. Vittorio shaves and his friends find him clean underwear, a shirt, shoes, a suit. Nothing fits: even the hat is too small, but at least it covers his head wounds.

Tina and Vittorio take the train to Paris, riding third class.

"I feel ridiculous in these pants."

"Who in the world do you think cares?"

When they reach International Red Aid in Paris, they find everyone suffering from the same sense of profound loss. Where to live? What to do? Marcel Villard, a good friend who had organized the campaign to save Georgi Dimitrov with Vittorio in 1933, offers them a room in his house.

At an International Red Aid meeting, a French comrade takes the floor. "The Spanish refugees ought to understand that they lost the war, and accept the consequences."

Tina, stunned, exclaims, "You, too, lost the war against the

Nazis! The defeat of the Spanish people is the defeat of anti-Fascists everywhere."

Tina's disillusionment during this first meeting of the Red Aid Committee to Help Refugees is profound and will affect her entire stay in France.

Since January 28, 170,000 women and children and 60,000 men—10,000 of them wounded—have arrived.

When André Marty, vice president of Red Aid, sees Vittorio, he tells him there is a message from "la vieille." Stasova orders him to remain in Paris until the arrival of Tom Bell, an English comrade from the Comintern. That same day Tina and Vidali have dinner with Vittorio Codovilla and walk with him for hours along the Seine. They pore over how they could have organized the defense of Barcelona along the same lines as the defense of Madrid.

Later Julio Alvarez del Vayo, Negrín's Secretary of Foreign Relations, comes to André Marty's office and comments on Azaña's resignation and on the generals, among them Vicente Rojo, who refuse to return to Madrid: they consider the war lost. To return to Spain would be an act of madness, suicide. Alvarez del Vayo tells them that Dr. José Puche has escorted Antonio Machado safely to France, and helped him get settled in Collioure.

On February 17, Tina travels to Collioure and returns with an even heavier heart. The border crossing was horrendous, and France has treated Machado and his mother egregiously. A few weeks before Tina's visit, Don Antonio had still been able to walk along the cliffs of Collioure, a fishing village twenty-five kilometers from the Spanish border, but now he is no longer able to leave the hotel. Machado's brother, José, doesn't know where to turn for help. The poet is too sick to travel; he is dying.

Despite their exhaustion and low morale, Vittorio and Tina join Secours Populaire, a French solidarity organization working with Red Aid. Moscow's instructions: give moral and material support and legal advice to the Spanish and the international refugees.

Tina's first case is Machado. She won't give up trying to do something for him. She argues that the French authorities must intervene, that he is a great poet, a truly great Spanish poet. But the French only shrug their shoulders. In Collioure, Jacques Baille, a worker at the hotel, is the only person who knows who Machado is and offers to help him.

On February 22, Antonio Machado dies and nobody seems to notice. Julian Zugazagoitia delivers the funeral oration in front of the coffin covered with a Republican flag. Soon thereafter, the poet's mother follows him to the grave. A few weeks later, with the help of Tina and Secours Populaire, Machado's brother, José, and his wife travel to Chile with other refugees.

For Tina, Antonio Machado's death makes the defeat even harder to bear. She wants to leave France at all costs. Tina asks the leader of the Foreign Center of the Italian Communist Party, Giuseppe Berti, if she can return to Italy. "I know how to live clandestinely. Set me up as an agent."

"You are asking to do this now because you are desperate. You would be arrested immediately."

Vittorio also has trouble defining his future. He is in poor physical condition: he is being devoured by lice, his skin burns from a merciless rash, and his wounds refuse to heal.

Once again, Stasova in Moscow suggests a course of action. Tom Bell, Stasova's messenger, offers them a choice. They can go to the Soviet Union and rest for six months in the Crimea, or they can leave for the United States to organize assistance for 300,000 Spanish and international refugees. Stasova's discreet but explicit advice is to choose America.

"I was deported from the United States. To go back illegally would mean to risk being deported to Italy." Vittorio objects. "It would mean living in hiding again. Tina and I have never led normal lives."

"Remember, comrade, private lives do not exist."

Vittorio leaves the office with a heavy heart. Alvarez del Vayo asks him, "What are you going to do, Carlos?"

"Go to America, as I've been ordered."

Vittorio returns to the Villards' house and packs his bags; he will travel by train to Cherbourg to catch the boat. Tina will remain to help Melchiore Vanni and see Isidoro Acevedo off when he boards the train to the U.S.S.R.

"I want to do at least one thing well," she says gloomily.

"The next boat leaves in four days," Vittorio says. "I'll meet you in New York."

It is colder in Cherbourg than in Paris; the gray water is as heavy as his soul. Vittorio hears from a fellow traveler that Galán has rebelled in Cartagena and that on March 8, 9, and 10 the anarchists and the Communists were bent on destroying one another. The Communists executed Colonels Pérez Gazzolo, Fernando Urbano, and Otero Ferrer. Casado executed Barcelo, Conesa, and Meson. Vittorio wonders what has happened to Matilde Landa. The uprisings continue, a civil war within a civil war. England promised to evacuate the Republicans but didn't send enough ships. The forty-six Republicans who were left behind killed themselves on the docks of Valencia.

Vittorio thinks Tina, in her obsession, might even have returned to Spain. You never know what women are going to do. Tina has become such a fanatic he hardly recognizes her.

On March 23, Vidali's ship enters New York Harbor. He looks around at the skyscrapers and the proud profile of the Statue of Liberty. When he first arrived in America twenty years before, he was illegal; he carried a cardboard suitcase and wore shoes that were too tight for him. He didn't have a single friend in New York. Now at least he has comrades and, as his passport indicates, he is a professor of history born in La Coruña. From his small hotel near the dock, he contacts his friends and Communist leaders, Earl Browder and William Z. Foster.

Vidali lives only for news of Spain. The first thing he does every morning is turn on the radio. More than 100,000 Republican soldiers have surrendered. Forty-two Republican planes are grounded in Nationalist airports. A few hours before, the Nationalists occupied Cuenca, Guadalajara, Ciudad Real, Albacete, and Jaen. Two days later they take Almería, Murcia, and Cartagena. Where on earth can Tina have gone?

On April 1, 1939, Francisco Franco declares the war is over.

Vidali establishes himself in the house of his friend Rose Baron.

The Abraham Lincoln Brigade in New York is organizing a march to demand that the U.S. government take a strong position against Franco. Vittorio attends the demonstration with Browder and William Z. Foster.

Wearing a hat and wrapped in a scarf that almost covers his face, Vittorio watches the people marching and shouting slogans. When he sees the veterans of the Abraham Lincoln Brigade in military formation led by their commander, Milton Wolff, and hears them singing war songs, he realizes that he is crying. Across the ocean Madrid is going through the last hours of its tragedy; here in New York, they sing and cheer the Republican army that has endured the dangers of Fascism.

On board the *Queen Mary*, waiting to disembark along with the other Spanish refugees, Tina senses that something is wrong. Her passport number 23922, issued in Barcelona to Carmen Ruíz Sánchez, teacher, is valid for travel anywhere except Germany, Hungary, Austria, Italy, and Portugal. Her visa from the U.S. consulate should be in order. Suddenly she is told that she will be held in New York until passage is booked for her return to Mexico.

"You are being sent to Mexico."

Tina begins to tremble. "I can't go to Mexico."

Through one of William Z. Foster's messengers, Tina receives word from Vittorio, who is under FBI surveillance. Vittorio will meet her in Mexico; she shouldn't worry, everything will be okay, there is no reason to be discouraged. Vittorio, Browder, and Foster breathe a sigh of relief when they know her ship has weighed anchor and is on its way to Veracruz.

Tina's boat will arrive on April 19. Nobody in Mexico must know that Carmen Ruíz Sánchez, a Spanish national, a teacher, is the supposed perpetrator of the failed assassination attempt nine years ago of then President of Mexico, Pascual Ortiz Rubio.

And nobody will recognize in Carmen Ruíz Sánchez, with her sunken eyes, wrinkled skin, and trembling hands, the Tina Modotti who was deported in 1930. When an inspector sees her faltering on deck, he shouts to his assistant, "Give the old lady a hand, man. Can't you see she needs help?"

3 1

In Veracruz people buy, sell, and eat. They waste time and food. As Tina sits under the white portals of the arcade eating break-fast, she remembers a night a thousand years ago when she was serenaded in the same spot.

> *In the sweet sugar cane,*
> *in the tall sugar cane,*
> *give me your sweet mouth*
> *so I can kiss it.*

A different woman has returned to a changed Mexico. Not even the lottery-ticket vendors approach her; they are intimidated by her aura of deep mourning.

She always loved the benches in the plaza. She and Weston had wanted to donate one to the city, but they'd never had enough money. She looks at the streets, the white pier, and the children who come to offer their maritime harvest: jewelry boxes studded with seashells, mirrors framed in clamshells, tortoiseshell combs. Then the candy vendor comes, carrying his sweets in a tray hanging from a strap around his neck.

She remembers how people used to flock around her in the markets, the pleasure it gave her to sit on the stones heated by the Mexican sun. She recalls the stone metates for grinding corn, the stone mortars, the earthenware tortilla pans, the stones that absorb the heat of the sun, retain it all night, then release it the next day.

But when her mind's eye turns toward Spain, she becomes blind to the light of the Mexican afternoon, and to her own past.

The vast Mexican night falls over her. She had forgotten its immensity, its ardent vapors, its hundreds of thousands of crickets, the flowers devouring the earth. She had forgotten how red and yellow the nights were. Far-off shouts, a firecracker exploding, a bugle at dawn.

On the train she thinks: "I am an old woman." The vendors who so fascinated Weston still raise their gardenias, their tamales wrapped in banana leaves, and their brown-sugar sticks up to the train windows. "What a country of extremes! Once it was part of me, but I no longer carry it inside."

When the train arrives at the Buenavista station, she remembers Lola Alvarez Bravo holding her child up to her, Manuel, so firm and transparent, and Luz Ardizana. What has become of them? She doesn't want to see them again. Not even Luz. She doesn't want anybody to meet Carmen Ruíz Sánchez. Her fear sharpens like a hook that will not release her. She hopes nobody will come to meet her, that Vittorio doesn't bring anybody with him: she just wants to be left alone, to be forgotten. Isn't she entitled to a little peace? Don't she and Vittorio have the right to a moment of rest?

Vidali's square, solid figure welcomes her, but Tina pulls back. For a moment she is enveloped in a black, heavy cloud of paranoia and she sees him as a trap, too.

Vittorio smiles from ear to ear. "A wonderful couple, the Díaz de Cossios, have offered us a place to stay. They are working with refugees. You can't imagine how dedicated they are. He is a Cata-

Ionian nobleman who heads the welcoming committee and treats refugees like princes."

When they arrive at the house in the southern part of the city, Martin and Isabel greet them warmly. Tina is unaccustomed to refinements, and she suddenly feels the pleasure of a bouquet of scented flowers, an embroidered tablecloth, the lace-trimmed sheets on the bed, things that return her to a world she lost so many years before.

"Surely you will want to bathe. If you need anything, just ask."

A kimono identical to the black one in which she posed for Weston so long ago hangs in the bathroom. "Everything passes, everything returns," she thinks, but she doesn't put the kimono on. Nothing related to idleness has a place in her life now. Well disciplined, without the least pity for herself, she subordinates her desires to the principal goal: the struggle. She has given her body and her will to the Party.

Isabel comes and goes in the house. She is always rushing about, but will suddenly break into a happy song. "Let's go trim the geraniums on the terrace, come on." But that is not all there is to her: Isabel devotes most of her time to the Communist Party.

"Don't you think she's nice?" Vittorio asks Tina.

"Very, but if she weren't a militant, I wouldn't stay at her house."

Pain and anger are Tina's intransigent companions. She is outraged that Mexico has given asylum to Trotsky, and even more that Diego and Frida have helped him get settled. After so much death, she cannot accept betrayals like Diego's. Incompetence drives her crazy. Even anecdotes about the follies of others irritate rather than amuse her.

Isabel worries about Tina's health. She looks so pale, so worn out, so spent, and she is surprised that an outgoing man like Vittorio would have a comrade who is so withdrawn. "How different they are. She is so quiet and he even thinks out loud!"

Tina lives in constant fear of being recognized. Her return to Mexico has been a fresh encounter with memories she had thought long buried. At night, the defeat of Spain turns her stomach inside out: she jumps out of bed thinking she hears an ambulance siren. Meanwhile, Vittorio snores. During the day, every person who enters the house, every phone call sets her on edge. Her nerves were bad in Spain, too, but there she awoke each day to an urgent task that helped her forget her fear. In Mexico, she is constantly on the lookout for snares. Mexico is deceptive, rapacious. In her black skirt, white blouse, and black jacket, she sits alone in the shade, hoping nobody will notice her, hoping nobody will ask anything of her.

The problem of her identity is a source of constant anxiety. Vittorio shows compassion for a while, then he flees. For him, Mexico is a large sunny patio, an open square. He makes friends, drinks coffee at Lady Baltimore's and Sanborn's. He praises the Mexican beer, the Mexican beauties; he's an incorrigible womanizer. As he opens up, Tina shuts down. "That's Mexico," Vittorio asserts. "Or don't you remember? You'll get used to it again."

On the first of May, at Mexico's official workers' march, Tina feels a moment of renewed enthusiasm when she sees the outpouring of ardor. She and Vidali march with the other Spanish refugees, and raise their fists as they pass in front of President Lázaro Cárdenas. Their large banner thanks President Cárdenas for receiving the soldiers of the Spanish Republic. The crowds cheer the marchers on.

Tina's eyes fill with tears.

"There is the same vitality in Mexico as there was ten years ago, but now there is more social conscience," Vittorio points out.

On the presidential balcony, Cárdenas looks like a saint. On other balconies and windows of the National Palace, red banners and flags are fastened to the balustrades. Tina's black felt hat hides her and protects her from the sun. In such a crowd nobody would recognize her; there's nothing like a crowd to lose oneself in, nothing like a crowd to make one feel part of things. "Ices!" "Lemon!" "Mango!" "Fresh juice!" Mexicans never miss an opportunity to sell something. Tina recognizes many militants, but nobody recognizes her: she can raise her voice and her fist with total impunity.

Tina's desire for anonymity grows stronger. Adelina Zendejas, the feminist journalist and social militant, comes to dine at the Díaz de Cossíos' house. When she sees Vidali, they hug fiercely: how much they have in common! Isabel introduces her to María. Adelina doesn't recognize her as Tina Modotti and is shaken when

Isabel takes her aside to reveal María's identity. "It's impossible, she's another woman!"

Tina's silence grows. She feels no need to communicate; it is enough for her to listen. She keeps both her sadness and her infrequent moments of pleasure to herself: the wind blowing a curtain; the breeze brushing against her skin on the balcony of the Cossíos' house; a child's laughter ringing through the trees. She observes herself as if from a great distance. When she sees another woman, she wonders, "Will Vittorio fall in love with her?" She wants only to be left alone, to live within that silence and try to ward off images of a dead child, an open trench, a soldier clutching his intestines with his hands. She has become so withdrawn she almost disappears, a nonexistent woman, without breasts or thighs, always dressed in black.

Adelina Zendejas begins to take an interest in the Tina–Vittorio case. Then she invites them to come live at her house. Tina accepts provisionally. "But I don't want to stay in Mexico, Adelina, I want to work in the United States, where I will be more useful."

Tina floats through the rooms, making a great effort not to disturb anybody. She is helpful, but she remains reserved, in a kind of tense passivity. When Adelina comes home, she finds the table set, always with some special touch. She praises her servant.

"It wasn't me, it was Señora María."

Her gentleness contrasts sharply with Vidali's manner; he is loud, extroverted, and uses crude language in both Spanish and Italian. He doesn't want to dwell on anything. A revolutionary always moves forward; a revolutionary does not waste time in the past.

Adelina notices that Tina is growing alarmingly thin. "How lucky you are not to have to worry about your figure, so slim, and look at me, I just smell the soup and I get bigger around the middle. But I don't like your color: I can see right through you, Tina."

One day, Tina has an idea: she remembers Mary Doherty and is certain she would let her use her passport. She would only have to change the picture. And she knows that Martha Dodd would welcome her in her home in New York.

"Adelina, where can I find Mary Doherty?"

"In Mixcoac, at Katherine Anne Porter's house. Or maybe in Cuernavaca."

Vittorio writes articles for the magazine of the Anti-Imperialist League of the Americas and keeps a journal. He has learned to hold his pen between his index and middle fingers; before going to sleep, he writes down what he did that day and what he plans to do the next. He tires more quickly now, so he writes less than he used to at the Soyuznaya Hotel when Tina, lying beside him, would smoke her last cigarette of the day.

Vittorio comes and goes. His way of guessing others' motives, of being the cleverest, now irritates Tina. "I am no longer impressed by his astuteness." She is amazed that Vittorio, despite his physical weakness, still takes such a passionate interest in life.

Tina takes dictation from Vittorio on a Remington for *El Popular*. The Giuseppe Garibaldi Anti-Fascist Alliance asks her to translate a book by E. Varga about imperialism. She translates Italian editions of works by Lenin—until then unknown in Mexico—and some memoirs from the Party congresses in the Soviet Union. Later, she will go over her translation with one of the secretaries at the Russian Embassy, where Constancia de la Mora works. On one wall of the Embassy hangs a photograph she took and gave to Alexander Makar more than ten years before. She looks at it with curiosity; she no longer recognizes that Tina.

One day, at the main post office, B. Traven sees her and approaches her; Tina holds him off. "I'll call you later," she says.

Miguel Covarrubias can't believe his eyes. "That was Tina, I'm sure, I recognize her by the way she walks, but she pretended not to know me."

"Of course it's Tina," Juan de la Cabada says. "When I saw her in Valencia she already seemed lost, poor thing."

The same thing happens with Baltasar Dromundo. She is riding in a taxi. Dromundo looks at her, puzzled; Tina hides her face. Then he is sure of her identity.

Tina doesn't want to see anybody, except perhaps that young photographer, Manuel Alvarez Bravo, to find out what he has been doing all these years.

When Manuel Alvarez Bravo opens the door and sees Tina at his doorstep, his eyes fill with happiness. He shows her the place of honor he assigned to the photograph, *Flor de manita*, that she gave him in 1929. Weston had also loved that small flower shaped like a beggar's hand.

"I'll always keep it with me, Tina. Wherever I am, it will follow me."

Manuel doesn't even ask how she's been. He is too sensitive for that. He doesn't talk about himself or Lola or their son. For Tina, Manuel is a welcome respite. He shows her photographs of magueys, his room at midday, a black mountain and a white cloud, horizons of the landscape, portraits of the eternal.

"Tina, you always liked the Graflex, I have one you can use. And my darkroom."

"No, Manuel, not anymore."

No papers, no country, no children, no family. And in Mexico she experiences the death of sexual desire. Vittorio doesn't seem to notice.

3 2

The headlines in all the newspapers in Mexico are the same: the Nazi–Soviet Pact has been signed.

All day, Tina is glued to the radio, waiting for the news to be denied. She doesn't eat a bite of food.

Vittorio tries to reason with her. "Tina, you must be calm."

The next day, the word is confirmed.

"I don't understand, I don't understand anything."

El Popular continues calling Stalin the champion of peace and of the independence of the people.

"I want to rip up my card. Many others will, too."

"Try to analyze the events calmly. Look at the world situation."

Tina shouts in a frenzy. "This is a betrayal, a betrayal of everything we have struggled for!"

"There will be debates, Tina. Let's wait and see what reasons they give. I'm also stunned, but I'm not going to lose my head. Calm down."

"And the dead? And the families of the dead? Who's going to calm them down? You know how I love and admire the Soviet Union, you know I adore Stalin. But an alliance with Hitler? Never! Just the thought of him shaking Hitler's hand is unbearable!"

Trotskyists, anarchists, anarcho-syndicalists express their indignation and launch their attacks. "Filthy Communists, bastards. Now let's hear you explain this little ruse of your Uncle Joe. How do you justify this 180-degree turn?"

El Popular, *Bandera Roja*, *La Voz* defend the pact. They proclaim Joseph Stalin a visionary.

"We can't discredit the Soviet Union. It's all we've got," Vittorio explains to Tina.

"I'm going to resign from the Party," Tina tells Vittorio.

"Do you think that would make any difference?"

"I know perfectly well that I'm not important, but I just can't stand feeling like a hypocrite."

"You weren't so virtuous a few years ago."

Even Vittorio has turned against her.

September 1, 1939: Germany invades Poland. *September 3, 1939*: England and France send their ultimatum. When there is no response, they declare war on Germany. *Le Temps* writes: "The Hitler–Stalin Pact, on the eve of Hitler's unleashing of a world war, is outrageous. We will never accept it."

Tina's withdrawal is complete. She refuses to attend meetings or participate in political discussions that always end in fierce arguments. She trusts nobody. She devours newspapers and lives by the radio. In the evenings, Vittorio brings her *El Popular*, and Tina reads an article that describes the pact as a masterly maneuver. She is torn between loyalty and outrage.

In Mexico, some refugees say that the war could be advantageous for them. Industry will benefit. Tina goes from one disappointment to another. She sees Frances Toor, her neighbor and almost a sister from the old days, who tells her that Anita Brenner helped Trotsky settle in Mexico. She is infuriated by Frances's decrying "the destruction of works of art by the Republican militias. The palace of the Duke of Alba had priceless treasures, the patrimony of the world community."

"You are completely uninformed. The palace was destroyed by a Fascist bomb. It was the Republican militiamen who safeguarded the national treasures."

When Frances insists, Tina argues back. "No, Paca, no. The government of the Republic saved works of art."

Then Frances mentions the burning of relics, of medieval churches, broken statues, desecrated Christ figures, baptismal founts overturned, pillage and profanation by barbarians—until she finally asks Tina how she could possibly have gotten involved with people as horrible as the Spanish Republicans.

"You have no idea what you are talking about. If there is a brave, generous, cultured people, it is the Spanish people. And your greatest misfortune is that you will die without having known them."

Tina simply cannot get used to Mexico. People in the street greet each other joylessly, if they greet each other at all. Before, in Tacubaya, greetings would echo through the streets, bounce off walls, to be carried away by the flouncing of skirts, the fringe of shawls, the brims of straw hats. Mexicans took their smiles everywhere. Did the Revolution get stuck? The Revolution that had so moved Tina? She remembers the fervor with which she had tried to capture the symbols in her photographs: the cartridge belt, the sickle, the huaraches, the hats. The ear of corn was better, the sickle, a hat again, the mother carrying the newborn baby wrapped on her back. The images of Mexico have changed. Tina no longer sees the fierceness in the eyes. Before, when a band of peasants arrived in the city, people in the street would step aside in fear and respect; now all she sees is a Mexican wrapped in a serape huddled in a corner trying to find some shade.

Where are the outdoor art schools envisioned by Ramos Martínez? Nobody speaks about mural art anymore. Art used to be a collective event; passersby would stop at the Ministry of Education to see the murals and those murals would become theirs. Why would they want to take a painting home with them if the murals belonged to them? There on the wall, the figure of their indigenous grandmother comforted them, showed them their heroic lineage, reconciled them to their past. Or they could take a nap in front of those enormous public spaces guarded by Cuauhtemoc, Hidalgo, Zapata, and the heroes of the Mexican Revolution, the history of humanity in all its blood and breath.

Now there are more cars than people on the streets. Industries, monopolies are born; commerce grows.

"I think people drink more now than they did ten years ago."

"It's the same," says Vittorio. "You just got out of practice during the war."

"I think the Mexicans have forgotten their Revolution. They no longer want to create a better world. They just take advantage of each other."

"I don't agree. Look at what Cárdenas is doing."

"Cárdenas gave Trostky asylum, that's all I know. I don't like the new Mexican reality. I want to get out of here."

In Mexico, Tina feels stripped, exposed, vulnerable. She is sickened by these Mexicans who use coarse language when speaking about women. Didn't Andrés Henestrosa say that the women in the Communist Party couldn't tell the difference between Red and bed? In Mexico, women are held in contempt; they are consumed, ripped apart, stigmatized, hung by their necks on the patriarchal tree and left to swing, their tongues hanging out and their sex in the air. And she, could she have defended herself in 1929? Mexican society declared that it was ashamed of her. Modotti, daring, sexy, insolent, indecent, foreigner, dangerous. That's why she doesn't want anybody to see her, to recognize her, to touch her. One must be like those pretty women she used to take portraits of in the twenties: silent blank pages, private, good people who never speak their minds.

Blessed old age, then, blessed voyage nearing its end. Now she looks forward to experiencing her own death, to not being blown to a thousand pieces on the battlefield. She does not want to be surprised by death, for she is sure she will find the transition beautiful.

In the meantime, if she left for the United States, she would also avoid watching Vittorio fall in love with other women.

Tina and Vittorio move out of Adelina's house and into an apartment in the Tabacalera neighborhood. Vittorio leaves early in the morning, and Tina stays at home reading. She wants to absorb as much political theory as possible. As with everything in her life, she is in a hurry. Always, as a child, as a teenager, she has had this feeling of wasting time; she's always trying to force the future by shoving it into the present. At night, she prepares a frugal supper in case Vittorio comes. Vidali flees from the opaque, depressed Tina. "Let's not talk about Spain, Tina. Please, I don't want to go over that again. Go out, get together with some of your old friends. You used to have so many."

But that is just what Tina doesn't want to do.

On November 12, Tina takes the train to New York, to see if she and Vittorio can join the Committee for Aid to Political Exiles, which is more active in the United States than in Mexico. She travels with Mary Doherty's passport.

Earl Browder and William Z. Foster meet her at the station. After a careful analysis of the situation, the committee in charge of the case decides that it would be too dangerous for Vidali to enter the United States illegally.

In New York, Tina stays at Martha Dodd's house. She does not attempt to communicate with her sister Yolanda in Los Angeles. Benvenuto, on the other hand, is able to see her, because he is a Party member. "I want to live here, with you," Tina tells him. "That's impossible, sorella. You must obey the orders of the Party. The Party knows best. Here, your life is in danger." She takes the maximum precautions. Martha Dodd leaves her very much alone. She and her husband go out almost every evening.

"You look very tired, there must be something physically wrong," Benvenuto says. He looks at her with great concern. Benvenuto is critical of Vidali. "I just don't understand how you could have gone from Mella to Vidali. Vidali is the opposite of Mella. Mella is Danton and Vidali is Robespierre, the secret man, who belongs to clandestine committees, meetings in cellars, coded messages. Why did Vidali go to Mexico in the twenties? To radicalize, to push the Mexican Communist Party, to impose himself. The new line of the Communist International is that there should be friendship between the Soviet Union and the United States. Vidali will find that difficult to accept."

In her luxurious quarters at Martha Dodd's house, Tina has a nightmare in which the room smells of urine, sweat, and ether. She is sitting by a bed in the Hospital Obrero, listening to the uneven breathing of a wounded man. A low rattle comes from his throat. She can see his chest rise and fall. She would like to sleep, but no, she must wait until the rattle gets stronger, then she will know that the end is near. She will take his hand, just a little pressure from her fingers so he'll know that she is there. How the wounded man stinks! But there's no reason to change him. He has opened his mouth, gasping for air. And then he dies.

Matilde passes by. "We need the bed, María," she says vehemently.

Tina walks over to the window and opens it.

"What are you doing?"

"Letting him leave."

Tina wakes up, drenched in sweat. She cannot even shout. She spends the whole night sitting at the window counting her breaths, one, two, one, two. Her chest expands and contracts like the dying man's in the dream; like him she desperately gasps for air until she sees the first light of dawn over the New York City skyscrapers.

When Tina returns to Mexico, she and Vittorio move into a studio apartment on Ejido Avenue. The Communists have waged a campaign against Trotsky in the pages of *El Popular* and *Bandera Roja*, ever since he came to Mexico. What is he doing in Mexico? Why should he contaminate the country with his presence? How was Rivera able to deceive Cárdenas and convince him to give Trotsky asylum in Mexico, when the only possible asylum for him is hell? How shameful for Mexico! Avid anti-Trotskyists pour onto Ejido Avenue and make their way toward the Palacio de Bellas Artes. The whole Party is out in force, demanding Trotsky's expulsion.

There is no doubt that in Mexico Trotsky will attempt to intervene in politics, as he did in France during the Spanish Civil War, and everywhere else. He has followers in every country. For Trotsky, political exile is another form of intervention. He respects nothing. His fortress in Coyoacán, guarded night and day by U.S. bodyguards and Mexican police, costs the Mexican government a fortune.

More bad news comes from Spain. Franco is pursuing the Republicans into France, taking them out of the concentration camps and executing them after a summary trial. Julian Zugazagoitia was sentenced to death and executed on November 9.

Some time ago, Tina wrote a letter to Ignacio García Téllez:

> *Your secretary informed me that my deportation was the result of a presidential decree and not an administrative act. I understand that this may make it easier to legalize my status. I have been in Mexico for a number of months and still have no official status that will allow me to move about freely or look for work . . . I deeply appreciate the gracious hospitality your country has already offered me. I now turn to you as the only person who can officially resolve my case.*

She still has received no response.

Tina and Vittorio eat frugally. On special occasions, she makes pasta.

One Thursday, Vittorio arrives late. "Close your eyes. I brought you a surprise."

"María, María, it's me, María."

Tina throws herself into Eladia Lozano's arms.

"I found her at the Spanish Communist Party."

"Eleven months in the concentration camps, and now I live less than a block from you. I just arrived in Mexico with my mother."

Tina, glowing with happiness, showers her with questions, kissing her again and again. Vittorio sees Tina's transformation, with surprise. After all, Eladia was only a young, slender blond girl who gladly made packages for the soldiers in Valencia. Why has Tina endowed her with so much importance?

Eladia visits Tina frequently. They sit in front of the window where they can watch the falling twilight. "The sky in Mexico is so special, don't you think, Eladia?" Eladia has such an enthusiastic, eclectic way of talking; in her conversation she moves from the concentration camps to the joys of French cuisine, from fleas to the sea, the Andalusian countryside to the Montjuich Castle in

Barcelona, to the air raids. "You know, María, I never went into a bunker. My father had an injured leg and my mother wouldn't leave him, so neither did I. Can you imagine? And we lived near the storage tanks which were a prime target. Our house shook from the antiaircraft fire."

Tina tells Eladia about her past, about how her family was so poor that at her house they ate only polenta. She also relates the story of a nobleman who lived in a castle in Udine. Unusually progressive, he sent his daughter to a public school. The child became friends with Tina and invited her to their house for a meal. She sat at the table and was served by the servants, and when she got home, Tina's mother said she should invite the nobleman's daughter to her house.

"No, Mama, not to our house."

"If she is your friend, she will like your house, whatever it is."

The girl accepted the invitation and ate polenta. They were friends until Tina left for the United States at sixteen.

Sundays are relaxing for Tina. Eladia reminds her of the good part of the war. Tina finds she can replace her most painful memories with ones that are less disturbing. Eladia, for example, does not feel bitter toward the French.

"More than half a million people descended on France in just a few days. At the train station, the refugees were shitting on the platform. I was so mortified I began to apologize to the border guards."

"This is no time for manners, my dear, don't be ashamed. In the war of 1914 we did worse things than shit on train platforms."

Tina laughs when she is with Eladia, even though she is not sure why she is laughing. Eladia spends Sunday afternoons with her because Tina is a grateful listener. Eladia sees her own story reflected in Tina's eyes. Tina hangs on Eladia's every word.

As Tina grows closer to Eladia, her bond with Spain strengthens. Meanwhile, Vittorio is getting more involved with the people who work at *El Popular*. He is amazed by how frequently they are arrested, how they go like lambs to the slaughter on their way to jail. He cannot understand why they don't protest.

He asks his comrades if there isn't something they can do about it. The answer is clear.

"No matter what we do, they get us. That's justice in Mexico."

The political climate in Mexico City turns red-hot. There are international repercussions to the attack on Trotsky's house by an armed commando on the night of May 24, 1940. According to *El Popular*, Trotsky is waging a war of nerves in Mexico: "The attack was international blackmail."

On May 25, 1940, Vittorio walks down the Alameda, and only seconds after he notices that he is being watched by a policeman, he is surrounded by four men. There is no escape.

"Are you Carlos Contreras?"

"Yes, sir."

"What is the license number of your car?"

"I don't have a car."

"What is the number of your bank account?"

"I don't have a bank account."

"Where do you live?"

"I'm not going to tell you where I live."

"Very well then, we'll tell you. Just follow us."

"Do you have a warrant for my arrest?"

"For someone like you, we don't need one."

"Okay, without a warrant, I'm not going with you."

One of the policemen shoves a pistol into his side. "You don't have any choice."

In the middle of the night, they take him out of his cell and to the office of Miguel Zeta Martínez.

"Are you the Spanish refugee Carlos Contreras or the Italian Enea Sormenti?"

Vittorio has not used that name for years. It's a bad sign that it turns up now.

At night, after he has fallen asleep, two policemen wake him up and load him into a van.

"Are you taking me for a ride?"

In Spain during the war, taking someone for a ride meant shooting him.

No answer.

"I have the right to know where you are taking me."

The policemen don't even look at him.

They take him far outside the city, or at least that's how it feels to him from inside the van. They arrive at El Pocito, a provisional jail in the mountains used for those awaiting trial. It is a sinister and fearful place.

"May I make one phone call?"

"Only if the Comandante gives his permission."

At El Pocito, Vittorio's life depends completely on Comandante Jesús Galindo. He is not allowed to read, write, speak with his guards, let alone make a telephone call. They put him in the worst cell he has ever been in, and he has been in quite a few, from Trieste, when he was just a kid, to Paris, Berlin, and New York.

It is nothing more than a fetid hole with a dirt floor and damp walls; there is no window, not even a peephole. There is no bench, toilet, or cot. They give him newspaper pages for bedsheets. Every two days he is given four tortillas and a bit of water, which he eats right there amid the excrement. He tries to defecate near the walls, but the rats crawl all over his body. When he lies down, his head hits the wall. He thinks anxiously about Tina, and is sure that she and the Party comrades have denounced his disappearance and begun to look for him. The people at *El Popular* must be working on his release. This thought gives him strength and helps him stay alive.

Vittorio refuses to give in psychologically: he must keep his mind occupied. Immersed in darkness, he writes sentences and paragraphs in his head, sifts through his memories, composes poems and songs, sings them aloud. First he goes through all the Spanish war songs, then he repeats the Mexican rancheras he taught the militiamen of the Fifth Regiment. He struggles to keep track of time. He would exercise if he could, but each time he tries, he steps in his own excrement.

For more than twenty-five days, Vittorio has no contact with the outside world.

He begins each morning by talking to himself. He tells himself the news, then begins to narrate his childhood, recite Dante's poetry, the multiplication tables; from there he goes to the works of Alessandro Manzoni, Antonio Machado, Pablo Neruda, and Rafael Alberti.

He repeats Machado so many times that the guards learn the verses by heart:

> Caminante, no hay caminos
> Se hace camino al andar.
>
> Wanderer, there's no road,
> You make the road as you walk.

He remembers some words from Vaillant-Couteurier and repeats them to himself: "Communism is not only the future but also the youth of the world."

And he recites Martí: "With the poor people of the earth, I wish to cast my lot . . ."

He repeats: "I am a sane man, I am a vigorous man."

There are long days of solitude, nights when he sleeps hugging the wall in the fetal position, praying to all the saints to keep him from moving so he won't soil himself.

Suddenly, one morning, they drag him out of his cell.

The light assaults his eyes with unbearable violence. He can barely stand up.

"May I clean up a little?"

"There is a fountain outside. But don't dirty the horses' water."

Two men are waiting for him in a semi-dark room. One is Mexican and the other is some kind of blond giant sent from Washington by the FBI. Vidali recognizes the Mexican: he is the son of the former senator and signer of the Constitution of 1917, Luis Monzón, a friend of Vittorio's during his first stay in Mexico when Luis was granted membership in the Communist Party. The American begins by asking questions in English: name, age, passport number, illegal visits to the United States in 1939, and ends up threatening Vittorio with the prospect of jail.

"I am under the protection of the Mexican government."

"But our power is enormous, Sormenti."

"I know, I probably have the FBI to thank for my stay in this place."

"Probably," the man answers with disdain.

"Who's helping you? Diego Rivera, secretary of the Fourth International?" Vittorio asks, losing his patience.

The American doesn't deign to answer.

Finally Vittorio says, "Enough, I'm on Mexican territory, and I refuse to answer one more question."

The American agent goes out to talk to a couple of policemen. The interrogation continues. They confront him again and again, but he confesses nothing. Young Monzón looks at Vittorio as if wanting to apologize.

"It must be difficult for you to be part of the secret police and maintain your father's democratic spirit. If you do, that is. Do you know anybody in Lecumberri Penitentiary, Monzón?"

"Sure, I've got buddies there."

"Guards?"

"Of course, not prisoners. I'm not a snitch. Guards and officials. I can see anyone I want."

"Can you get a message to David Alfaro Siqueiros?"

Young Monzón is good as his word. He goes to Siqueiros and informs him that his friend Carlos Contreras is in El Pocito jail and is in grave danger. This sets in motion the rather absurd Mexican political system of alliances.

From jail, Siqueiros telephones to request an interview with the presidential candidate Manuel Avila Camacho. Siqueiros is brought to him, and Avila Camacho recognizes the young revolutionary lieutenant. He hugs him affectionately. They reminisce nostalgically about the days when Manuel was captain and David a lieutenant in the Mineros Division. Siqueiros tells him, "You are holding Comandante Carlos Contreras, loyal Republican, anti-Fascist, and hero of the Fifth Regiment, prisoner in El Pocito. You must have heard about the military feats of the Fifth Regiment in the defense of Madrid, mi general. Thanks to him, Mexican corridos were sung during that war, the same ones we sang in Jalisco during the Revolution. How can you hold a man like that in jail, mi general?"

"Yes, I've been getting telegrams from Central and South America: 'Where is Carlos Contreras?' The Communist Party is organizing the campaign."

"And soon you'll be getting telegrams from the United States and Europe. We're talking about an international case. The eyes of the world are on you."

When Siqueiros leaves, Avila Camacho gives the order. "Get the Italian out of El Pocito immediately."

The next day, all charges are dropped against the Italian Communist. Vidali is escorted to Internal Security by two policemen. Waiting for him are comrades from the Party and *El Popular*, with whom he is allowed to speak for a few minutes. He ask about Tina.

"Once she sees you, she'll be better."

When he reaches the fifth floor and enters their apartment, he sees how much Tina has suffered. She has the same tragic expression she had during the last days of the war in Spain. She doesn't even have the strength to embrace him. Isabel Carbajal brought her fruit and vegetables, but she barely touched them. She just sat and waited, her eyes on the door.

Ignacio García Tellez helps Vittorio legalize his status in Mexico.

"What *is* your name? In your file it says Vittorio Vidali, born in Odessa, Austrian citizen; Peruvian Jacobo Hurwitz or Zender, born in Lima, professor of history; Carlos J. Contreras, born in La Coruña, Spain; and Mr. Raymond, Parisian; not to mention Enea Sormenti."

"My real name is Vittorio Vidali."

"So what do you say we just burn the rest of the file? It will make things simpler."

After eighteen years, he finally recovers his identity: Vittorio

Vidali, native of Muggia, an unknown Italian village on a hillside overlooking the Adriatic. Tina will soon recover her identity, too.

Vittorio sees no improvement in Tina's health, and suggests that she consult a doctor. Tina responds with an apathetic "Okay" and doesn't mention the subject again. Vidali, strong and healthy, busies himself with one activity or another. He is constantly being sought for a consultation, an interview, a recommendation, a conference, a meeting. Vittorio makes so many commitments he can barely fit them into a day. Tina attends meetings only at the Giuseppe Garibaldi Alliance, and on Sundays she goes to the country with Vittorio and their friends. Sometimes during those excursions, Vittorio catches her smiling. Tina doesn't tell Vittorio that the doctor recommended she leave the city. How could he change his way of life? How would they survive outside the city? Vittorio comes home late every night. He is still a full-time activist.

On June 25, a month after the attempt on Trotsky's life, the body of Robert Sheldon Harte is found in Siqueiros's country house. Harte, Trotsky's bodyguard, had opened the door to the attackers.

On August 20, 1940, as he sits at his writing desk, Trotsky is attacked from behind by Ramón Mercader, who drives a pickaxe into his head.

Outside, Mercader's mother, Caridad Mercader, and Naum Yakovlevich Eitingon, special envoy from Moscow, await him.

The old Bolshevik fiercely clings to life. He dies on August 21, never having regained consciousness.

Concha Michel, who still remembers her trip to the Soviet Union, gives Tina a little book that she has written called *Two Fundamental Antagonists*. Tina looks through it and reads how patriarchal society enslaves women just as it enslaves workers, how it represses women at every opportunity. "The ancient prostitutes were allowed a certain amount of education in the arts and sciences, so that they would be more attractive to men and give them more pleasure. Women as mothers are denied all access to culture." Suddenly her eyes fill with tears which spill over the book, over Concha, over herself, a wrenching cry that comes from afar and has no reason to ever end. Still in tears, she begs forgiveness of the emptiness around her. Isn't she that prostitute who was allowed a certain amount of culture? Haven't the women comrades involved in the Party been used, made fun of, been beaten, not even knowing the difference between Red and bed? The men have no real affection for them, they don't know "the potential of a high level of love," as Concha writes. Otherwise, how to explain that nobody has bothered to teach Benita Galeana to read and write. Tina remembers Concha Michel in Russia, singing with her son at her side, touching her listeners with her youth, her colorful hat, and her melodic voice. "My guitar is an extension of my body," Concha told her once. But who pays any attention to Concha? And Tina, who will remember Tina?

"How Concha has matured! Or was she always like that? Probably nobody else has noticed." In her book, Concha talks about Darwin's theory of evolution and the constant movement toward renewal. She quotes Engels's *Anti-Dühring*: "At every instant an organized being is the same and not the same; every instant, the cells of the body decay and others are formed. After a more or less specific length of time, the substance of the body has been completely renewed, replaced by other atoms, in such a way that an organized being is constantly the same and yet another."

But for Tina, nothing remains of the powerful woman who made decisions, devastated suitors, made a way for herself in the world.

On Mesones, the Mesones of the good old times, a tall young man with broad shoulders approaches Tina, greets her, and asks if she needs anything.

"No, thank you."

"I admire you greatly."

Tina blushes but does not ask his name. Suddenly she feels a chill and rises to get her jacket from the coatrack. The young man jumps up to get it for her. "Why didn't you tell me? I would have brought it to you. You're too proud to ask." And he flashes a smile under his mustache.

Tina allows him to help her with her jacket. He takes her hand as it comes out of the sleeve, holds it between his, and kisses it.

Something about him touches her deeply: his solicitude, the

3 4

At the request of Constancia de la Mora, Tina accompanies an American photographer named Condax and his wife on a tour of Mexico. When she returns from their trip to Michoacán, Tlaxcala, Puebla, and Veracruz, Vittorio thinks she looks better than ever.

"Did you take photographs?" Vittorio asks her.

"No," Tina answers, "but I helped John Condax, who doesn't speak a word of Spanish. I made hotel reservations, talked to people. He had a Graflex. It thrilled me to see Morelia, suspended between earth and sky, serene as ever. The palaces there are so exquisite it looks like the whole place will simply elevate." Tina does not tell Vittorio that she had again felt a little of the pleasure of her trips with Edward. The Mexican countryside was even more beautiful than she remembered it. The luminous landscapes, the sun-drenched stones, the sweetly innocent men and women were like a balm to her.

"Great. So you're going to develop your pictures?"

"No, Vittorio, I didn't take pictures. I just told you."

"Bene, bene, at least you look healthier."

"You look well, too."

"Yes, Mexico is good for me. I love *El Popular*."

Tina does not tell him that she has had a welcome rest from him, from what she and he mean together, and what she and he represent to each other, from her constant awareness that there is no power in the world that will stop Vittorio from fixating on other women. He likes women so much that once, in the Soviet Union, he described to her in detail how he had to bathe in cold water during his trips in order to lessen his desire for the women he saw on the street. "The Party even controls my erections," he said, flashing his wide conqueror's smile.

Besides Eladia, Cruz Díaz and Constancia also come to visit Tina. Pablo O'Higgins stops by from time to time. She is slightly less isolated than before. It's possible that René d'Harnoncourt, her companion and Weston's on so many trips through the country, will come to Mexico. Tina would like to see him; she remembers his drawings of the Mexican people as sensitive and insightful.

One afternoon, Eladia talks about her suitors: Santiago Alvarez and Enrique Líster. "They followed me around like shadows." Tina laughs because now Count Frola, an anti-Fascist who attends all the meetings of the Giuseppe Garibaldi Alliance, is also smitten with Eladia. "Have you noticed, María, how he makes a deep bow when he kisses your hand? There's no doubt about it, having a title is a sign of good manners."

Suddenly, Eladia asks, "María, did you have any boyfriends before Carlos?"

"Yes, but they're not worth talking about."

Tina and Vittorio resume their Sunday trips to the countryside. She returns to familiar places: Xochimilco, the pyramids, her beloved magueys. One day, Vittorio notices that her tanned face glows with a smile and there is a new vitality in her eyes.

As she walks along, Tina puts her arm through her comrade's and says, "We are beginning a new life. We can leave the ghosts behind."

At home, she takes a straw hat off a nail on the wall. On the table is a small earthenware vase with a few daisies.

"Come here, put on this hat," Tina says to Eladia, "I want to see how it looks on you." She looks at her affectionately. "Let's go next Sunday and have your picture taken."

Vittorio says, "You know, Eladia, Tina is a very good photographer."

Eladia's question to Tina about her boyfriends echoes in her head. Many boyfriends. She remembers them less well than she remembers the subtlety of her feelings for each: the compassionate love she always felt for Pepe Quintanilla; her love-hate for Vittorio; her immense admiration for Edward, her sexual attraction to him. Each one gave her a different sound, a different rhythm, spirit, stature. Each one walked across the waves to her, and she rested her head on each one's chest in turn. She never wanted to know what the future held: this ignorance was part of her freedom. They all wanted to seduce her forever, to make plans, but not her. "I want you to be mine," they would say, though she never felt any exclusiveness. To keep, possess, to think of herself as possessed was alien to her. Surely the same thing happened to men, each lover discovered himself in the confines of her vagina, the intuition behind her brow, the terrible or brutal or haughty mystery in those eyes, the immeasurable marvel of the human mind resting on that pillow. Eladia—audacious, beautiful, flirtatious—has many suitors, as Tina once did. But God forbid she should ever have one die on her, have a Julio Antonio who would beat in her heart forever.

Tina and Vittorio decide to move. They walk through the streets looking for new quarters. Finally, one day, Tina returns with her eyes shining. "I found my home."

In Colonia Doctores, at 137 Doctor Balmis Street, right across from the main entrance to the General Hospital, Tina climbs up the stairs, followed by Vittorio. On the roof, there is a little gingerbread house with two tiny windows like eyes, a little door, and eaves made out of tin sheets. One bed can fit in the main room; in the other room there is space for a table, a chair, and one person; in the kitchen there is room for a sink and half a person. Whoever is eating must do so alone and standing up.

Vittorio is clearly disconcerted. "This is a nest for Snow White and one of her dwarfs."

"This isn't the real house. Look in front."

The snow-covered volcanoes sparkle in the sun. The terrace seems to lead to the mountains that beckon from a distance. From this lookout, one can see Mexico in all its splendor, the valley and the mountains. The rooftop is connected to the lower floors by a stairway, but nobody bothers to come up there to hang clothes out to dry.

"So, what do you say? We even have a bathroom, but it is so small you can hardly see it. We have everything we need up here: the starry vault of heaven, the sun king, the volcano brothers, our guardian angels, the company of swallows and sparrows, the spiritual terrace, the view, and clouds whenever we want them. And the rent is so low we can pay it ourselves."

"Ma . . . e molto piccolo."

Tina's face is so full of excitement that the "no" gets stuck in his throat.

"We are going to live in an enchanted castle. Chapultepec or Montjuich can't hold a candle to this."

Within a few days, the residents of the enchanted castle multiply. Tina finds a little white dog in a bundle on the doorstep downstairs. Soon after Suzi's arrival, a yellow cat they call "Kitty" shows up at the window. Now they are a family.

On the terrace they discover a plant used in religious rites, "the crown of thorns": the thorns sprout red flowers that look like drops of blood. The previous tenant, who went off without paying the rent, left it behind.

When it rains, the castle is an echo chamber; the roof leaks in the bedroom and the kitchen. In one corner of the terrace, a small vine of climbing geraniums hides their home from the taller buildings. When the sun shines, Tina and Vittorio can lie naked beneath it. The terrace is their balcony, their promenade, their rendezvous, their moonlit eyrie; from here they can admire the big city lit by fireflies and hear the music of cobblestones and organ-grinders rising from the street below.

When they drink coffee in the early morning, the outlines of the volcanoes appear sharp, their peaks eternally white. Tina's problems shrink in the face of such grandeur. After all, who is she to suffer so much? In the shadow of the snow's brilliance, Tina feels minuscule. The volcanoes speak to her, tell her they will not allow the war in Spain to ruin her life. They are like people: the Popo and the Ixta. There, hovering on the peaks, are Weston's clouds, clouds that travel quickly, sweeping the sky clean.

When their friends come to visit, they are surprised by their choice of abode. "What kind of house is this?" says Mario Montagnana. "Do you think you are eagles?" "The sky is going to fall on you," Hidalgo de Cisneros says. But they all admit that the view is incredible, that the sky and the mountains merit some kind of sacrifice.

After initial disagreement, the other two residents establish a decorous harmony. Kitty disappears at night and returns dirty and scratched from bouts of love. She lies down in Suzi's box and closes her eyes until nightfall, when she is ready to take up where she left off. None of her suitors comes up to the roof. Suzi scares them away. The house is sacred. Suzi remains single until she gives in to the flirtations of a male from the neighboring house. Two months later, Vittorio and Tina are living with two pregnant females. Soon their owners are distributing black-and-white puppies and yellow kittens among their friends.

At mealtimes, guests bring chicken, bread, cheese. They toast with many glasses of water. Vittorio suggests adding vinegar, "as we did when I was a kid." Nobody is very enthusiastic about the idea. Wine is too expensive, and they drink it only on special occasions.

Eladia thinks the house is worse than the place they lived in before. It is, in fact, a servants' quarters. In a tiny entryway is a hard couch on which Tina collapses after climbing the stairs. Sometimes she removes her shoes from her swollen feet and leaves them there. In one corner, there is a toilet and a shower that gets the whole room wet when it is used.

Vittorio and Tina live a life of monastic austerity. It is touching to see how Tina manages to buy a few flowers, even if they are the cheapest ones available. Their furniture consists of a tiny table and two chairs they bought at a flea market. Tina tries to soften the hard couch with a blanket she made herself. Everything is inexpensive. When Eladia visits, they always invite her to share a meal. She is never sure if she is consuming Vittorio's or Tina's supper.

In the evening, Tina types Vittorio's articles or her translations while waiting for him to return from *El Popular*. She goes to meetings of the Hands Off Nicaragua Committee, and brings work home with her.

One morning, Constancia de la Mora comes over and announces, "I have a two-week vacation from the Soviet Embassy. Why don't you and I take a trip around Mexico?"

"Why not?"

It seems a magnificent idea to Vittorio. He hopes that the passionate woman he once knew, whom he now sees glimpses of when she turns her eyes to the sky, will finally return.

But the trip is cut short and on their return, Connie de la Mora confides to Vittorio. "She's not well. She's always short of breath."

At night, when Vittorio stays late at *El Popular*, Tina loves to take walks, to look deep into the vast emptiness, deep into time, deep into herself. She is enthralled by the stars, by the soft air as it caresses her face, and for moments she actually forgets the Spanish war. Then she walks more freely, almost as when she was young. But now no one even seems to notice her slim black silhouette moving slowly through the night.

"Maybe we are all particles of this luminous mass called earth and we shouldn't worry so much," she thinks. For her, space has no density; it is light on her shoulders and light on her thoughts. Every day she waits for the hour when she can go down into the streets of Mexico. The only trouble is climbing back up the stairs. The stairs take her breath away. But if she does it very slowly, and summons the help of the stars, she can reach her rooftop and find the stars ready to greet her over the home she has chosen above all others.

Vittorio and Tina go to Texcoco to visit the chapel at the Chapingo School of Agriculture painted by Diego Rivera. Tina appears twice in the murals: once, naked and lying down, her face hidden by her hair, she holds a plant in the palm of her hand that represents germination; in the other, she is also naked, emerging from the roots and the trunk of a tree, her breasts exposed.

Though he understands little or nothing about art, Vittorio stares at the vault of colors, enchanted.

3 5

On New Year's Eve, 1941, everybody proposes a different toast.

"To the Allies," Cruz Díaz says.

"No, to the Red Army," Constancia de la Mora insists.

"To Stalin, to Stalin, to Stalin," Eladia pipes in. Tina hesitates a moment before joining all the others who toast Stalin's health.

Tina seems happier than usual that evening at Pablo and Delia Neruda's house. She is comforted to be with her Spanish friends. There are also Latin American, Italian, French, Swiss, German, Polish, Rumanian, and Czech exiles. At midnight, they all sing the "Internationale" and embrace.

It has been an unforgettable evening, a wonderful New Year's party. Arm in arm, Vittorio and Tina walk home with Simone Tery.

"Let's go watch the sunrise from the Paseo de la Reforma,"

Vittorio suggests. "The Chapultepec Castle on the hillside reminds me of a castle in Trieste."

As they cross the Paseo de la Reforma toward Doctor Balmis, Tina sees a man lying on a bench.

"Just a drunkard," Vittorio says.

Tina moves closer. The man seems sick, not drunk.

"We have to do something. Call the Red Cross."

Vittorio and Simone follow Tina to the General Hospital in front of their house.

At the hospital, the staff tells her they don't have anybody available to pick him up.

"The man can't stand, he's too weak."

"Our hospital doesn't take emergencies. Go to the Green Cross."

Tina calls the Hospital de Jesús.

"Right now, we don't have any beds."

"I beg you, he's going to freeze to death."

Tina calls other hospitals; finally the Green Cross admits him.

Simone Tery says goodbye, and Vittorio accompanies Tina. Finally, they manage to get the man into a hospital. They go to bed at six that morning. Tina is pleased that they've saved an old man's life. Vittorio is happy just to lie down.

"For four nights now, you have been talking in your sleep about the sea. 'Where is the sea?' you keep asking. You yearn for the sea, Tina. Let's go to Veracruz."

Tina smiles. "Don't worry, I carry the sea around with me. Its waves break against our castle walls. I can hear it breathing down in the streets."

The first few days of January are very busy. Tina prepares the distribution of toys to the Spanish refugee children in Mexico with the help of Eladia, who is pregnant. "Let's hope it's a girl," says Tina.

Tina calls Adelina Zendejas to invite her over for the Feast of the Magi. "I can't. I have too much to do. But we'll see each other later. Come have a cup of coffee the day after tomorrow."

Tina and Vittorio had promised the Bauhaus architect, Hannes

Meyer, that they would visit him at his apartment at 46 Villalongín. In the sitting room, Meyer has set up an exhibit of his typographic designs, models, projects, and pictures. The evening is clear and cold, and the sky is lit by a full moon. At Meyer's house, Vittorio and Tina meet their friends, Ana María and Mario Montagnana, Colonel of the Spanish Army, Patricio Azcárate and his wife, Cruz Díaz.

Tina sits next to Cruz, whose presence gives her confidence. To be with Cruz is to be in familiar territory. Tina confides to Cruz that she has been having heart palpitations ever since Vittorio was in El Pocito, but she doesn't want Vittorio to know.

They talk about the quintet of Dmitri Shostakovich. "Art does not point toward the future, nor is it prophetic. Art determines the future," Hannes says. They talk about the Soviet anti-tank trenches, at which point Cruz turns to Tina and scolds her. "Don't let yourself go like this. Since you arrived in Mexico, you haven't looked well. Go see a doctor. You're all skin and bones. I'll go with you, if you want. I love you like a sister, Tina, and you musn't neglect yourself this way."

Tina, her eyes on the toes of her shoes, doesn't respond. She wants to say that she has done everything she can to forget the war. None of the other comrades thinks of the defeat of the Republic as a tragedy. Even the refugees are adapting. She still doesn't understand. Now she doesn't even want to return to Italy.

The word "love" draws her attention when Vittorio remarks: "All wives are the same, but each lover is different." His words sadden Tina. Hannes Meyer's warm, encouraging voice brings her out of herself. "Let's plan a trip—to Madrid, Genoa, Udine. Soon Franco, Mussolini, and Hitler will be defeated. There will be no more Fascism in the world."

Hannes Meyes gives her hope for the future.

Vittorio excuses himself. They are waiting for him at *El Popular* to set up the international page.

"I'm leaving." Vittorio kisses Tina on the cheek. "I'll see you at home."

"You should write, too, Tina," Cruz says to her. "Look how good it is for Vittorio."

"It's very hard for me. I keep crossing things out. I do too much research, and I'm never sure of anything."

"You are so pale."

"I'm feeling the exhaustion of the last days of the year."

"But you looked so well at the Nerudas' on New Year's Eve."

"It's old age." Tina smiles.

At midnight, Tina says goodbye. "See you later." She gives Cruz a hug.

"See you later," she says, holding out her hand to the others.

The young painter Nacho Aguirre gets up. "I'll come with you. I heard you tell Cruz that you felt tired."

"Don't worry. It will pass."

"You're okay on your own? You don't want me to come?"

Vittorio walks to *El Popular*. When he enters the building, he hears the sound of Remington typewriters. "Life! Reporters write against time and about time." When he returns to their castle, it is after midnight, and he is invigorated.

Vittorio reads as he waits for Tina. The doorbell rings, and he sees that it is after 1 a.m. He goes downstairs. Maybe Tina has forgotten her keys. Two gentlemen ask for the husband of Tina Modotti.

"I am her husband. Where is she? Did something happen to her?"

They pause, look at one another, then say flatly: "She's dead."

"What are you talking about?"

"Your wife, Tina Modotti, died in a taxi parked out in front. The taxi driver took her to the Green Cross."

Vidali is speechless and follows them, dazed.

On a table in a badly lit room Tina lies dressed as she was when Vittorio left her at the Meyers' house: the black skirt and jacket she wore on so many trips, her white blouse. Her hair, parted down the middle, frames her sweet face.

There is still some color in her cheeks.

Vittorio thinks this is how her face probably looked when she was twenty. Her teeth show through her half-open mouth; her soft hands are folded over her belly, waiting for somebody to come and caress them.

"Do you recognize her?"

"Yes."

"Is this your wife?"

"Yes."

"We need two witnesses."

Vittorio follows the instructions of the two funeral-home employees. He fills out a questionnaire in triplicate. He wants to ask, "Hey, Tina, what illnesses did you have as a child?" and he realizes that she really is dead.

"Is that all?" he asks the men.

"For now, yes."

Vittorio kisses her brow and leaves. He goes to his friend Pedro Martínez Cartón, who, with Isabel Carbajal, identifies Tina.

When the taxi stopped at the corner of Insurgentes and Villalongín, Tina gave the driver the Doctor Balmis address and he asked, "Where is that?"

"Right in front of the General Hospital."

Nacho Aguirre and Hannes Meyer, who had come down with her, heard her say as she leaned into the back seat, "See you later."

In the taxi, Tina feels she is flowing like a river. Julio's body comes toward her. "Julio, don't die, I love you so much." Her sex is waiting for Julio, Julio and the sea that has enveloped her ever since. "It is good to go like this, wrapped in water. It doesn't hurt, it doesn't hurt to die. Why am I crying if it doesn't hurt?" The water is Julio, the water is rest, the water is infinite like the reflections of the sun on the Danube the afternoon of her mission to Budapest; when the gold of the Danube gilded her, she forgot about the danger of the mission and thought about the splendor of the world and her eyes grew damp with gratitude.

A new Tina observes her, accompanies her. She is sweeter, more tender than the Tina of the last few years; she advises her gently: "Let yourself go, that's it, all by yourself, don't make any effort, just let the current carry you." Her lungs are bursting, but there is no feeling of suffocation, no reason to struggle. The silk scarf her godmother gave her in Udine floats on the water, her only item of luxury. Tina stretches out her hand and picks it up with fingers aching from twelve hours at the loom. "Don't you want to buy it? It's the most beautiful thing I have." The scarf disappears. With

345

that money, there will be bread, ham, and oil. She will see the surprise in the faces of her mother and brothers and sisters when they sit down to eat. José Guadalupe Rodríguez from the Central Committee of the Party comes in. "Go ahead, comrade, you have the floor." Yelena Stasova is wearing that horrible felt hat, and she runs out into the street. Tina wants to catch up with her, but many hands hold her back. They cling to her black skirt. A loaf of bread, a bandage, a chair, a glass of water, give me, give me, that child's face is burned, his hand is bloody, the wounded and their demands, the stretcher-bearers in the muddy trench, pick him up, comrade, don't let him rot, give me your hand, I want to die looking at a beautiful woman, the smell of the dead, the stench of war, of urine, of excrement, of vomit, the wounded, the dead, their blood on her hands, their blood on her skirt, letters begin to fly up in the air, a piece of paper goes into her mouth and sticks to her palate. "I am beyond good and evil," she once said, laughing in Vittorio's face. "Oh, really. That's why your friends in Mexico said you were an expensive whore." I'm falling to pieces. Leaves, shouts: "You didn't make a copy. Where is the translation?" Steam surrounds her, doesn't let her move, the steam from the boiling pots, she can't explain that it hurts, that the pain is intolerable, horribly intense and doesn't stop, each second it gets worse, dear heart, where are you?

She throws back her head. She sees the sky, black and star-studded, through the window. "Oh, I'm dizzy! What strange things am I thinking? Am I dead or alive?" "Comrade, your documents. Are you the one in the photo? The picture was taken when you were young? Please sign again, we must compare the signatures." The borders are closed, but the sea is vast and open. "You've never gone naked into the sea?" "You haven't felt the ineffable joy of the ocean?" The sea, the sky were not for her. The ships point down toward the horizon. Total blackness, abyss, bad water. The stars go crazy, an avalanche of light on her eyes. She feels like vomiting and stops herself, but something must have come out, because she tries to wipe her chin. Her right arm doesn't respond. Her left arm aches. Again she opens her eyes and the brightness of the stars forces her to close them. The pressure on her right side diminishes. "It is so easy to die," she thinks, "I am going, I am going. Mamma is calling, she tells me to follow the Milky Way. Mamma." The stars are filling her belly, they give off sparks, a swarm of fireflies awaits. "Julio, what a good death, do you remember, Julio?" She tries to see him when a last star closes her eyes.

The taxi stops in front of the General Hospital.

"Here we are, señora."

The driver hears a soft moan. When he opens the back door, he says again, "Señora, we're here."

She doesn't move. He runs into the hospital and points to the taxi. He insists, and two nurses come with him.

"It's too late, she's dead. Take her to the Green Cross."

A reporter is present when they open the dead woman's purse. There is no compact, not even a comb, only a crumpled handkerchief, a one-peso bill, some keys, an oval photograph of a young man with curly hair, and a document with the name Tina Modotti Mondini, 137 Doctor Balmis.

Isabel Carbajal thinks Tina looks more beautiful on the marble slab than she has ever seen her, as if she had finally attained some kind of peace.

There would have to be an autopsy.

At six in the morning, Concha Michel calls Adelina. "If you want to see Tina for the last time, go to the Green Cross immediately."

Adelina hails a taxi, desperate.

Tina is taken to the Juárez Hospital, the same place where Julio Antonio Mella was thirteen years before. Totally naked, her gorgeous body looks much younger than her face.

Vidali, grief-stricken, knocks on Hidalgo de Cisneros's door. He tells Constancia and him what happened and collapses: he can't face the death of his compañera. His bull's head is bowed.

"Stay here. We'll put you up."

Tina's wake is held at a funeral home for the poor across from the Juárez Hospital. Just as thirteen years ago, the press unleashes a campaign against her, instigated this time, according to Vittorio and his comrades, by Spanish Trotskyists in Mexico.

"Don't go out, Vittorio. They are doing everything they can to blame you. They have an opportunity to slander the Communists. They're going to be all over us."

Eladia Lozano sees Tina's face in *Extra* and reads the caption under the photograph: "The Communist Magdalene." She rushes to Cruz's house. "But I just saw her a little while ago, we were going to get together this week," Cruz cries in disbelief. The two of them go to look for Concha Mantecón.

"So her name wasn't María? Have you seen what the newspapers are saying?"

"They're all lies."

But Eladia reads that Tina was Mella's woman, that she lived with Xavier Guerrero, that she was implicated in the attempted assassination of Pascual Ortiz Rubio. It goes on and on. The mysterious "Mata Hari of the Comintern" had always led a licentious life: she posed naked for Weston and Diego Rivera, and was the lover of both.

"Don't read any more, it will just upset you."

The following news item appears in *El Universal*:

Tina Modotti, known in Mexico as a Communist leader and for her suspected implication in the assassination of her lover, Julio Antonio Mella, also of radical tendencies, died suddenly in the early hours of the morning, the day before yesterday.

Tina Modotti lived at 137 Doctor Balmis Street, apparently with Carlos Jiménez Contreras. According to our investigation, she suddenly began to feel strong stomach pains and hired a taxi to take her to the General Hospital near her house. She died on the way there.

It is hoped that the results of the autopsy will clarify suspicions regarding the circumstances and cause of her death. It is rumored that she may have been poisoned. The case is now in the hands of the Mexico City district attorney.

La Prensa *says:*

Her lover, whose real name is Carlos Sormenti, is a fanatic agent of the GPU and is thought to be responsible for her death.

Many wonder why Tina's lover, Carlos J. Contreras, has disappeared, and blame him for her death. A rumor spreads that Vidali, an assassin, could have poisoned his comrade because "she knew too much." Tina led a "mysterious life" and the proof that

Vidali or somebody else poisoned her lies in the fact that she gave the taxi driver the address of the General Hospital. But who doesn't give a public building as reference if their own house is close by?

The attacks become more direct.

The death of Tina Modotti has all the characteristics of a Communist "elimination."

Veterans of the war in Spain who are not afraid of the GPU point to Sormenti–Vidali–Contreras as responsible for many political assassinations; there seems to be little doubt that he took part in the crimes against Ignacio Reiss in Switzerland, and Andrés Nin in Spain. This terrible man is a longtime member of the Communist Youth and a founding member of International Red Aid. He spent time in prison for his political activities, then went to Switzerland and other European countries, then came to America apparently as a member of International Red Aid, concealing his true identity as an agent of the GPU.

Vittorio can't stop torturing himself. "I always forced her to live in danger. She never felt sure of anything, not even of me." He sobs. "You know, Pedro, I just cannot bear this feeling of remorse." "Vittorio, we are men, not saints." "If I had just paid more attention. I never even answered a simple 'How did it go?' She was always tense, poveretta. If I had insisted on going to Cuernavaca, somewhere that's at sea level, she would be alive now. But I couldn't face the idea of leaving the city, so I let Tina stay at this altitude, on the razor's edge, her poor heart. One afternoon she told me that her heart was like an old shoe, that it ought to be tossed in the trash. And she laughed. 'Can you imagine, Toio, finding a heart in a trash can?' I didn't pay any attention, I didn't hear her or see her. How many times did I call her old, old, old, to myself. And she was too sensitive not to notice that she irritated me. I didn't realize she was so sick; she never complained, never asked me for anything. That's what I can't stand, Pedro, that she never even raised her voice!"

Vittorio's friends don't know what to do to console him. "Tina," he begs. "Tina. Tina," he cries.

Vittorio raises his eyes full of tears to his friends, seeking absolution.

The newspapers dig up the "Mella case," the case of the Communist leader assassinated in the arms of his Italian lover in 1929.

She was deported in 1930, accused of conspiring in the attempted assassination of Pascual Ortiz Rubio. The co-conspirators met at her house, but the deportation of the dangerous Italian was due as much to her licentious behavior as to her political activities.

Moreover, her first husband died inexplicably while traveling with her in a sleeping car between San Francisco and Los Angeles. He died because he knew too much.

In *La Prensa* it is revealed that Tina had an Italian passport, something that could have been possible only through the personal intervention of Mussolini. *When she left Mexico in 1930, she traveled first to France, then to Fascist Italy, and then, passing through Germany, she went to the U.S.S.R.*

The author of the article presents an image of a depraved and dangerous woman involved in numerous assassinations. He also accuses her of being a spy working for the Italian Fascists.

The newspapers all discard the possibility that she might have died from a heart ailment. Tina was poisoned like so many others before her. Either the autopsy was not performed correctly or Mexican science is just not up to snuff, or both. The poison was instantaneous and left no trace. Vittorio Vidali, or Enea Sormenti, a terrorist working for Stalin, knows better than anyone. Wasn't he the mastermind behind the assassination of Trotsky? Couldn't he also have assassinated her?

"Don't go out, I'm telling you, don't show your face on the street, Vittorio," Hidalgo de Cisneros insists.

"What about the house? And the animals?"

"Isabel Carbajal can feed them, don't worry."

"They'll murder you if you go out, don't do it."

Benvenuto Modotti publishes a statement in an Italian-American newspaper regarding the rumors about the "inexplicable and mysterious death" of his sister.

I am Tina Modotti's brother. My sister took part in the war in

Spain and managed to survive. She came to the United States for two months; she wished to remain but the government would not give her permission. One night—I'll never forget it—she said farewell. I asked her why farewell and not "See you later." And she said, "Impossible, I'm already dead, I cannot live long in Mexico." She knew that she had a bad heart, and that was the cause of her death. Anybody who says anything to the contrary is a liar. I do not share Vidali's political convictions, but the truth about my sister's death is just what I have stated.

Pablo Neruda writes a poem and sends it to the newspapers. To his surprise, they all print it.

Tina's funeral is presided over by Doña Leocadia Prestes, Simone Tery, Pablo Neruda. Mario Montagnana and Enrique Ramírez y Ramírez, the young director of *El Popular*, speak on behalf of the Mexican Communist Party.

"I wish only to say what I believe she would most have wanted to hear: that she attained the highest honor all Communists covet, that when her body is returned to the earth, it be covered with the flag of the Communist International.

"Because Tina was, from the year 1927 until the last day of her life, until the last minute her heart beat, a member of our Party; she is, for us, Mexicana ad honorem. She has every right to be considered part of the history of the Mexican Revolution."

Vittorio does not attend the funeral.

They bury Tina in the Panteón de Dolores. The comrades are unable to collect enough money even for fourth class, so she is placed in the poorest section. Fifth class, fifth section, row 28. A narrow grave, barely a gash in the earth. Leopoldo Mendez promises to engrave her profile on the stone on which Pablo Neruda's poem would also be engraved.

> *Tina Modotti, sister,*
> *you are not sleeping,*
> *no, never sleeping.*
>
> *Perhaps your heart hears*
> *yesterday's rose growing,*

yesterday's last rose,
the new rose.

Rest sweetly, sister.

Pure is your sweet name,
pure your fragile life:

with bees, shadow, fire,
snow, silence, foam,

steel, line, pollen
was made your firm,

your delicate frame . . .

El Popular publishes protests against the campaign unleashed against Tina. Workers' organizations, peasant leagues, and refugee groups write letters in her support.

The textile workers in Puebla give the name Tina to a new factory. The typographers in Mexico City use her name for a modern linotype. Groups of militants take her name for sections of the Party and the Anti-Imperialist League.

Vittorio climbs the stairs to their "castle." Benigno Morilla and Cruz Díaz accompany him. They find the house neat and clean, as if Tina were still taking care of it. Vittorio hands over to Cruz all of Tina's things, but Cruz warns him that she'll turn the best of it over to Eladia. Vittorio gives Morilla, who is about to get married, the hard sofa and the kitchen utensils. They look for the cat, but Kitty has left. Vittorio offers the dog, Suzi, to Morilla as she stares at them with pleading eyes.

He takes one last look at the terrace. He walks around it as he did the first time, when Tina was waiting for him to say yes, Tina, yes, I love it, we'll stay here. It was the only time he had seen her genuinely excited during their second stay in Mexico.

He opens his eyes wide to take in the far-off circular city under the sun, the snowy peaks of the volcanoes, white on blue. Life goes on. Everything remains the same. The rooftop on which his steps echo is hard, sturdy. The world is hard. It is sturdy. Nothing will change it. He takes one of the red flowers from the thorny plant and holds it in his hand. He presses the thorns and the flower into his flesh.

Cruz and Benigno wait. "Shall we go?" They hurry down the cement stairs, and when they reach the street, Vittorio shuts the door behind him.

Photo Credits

1. *Julio Antonio Mella.* Tina Modotti, 1928. Courtesy INAH, Pachuca, Mexico.
2. *Mella's Typewriter.* Tina Modotti, 1928. Courtesy the Museum of Modern Art, New York. Gelatin silver print, 9⅜ × 7½ in.
3. *Mella, Dead.* Tina Modotti, 1929. Courtesy INAH, Pachuca, Mexico.
4. *Woman of Juchitán.* Tina Modotti, 1929. Courtesy INAH, Pachuca, Mexico.
5. *Temptation.* Roubaix de l'Abrie Richey, 1920. Illustration for Ricardo Gómez Robelo, *Sátiros y amores.*
6. *Staged Marriage Portrait of Tina Modotti and Edward Weston, Mexico.* Unknown, 1925. Collection of the J. Paul Getty Museum, Malibu, California. Gelatin silver print, 5⅝ × 3¹⁵⁄₁₆ in.
7. *Tina, Nude Torso.* Edward Weston, 1924. © 1981 Center for Creative Photography, Arizona Board of Regents.

8. *Tina Modotti, 1924.* Edward Weston, 1924. © 1981 Center for Creative Photography, Arizona Board of Regents.

9. *Diego Rivera, San Francisco, 1930.* Edward Weston, 1930. © 1981 Center for Creative Photography, Arizona Board of Regents. Print courtesy Throckmorton Fine Art, Inc., New York.

10. *Weston and His Camera.* Tina Modotti, 1923–24. Courtesy INAH, Pachuca, Mexico.

11. *Calla Lilies.* Tina Modotti, 1925. Courtesy INAH, Pachuca, Mexico.

12. *Campesinos Reading "El Machete."* Tina Modotti, 1929. Courtesy INAH, Pachuca, Mexico.

13. *Misery.* Tina Modotti, 1928. Courtesy INAH, Pachuca, Mexico.

14. *Tina Interrogated by Police.* Unknown, 1929. Courtesy INAH, Pachuca, Mexico.

15. *Vittorio Vidali on the Deck of the "Edam."* Tina Modotti, 1930. Courtesy Carlos Vidali.

16. *Hands resting on tool.* Tina Modotti, 1927. Collection of the J. Paul Getty Museum, Malibu, California. Platinum print, 7½ × 8½ in.

17. *Couple at the Zoo, Berlin.* Tina Modotti, 1930. Courtesy INAH, Pachuca, Mexico.

18. *Corn, Guitar, and Cartridge.* Tina Modotti, 1927. Courtesy Throckmorton Fine Art, Inc., New York.

19. *Crystal Glasses.* Tina Modotti, 1925. Courtesy INAH, Pachuca, Mexico.

20. *Hands with Marionette (Mildred from "The Hairy Ape").* Tina Modotti, 1929. Courtesy the Museum of Modern Art, New York. Gelatin silver print, 9½ × 5⅜ in.

21. *Man with a Beam.* Tina Modotti, 1928. Courtesy INAH, Pachuca, Mexico.

22. *Convent of Tepotzotlán (Stairs Through Arches).* Tina Modotti, 1924. Courtesy INAH, Pachuca, Mexico.

23. *Nopal Cactus.* Tina Modotti, 1925. Courtesy INAH, Pachuca, Mexico.

24. *Tank No. 1.* Tina Modotti, 1927. Courtesy INAH, Pachuca, Mexico.

25. *Workers Parade.* Tina Modotti, 1926. Private collection, San Francisco, California.

26. *Flor de manita.* Tina Modotti, 1925. Courtesy INAH, Pachuca, Mexico.
27. *Woman with Flag.* Tina Modotti, 1928. Courtesy the Museum of Modern Art, New York. Palladium print, $9\frac{3}{4} \times 7^{11}\!/_{16}$ in.
28. *Child with Bucket.* Tina Modotti, c. 1928. Courtesy Francisco Luna.
29. *Geranium.* Tina Modotti, 1924–25. Courtesy INAH, Pachuca, Mexico.
30. *Elegance and Poverty.* Tina Modotti, 1928. Courtesy INAH, Pachuca, Mexico.
31. *Sugar Cane.* Tina Modotti, 1929. Courtesy INAH, Pachuca, Mexico.
32. *Niña pobre.* Tina Modotti, 1929. Courtesy Francisco Luna.
33. *Concha Michel with Guitar.* Tina Modotti, c. 1925. Courtesy Centro de la Imagen.
34. *Tree and Shadows.* Tina Modotti, 1924. Courtesy INAH, Pachuca, Mexico.
35. *Roses.* Tina Modotti, 1924. Courtesy INAH, Pachuca, Mexico.

FOR THE BEST IN PAPERBACKS, LOOK FOR THE

In every corner of the world, on every subject under the sun, Penguin represents quality and variety—the very best in publishing today.

For complete information about books available from Penguin—including Puffins, Penguin Classics, and Arkana—and how to order them, write to us at the appropriate address below. Please note that for copyright reasons the selection of books varies from country to country.

In the United Kingdom: Please write to *Dept. JC, Penguin Books Ltd, FREEPOST, West Drayton, Middlesex UB7 0BR*.

If you have any difficulty in obtaining a title, please send your order with the correct money, plus ten percent for postage and packaging, to *P.O. Box No. 11, West Drayton, Middlesex UB7 0BR*

In the United States: Please write to *Consumer Sales, Penguin USA, P.O. Box 999, Dept. 17109, Bergenfield, New Jersey 07621-0120*. VISA and MasterCard holders call 1-800-253-6476 to order all Penguin titles

In Canada: Please write to *Penguin Books Canada Ltd, 10 Alcorn Avenue, Suite 300, Toronto, Ontario M4V 3B2*

In Australia: Please write to *Penguin Books Australia Ltd, P.O. Box 257, Ringwood, Victoria 3134*

In New Zealand: Please write to *Penguin Books (NZ) Ltd, Private Bag 102902, North Shore Mail Centre, Auckland 10*

In India: Please write to *Penguin Books India Pvt Ltd, 706 Eros Apartments, 56 Nehru Place, New Delhi 110 019*

In the Netherlands: Please write to *Penguin Books Netherlands bv, Postbus 3507, NL-1001 AH Amsterdam*

In Germany: Please write to *Penguin Books Deutschland GmbH, Metzlerstrasse 26, 60594 Frankfurt am Main*

In Spain: Please write to *Penguin Books S.A., Bravo Murillo 19, 1° B, 28015 Madrid*

In Italy: Please write to *Penguin Italia s.r.l., Via Felice Casati 20, I-20124 Milano*

In France: Please write to *Penguin France S.A., 17 rue Lejeune, F-31000 Toulouse*

In Japan: Please write to *Penguin Books Japan, Ishikiribashi Building, 2-5-4, Suido, Bunkyo-ku, Tokyo 112*

In Greece: Please write to *Penguin Hellas Ltd, Dimocritou 3, GR-106 71 Athens*

In South Africa: Please write to *Longman Penguin Southern Africa (Pty) Ltd, Private Bag X08, Bertsham 2013*